The First Day After Life

A Spiritual Adventure about
Why Bad Things Happen
&
How to Shape Your Future

Cristian YoungMiller

RateABull
Books

To everyone who may have asked themselves why their devotion to their spiritual and religious practices didn't result in them achieving what they wanted most out of life.

<u>Happiness Thru the Art of…</u>
<u>Penis Enlargement</u>

A 'Novel Guide' to Jelqing, The G-Spot, How to Last Longer
in Bed & Other Sexual Secrets

Ben, a good-natured guy, has lived his entire life with an alcoholic, verbally abusive penis named 'The Brotha'. The story begins when the Brotha finally goes too far with his dictation over Ben, and both admit to being unhappy with their life. As a result, both start a journey toward happiness which leads to their finding a guide to penis enlargement. Following the guide, they increase the Brotha's size, and learn sexual secrets which turn out to be only the beginning in their journey towards happiness.

<u>Everybody Masturbates</u>

'Everybody Masturbates' is the perfect gift idea for anyone from ages 8 to 42 yrs old. In the style of the classic book 'Everyone Poops,' 'Everybody Masturbates' is designed to make boys and girls of all ages feel comfortable about masturbation. (It also makes a great party gift for adults.)

<u>Everybody Masturbates *for Girls*</u>

'Everybody Masturbates *for Girls*' is the perfect gift idea for girls between the ages of 7 to 38 yrs old. Also, in the style of the classic book 'Everyone Poops,' 'Everybody Masturbates *for Girls*' addresses the specific issues that girls have accepting their emerging sexuality. (It also makes a great party gift for adults.)

Contents

Acknowledgements

Writing this book required a tremendous amount of self-reflection. But as strange as it might seem, I am not the character Tian. But there is enough of me in the character Tian that I know that I need to thank my friends and family for the support that they gave me over the years. It was support that ultimately allowed me to pursue my deepest desire which was to create stories. No man is an island and I thank everyone around me for all that you have given me.

And most of all I would like to thank my mom, that beautiful, smart, independent woman who supported me and loved me unconditionally even when I didn't think that I deserved it. Thanks mom!

The First Day After Life:

A Spiritual Adventure about
Why Bad Things Happen
&
How to Shape Your Future

CHAPTER 1

Tian looked up at the sky to find a clear night. He loved these nights in Los Angeles. To him it meant that the city had recently been cleansed. The smog that perpetually covered the city wasn't necessarily the residents' fault. It, like many of the city's problems, was a matter of geography.

Los Angeles sat in a valley surrounded by hills and mountains. During the winter the winds blew in at downward angle over the Hollywood hills. These diving winds whisked away the state regulated smog from L.A.'s million plus cars.

But during the summer the San Andreas wind changed direction. During the summer the winds traveled down southern California closer to the ground. So eventually when it reached L.A.'s Hollywood hills, the winds had no choice but to roll up the northern hillside. Once it reached the most expensive hilltop homes, the winds would shoot off over L.A. creating an impenetrable canopy.

During the summer, the same million cars releasing state regulated amounts of smog had a different result on the city of angels. Instead of being blown away, the smog lifted up to the wind canopy and then was rolled like dough in flour. The smog then built up and thickened into the brownish haze that got so dark that it hid the Hollywood sign from less than a quarter mile away.

But as Tian looked up at the stars he couldn't remember the windy day that proceeded this clear night. There was no summer rain that could explain why he could see every star and constellation as if it were drawn on a map.

'It must be the mountain air,' he thought. Tian had taken a trip from L.A. to the Azusa Mountains to relive one of his fondest memories. Just eight years earlier Tian was a movie director. And during a night that showed his mettle, he had lead his crew through their own fatigue, and their fear of what could be lurking in the dark, to these woods to shot the crux of his film. It was the scene where the hero of the story seduced his love interest, getting in body what he couldn't get in mind.

Tian had often thought about returning to this spot in the darkness of night with only the hollow sound of the wind surrounding him. But now, as he sat under the trees amongst the pine needles and cones, there was no mistaking that something was definitely wrong.

He had recognized the spot where he had parked his motorcycle so he knew that the location was correct. The uphill climb to the spot made his legs burn like it had eight years before so he assumed that that too had to be the same. But it was the camp ground at the end of the path that made him wonder. The camp ground was non distinct and hence unfamiliar, but Tian figured that this too had to be correct because it, like before, was the only one there.

'No, there's something missing,' he thought. 'It's the people.' Tian thought about the 15 cast and crew members that had volunteered a month of their life to work on his epic.

There was the production manager who had recently taken a course at a community college and wanted to practice what he had learned. He was the most delightful born-again Christian that you could imagine. And he, being a forward thinking middle-aged father, wanted to also get experience for those that might make up a new family business.

To that end the production manger recruited his 19 year old son as first assistant director, his nephew as an assistant cameraman, his daughter as an on again – off again costume assistant, and their church family friend as a grip. Together, the rest of the crew referred to them as the 'God Squad' and they liked it.

The director of photography was a woman with long, bright red hair and black nails. She was a recent transplant from the New York punk scene with eyebrow and nose piercings, pale skin and a 'get it done' attitude. She saw life in a much more spiritual way than religious. In fact, she mistrusted the God Squad at first. But as a whole, the family was so sweet, and so kind that by the end, not even she could imagine a better group to work with.

The last of the large personalities was the lead actress who acted opposite Tian. Tian had cast her over a TV star because although both actresses had the same general look, Tian didn't want to have to pretend to be in love. As the lead actor, director and producer he wanted one less thing on his plate. With the love in place then he could focus more on the directing and lines. It wasn't until after the production started that Tian learned that she was a devout Scientologist.

These were all of the beliefs that made up the crew. It wasn't surprising to Tian that everyone was so diverse because Tian thought all beliefs held a shared wisdom. And it was that shared wisdom that he had written his movie around. The movie talked about faith and about a higher power. The movie was about a love triangle between a woman who lived on the other side of death, a psychic, and the living woman whom the psychic loved. It was about how the world after life interacted with the living. And it was about the idea that even when the universe brings you to your lowest point, it is working to create your greatest good.

But Tian had made that movie a long time ago. Stories like that were no longer true for him. Major undertakings like making a movie were no longer possible for the man that Tian had become in the interim. Los Angeles was rightly referred to as the city of dreams. But what no one ever talked about was what happens when the dreamer woke up.

Tian had woken up staring at the stars. Looking up he realized that real life didn't look much different from the dream. He got up from where he lay, looked around the woods and instead of going back to the street, walked away from everything that he knew.

The woods were not hard to navigate tonight. The moon was surprisingly bright. 'It's bright enough to drive by,' Tian thought. What also made it easy were the branches of pine needles above. Not only were the needles not thick enough to block out the moonlight, but over the decades the needles had carpeted the ground preventing anything denser from growing.

Tian took stock of what he had with him. It wasn't much. Other than the crotch length leathers he wore as a motorcycle jacket, he had nothing to protect him if the night turned cold. He remembered that he always kept an energy bar in his jacket pocket but he knew that once that was eaten he would have to survive on what he found.

Tian knew from experience that hunger would be the first thing that he felt. But he was sure that it wouldn't be the thing that would eventually get him. Unfortunately Tian never carried water when he rode his cycle. And although his car always had at least two bottles in it at all times, they would be of no use to him now.

After walking for a while, Tian stopped and stood perfectly still. 'There is too much rustling to be just me,' he thought. If there was one thing that Tian could never get used to, it was the idea that the woods were God's country; And God let wild animals live in his country. Tian ran down the list of possibilities: 'Coyote, wolf, bear, deer and survivalists'. None of them were good options, but if he had to choose one, he thought it best to be a deer.

Tian remained still. He hoped that he would hear the rustling again. Continued movement would mean that it was a random animal walking through the woods. If the rustling matched his, it meant that he was being stocked; on his first day, within his first hour, he was being stocked.

He listened again and continued to hear nothing. There was no wind, there was no traffic. He couldn't even hear the sound of his own breath. It was like he had gone deaf. And as the loneliness started to seep in he took another step forward hearing only the sound of his steps bounce back.

'What is better,' he asked himself, 'the loneliness of being alone or the fear that came with knowing that you're not?' Tian choose the latter and as soon as he did he heard the rustling again.

This time he was ready to analyze it. It was coming from ahead of him so it wasn't an animal. If a deer had seen him it would be moving away. If it was a predator it would have waited for him to come to it. No, this person saw him and wasn't willing to wait for his approach. It was coming to meet him.

Tian was prepared for this. He was in part wondering what had taken so long. The last time this happened he had met someone almost immediately. 'The circumstances are different this time,' he figured. 'The last time was in a dream within a dream. This time it's in real life.'

Still, this wasn't how anyone else described it either. He had woken up alone in the dark, where as he was hoping to find his father standing next to him in the light. 'No, something is missing,' he concluded. And now he didn't know what to expect.

"You are not alone," a voice called out from the darkness.

"Hello?" Tian replied not sure if he heard the voice or just thought it.

The rustling ahead of him stopped. Tian knew that whoever it was was waiting for Tian to find him. "I'm sorry, where are you?" Tian asked. But the voice didn't call back.

Tian didn't really need the directions. What he wanted was the reassurance that he hadn't imagined it. Tian took comfort in what he thought he had heard. He also felt relief that his bad dream had finally ended and that his real life was about to begin.

Tian continued forward and entered what seemed to be a clearing. Standing directly in front of him was a man no taller than his own six feet four inches. But what Tian found unnerving was that the man barely seemed to be there. His blank look neither denoted welcome nor disagreement. His demeanor stripped Tian of the reassurance that the words had given him. And in the worst of all possible options his loneliness remained in spite of the fact that he knew that he wasn't alone.

The moment of silence before either of them spoke drew out. Tian didn't know what to say while the man seemed content to stand there for hours saying nothing. 'What am I doing here?' Tian thought. 'What was I expecting? Something's definitely missing. This isn't like it was before.'

"Can you help me? I think I'm lost," finally rolled out of Tian's mouth.

"Where is it that you wanted to go?" The man answered back.

A dread filled Tian's body. He didn't think that he would have to know. Through all of the years and dreams, through all of the failures and successes, he was never quite sure where it was that he wanted to go. And now at the end of his dream, he woke up and the first question he was asked was for the answer that he never knew.

"I don't know."

"Ok."

In a few more moments of silence, both men disappeared.

CHAPTER 2

Although Tian had always thought of himself as a calm guy, the years leading up to his college graduation were filled with anxiety. As a child he had witnessed the financial collapse of his family and he feared that his family's fate would again be his own.

When Tian was eight years old, his father Frank abruptly left his high-level bank job for the opportunity to control his own destiny. Frank saw his future as the king of fertilizer. Once Tian became old enough to think about such things, he thought it an odd choice. But the older that Tian got, the more he admired how well thought out his father's plan was.

Living in the Bahamas, Frank's venture came only a few years after the country's independence from Britain. And the new Bahamian government, wanting to encourage local entrepreneurship, created a law saying that the government must purchase over foreign products any item manufactured in the Bahamas by Bahamians.

Frank, a man whose every decision beforehand had led to success, saw this as his greatest opportunity. Frank knew that the one industry that would never end was farming. And a guaranteed contract to supply fertilizer for the nation's subsidized farms was a stroke of genius. So after Frank mortgaged his beautiful two story hilltop house, the home that had ocean views from both the pool and tennis court, he partook in what seemed to him to be a sure thing.

As an eight year old boy Tian didn't know what actually happened to his family estate. Tian had heard a lot of arguing between his parents and then an accusation about an affair. But when his parents began discussing leaving the only place Tian ever knew as home, he learned an important lesson; 'No matter how prepared or well planned you are you can always end up homeless.'

That was the lesson that feed Tian's fears as his college years in Wisconsin progressed. What drove Tian's fear even more was his decision to become an actor. He had turned professional during his sophomore year and booked 80% of his auditions. But those Wisconsin jobs only paid between $200 and $800 a month. Tian didn't know how much an apartment cost or what a month of food cost, but he knew that his acting jobs wouldn't be enough.

This was the dread that filled his thoughts as he drove his 1982 Ford Escort from Wisconsin to Toronto, Canada the week after graduation. 'The plan', he thought, 'would be simple. Find the inexpensive part of town and then find a motel. Spend no more than a week in the motel while I secure a job and a room to rent.'

The plan seemed simple. Millions of people had followed this path before him. So with the inexplicable luck that he had always had, he knew the move shouldn't be a problem.

The first part of journey ended fine. He had found a motel in the worst part of town. And because the worst part of Toronto had no comparison to the parts of Chicago he had been exposed to, he felt safe.

But it wasn't his plan that fell apart on him, it was the addition of the unexpected. Tian had always felt connected to the mystical and in touch with his dreams. But past a few dreamy déjà vu's and coincidences they didn't require much note.

After the first full day of apartment hunting Tian returned to the mildew smell of his motel room. He found it tiring to drive the unfamiliar streets in a commuter's town. And Tian didn't want to do anything more than climb into bed and go to sleep.

But that night was a little different than any he had ever had. That night Tian woke up from his dream having aged 30 years. He didn't know how he got there but his first steps were into his brother's Bahamian home. His family had all gathered to celebrate his latest accomplishment which had finally achieved everything that Tian had set out to do.

Tian stared at his favorite nephew Benny, who minutes ago was 10 years old but who was now in his 40's. He was one of the five nieces and nephews from his only brother Pat. Pat had died a few months earlier and only a few of his kids felt up to joining the celebration. But the ones that did come brought their kids and there were enough people there to fill up the room.

Tian liked that everyone had come to meet him but he needed space. He had been hoping for a more intimate party. Tian would have been happier to let his accomplishment pass unacknowledged. Whereas his family only saw the success, Tian saw only the sacrifices that he made to accomplish it. And with everyone making a fuss over him, the sacrifices were beginning to take their toll.

He spotted a door that he guessed led to a den. Tian took leave of his guests and entered the darkened room. As soon as he entered, he spotted a female cousin that he hadn't seen in years. Neither of them decided to reach for a light switch, instead choosing to talk in the dark. They spoke for a minute or two until the door opened again. Tian didn't bother to look around because he could feel what it was. Tian wasn't sure how Pat had died but he knew that whatever or whoever killed his brother had just entered the room behind him.

Tian stopped talking and took a final look at the dark room illuminated by only the yard light next door. There was a lamp on an end table in the corner, and there was a couch next to it. There were some type of prints or paintings in frames on the wall but in the darkness there was no way of telling what they were of.

Tian felt a chilly isolation in the room that he hadn't noticed before. This room wasn't anymore lonely than any other room in any other house, but now its hollowness weighed on him. His shallow breaths stole the ease at which he tried to maintain for his life and without that relaxation the isolation of his life became clear.

Tian then felt a heavy blow across the back right side of head, and he dropped down dead. But although his body fell to the ground, Tian fell no further than 45 degrees before standing back up. Tian barely felt it as he slipped out of his body. But he did hear it as his body made a thud onto the tiles.

With his body laying on the ground everything in the room changed. The room was now evenly lit though Tian couldn't tell where the light was coming from. And the isolation he had just felt was gone.

Tian filled with an exuberance that he had never felt before. For him, it felt better than the best day of his life. In fact, it was the best day of his life multiplied. It was the feeling created from the day when everything was going exactly right and he felt he could do no wrong, and then that was multiplied by seven.

At that moment, Tian understood the reason humans didn't feel this feeling during life. He instinctually knew that the intense vibrations that accompanied this feeling of elation would shake the atoms in the human body apart. He felt like energy in motion.

Tian had another realization in those first few moments. Tian understood that everything that exists was made up of energy, and that energy felt closest to what people on earth referred to as love. Tian understood that love was more than just an abstract concept that men and women fell into and out of. It was the human equivalent of the energy of which everything is made.

Tian looked at the lamp that he had seen moments before and it emitted this love. The couch and the painting emitted the same. Tian knew that that energy was what was holding the particles in the objects together. Tian knew that that energy was a base substance that made up the universe. That energy could not be withheld by one individual; it was the equivalent of the atomic energy that made up life.

Tian made another observation, and this one made him laugh. Tian observed that everything in the room that seemed so real only moments ago were now laughably hallow. The lamps' existence which he had never thought to question was barely solid. The atoms of the object were so loosely packed that it was barely even a lamp. The couches that he had sat on so many times before, now looked like a projections of real things, and bad projections at that.

Nothing in that room was real and Tian couldn't believe that he had thought that they were for so long. Tian couldn't resist laughing. His own naiveté struck him as incredibly funny. Tian admitted to himself that he had believed the illusion, and there was never any harm done.

Now understanding where he was, Tian knew that the rules on earth didn't apply to him anymore. Tian decided that he wanted to float into the air and he did. Tian immediately knew that there was no limit to where he could go and what he could do. And when he realized that, the room around Tian changed. The furniture and other things in the room remained but the ceiling disappeared and the upper frame of the room changed into that of a church.

Tian looked to his right and saw a window. As he stared, a small white light appeared outside of it. The light was getting closer and eventually it passed through the window into Tian's room. Tian looked at the light and knew that it was his brother Pat. It didn't look like anything other than a light, but Tian could recognize his brother just as he had the countless times he had seen Pat in the past.

'Patrick!' he thought loudly to his brother. Tian quickly floated up to him and put his arms around the light. As they joined, Tian's exuberance, which he had thought of as seven times his greatest day, jumped to twelve times, and the two energies seemed to briefly become one.

Tian felt that his time on earth was growing short. He decided that there were things that he wanted to do before he followed his brother away. So without thinking about it, Tian transported himself in front of his favorite nephew. He had read in books on death that family members were often able to know when their loved ones had died. Tian hoped that it would be true in their case as well.

"Benny," Tian said.

Benny stopped what he was saying and looked around. He had heard Tian.

"Benny, I've died. And I want you to know what you have to do to get to where I am."

Benny seemed to understand the words and then replied with "why?"

Tian was about to launch into the amazing experiences he had had on arriving to the other side when he thought again about his nephew's question.

'Why indeed?' Tian mused.

Something was talking directly to his soul. Tian didn't recognize it as another person. It was instead a flow of knowledge that existed independently of everything else. The flow told him that his experiences were his own, and that they were no more right or wrong than anyone else's.

Tian stopped trying to communicate with his nephew. Tian turned away from Benny and held back another piece of knowledge as long as he could. Within a moment Tian knew that he couldn't deny it anymore. Tian let it seep into his consciousness before thinking it aloud, 'I have more to learn. It isn't my time.' With that thought Tian opened his eyes. He was awake in his motel bed and his entire body was still vibrating at an accelerated rate.

Tian accepted that what he had just experienced felt more real than anything else he had experienced during life. Tian accepted that he had just touched the real world and from that moment forward his life would change.

Unfortunately, Tian's life wouldn't change for the better. For years to come, every good day and exciting moment Tian had was held in comparison to what he referred to as the first time he died. And unfortunately for Tian, none of those fleeting life experiences ever came close.

For the first few years after the dream, he yearned to go back. And it wasn't until after the vividness of the memory faded that he began to fully engage in life again. But even with the ravishes of time he knew that earth wasn't where he wanted to be. He never forgot that life wasn't the real world. And now, in the woods, after over a decade had passed, he was again awake yet this too felt incomplete.

When Tian looked around again he was in a very familiar place. He was standing on the snaking driveway of his childhood estate back in the Bahamas. He looked over at his travel companion for assurance that what he was looking at was real. He got none in return.

Tian looked to his right and there was the sand pit. It was a staple of Tian's childhood after having been put there for the construction of the barbeque pit next to the pool. Up ahead was the carport with a decaying ping pong table laying on its side.

As Tian scanned the front yard that his mother had spent hours working on, Tian heard barking. He turned his attention back toward the front gate and could hardly believe his ears. He ran into the carport to find the same wrought iron gate that his father had built to keep the dogs in. And behind the gate were two familiar sights.

As two dogs excitedly poke their noses through the wiring, Tian was filled with warmth. Snowby, the medium sized, short white-haired dog with the pink and black nose was what Bahamians referred to as a potcake breed. But this wasn't a breed at all.

In the Bahamas, peas & rice was a dish which had been made for generations. It was rice cooked in tomato paste, sweet pepper, onions, pork fat and black eyed peas. But when the rice cooked for too long, a lot of the heavier ingredients sunk to the bottom. Caked at the bottom of the pot the ingredients burned.

When the rice was done and all of the loose peas & rice was removed, there was left a cake of rice with a mix of all of the tastier ingredients. Some Bahamians scooped the potcake out and threw it away, while others thought of it as their favorite part. That was the type of breed that Snowby was. She was a continuous mix of every breed until nothing was recognizable. She was a pure breed potcake.

Teddy was a potcake as well, but he looked like a terrier. He was a medium sized dog with long wavy brown hair, and somehow this little dog ruled the neighborhood. Dogs were not often fenced in the Bahamas and amongst the dogs that ran wild, Teddy was king.

These were the two dogs that Tian's family had during what Tian thought of as his family's golden age. This was the time before his father left the bank but during the excitement of his planning it.

Tian stepped through the gate with the dogs jumping all over him. The porch that the gate protected was exactly as he remembered. On his left were the outdoor sinks and on his right was the path that led to the rain water tank and the tennis court.

This was not the way it looked a few years ago when Tian visited his old house. When he visited then, the new owners had turned the porch into a foyer and the tennis court was a decaying basketball court. No, this was his home as it existed in 1979. Looking out onto the place where he had grown up, Tian understood that they hadn't just traveled through space, he and his companion had also traveled through time.

CHAPTER 3

Tian walked through the porch to the side of the house where the mulberry bush once again stood. Just like in the summer of '79 it was in bloom. That summer the bush began to more resemble a tree. And out of concern for the house's foundation, Frank cut it down the following year. But now, as it had before, the mulberry bush was there and in bloom.

Tian looked across the yard to the pool and once again the guava tree stood next to it laden with fruit. Tian stepped onto the grass taking in every familiar step. He rounded the house to see what fruit trees were left there. And just like he remembered there were the eight avocado trees and the scarlet plum tree behind them. And like mulberry bush, everything was in bloom.

Tian remembered this summer. He had spent most of this summer in his Speedo swim trunks. It became a contest between him and his friends for which had developed the most contrasting Speedo tan. Tian was naturally a milk chocolate, but after that summer he was proud to show off his dark chocolate brown.

Tian wanted so much to return to this time of his life. This was the summer before self-reliance and change. As an adult he often dreamed about this time. And in his dreams this place symbolized home. But as Tian got older he reluctantly accepted that time always moved forward. So he locked that summer into a capsule in his memory never to be cracked open again.

Tian took a breath in and considered where he was. 'How real was this place?' he thought. It felt, smelt and looked like the place of his childhood. But as much as he wanted it to be real, it didn't fit. The proportions were no longer the same.

Even though Tian had always been tall for his age, it wasn't until after they moved away from this house that he shot up to 6'4".

The house seemed smaller now. The mounds in the yard that had been so hard for the young boys to ride his bicycle over where now mere humps. And when he allowed himself to consider what the interior of the house looked like, he realized that the rooms had probably shrunken just as much.

Tian crossed back to the driveway where his travel companion stood. The dogs escaped through the gate behind him and immediately ran into the street barking with excitement.

"What is this place?" Tian asked the man.

"This is where you wanted to go," the man replied.

"So is this a memory? Is this real?"

"It's both."

"How can it be both?" Tian rebuked. "Memories are memories. But I can touch this place. I can smell it."

"This is as much the place you lived in when you were a child as where you fell asleep on your 7th birthday."

"Then where is everybody? There was always someone home. And where am I right now?"

"You are right here."

"I don't mean me. I mean the seven year old me."

"First, those dogs are your dogs. They wanted to be here for you. They knew that seeing them would help you understand where you are. You didn't want your family here. If you had wanted them, they might have come. And I would like to point out that you are standing right here."

Tian turned to look at Teddy and Snowby as they ran towards him. Still unsure he kneeled down and allowed the two to plaster his face with their tongues. Tian grabbed onto the two of them and the dogs jump back into the playful game of keep away that they all had once played together. Tian got down on all fours and Teddy stood still in front of him. Teddy waited for Tian's first move.

The kneeling man slowly leaned his body to his left and Teddy delightfully jumped to the right. But Tian had tricked him. He then jumped to his right grabbing Teddy and rolling onto the ground with him. Snowby came over and barked at the two on the ground. Teddy struggled for a while but then relaxed into another bath of licks. Tian loosened his grip on the dog and began to cry.

Tian made it to his knees and just held his two childhood companions. Tian's appreciation for being able to hold them again was overwhelming. He hadn't allowed himself to remember how much he had missed them until now. Each of them had died a tragic death. But at age 11 and 12 Tian had thought of himself as too old to cry. So instead Tian locked his feelings away only for them to resurface as a flood of emotion now.

Turning again to the man, "Where am I? Am I dead?"

The man didn't say anything.

"Is this a dream?"

"This isn't a dream. Nor are you dead… yet," the man replied.

Tian stood letting his friends go. The two dogs trotted off through the wrought iron gate.

"I'm not dead yet? Is that why I haven't seen the light? I did the last time. Was that real? The death dream I had after college, was that real?"

"If you want to understand what you experienced back then, you have to loosen your definition of what a dream is and what you consider to be real."

"What do you mean?" Tian retorted.

"Answer me this," the man replied. "What makes an experience real?"

Tian thought for a moment. "I guess if I can actually touch it and see it, and others can touch it and see it as well, then it's real."

"So is this place real?" the man asked.

Tian looked around at the trees shading the driveway which did not exist the last time he drove by this house. He looked up at the roof of the carport which was lined with Christmas lights which were long taken down. And he looked at the basketball rim and wooden backboard that hadn't been there for decades.

"I don't know if this is real or not."

"Use your definition. I can see this place and I can touch it. By that definition mustn't this place be real?" the man prodded.

Tian looked at the man again. "Who are you? I don't recognize you. If I died, or even if I'm just dying, shouldn't I have been met by someone I know? Why didn't someone come to meet me? All of the books I read said the same thing. Am I being punished?"

"All of the books you read are written by people that nearly died. They developed memories that they were supposed to take back with them."

"So either I'm not supposed to remember this experience or I'm not going back." Tian looked at the man for confirmation and got none. "Can you not tell me that?"

"I am here to answer the questions that you don't know."

"Ok, then what's your name? I don't know that."

The man uncomfortably pulled a name from his memory. "You can call me Irabell."

"Is that not your name?" Tian asked after seeing his hesitation.

"It was. But I have had so many that by giving you just one I'm helping you to see me in a particular way instead of helping you to see me for who I am completely."

"Then what do other's here call you?"

"They don't have to call me anything. When they think of me and I am available, I come."

"Is it like when I saw my brother in the death dream? He didn't look the same, but I felt him and knew that it was Pat."

"Yes. The feeling you had when he was around you was him. It wasn't his name or looks or his smell. You, I, the dogs, everyone is more than just what you see and touch. They are all multi-dimensional."

"Do you mean that they have different facets to them, or do you mean it in the Star Trek sense?"

"I mean both."

Tian looked at Irabell with a heavier heart. Tian had grown to hate this metaphysical double speak that he had read in the books of his childhood. All of them spoke is such twisted logic that no one really understood. Ruth Montgomery, A Course in Miracles, the Conversations with God books, they were all metaphysical nonsense to Tian. And here he was on his deathbed, with the secrets to the beyond being withheld by a man with the same double speak. Tian felt the same learned helplessness that he had felt during the latter years of his life.

"You brought us here," Irabell abruptly injected.

"Did I?" Tian responded as the will to be there or anywhere slowly left him.

"You believe that everything that happened to you in your life had been dictated to you by forces beyond your control. Now you think that the same is true here in this world."

"I don't know. I tried so hard during my life to be good, and make things happen for myself. But I just couldn't. And I watched the people around me do so much better than I did even though I knew there wasn't anything special about them. Yet somehow I just kept failing. I just kept being pulled through life, and when I was too tired to walk, I was dragged.

I was so looking forward to coming back here. The dream I had about here felt so much more real than my life did. I felt like I could know anything in the dream. And now I'm here and I don't know anything more than what I knew before; which is nothing."

Irabell had a certain level of discomfort with emotions. He understood them and at one time expressed them, but now he couldn't identify with them. Irabell watched Tian as if he were watching a foreign film with no subtitles. Tian's emotions were real and heartfelt, but they didn't mean anything to Irabell.

"Would you like to know the truth?" Irabell causally offered.

"Well, I don't want to be lied to."

"No, would you like to know the truth about everything that ever existed?"

Tian looked at Irabell stunned. He couldn't be sure if he was offering Tian the answer to everything, but he didn't dare to move in case it caused Irabell to retract his life changing offer.

Irabell looked over at Tian who stared back at him with his mouth open and a look of awe on his face.

"You seem amazed. All that I'm offering you is what everyone is given when they come back here. It is the white light that they see. That white light is the brain being overwhelmed by information that it cannot process. So instead the brain interprets the information as a white light.

The feeling of euphoria that is often reported after dying is the brain releasing high levels of serotonin and oxytocin as it dies. It would be the same if a human lost a limb in a non-fatal accident.

Pain is not a punishment for having done something wrong. Pain is a part of an evolved survival process.

Pain has evolved into being because the animals that felt pain more quickly got themselves out of danger, and then coddled the part of them in pain. This coddling allowed their body to heal faster. The animals that had a lesser feeling of pain did not remove themselves from the dangerous event as quickly and hence died more often. The animals that died couldn't reproduce as often and hence didn't pass along their inability to feel pain.

So in the same evolved survival system, the animals that felt overwhelming pain after a horrific accident became stunned. This prevented them from pulling themselves out of the danger. Those animals usually died on the spot. But the animals that were relieved from the initial shock of tremendous pain were able to pull themselves to safety and survived more frequently. Those animals lived long enough to reproduce.

So in that same way, the feeling of euphoria that a person feels during death is the body's reaction to the fatal injury. There is nothing amazing about the white light process that follows death except the amount of deaths it took to evolve it. "

Tian stood processing the information. He wasn't ready for such an intricate answer. 'Serotonin,' he thought. 'I know this. It is the body's feel good hormone. And oxytocin was the drug that people got addicted to because it made people feel mellow and like everything would be ok.'

'Evolution?' he thought. 'Did I just die and the spirit that met me explained away the most mystical part of dying in evolutionary terms?'

As unusual as this seemed to Tian, this calmed him because it made sense to him. Tian remembered back to the sixth grade when he began to question his religious teachings. Tian had attended an evangelistic elementary school. In the Bahamas all of the private schools had religious affiliations. There were the Catholic schools: St. Augie's College, Xavier's, and St. Andrews School. There were the Anglican schools: Queen's College, St. Anne's and St. John. And there was the Evangelistic school Christsway Academy. This was the one that Tian attended.

Tian thought that Christsway was a tremendous amount of fun to attend. At various times during the day, the teachers would take breaks to sing the catchiest songs that Tian could imagine. And every Friday all of the classes would line up in front of the auditorium for something they referred to as chapel.

Every day during school time was set aside for Bible study. And each week there was a memory verse. This didn't seem unusual to Tian because it was all he knew. Bible study seemed no stranger to Tian than social studies and math. But because so much of an emphasis was placed on Bible study, he knew that this class was more important. This was the intent of Christsway. The school did its best to teach the kids that bible study was essential for the survival of their soul.

Christsway taught that every person had to take the Lord Jesus Christ as their personal lord and savior. When they did, God would allow their soul to go to heaven after they died. This process was called being saved and everyone would want to go to heaven. Heaven was described as a place in the clouds where everything was calm and everyone got along. And if you were really lucky you could walk around heaven holding hands with Jesus.

But if you didn't ask Jesus to be your personal savior then you would be sent to hell. Hell was a horrible place filled with stones so hot that they glowed red. In hell people would be shackled by the neck, wrist and ankles and would be tortured everyday and forever.

Christsway taught that God would test you to see if you were worthy to go to heaven. God would go as far as taking away everything that you own, killing your wife, killing your children and even asking you to kill your own children. And if didn't, or in some way showed yourself to be unworthy of joining him in heaven, then he would send you to hell.

Tian knew that he didn't have to ever worry about going to hell because, the one thing that you had to do to avoid hell was to ask Jesus to take away your sins. Tian had done this. And just for measure Tian had asked Jesus a few times. Tian was confident that he was safe, and it was in that safety that he found room to examine the logic of these most strict rules.

It was during Bible study class in the sixth grade that Tian first questioned his religious teachings. The class was on how God does not accept any soul into heaven that has not taken Jesus as their savior. The emphasis of the class was on 'any' soul.

Tian allowed his young mind to wonder on this for a moment. 'Any soul,' Tian thought. 'Well, what if there was a baby that didn't get the chance to hear the word of god before it died?' Tian remembered the answer to that one. In this case God would put them into a special heaven for babies that hadn't yet committed any sins.

Tian then thought about the natives in the parts of Africa that the missionaries hadn't gotten to yet. Certainly it wasn't their fault that they hadn't heard the word of God. 'Wouldn't that mean that those natives would have to spend their whole after life being tortured? Would God torture them for a reason that was no fault of their own?'

Tian received a thrill from asking this question. He had never felt as proud of himself as he was now. With this question Tian felt that he had out thought them, his teachers, Christsway and God himself.

There was no logical way out of it. They all said that God was compassionate and loved his children. They said that God would save the babies because they were too young to take Jesus into their heart. But what was also implied in all of the teachings was that God would let the natives burn. That was not a compassionate God.

Tian was beaming when he finally raised his hand to confirm what he had discovered. When called on he phrased his question carefully to get it right on the first try. Tian could tell that his teacher didn't see the question coming. Her mouth hung open like it did when she wasn't sure what she was supposed to do next. And then she said it.

"That is up to God," his teacher said.

Tian knew that he had her on the ropes. "But doesn't everyone have to accept the word of God to go to heaven? Then how could the natives go to heaven? They would have to go to hell."

His teacher's face relaxed into satisfaction. "That is up to God," she said.

But after seven years of teachings Tian knew the answer.
They would have to go to hell. By God's own rules, by the Christian
rules, they all would have to go to hell. Tian was sure of his logic.
Tian relaxed into the understanding that the God of Christianity
wasn't fair. And it was at that moment that Tian knew he was no
longer Christian.

After that year Tian went to the Catholic St. Augie's
College. The priests and nuns there were more thoughtful, but it was
too late. Tian was lost to their religion. In the next few years Tian
read metaphysical books that emphasized Hinduism, Taoism and
Buddhism, but what he enjoyed most about the books was the
psychic phenomena.

As far reaching as the psychic events seemed, they were
tangible. They were observable. They could be held to rules of
science. Tian received comfort from that. Now Irabell had explained
away the mystery of seeing the white light before your death in the
same scientific way. This made sense to Tian. 'Oh course this is the
way pain worked. Of course this is the way the euphoria before
death worked. It just makes sense.'

'But wait,' Tian thought. 'Why hadn't I felt that euphoria?
Why hadn't I been overwhelmed with that knowledge? Why was I
being left out from the knowledge that everyone else got?'

But before Tian could formulate the question, Irabell
interrupted. "Would you like to leave here now?"

Tian looked around at this place that had given him so much
comfort as a child and knew that real or not, it was a part of his past.
And if he didn't keep moving forward eventually he would be
dragged.

"Yes, I'm ready."

And in a moment they were both gone.

CHAPTER 4

The last time that Irabell had experienced an earth life was more than 800 years earlier. He was born to an old woman of 28 and her even older husband. The woman had been thought of as barren by the other villagers. It was a thought shared by her and her husband.

She had seen the lump of pregnancy eight times before, each time giving birth to a dead baby. By the time that she was pregnant with Irabell she had given up hope of having a live birth. The long trip necessary to get the blessing from the priests was not taken. The special herbs brewed to bring long life and luck to the child was not drunk. And the usual privileges given to the pregnant women of the village were not offered to her.

The mother didn't have these deviations from normal life this time. In fact, she didn't do anything outside of her normal daily routine. The last two times had been very hard on her. The heavy sadness that had enveloped her after her 7th pregnancy continued throughout her 8th. But after that she understood her role. She was to be barren. Her place within the community was to be used as an example of what happened to little girls who have been bad in their past lives.

Irabell's mother didn't pay attention to the other women's allegories that used her as the protagonist. If her children's deaths were caused by what she had done in a past life, then the damage was already done. All she could do was live her life out and prepare herself for the next.

Irabell's mother didn't think much of it when her brown belly grew larger than it ever had before. She didn't think much of it when she started to feel the pushes and kicks within her. The woman didn't even think much of it when the usual contraction pains were accompanied by an explosion of liquid from between her legs.

So when the time came and a fully formed baby was pulling out of her loins she was completely unprepared. She was unprepared for how difficult a live birth would be. And she was unprepared for the pain.

It was tradition that one of the prolific mothers past her fertile years would assist the young mothers give birth. But after so many miscarriages the mid-wives had become scared of Irabell's mother. They thought that whatever caused all the miscarriages would be passed on to the mid-wife, and the mid-wife would then take the disease home to their own young girls.

Irabell's father, however, saw his wife's pregnancy from a different perspective. He had been with her through all of the experiences, and had noticed the differences this time. He noticed how his wife's breast had stayed fuller longer. He noticed how his wife's hips had gotten wider. And he noticed that this time she had let him push himself into her with her belly still full. In fact, not only did she let him, but she craved it. Near the end, he actually allowed himself to believe that if a baby would be born, it would be born smiling from all of their marital relations.

So, when his wife started crying in pain and her fluids spilled onto their bed, he was a little more attentive. He didn't know what to do so he ran out into the village of tree-branch mud huts. He scanned all of the midwife's homes and chose wisely. Within a second he saw the home of the midwife whose husband had died. 'She is the person,' he thought. Irabell's father knew that she would resist as much as any of them would, but without a husband she could be forced.

The husband had to drag the woman into their hut kicking and screaming. And the combined noises of his wife and the mid-wife brought all of the villagers out of their huts. Some of the villagers had thought to help the midwife. But ultimately their compassion fell mostly onto Irabell's mother. They knew that someone had to deal with her latest embarrassment, and it was better this widow mid-wife than any of them.

After the midwife had accepted her fate, she rolled Irabell's mother onto her back. With a quick check, the midwife saw that the baby's head hadn't appeared even though her opening was wide enough. Thinking quickly the midwife decided to try something different. She signaled to the husband to help his wife onto her feet. She wanted to relieve some of the strain of pushing so she decided to have the mother stand while giving birth.

The husband helped his wife up. The midwife directed them backwards until the mother's back rested against the wall. The mother screamed as her legs burned with pain. She wanted to lie down, but her husband sensing his chance at fatherhood pinned her against the mud. The mother's legs wobbled one more time and then collapsed under the radiating pain. Feeling his wife fall onto his shoulders he held her even tighter. He felt like he was in a life or death struggle for the life of his child and he wasn't giving up.

The midwife ordered the husband to hold her still while she maneuvered her old, thin body between the two of them. "Push" the old women yelled. The head of the baby became visible. "Again" the old women screamed out. The mother let out a scream that the husband could hear even through his prayers. "The head is out," the old woman rejoiced.

The mother now knew that this birth was different. This time it hurt more. And this time her husband was holding her with one of the old women yelling at her to push harder. All of the other disappointments quickly left the mother's mind. This was all something new and if she was going to help this new life into the world, it had to start with her believing that it was possible. That was the moment she made the decision to believe.

The mother pushed again. Between the feelings of her insides being ripped apart, she felt the baby sliding out.

"Squeeze," the old woman said.

The mother grabbed onto her husband's neck and squeezed as hard as she could. 'Such pain' she thought. 'So much pain!'

After the throbbing pain came the burning. It felt like a cold breeze blowing against an open wound. It felt like fire being shoved into her. It was through this new burning that everything was reduced to silence. She didn't hear her own screams anymore. She didn't hear the old woman's pleas. There was just a ringing in her ears and a deafening silence.

The mother, whose eyes had been closed, knew that when she opened her eyes she would know her baby's fate. Delaying the disappointment of another still birth, she decided to first explore the room with her ears. The room would either be filled with the crying of her child or the absolute silence of death.

'Ranka' she thought. 'Live or die, this one's name is Ranka.'

The sound of static began to fill her consciousness. Her hearing was coming back. She dissected the static looking for signs of life, but she found nothing. Without thought the tears rolled down her cheeks. 'The baby is dead,' she thought. 'Ranka was her name and my baby is dead.'

The mother opened her eyes. Her first sight was the midwife moving her hands rapidly around her dear Ranka. Something had gone wrong she thought.

She could now feel her husband's shoulders rocking up and down. 'He's crying' she thought. 'My husband is crying.' The first sound to break through the static was her husband and he was crying.

The husband for the first time released his wife from the death grip. 'If Ranka has died then I don't want you to let me go,' she thought. But he did let go and she slowly slid down the wall onto the floor.

As she slid, the mother looked for her husband's eyes. They weren't visible on the way down but once sitting she found them as he pulled away. They were tired, sad eyes and they seemed to show signs of struggle as he helped her back onto the bed.

'Tell me whether my baby's alive,' she yelled with her eyes. But the father didn't hear. Instead the father turned to the midwife, the miracle midwife, and gently took his son out of her hands.

Carefully he walked his bundle over to his beautiful wife and sat next to her. "Do you see what you have done? Do you see your beautiful baby boy?"

The wife could barely understand his words. Who was the beautiful baby that her husband held in his hands? "This is your baby boy. Do you see the miracle that you created?"

'My baby,' she thought. "My baby?" she finally said aloud.

"Yes, this is your baby."

She looked down at this squirming, screaming creature and wept. Her husband transferred the boy over to the mother's arms and through her tears she said "your name is Ranka." The mother, looking into her baby boy's eyes, was suddenly filled with warmth and euphoria. The mother knew that she was now in love and she liked it.

Even after four years the old woman was known in the village as the miracle midwife. Not only had she helped the barren woman to give birth, but the baby had grown up to be beautiful and very talkative.

The villagers had begun to worry about the family when the father lost a lot of weight after his wife's birth. But what they didn't see was that the husband had broken with the villagers' traditions. When food was collected for a family it was divided into parts. Since the men needed their strength to lift, build and find more food, two parts were given to him, while one part was given to the wife.

But in this family, the husband fearing an early death by his child insisted on the two parts being eaten by his wife. He claimed that she was eating for two and therefore needed it. And as a result his wife grew surprising fat while the husband became skeletal thin.

Two years later when Ranka left the nipple the villagers noticed that the husband gained a little of his weight back but then the mother became thin. They all just looked at the family as cursed, but the one saving grace was that their child was fat and healthy. Ranka seemed to crawl sooner than the other children. He spoke before all of the other children and he seemed to fear almost nothing. In fact, neither the men nor women minded it when Ranka stopped them to engage in conversation about a passing beetle or lizard.

Ranka's qualities were also what the high priests noticed when they visited the village. The priest weren't impressed with the thin poor parents, but they were taken back by the vivacious boy that they were raising.

None of the four priests were young. It was the tradition of the priests that by age 35 they identify the temple's next high priest. Their age was important because it took at least 15 years to train the new priest and no one was guaranteed life after 50.

All of the four priests were found during times when the villages were flourishing. And it was always thought better to have more than one priest trained incase tragedy struck and one died. But for the past ten years healthy children were not so plentiful.

Tradition held that all of the new candidates meet certain criteria. They must all have very balanced faces. It was thought that a balanced face was more beautiful and was a sign of a healthy child. The child had to have an impressive grasp of language for their age, because it was language that would be their trade for the rest of their life. And third, they must express a basic curiosity. It was this curiosity that would drive them to continue learning even after they had been taught everything they needed to know. Ranka met all of these criteria, and it was to the relief of the priest when they found him.

The ritual that was enacted when the child was taken from the parent was originally designed to bring status to the parents of the lost child. The parent of a temple child was held in the highest esteem. And the loss of one of nine kids was a small price to pay for the material wealth that would be showered on them by their village.

But the ceremony didn't seem to comfort Ranka's two parents. Even the husband openly wept. The priest continued on without empathy knowing that this was how they were initiated. They knew that once removed from their village their parents had prospered.

It almost drew ire from the priests that the parents failed to understand the role their child would play in society. They had to remind themselves that the parents didn't know that Ranka would probably be the only priest trained during his generation. And as the only priest he would lead not just their village but a hundred other. The priests almost hated the parents for their ingratitude. But instead of reacting to their blubbering, the priest continued the ceremony as it was designed.

After the ceremony the mother lurched for Ranka and it took one of the priests to pry them apart. After that the husband lurched for his little boy and it took a number of hits across his head to get him to let go. A hysterical Ranka reached for his mother and dad as they cried for him. He did his best to wiggle out of the priest's hands, but they were too strong and there were too many of them.

Ranka sensed some sort of finality to this moment that he had never experienced before. And in that he was right. He would never see his parents again. And the only thing he would remember about this event in the coming years would be the sounds of his mother's emotions spilling out into the room.

The priests carried Ranka for the first five miles, and then insisted that he walk. four miles later he was again on Cedra's back. Cedra was the youngest and would become Ranka's favorite priest. Of all of them Cedra would be the closest to a father and it was Cedra that carried Ranka for the next 20 miles.

Ranka could see his new home miles before it stood above them. Incredibly the main temple was a four-story stone, almost gothic structure carved into the side of a cliff face. The entrance to the temple was a 200 foot ladder that assured the temple's safety for a hundred years. The 50 feet of cliff face above the temple made attack from the top near impossible. During its time the temple never faced invasion from those who had their eyes on conquering the world. So it was more than an adequate way of warding off attacks from nearby villagers that thought they could better control the priests' land.

From a mile away the caves around and below the temple looked like knots in a tree. But they were all large enough to house a family of five. The knots were the homes of the temple servants. The high clerics and temple prostitutes who lived within the temple made sure that the servants were always on call whenever they needed them.

The cave of the cook was directly below the temple and was connected to the temple by stone stairs within the cave. The kitchen help lived below the cook and was connected to the temple by a rope ladder that ran up the face of the cliff. And the cleaners and food gatherers lived at the bottom of the cliff face giving them easy access to the land.

These were the people that Ranka would learn from and then eventually lead. During his younger years he befriended a few of them. And throughout the next 15 years, Ranka's heart remained surprising open to the ones that he considered friends. Ranka learned compassion from the servants, and true dignity from the cook.

Added to his quick absorption of the priests' teachings, Ranka was showing signs of being a great leader.

It was around his 20th year when he prepared to ascend to his position as Supreme High Priest. It was customary that during the ceremony the Supreme High Priest named his teachers as his high counsel. The four High Priests were sure to teach Ranka this.

But when the time came Sri Ranka didn't make the gesture. Throughout his years he had grown to see the priests as corrupt. Many of their decision were based around maintaining the temple's power and their own aggrandizement. Ranka decided that the priests would stay as they were so that a new era could emerge.

As the High Priests had predicted, Sri Ranka soon learned that he wasn't ready for all of the responsibilities that came with dictatorship. The priests had given Ranka a moral basis, but each problem that arose was new to him and they had to be figured out each one from scratch. This wore on Ranka more quickly than anyone had imagined. Within months of taking power Ranka began to spend inordinate amounts of time with his favorite temple prostitute. This left decisions unmade and soon the villages began to suffer.

The woman that Ranka was with was no more beautiful than the rest. All of the temple prostitutes were chosen for their beauty and they were all taught the arts of pleasure. But what Ranka enjoyed about this woman was the excitement he saw in her eyes when she looked at him. He liked how her back arched and her toes curled when he lay with her. She seemed to truly enjoy him and he appreciated her for it.

But after months of mutual pleasure even she noticed how he left important things undone. Soon even she asked Ranka if he was needed elsewhere. And finally when she asked, Ranka considered it.

Upon examination it didn't take Ranka long to realize that his teachers were once moral men as well. The realization came as he began to see his own future in them. But what Ranka feared most was that his own fate would be worse. Whereas power corrupts, Ranka began to see that his absolute power would corrupt him absolutely.

The decision Ranka made resulted after a night of looking into his lover's beautiful eyes. In her eyes he found more than just love. He saw her needs as well. He saw her desire for safety, and her own ambition.

Ranka didn't think that any of these were bad things. All of Sri Ranka's people wanted the same for themselves. They all wanted to live as grand a life as their High Priest could afford them.

But in his lover's eyes, Ranka felt all of the temptations allowed by his youth. In his desire to give his lover everything she wanted, the balance between what was good for him and what was good for his people became too hard to maintain. And the only clarity that appeared after that was that he had failed the one test that his people had most needed him to pass. Ranka had failed to be humble.

As Supreme High Priest, Ranka rectified his missing humility with a decree. "Starting immediately the High Priests are to again lead the people. I will be their lowest of servants and will assist in the maintenance of the temple. My favorite one will be banished from the temple and this will be how we will end our days."

This was an unprecedented move. No one had ever so completely given up their powers before, but Ranka had thought it through. He loved the servants. He knew each of them by name and even knew the highlights of their life. Ranka's decision wasn't completely selfless, it was self-preservation. He felt that these people could give him a place to belong, a family that he never had. With them he felt that he could hide. And without the deep eyes of his lover, he could escape from all the demands that awaited him in the life he abdicated.

However, the new life wasn't what he expected either. It was backbreaking work and the servants hadn't accepted him like he thought they would. Ranka wasn't their brother. He was their embarrassing uncle.

A shame followed Ranka around as he wiped the floors he once spat on and emptied the buckets he once shat in. And the shame was only highlighted by the heartbreak he felt. In her absence, Ranka had fallen in love with his lover. And with his mind now freed from tutorship and decisions, she was all he could think about.

The High Priests didn't notice Ranka's decline. They were too busy engorging in their regained power to notice the seriousness of their situation. The fact still remained that they were very old and the village needed a leader after they were gone.

They didn't think much about it when they heard that Ranka snuck his lover into the temple for quick visits. They didn't think to question the time Ranka spent with the apothecary. And they didn't think to look for Ranka when he didn't show up at the temple when he was supposed to. And because none of the servants really thought of him as constrained to the same rules as they were, none of them checked when the second day passed without him.

But as a stench filled the air outside his cave they went looking for him. What they found was that the young leader had seemed to die in his sleep. As was tradition, they opened up his body before burial. To the trained eyes of the high clerics it seemed that Ranka's heart had exploded. This was an unlikely outcome for such a young and healthy man.

What was more likely, though undetectable, was that Ranka could no longer live the life that he had created for himself. Ranka had visited the apothecary for what seemed to the apothecary as a means to regain his natural place as leader. But the young priest used the undetectable poison on himself.

When Irabell's heart stopped he woke up in the world in which he now lived. But unlike Tian he was filled with the knowledge of everything. It became immediately clear to him that the High Priests wouldn't have enough time to train a new successor. So when their land grew unfertile, and Cedra, the last of the old High Priest died, the community wasn't prepared for the devastating earthquake that quickly followed.

80% of the villagers had died during those times. And after Cedra's death, most of the temple's traditions were lost. But what hurt Irabell the most was that if he would have hung on for just two years more the priests would have realized that they needed Ranka. And slowly the priests would have begun to bring him back into the fold.

Five years after that Sri Ranka would have again become Supreme High Priest. And with a combination of humility, compassion and wisdom Sri Ranka would have been able to save almost all of his people's lives. That was the realization that shaped Irabell the most. And that is what drew Irabell into the woods to Tian.

When Tian opened his eyes again, everything was dark. He could feel that things had changed around them but he couldn't tell how much. He was sure that there were more people than there were before, but he couldn't tell how many.

"I can't see," Tian mumbled.

"That's because there is nothing here to see with your eyes. We are in a new place now. Don't try to use your ears to taste. Explore what you're perceiving and figure out where the stimuli are coming from."

Tian took stock of himself. His eyes perceived nothing. His ears heard nothing except what sounded like sparks. He could smell something though. It smelt like an old place, like a library. Specifically, it smelt like the decaying books in his college library. And as Tian focused more, he realized that it was less of a smell and more of a feeling. It felt like the feeling he got as he walked down the fluorescent lit stacks of his college days.

'That's it,' he thought. 'It smells like fluorescent lights. No, not smell like them. It tasted like them.'

Tian rolled the feeling around on his tongue. It was more than taste, it felt like them. He felt it on his tongue and it traveled though his body. He shut off his sight and his hearing and concentrated on the feeling, on the thought of the feeling.

Tian stood in the dark for a second and then took a deep breath in. No air filled his lungs. Instead Tian expanded and filled up more space. On his release there was a flash. It was clear. It was complete. And it was just a flash.

Tian tried again and this time he held it. The image was dim but he could make out a light. It was an ocean of white light churning on the ground far in front of him. He looked over at Irabell who didn't look the same. He no longer looked human. Irabell looked more like an amoeba of light. He still had some human characteristics like projections where his arms and legs would be. But there were no hands, no feet, and his clothes were gone.

"Where are we?" Tian asked Irabell.

"In general or specifically?"

"Both."

"We are standing in front of the knowledge of everything that has existed," Irabell replied casually.

Tian looked trying to make out more. "The light, is that a library?"

"No, those are the people. Where they stand is the center of all of our knowledge. Everything that we have learned from the time of our second birth has been stored here."

Tian considered the phrase 'second birth.' "What do you mean second birth?"

"When we first became self aware we didn't know to record any of our experiences. But eventually we learned. At first we recorded everything like they did on earth, on decaying energy similar to earth's paper. Then we created a technique that would hold knowledge for millennia. But after millennia it too started to fade away.

We consider our second birth our enlightenment. Now every living memory that we have and have had for millions of years have been cataloged and stored for all of time. Every decision and thought that you've had will remain preserved and unchanged from the time that you made it to the end of us all."

That didn't appeal to Tian. There were many thoughts that Tian had that he didn't consider worth preservation. There were ugly thoughts that didn't present him in the best light. There were brief moments when he was the problem with society and not a positive force for it. And worst of all there were things that he did that he couldn't stand to live again. The thought of others flipping through the book his life choked him and dimmed what he was seeing even more.

"Why does everyone look so different here?" Tian asked trying to get his thoughts away from himself.

"That is because we are all different species of life."

Irabell's words just hung there. Tian turned around and looked at him. "As in different types of humans?"

"As in aliens."

"As in flying saucers?" Tian asked.

That was a hard question for Irabell. There were so many details that needed filling in before he could answer that question accurately. But after a moment Irabell decided that accuracy wasn't as important. Not at this stage.

Irabell gathered his words carefully before laying them out before him. "We are a species of alien that would visit earth from another dimension."

Within the bundle of all the things that Tian was prepared to hear, these words weren't among them. Tian examined the alien body that stood in front of him. It was richer than he first noticed. If it were color it would look like a swirling mix of hue dancing within a synchronistic breath.

If it were color there would be 30 different shades of red yet each would be distinguishable from the next. There would be 20 different blues, 15 different yellows, and a matching number of greens, purples and oranges.

There was a tremendous amount of depth to what Tian saw, but he really didn't see it in color at all. What he saw, he was actually feeling. And what he felt was an opera of experiences full of sound and fury performed on a stage that was as old as life itself.

Tian now turned his attention to the people in the ancient library. It was all clear now. He wasn't seeing them. Tian knew that if he was seeing them, the people would lose their definition as they got further away. But looking at what had to be a billion people, he could see each one with the same clarity that he could see Irabell.

In front of, and behind the ocean of light were what looked like grass and shrubs. But in each case the green colors were replaced with a song that hit Tian with the feeling of a perfect spring day on a grassy mountain side. It reminded him of hiking in Yosemite National Park, or the Redwood National forest. It felt like old, content life.

Past the shrubs were rolling hills that were like what he imagined ancient Greek gods to be, unforgiving and hard. The hills screamed out that they challenged anyone to climb them. And if you took the challenge you would be tested. Tian respected those hills and briefly bent his head to them.

Tian's sight continued up the landscape. And what surprised him the most was that there was no sky. There was no blue, no clouds and no black. There was only a void. But this wasn't the emptiness of space. This void was welcoming. Tian felt at home within the void. The emptiness felt like a world full of people holding a deep breath and thinking of one thought. The void felt like the release.

It was unmistakable. This was an alien world. The people, the landscape, the planet itself did not belong to the universe that he knew. Tian even admitted that this could be a different dimension like the ones seen on Star Trek or 1950's American movies. But the question that Tian could not resolve was why he was there. Why did he wake up and find himself among aliens within a different dimension?

Without being prompted Tian felt the answer come to him. It was Irabell's voice, or at least his thought. Tian held the answer and rolled it around in him before digesting it. It was hard to swallow, but once it got down it stayed down. Tian could still taste the thought on his tongue though. He examined it for its individual flavors.

"Because you are one of us," the voice had said. "And this is your home."

Tian tried to wash away the taste of it. He swallowed hard to get the last of it down.

'I don't know this place,' he thought. 'How could this be home?'

Chapter 5

Tian always felt a difference between himself and others. The first time was sitting in his sixth grade classroom. But it wasn't when the 11 year old boy denounced his Christian faith, it was in the thought that followed. 'Wouldn't it be cool if I started my own religion where I was the Jesus?'

Even he knew that this wasn't normal. 'Eleven year old boys don't think like this,' he thought. But he looked around the room and wondered how all of the kids in the class would feel following him to salvation. 'It isn't that crazy,' he decided. 'There isn't anyone special here. They're all ordinary. They will follow someone, why shouldn't it be me?'

Tian put the thought down like it were a machete in the jungle. He didn't pick it back up until three years later when his brother's girlfriend introduced him to a series of books by the author Ruth Montgomery. They opened up a world that he never imagined. The first book that he read was a book called 'Aliens Among Us.' It was about phenomena that Montgomery called "walk-ins". This was when a soul on earth wanted to leave their body and another soul from another planet agreed to take over their body.

The concept was fascinating to Tian. And as everyone who read the book wondered, Tian asked himself, 'could I be an alien too?' Montgomery's criteria to be a 'walk-in' were very strict though. All of the walk-outs had to have gone through some sort of traumatic life experience that propelled the exodus. And once the new soul took over their life had to immediately change.

Tian had had no traumatic event in his short life that could equal the carnage and disaster that accompanied the walk-outs in Montgomery's books. So what Tian carried away from the book was about the author herself. Ruth Montgomery was renowned, and she had drawn to her a following. What she wrote, her followers believed. Her readers would change their lives to follow her teachings and Tian liked that idea.

Tian did everything he could to get his hands on all of her works. He kept his eyes open every time he visited the United States and he always asked his friends to visit the bookstore whenever they traveled. After two years Tian had read all eight books and what he read within its pages was the rise and the fall of a movement.

Ruth Montgomery, respected new reporter, meets a spiritualist that shows her amazing things about the psychic world. Moved by what she sees she gambles her respectable career for the possibility to help others find their spiritual way. Mockery comes but it is also accompanied by financial success and followers. She leaves her respectable career and the topics get wilder and more elaborate.

In the second act, she joins forces with other icons that she herself helped to build. However, after exhausting every angle, the topics begin to be repeated and refuted. But by the time Montgomery is an old woman her mistakes become overshadowed by her body of work. And for the most part, her body of work has been praised and honored. Over her career she has been showered with riches for having shaped the lives of millions. And in the end, Ruth might not have started her own religion, but it was close.

Tian admired Ruth while finding her topics fascinating. There were some things that not even he at 15 could believe, but the genre itself called to him. He then read the works of Shirley Maclaine and Dammion Brinkley. And he read books like 'How to Channel,' and 'Wiccan Witchcraft'. But by far the ones that held his interest the longest were the books on Parapsychology.

Parapsychology, as Tian learned, was the scientific study of psychic phenomena. It existed at the intersection of amicable and amazing. Parapsychology offered something that Ruth Montgomery never had, respectability amongst the thinking class. Ruth's work spoke to the feeling class and it was with them that she left her mark.

The great discovery of where physics met the human will was still a few years off, but Tian felt the same sort of draw towards physics all the same. The moment the love began was when Tian was still 13 years old. One day after school his brother came home and with an excitement that Tian had never seen in his brother before, announced an amazing thing that he had learned. His brother proclaimed the discovery that color did not exist.

At first this didn't make sense to Tian. Of course color existed. It existed all around him.

"No," Patrick proclaimed. "The dining room table isn't brown. It isn't any color. What happens is that the atoms in the table are vibrating at a particular frequency so that when light hits it, it absorbs some of the energy in light and reflects the rest in all directions. That energy then goes into your eyes and your brain imagines it as the color you see as brown."

It amazed Tian. This was a revelation to him. In that moment he understood that the universe wasn't as it seemed. It then came as no shock to him when weeks later Patrick came home with another announcement.

This time Pat had proclaimed that nothing we saw was solid. "Everything that exists is made up of more empty space than solid object." Pat punctuated the point by saying that "if you were small enough, you could pass right through a wall." Tian had a harder time coming to grips with this idea, but after learning about light he accepted that anything was possible.

When Tian was finally allowed to choose his high school electives, physics, chemistry and biology were all among them. But physics was his favorite by far. There was something orderly about it. Every turn of the universe could be explained. And even the largest of thing could be broken down to the same small things; protons, neutrons and electrons.

Protons have a positive charge and live in the center, or nucleus of the atom. Electrons have a negative charge and circle the nucleus like planets around the sun. An atom always wants to be in balance. That means that it always wants to have as many positives and negatives. And in their natural state they are balanced.

But an atom has a competing force. It also wants to have just the right amount of electrons circling it. An atom is in many ways like the humans that it combined together to create. Without balance in our lives between exercise and rest, work and play, happiness and discontent, our bodies and our lives break down. But even though this balance is necessary, humans still choose to only show the world success, strength, power, beauty and others positive leaning characteristics.

At the atomic level the balance was a fight between two competing forces. The atom has a drive to be negatively and positively balanced as well as the drive to have a particular amount of electrons in its outmost orbit. And usually if an atom is balanced negatively and positively then it is not showing the correct amount of electrons in its outer orbit. And if an atom is showing the correct amount of electrons in its outer orbit it is not balanced between its positive and negative forces.

When an atom is unbalanced it does a very human thing. An atom will look for mates that have what it is lacking. So if an atom is balanced negatively and positively but isn't showing the correct amount of electrons in its outer orbit, it will find another atom and share the electrons in its outer orbit allowing both to become balanced. But with the addition of borrowed electrons the atom goes out of balance because whereas before the negative and the positive charges were in balance, now there are more negatives than there are positives.

Now each of the atoms goes in search of other atoms or groups of atoms that are more positive than negative. For humans that could be more work, more play, more happiness, more challenge etc. And in both cases they will go off looking for that other thing until a balance is reached.

In the atomic world there are also the loners. There are those atoms that are born positively and negatively in balance while having the perfect amount of electrons shown to the world. They don't need anyone else or want anyone else. They are content and rise above it all.

Tian knew that he wasn't one of those loners. His young life felt in balance before his first thoughts of being a savior. But after that he could feel himself drawing on the praise and admiration of others. With that drawing, he became very negative until he almost wanted to end his life. But with the discovery of Montgomery's books, he discovered meditation and it was like magic how much that put his life in balance.

But after all of the years of his studying the spiritual books and the books on physics, a stone cracked the surface of his peaceful mind. 'A loner stays alone, wants for nothing, and affects nothing around him. A discontented person constantly reaches out to others drawing them closer and then pushing them away,' he considered.

'A discontented person is driven to search for more and has an effect on others. That person goes up and down. And more importantly, that person's discontented life is like all of the other discontented lives that are reaching and pushing through the malaise.' Tian knew that if he were to become the savior he imagined himself to be, he had to let go of the balance and be whipped through the atomic winds.

During the summer between high school and college Tian took his final deep meditative breath. It took almost a year for the negativity to return but when it did it was more powerful than it ever had been. Tian spent hours thinking about bloodletting himself in his dorm room sink. Hours more were spent imagining himself the biggest acting star in the world, and more still exploring every sexual thought imaginable.

Tian was slowing transforming into pure ambition and desire. It was then that he realized that he wanted three things: a connection with someone else; he wanted to create something that changed the world; and he wanted the financial success that came with it. Tian decided that this was what his new life was going to be about. And true to that thought, that is where Tian's every decision was orientated.

Tian spent his senior year of college preparing for the leading role in a television show in which he was cast. And when the show didn't happen he focused on his senior thesis for his psychology degree entitled: The History of Parapsychology.

When graduation rolled around he was apprehensive about his after college survival, but ready. The drive to Toronto was long but it was also good thinking time. Tian felt destiny pushing him through life and the glory of it all was about to begin.

Tian knew he was young, smart, good-looking and tall. He had all of the genetic advantages that anyone could wish for. And more importantly, he now had destiny on his side. It was two days later that he had the death dream.

Tian looked at Irabell with his swirling depth and undefined features and saw the alien in him. But Tian wondered where the alien was within himself. Certainly Tian always felt the difference between himself and others. 'But where did the normal characteristics of humans leave off and his own alien-ness begin?' he wondered.

Irabell turned and walked toward the ocean of people below. Tian noticed how Irabell didn't as much walk, as he floated away with his legs flowing back and forth in alternating motions. Tian followed him but was sure to make each of his feet touch the ground.

"We have existed for a long time," Irabell began. "We were created at the same time as the human universe, at the time of the big bang. We weren't the same then as we are now. It took us a time to evolve."

"From what?" Tian interjected.

"From what we were before. We were small and noncomplex. We weren't self aware. We weren't conscious of ourselves as individuals."

"What happened?"

Irabell stopped moving and turned toward Tian. "The human universe created life."

Tian didn't understand. All of these words meant nothing to Tian. 'They evolved out of the big bang and became conscious because of life on earth?'

Tian felt his human-ness returning to him. Answers, facts, understanding, these were the things that meant something to Tian. He always needed takeaway nuggets that when put into his pocket fit with all of the other nuggets that he had gathered.

Irabell turned away from Tian without a word and continued toward the ocean. Irabell's pace increased and soon Tian had to let go of the solid feeling underneath him in order to keep up. The flying was effortless. It felt no more difficult than having the desire.

As Tian got closer to the edge of the crowd he felt something unusual. It felt like the vibrations expelled from the mumble of a crowd. He was moving too quickly to accurately process it, but when Tian entered the edges of the ocean, the suddenness knocked him back like a 50 foot wave.

In an instant Tian was overwhelmed by the presence of everyone. It reminded him of his experiences walking into an incense shop. First there was nothing, but then there were a hundred different smells that took your breath away.

Tian struggled to regain his footing causing him to fall further behind Irabell. There were more than just the thoughts and feelings of everyone around him, there were words and phrases that popped into his head. Words like 'Henry', 'Horse', '1698', 'Wife', 'Fight', 'Child', ' Food', 'Bread', 'Sex'. But a second later there would be 'Henry', 'Horse', '1698', 'Wife', 'Fight', 'Child', ' Food', 'Bread', 'Table'. And then the change would be the word 'Bread' which became 'Peasant.' And then the last word would change again.

It was all too much for Tian and in a moment all he wanted was quiet. So in another moment, that's where he found himself. Tian looked around and everything was familiar again. He found himself standing on a hill looking over a field of rolling green.

The scenery touched Tian in a way that was unfamiliar to him. Tian thought about how he and his ancestors had all been born here. He thought about how his child would soon be another in a long line of proud Liquiduses. He thought about how he wanted to name his child Henry like himself and his father. But he also thought about how his wife had objected.

'Who was she to deny his heritage, his birth right?' Tian thought about how much he wanted to kill his wife, but also about how much this vista always calmed him. 'She was not a selfish wife,' he thought. 'She did her womanly duties and her dowry was abundant when they had married.'

It was her father that she wanted to name the baby after. She thought that it would cause her father to look favorably on them to help ensure that his name would live on. 'There is a wisdom in her thinking,' Tian thought. But what the name Henry could give his son would be the same proud heritage and solace that it gave him on troubling days like today.

"Come with me."

Tian heard a voice interrupt his thoughts. "Listen to my voice and come to me."

Tian looked around for Irabell and then found him standing behind him in much the same stance as he had found him in the woods.

"Irabell?" Tian announced with some surprise. He had forgotten all about him.

"Focus on me and walk toward me," Irabell said with sternness that Tian didn't come to expect from him.

Tian did what he was told. He looked at Irabell and walked toward him. In a moment they were both among the waves of people whose thoughts again crashed down on Tian with a thunderous 'whoosh.'

"You have to be careful of what you think about here. Every moment of life has been indexed and the system is designed to work with your thoughts to take you to exactly what you are looking for. You were standing within the life of Henry Liquidus, so your next thought took you to the nearest entry that matched. This isn't a place that you should be for very long, because it can change you too much."

Tian could hear Irabell's voice loudest amongst the bramble and wondered how much longer he would have to stay there.

"I wanted to answer your question," Irabell continued. But at this point Tian couldn't even think of what the question was. "You wanted to know what we are, but I can't show you here." Tian took that as Irabell's prompt to keep moving, so he did.

Topic after topic filled Tian's mind. At one moment it was a child in the jungles of Brazil and in another a bee in Africa. Tian equated this experience to walking through a grove of palm trees back in the Bahamas. As soon as he past one branch, another was there to hit him in the face. And after the initial hit came all of the individual spines which poked and itched. Tian never thought of himself as an outdoorsman. And it was this feeling of discomfort that kept him confined to comfortable hotel rooms.

Tian sped up and pulled himself closer behind Irabell. He chose to focus on the narrowly defined creature that floated in front of him. 'How did I get here?' he thought. 'Where are we going?'

Tian cleared his mind remembering what had happened when he wished for quiet. Instead he focused on all of the creatures he passed. They were all of different shapes and each of them had their own emotional signature. There was more than just one feeling of contentment among them. Their contentment came in millions of different shades. But Tian also noticed that their feelings of uneasiness came in a million more.

The words continued to whip through Tian's mind until they became unfamiliar to him. He welcomed this change. In place of the words were now feelings of pops and snaps. There weren't any less of them, but together they almost made a song. Tian imagined that if a person's life was a song, this must be what it sounded like.

'Does my life have a song?' Tian wondered. Heaviness filled him as he realized that if it did have a song it would be a sad one. Tian imagined the joy and majesty of what some life songs would sound like. He hoped that those more joyful songs quieted the sounds of his own.

Irabell slowed to stop. As Tian stopped behind him, Tian realized that there hadn't been words for a while. There were also less people, or whatever they were, in this part of the ocean. Tian moved around the space to find the subject of the area they were in, but only saw what could be described as pictures of lightning flashes.

"Where are we?" Tian asked.

"This is the moment when we made the greatest discovery about ourselves. I want you to see it. It will explain to you who we are."

Tian was excited about this prospect. He wanted something tangible. He wanted a gem that he could put in his pocket. "What do I do?"

"Think about the atom," Irabell said.

'The atom?' Tian wondered. He searched his mind for an image or time that would trigger a thought of an atom. He recalled a memory. It was of the first time that he imagined what an atom looked like. He concentrated and conjured the image in his mind.

At that moment Tian saw a small light coming from a very far distance away. As the light passed by him his attention latched onto it.

This light was smaller but much more active. It traveled through space like a plane caught in wild turbulence. The light climbed up only to be dragged down lower than it had started off. 'It's like a drunk bumble bee in a rocket ship', Tian thought before smiling to himself.

Suddenly Tian's mind let go and he felt himself floating weightlessly. He could feel that who he was had changed again.

Everything seemed to be dark but as Tian thought again everything was illuminated. Tian could at once see, or more accurately, feel everything happening around him. It was like there was a force field extended far off from his body and he could feel the objects that penetrated it.

Tian's first thought was of excitement which brought with it a widening of his field. On the edges of his perception was a pool of live creatures that would be breakfast. Tian turned his thoughts toward the creatures and a distortion developed in the field.

Tian thought about the day that everything changed for the creature that he had become. He, the creature, had been feeding on the electrolyzed rocks next to the heat streams when something unidentifiable broke into his field of perception. Tian was startled because this thing had a much larger charge than the rocks that sometimes entered their ooze from the outer space.

While Tian could feel all of his fellow creatures look for safety outside the disrupted field, Tian was drawn toward the source of the disturbance. Tian pulled in his tentacles with the sticky lace hanging down, curled them within the flap of its bulbous body and warmed the top of him. By warming the top of him he created a charge within the ooze that pulled him toward the next negatively charged cloud.

Tian moved like a spider shooting invisible lightning bolt webs. Tian sprayed his webs outwards until it found an area of negatively charged ooze. Afterwards it would latch onto the cloud and Tian would use the attraction to pull himself forward. As Tian got closer to the cloud, the cloud would become neutral and he would attract another cloud further ahead.

Tian could feel that he was quickly approaching the cause of the distortion. Even from a distance Tian could tell that it was large and put out a lot of charge. What surprised Tian even more was that the object wiggled as if it were alive. This was a surprise because his force field told him that the creature didn't look like anything that he had encountered before. So when Tian eventually found himself in front of this strange new creature Tian didn't know what to do.

Tian swam around the creature and scanned the creature from all sides. The object was as big as Tian when he stretched out his tentacles all the way out. And although it released an incredible amount of charge, it didn't seem to think or move in an intelligent way. Instead the strange creature floated there spasming and sucking ooze into it. Tian decided that this was the result of having entered the ooze from outer space.

'Maybe its journey was unintentional,' Tian thought. 'Maybe something had sucked it into this world from the outer world and now it was dying.'

Tian reached out his tentacles and allowed his lace to dance in the current of the new creature's oscillating charges. In a moment of unbridled curiosity Tian let one of his tentacles touch the creature. Tian got a charge that he had never experienced. And at the small spot at which Tian touched it the creature seemed to explode into a shower of energy and then dissolve. It was exhilarating to Tian.

Tian had 17 tentacles that were all used for different things. Tian could barely stop himself when he wrapped all 17 of them around the body of this cylindrical creature. Tian didn't know how each of his tentacles would affect the creature, but the exhilaration that Tian felt when he first touched it was too compelling. Tian wanted more of it and he couldn't stand to dole out the experience. He wanted it all and he wanted it at once.

When Tian touched the creature he devoured it. With some tentacles Tian exploded its surface. With other he used his atomically thin hairs to pry apart the smallest part of the smallest particles of the creature. And each time the creature dissolved Tian was covered with a micro second of vibrating showers that would quickly go away.

Tian could remember and pick between every minuscule moment in those micro seconds. But because the creature was so big he didn't have to savor the moments. The creature seemed to have an unlimited supply of those minuscule moments to share. And each group of moments seemed to paint a picture in Tian's mind about what this creature was and what went through its mind.

Tian's laced covered tentacles discovered a lot about the wayward creature. The creature did not naturally live in the thick ooze that Tian had always lived. It lived in much thinner and uncharged ooze. The creature didn't use an electrical charge to pull itself forward, it normally moved in a wave fashion that pushed it.

Tian even found out that there was an enumerable amount of these creatures outside the ooze. In fact, the creature's last thought before entering the ooze was of finding an escape from its crowded home. It was with a clear intension that the creature propelled itself through the barrier. The creature didn't know what it would find, but it hoped that it was better than where it was.

Since that is where the creature's thoughts stopped, Tian suspected that there was something about the ooze that the creature couldn't stand. Tian suspected that it was the charge of the ooze. It seemed to overwhelm the creature's body when it came in contact with Tian's world.

But that wasn't all that Tian learned from the creature. With its atomic hairs on the shortest of its tentacles it peeled apart the smallest parts of the creature. And at the creatures smallest part were three different particles that when pulled apart, snapped back together with an explosion and then a pop. It was the explosion that Tian liked. It created bubbles within Tian's insides.

The vibrations made Tian's body dance and just as quickly as it started it stopped. This was the feeling that Tian had never experienced before. And this was a feeling the Tian craved again.

Tian guessed from the creature's thoughts that there would be more of its kind that would try to enter the ooze. But if any other tried they would suffer the same quick fate. So with a moment of thought, Tian knew what he had to do. Tian had to make a pool of uncharged ooze within the ooze near the barrier between their two worlds. That way when the next one entered Tian could quickly place it in the pool and examine it. Tian knew that this was the only way to take the time to understand its tantalizing vibrations.

Tian long observed that when the rocks next to the heated stream warmed, it created an area above the rocks that wouldn't carry a charge. It was a dead zone for Tian where if entered he couldn't latch onto a charged cloud to pull himself out.

The charge in the ooze seemed to be what disabled the creature. So Tian decided that if he could move these heated rocks near the barrier between their worlds then when another creature entered, Tian could move the creature into this dead pool and observe how it lived.

After a few attempts Tian learned that placing the rocks in a circle created the largest neutrally charged area. And after the pool was created there was nothing left for Tian to do but wait. With his heated rocks there Tian had all the food he needed. When Tian got hungry he would wrap his short tentacles around the still warm rocks. With his atomic sized hairs he would tear the electrons from their orbits around the nucleus within the atoms of the rocks. And as Tian did, there would be a release of energy that Tian fed on.

Tian's species once fed on secondary energy sources like plants and animals, but eventually the ooze grew barren of all life accept Tian's own species. And the creatures that couldn't break apart the atoms of the rocks for a direct infusion of energy died off. The creature that Tian observed was the first other species in the ooze during Tian's lifetime.

Tian spent most of his day in still alertness with his field extended as far as possible. It took a long time for him to feel another disruption and when he did it wasn't close. Tian took off after it, but knew that it would be a very difficult task to get there, grab it, and then bring it back to the pool.

Tian's electric webs pulled him through the ooze until eventually the wiggling and flopping creature floated before him. It was smaller than the first one which Tian knew would make it easier to carry back. Carefully Tian reached out its long tentacles and gently embraced it like nothing it had held before.

Tian raced back aware of every part of the creature's surface that dissolved at the touch of his tentacles. Tian felt the creatures memories pour out of it. And it was then that Tian reached its short tentacles toward it.

When Tian felt the creature's struggles lessen it became hard to resist devouring it. Even as Tian approached the pool, Tian's long tentacles pulled the creature closer to its more deadly short ones. But

Tian managed to allow only one pop and explosion before he shot himself into the pool.

The lack of control within the pool was disorienting to Tian. All he could do once he entered the neutral area was let go of the creature and flail around. Tian first threw his tentacles left causing him to move upwards. And then Tian threw his body right causing Tian to move downwards.

It didn't take long before Tian stopped struggling. He instead focused on the creature that he had brought with him into the pool. The creature was seemingly conscious. It was moving and it was swelling and contracting its body in a rhythmic fashion. Tian didn't know what to make of the behavior. But Tian decided that he should get out of the pool when the creature moved itself within a tentacle length of him.

Tian didn't like this feeling. He had captured the creature. Tian had rescued it, but here he was at its mercy. Tian knew how to attack. Its species was very territorial and he had to defend his area more than once over its lifetime. So when the creature moved away, and then approached Tian at an even quicker pace, Tian reached out its long tentacles and grabbed hold.

This didn't stop the creature and the momentum from its attack moved Tian's bulbous head to the edge of the pool. This was close enough to shoot out an electric web that found a cloud just outside the edge. Tian pulled himself toward it and then threw out another web that pulled Tian even further out.

Tian let go of the creature but not before the creature had bitten off a part of one of its long tentacles. Tian knew now that these creatures weren't exploring out of curiosity. They left their world in search of new sources of food and Tian's species could be that.

Tian observed the creature for a long time. Tian saw how the creature would dart around the pool at incredible speed. And Tian saw how after a little while the creature would remain motionless within the pool, only to start darting around a while later. 'If the creature could survive outside the pool, it would be a fight,' Tian thought.

Tian also kept watch on the barrier between the two worlds. And when a second and then third creature entered the ooze, Tian was careful to wait until the creature was almost completely still before he took it to the pool. They all recovered, and eventually Tian had five of the creatures captive.

He noticed a change in their behavior in groups. They all darted about in symmetry. And at certain times the larger ones would eat the smallest one.

But the day that Tian became this jellyfish creature, was the day that the experiments were to begin. Tian took his time to decide which one he would grab. He decided on the bigger ones, because they had more surface area and would probably live the longest. Tian also came up with a plan. He wasn't going to drag the captured creature out of the pool. He wanted to pull the creature close enough to the edge that he could get his short tentacles on it and begin.

However, whenever Tian approached the pool the creatures always darted around faster. And when Tian splayed his tentacles around the edges of the pool to pluck one out, the creatures just responded by splitting up in opposite directions.

Tian decided that patiently waiting for a large one to enter his strike zone wouldn't work. So instead Tian rotated around the outskirts of the pool with his tentacles splayed. But with every movement Tian made, the creatures would counter.

Noticing the creature's reactions Tian adjusted becoming more random in his movements. This seemed more effective. This would sometimes send some of the creatures in one direction and the rest in another. And all Tian needed was one bad decision by any of larger creatures and he would have them.

Tian rotated left upwards then down toward the right. He then shot around to the other side and then back again. Tian kept repeating this pattern until the creatures began to anticipate it. Left up, down right, swing around and then back again.

Tian observed how they stopped reacting to the movements and started engaging in the habit. Here would be Tian's opportunity. Tian moved left upwards, then down toward the right, then moved to the other side. But when the creatures crossed the pool Tian abruptly moved back. Before the creature could react, Tian shot its longest tentacle into the pool and grabbed one. The creature pulled Tian in but not before Tian got a web onto one of the outer clouds and pulled his prey to the edge.

The other creatures darted around the pool randomly but none of them got into what they saw as the strike zone. And with the gripped creature wiggling and struggling in Tian's grasp the experiment began.

With deliberate movements Tian reached out his shortest tentacles. The thin lace that hung from it rocked back and forth in the currents created by the creature's struggling. As Tian's short tentacles got closer he focused on the atomic pull being created by the nano-sized hairs on his short tentacles and the creature's skin.

Tian enjoyed the attraction between the two. There was a sort of electrical exchange going on. The creature's body drew Tian's short tentacles toward it and when the two finally touched there was a crackle. Tian couldn't be sure of what the crackle was, but if he were on the outside looking in, he would have seen that that crackle was the sound as the atoms of the creature's body rearranged where Tian touched it.

Tian then focused even more on what his short tentacles felt. He could feel the same atomic structures as when he grabbed the rocks, accept this time the atoms were much more varied. In one area atoms had both large negative and large positive charges. The creature had atoms where a lot of electrons circled the nucleus as well as atoms with only one or two. But as unique as this was for Tian, this wasn't what he was looking for.

With one of his tiny atomic sized hairs he reached out to one of the atoms. Tian could feel the little negatively charged energy brushing over the hair. The energy was smooth and constant.

Tian then used one of his nano-sized hairs and plucked the electron out of its orbit. For a brief nanosecond afterward the electron's movement changed. As it pulled away from the atom both the nucleus and the electron wobbled. But very quickly after the electron left the orbit, both the electron and the nucleus stabilized.

Tian had mined many rocks for food, but had never experienced this momentary vibration before. Within the rocks there was also a slight wobble that Tian couldn't account for, but Tian had just accepted this wobble as unexplainable. But within this creature it was pronounced. And Tian immediately concluded that the difference between the two wobbles was the presence of life.

Tian ran the same experiment again and again. And each time there was the same wobble of both the electron and the nucleus. 'Why is this happening?' Tian thought.

Tian's body was a highly refined instrument for measuring the exchange of energy. Tian's species had evolved that way. This species' body could feel every micro jolt of energy and account for it like the rocks at the bottom of the pool. But there was something more profound about what Tian was experiencing now.

Unfortunately before Tian could completely understand what was going on the creature stopped wiggling. Soon thereafter, the creature's body stopped swelling and contracting. And soon after that the extra wobble that occurred when Tian plucked out another electron stopped occurring. Tian hypothesized that the creature was now dead.

Tian pulled the creature outside the pool and engorged on it like it was one of its heated rocks. Tian's long tentacles pulled soft material from hard while the short tentacles strummed across the creature's atoms like the strings of a musical instrument.

Tian saved the memory packs for last. Tian popped the outer pouch and felt the creature's experiences cover him like a fine mist. The creature had been disturbed when it found itself in Tian's pool. Tian felt how the creature's thoughts were chemically altered as it began to panic. But Tian couldn't interrupt the emotion that came with the panic. That like most of the creature's emotions was outside the vocabulary of Tian the jellyfish.

Tian stopped for a moment and thought about how it was that it was experiencing the creature's thoughts. Tian's body was a highly tuned instrument, but the only thing that it could read was energy. Tian had never felt this type of thought energy before and it had never felt the wobble.

At that moment Tian felt a bubbling develop within him. This too was a new feeling, but it didn't disturb his concentration. Tian let go of what remained of the creature and allowed it to float away in the ooze. Without intension Tian began to slowly roll in the energy clouds. And like the bubbling this feeling didn't distract him either.

Tian thought 'why would the atoms wobble when they are pulled apart in a living creature? And why would the wobbling quickly stop?'

Tian ran through the experience again in his mind. He accounted for every scrap of energy that pulled toward the nucleus and then pulled away from it. It was all constant. But yet there was a wobble that started on its own and then spontaneously stopped.

'New energy!' Tian thought.

Tian's spinning slowed, but now a swelling was developing on the bottom of Tian bulbous head. The swelling was right in between the area in which all of his tentacles curled into when he moved. When Tian's spinning stopped his tentacles automatically curled into his body. Tian's body was now upside down and a flap retracted right where the smaller more centered tentacles protruded. And as the flap moved, the inner tentacles pulled away from Tian and his bulbous head caved in.

However, none of this distracted Tian. He continued to think about what he had experienced. And Tian concluded that there must have been a new energy source that he never before considered. There must be an energy that was immediately drawn to the electrons and atoms of living things. This new energy was what stabilized the living creature but was only needed while it was alive. After the creature dies, the energy is no longer needed so it is no longer drawn to it.

Tian considered how he had felt small wobbles when feeding on the heated rocks but had never felt them as he had now. 'Volatility!' Tian thought. The more active the atoms are, the more atoms join together and are broken apart. The more atomic process that occurs within an object, the more of this new energy is needed to stabilize the atoms.

'This new energy is what slows down the parts of atoms enough so that it can interact with each other.' Tian thought.

This was a new energy that Tian had never accounted for before. And Tian's first thought after coming to realize something that no conscious being had ever thought before, was how he could use this new energy as a new source of food.

Tian's shorter tentacles with the atomic hairs succeeded in pulling way from Tian's body. As it did Tian's bulbous head decreased in size. The smaller tentacles were now being guided by its own bulbous head. But the majesty of birth was lost on Tian. What was more important to him was the fact that his experiments were now over. And what also crossed his mind was that the creatures in the pool were now nothing more than food.

Without his shorter tentacles Tian would no longer feel the explosions and pops. His longer tentacles were the only ones left and they were much less sensitive. So with nothing else to do Tian pulled himself over to the pool and splayed its tentacles around the edges. His dance began again with the same rhythmic beat; left upwards and then down and to the right.

The memory ended and Tian once again found himself standing next to Irabell in the less populated part of the ocean. Tian looked down at himself and everything had once again returned to how he remembered it. His legs were still long. His fingers were still gangly.

But there was a slight, however slight, change that Tian could barely see. It was more noticeable as a feeling. Tian felt less human. He couldn't pinpoint why, but he knew it was there.

Irabell waited for Tian to regain his bearing before speaking. "Did you understand?"

"Was that me? Did I experience that?"

"You experienced it, but it wasn't you. It was someone else's memory"

"Was it a squid?"

"It was nothing that you might have encountered on earth. It is a creature that has no name. It existed in the physical universe for millions of years. But that memory is one of our most cherished.

That was the first time any living creature first noticed our existence. We like to say that is the moment when we became conscious of ourselves."

Tian heard what Irabell had said, but he was having problems fitting it into his understanding of the universe. "So that creature lives on a different planet?"

"It is from a time long ago, on a different planet, which revolves around a different star, which exists in a different galaxy. But it still exists within the same physical universe as earth."

Tian thought for the moment allowing all of this new information to settle. "So what was the new energy that it found? Wasn't that the point of the memory?"

"That new energy was us." Irabell broke the moment by turning away. Within a blink both he and Tian were again gone.

CHAPTER 6

There were few things that would shape Tian's life the way Ruth Montgomery's books would. What impressed him the most about her books was that they were all consistent. With their stories and insights they brushed aside Christian theology and instead emphasized a belief grounded in ending life. But it wasn't each individual life that the reader had to break away from, it was the cycle of lives.

Montgomery, who as a channel would communicate the teachings of her spirit guides, said that we all have lived many lives before. And each of those lives built up karma, or debts that we had to pay off. So for example if you killed someone in one life, you would either have to be killed in another, or you would be born with a defect that sufficiently enough hindered your life.

Ruth's books bypassed the presence of a judging God and instead relied on an innocuous thing called: the Universe. And she, because in Ruth's books the universe was always 'she', would see everything, and account for all of the injustices that were missed by human eyes. And the most effective act to escape the never ending cycle of mistakes and reconciliation was meditation.

Tian adopted this philosophy because it spoke to his young mind. Life was bad, ending life was good. But to end life intentionally was bad because your life was designed to teach you a particular lesson. And if you ended your life early you would just be forced to come back in even more difficult circumstances to learn the lessons that were set before you the first time.

Meditation allowed you to learn your lessons quicker. Montgomery stated that meditation could shave lifetimes off of your reincarnation cycle. Meditation allowed you to make contact with your higher self and your spirit guide. With meditation you could turn your psychic potential into psychic ability. Meditation opened a window that allowed you to talk to the dead, see into the future, astral project to different places and realities, and to read the thoughts of others. To Tian meditation was the secret passageway to a magical world and it was too alluring to resist.

Tian learned his meditative style from a book by the legendary actress Shirley Maclaine. Maclaine claimed to be taught about the spiritual by an alien inhabiting a human body. The man was a walk-in as described by Ruth Montgomery so to Tian the two worlds of spiritual teachings seemed to fit.

Maclaine's brand of meditation was called chakra meditation. Chakras were energy centers around the body that corresponded with different colors and stages of life. The lowest chakra was the base chakra. It was located at the base of the spine, was red and corresponded with the adrenal gland. This chakra corresponded to the first seven years of life and regulated the fight or flight mechanisms within the body.

The next was the orange chakra. This was located within the testicles of a man and over both ovaries of a woman. This regulated testosterone and estrogen controlling both your sexual and creative energies. This chakra governed life from age 8 to 14.

The third chakra was the solar plexus. This was a yellow energy center that sat in the center of your torso and regulated digestion. This controlled the way that you dealt with transition and governed ages 15 to 21.

The fourth chakra was the heart chakra. This was a green energy center that regulated love. It regulated the glands that released oxytocin and vasopressin and governed the ages 22 to 28.

There was next the blue chakra that centered in your throat. The blue chakra was the healing chakra and regulated the thyroid. This chakra was responsible for things like metabolism and healing. The blue chakra governed the ages of 29 to 35.

The next was the lavender chakra known as the third eye. It was located between the eyebrows and monitored the information that you gained psychically. This governed ages 36 to 42.

And the final chakra was the crown chakra. This chakra was white and governed the pituitary gland. As the white color was a combination of all the other colors, the pituitary gland told all of the other glands of the body when to release their hormones. The pituitary was the body's master gland and the crown charka was the body's master chakra. The crown chakra governed life between the ages of 43 and 49 leaving age 50 as the first year your life was released from the draw of any one chakra.

Tian liked this form of meditation because it gave his active mind a focus. And the benefits that Maclaine claimed was that after enough meditation you would start to gain power over the colors. One example that Shirley gave was that the color blue governed the clouds. So once you gained mastery over the blue chakra you could use the color blue to change the movements of the clouds. This appealed to Tian.

Tian began by meditating an hour a day. It was always after school before anyone else came home. But Tian often found himself falling asleep in the middle of it. So Tian pushed it to right before bed. It was at this time in the darkness that he began to feel the effects.

The first sign that the meditation was working came when he believed that he could feel the colors. Red was a low rumbling, while yellow was a higher pitched happier feeling. Blue was serious and orange… well, Tian didn't like to focus on orange because the sexual thoughts often derailed his meditation. But Tian eventually learned that orange was a fuller feeling that was almost as low as red, but not quite as cheerful as yellow.

The next sign that something was happening was that all of the dark thoughts that Tian had started to go away. Tian would often leave his meditative state with a warm contentment that was new to his life. Things stopped bothering Tian after he began meditating and it became easier and easier for him to turn the other cheek.

The final sign came after Tian began looking for proof that what Montgomery and Maclaine said was true. He wanted to glimpse into the future. And Tian decided that if what the two writers had written was true then seeing into the future wouldn't be that difficult. Both writers had claimed that everything was connected, so to dip into the future shouldn't be much harder than dipping into the past.

Tian increased his meditative regiment by adding a 20 minute outdoor meditation in the mornings before school. And after each session he made his desire clear by saying it aloud. "I want to be able to see into the future." Tian had read that it was very important to make your intension as clear as possible, and about this intention Tian had a singular focus.

After a few weeks Tian found himself sitting at the breakfast nook of the house that his family built after losing Tian's childhood home. It was a modest house but was a clear reflection of his mother's good tastes. His mother had designed the house with French double doors that had two columns in front of it supporting a roofed overhang.

There was a long window on either side of the door and there were matching long windows where the living room protruded out past the rest of the house. The beauty of the design was the symmetry. And it gave Tian a lot of pride when his best friend Ed gushed over the house's design.

The electricity went out often in the Bahamas and this Saturday day was one of those times. Tian and his parents were having a casual conversation about their neighbors when Tian heard the sound of the fridge turning on. It was always a welcome sound after a power outage because it also meant that the TV was back on as well.

"The power's on," Tian announced.

"How can you tell?" Tian's mother replied.

"The fridge turned on."

They had all been sitting next to it and Tian's mother was the closest. "No it didn't," Tian's father replied.

"Yes it did," Tian said with the stubborn adherence he believed necessary to ensure that his young voice was listened to.

"The lights aren't on," his father replied.

"The power's on. I just heard the fridge turn on," Tian insisted as he got up and crossed into the kitchen. "See," Tian said as he opened a dark fridge.

His parents looked at him with a knowing smile.

Tian looked into the dark fridge confused and embarrassed. He had insisted and had been clearly wrong. He had to figure out a way to rescue his young pride. He stood tall, closed the door and with confidence said "I guess that means that the electricity will be turned on any moment now." Before he had time to even take a step the embedded kitchen lights switched on followed by the whine that came as the fridge's motor geared up.

Delight filled Tian's person. "See!" Tian was ecstatic. Not only had he gained back his self-respect, he had did it as a prognosticator. This wasn't something that happened to him alone in his room. This had witnesses, doubting witnesses that had laughed at him just moments earlier.

"Did you see that? I said it would happen and it did. It didn't even take five seconds. I just said it and it happened," Tian bragged excitedly.

Tian's parents didn't like this. They already had concerns about how deeply their son had gotten into meditation and about the books he read. None of this was something that they were familiar with. They often stretched their minds to figure out how their son's obsession had begun. And after much thought they simply concluded that their son was odd and needed closer observation.

It was a few weeks earlier when Tian's father walked into the living room to find Tian meditating on the couch. Seeing Tian motionless in a strange seated position unnerved Tian's father. And when Tian slowly opened his eyes and looked at him with a look that his father could only compare to that of the undead, his father was creeped out.

Tian's father spoke to Patrick and his mother, but it was Pat who spoke to Tian about it. "What the hell are you doing? Worshipping the devil?" Pat yelled more than asked.

"No, I'm meditating. It's the opposite," Tian replied.

"Well stop it. You look like some sort of dead person when you're doing it. Where the hell did you get it from anyway."

That argument with Pat was one that Tian knew he wasn't going to win. But here in the kitchen on this particular Saturday he knew that he didn't have to hide what he had been doing. Not now. "You know, I've been meditating on trying to see into the future. And you saw it. I heard it happen before it did and I told you it would seconds before it happened. What do you think about my mediation now?"

"Sometimes these things happen," Tian's dad replied while looking out the windows in the French doors.

Tian didn't know what that meant. Did he mean that sometimes people can see into the future; or did he mean that sometimes people guess correctly? Tian was silenced trying to figure it out. "I said it was going to happen and it happened," Tian said again trying to rescue his moment of glory. But it was too late. The moment was gone.

Tian decided that whether they believed him or not the meditation had worked. There could be no clearer evidence. 'Now,' he thought, 'it was time for something a little larger.' Tian wasn't sure what though.

A year later after Tian's father had moved out for the second time, Tian found himself sitting in the quiet house watching TV. It was fall and Tian was watching coverage of a hurricane that was headed toward his island. Hurricane threats were an annual occurrence in the islands, yet none had hit his island since Tian was a child.

Hurricane Hugo captured Tian's attention because it was clocked with winds up to 135 miles per hours. That was considered a category 1 hurricane and at that speed would certainly rip roofs off of houses and kill dozens of people on any island it hit. Tian's friends often found potential hurricane landfalls thrilling, but this one was too dangerous to get excited about.

This one was headed directly for his island and as far as everyone was concerned, could be the one that shut down the shipping routes preventing food, water and gasoline from coming in. This could be the one that shut down the power for weeks. This could be the one that brought food riots to the 3rd happiest place on earth. This was a big hurricane and two days were all that stood in the way from The Bahamas being the focus of international headlines because of blood in the streets.

That night Tian watched the evening news before getting ready to meditate. He imagined the carnage that would occur in the next few hours as Hugo made landfall on Jamaica. It was then when he remembered what Maclaine had written in her book about meditation. 'Clouds were affected by the color blue,' he remembered. 'Would this be the ultimate test?' Tian asked himself.

'If what I read was real, if all of the meditation I did means anything, then I should be able to do something about Hugo.'

Tian shut off the TV and lay in bed. He went through his usual routine concentrating on each of the colors first. And then when the usual was done he tried for the extraordinary. He imagined the color and feeling of blue. He allowed the feeling to building up in his neck and body. And as his body began to vibrate with the feeling and he couldn't hold it anymore he imagined it shoot out of him into the clouds of hurricane Hugo.

At first he imagined the dark, powerful winds of Hugo. But then he saw the blue from his body join it. Tian didn't try to make the blue stop the hurricane, but instead to turn it. The hurricane was forecast to slice through the eastern end of the country. But what Tian imagined was his blue energy pulling the gale force winds east out to sea and out of the path of his country. Tian found the necessary focus draining, but this more than anything that he had experienced in his life, was important.

The blue energy continued to poor out of him and as he did he imagined the clouds spin out to sea. And when Tian began to feel the strain that accompanied the sustained concentration, he decided to end it. His teachings suggested that when giving off energy the giver should always end their session by encapsulating himself in a white light. So just before breaking the connection Tian imagined a white bubble cut off the connection between him and the clouds. After that Tian simply rolled over and fell asleep.

Tian slept well that night. His next day at school brought no surprises and his after school time was just as uneventful. Tian wasn't in a rush to watch the news that night because as much as he wanted the things he read to be true, as much as he wanted all of his meditations to mean something, there was a part of him that believed that it did not.

Within his normal nightly routine he flipped on the TV to watch the news. It was to Tian's marked surprise that shortly after landfall on the island of Jamaica, hurricane Hugo changed direction hitting only Jamaica's eastern seaboard. And the forecast had changed as well. Hugo was no longer going to hit the Bahamas. Its trajectory now placed the hurricane heading out to sea.

"What happened?" Tian spoke aloud to his empty bedroom. "Did I do this? No, I couldn't have done this."

Tian turned off the TV, laid back and thought about it. 'This is too big for one person to have done,' he thought. 'It couldn't have been me. But if it was me then I could do it again. Once is coincidence. Twice is when it becomes a miracle.'

Tian turned off the lights and went right to work. His routine remained the same. Each chakra received attention, and then all of his focus was on the color blue. When his body was full of the blue light again he imagined it flowing out of him and finding its way to Hugo's clouds. But this time instead of moving the winds, the blue energy was sent to do something more difficult, slow down the winds.

After the hurricane hit Jamaica its speed had slightly increased. It was customary for a hurricane to slow down when it hit land but Hugo had sped up to 136 miles an hour. 'If what I did was real, then it shouldn't be a problem to stop the hurricane all together,' Tian concluded.

But the idea was easier to conceive then the thought of it was to imagine. When the blue energy entered the clouds Tian first allowed it to swirl around with the imaginary winds. And after enough of the blue energy had entered the clouds he imagined that all of the energy suddenly stopped swirling. Tian imagined that the energy then repositioned itself into a wall that blocked the wind. But even in his own imagination he couldn't picture the wall having an effect.

Tian built up more blue within him and sent it out as reinforcements but still he couldn't picture it. Then he imagined himself standing behind this massive wall of blue pushing on it as well. This is when he felt some of the wind bounce back. He imagined a denser wall and a bigger version of him and this was when the wall began to hold. Soon the mental image didn't even need him in it. The wall held itself.

Tian found this was even more strenuous then the night before, but Tian held his focus even longer this time. Eventually though, there was no more he could give and his experiment ended. As instructed he again imagined the white light encapsulating him, but this time he couldn't do it. He couldn't imagine the white light interrupting the blue energy flowing out of his body. However Tian was tired so after five minutes of failing to imagine it, he gave up, rolled over and fell asleep.

It wasn't until mid morning the next day that Tian noticed how tired he was. It was like his mind was working in a thick molasses. He could perceive of everything in normal speed but his mind was working just a little too slow to react to everything. His body felt drained and what was most annoying to him was that he couldn't get his nose to stop running.

Tian thought about what he had done the night before and how he hadn't been able to break off the energy stream. 'It's silly to think that within the physical universe there was a role to be played by the wishes of others. Atoms bounce, they bond, and they change, but they do not listen and they do not obey. But still, what he was experiencing was similar to what Maclaine had warned about when a person expelled energy out but didn't encapsulate themselves afterwards. So coincidence or not, Tian decided that it was at least worth considering.

The symptoms dissipated as the day wore on. And by the time Tian made it home they were practically gone. However on this day Tian didn't wait for the evening to find out the latest on the hurricane. He turned on the news before he even put down his backpack. Tian sat on the edge of his bed waiting for the weather report to roll around. The weather in other parts of the world was normal, the report said. There was a pocket of warm air flowing over the Midwestern United States, and a full week of sunshine was predicted in Los Angeles. It seemed to take forever for the news to cycle back around to the important stuff.

"As our hurricane watch continues," the newscaster announced, "hurricane Hugo has dipped a little bit in its strength. Overnight the hurricane slowed to 131 miles an hour and now looks like it is headed for North Carolina."

Tian listened to the news very carefully. He replayed what he heard in his head. 'Overnight the hurricane slowed to 131 miles an hour…' He allowed the words to sink in. 'On the night that I tried to slow the hurricane, the winds dropped by five miles an hour. Where is coincidence in all of this?' Tian thought. 'What are the odds of me getting my desire two nights in a row?'

After a few moments his role in this national event stopped mattering and Maclaine's warning took precedent. 'What if all of this does have something to do with me; what if I had caused this to happen with imaginary blue light coming out of my body? What does it mean that I couldn't get the energy to stop flowing? What could that do to me?'

Imaginary or not, he knew what he would be doing that night. And as his self-imposed bedtime approached, Tian followed the rituals that he did on the other two nights. First he focused on all of his chakras, and then he focused on blue.

What appeared in Tian's third eye this time was a little different. Without even thinking about it an image of him lying on the bed with a constant stream of blue energy flowing out of him appeared in his mind. 'It never stopped,' he thought.

So this time, instead of trying to get energy to flow from himself to Hugo, Tian imagined pulling blue light from the clouds back into his body. It only took 15 minutes and he was able to again imagine the white light around him. This was a warm feeling for him. For the first time this image comforted him. He felt like a boy within an egg, protected and warm.

His dreams that night were uneventful as was his next day at school. But when he got home he was met by the news that reported that during the night Hugo had sped up by three miles an hour. Tian didn't know how to process these events or how he would tell his friends. But a few days later the decision became a lot easier when Hugo hit North Carolina and was responsible for a person's death and millions of dollars in damages.

This series of events would forever be Tian's secret to share as he may. Tian was sure that he couldn't replicate it and he could never prove that he had anything to do with it. But Tian couldn't help but think that although many more would probably had died if the hurricane hadn't changed course, he might have still played part in the death of someone that wouldn't have died if he had done nothing at all.

As time went on Tian began to reach back to his youthful desires of being a savior. He wasn't sure whether it was something that he wanted anymore. But what he was starting to believe was that there was a god. And more importantly than that, Tian began to believe that he was one of God's favorite sons. He began to believe that there was a destiny for him that others didn't have. He began to believe that there was a divine hand guiding his life.

The changes were unnoticeable to his family and friends, but they were clear to him. They were noticeable in the fact that Tian gave up on lying, warning all of his friends to beware. It was noticeable when Tian started doing charity work. It was also noticeable when Tian decided that he would work as little as possible in school because it was his destiny to go to an American college and all that mattered was his SAT scores.

It was a subtle thing that only his teachers noticed, but Tian pulled out of all of his O-level classes making him completely ineligible for the local college. He then only applied for one college giving no thought what would happen if he didn't get in. Tian felt that destiny and God was on his side so there was no need to apply to anywhere else.

Tian also didn't give much thought to a second school because it was actually a member of the board of the school that had suggested to his mother that Tian apply. Though their lifestyle had long become humble, Tian's mother still engaged in a high class social life. And it was during one of those fancy dinners that his mother was sat next to Mr. Albert Clear. When he mentioned to her that he was on the board of a college, she very quickly mentioned Tian's pending graduation. Mr. Clear then strongly suggested that Tian apply.

With his usual confidence Tian applied and it was with the same confidence that he opened his acceptance letter. The only real surprise that met him was that Mr. Clear had made sure that Tian received the Albert Clear Academic Scholarship along with a few others from the school. Tian knew that there were other students at his school that were a lot better students than he was and whose families were more in need. But Tian accepted what he had been given with grace because as a favorite child of God, he couldn't think of anyone who was more deserving.

Chapter 7

Whereas moments before Tian stood with Irabell in the ocean, now he was nowhere. Tian had no sensory input at all. He couldn't tell whether he was standing or floating. He couldn't see anything with his eyes and he couldn't feel anything around him. Time had no meaning to him here. And moments after arriving Tian couldn't tell if he had just gotten there or if he had been there for years.

Tian didn't feel lonely though. What he felt was more akin to isolation. He had gotten used to touching and seeing and feeling others. In this empty space he began to remember the good things about his life, the solidity of it, the camaraderie. Even if it was often unpleasant he felt something and something was definitely better than nothing.

With suddenness Tian felt something touch his shoulder. He was grateful for this contact. As the gratitude filled him he wanted to know who it was that had rescued him from the isolation. He stopped looking and tried to feel the person's identity. It was Irabell.

Tian concentrated on the touch and imagined where Irabell might be standing. 'He's next to me,' he thought. 'I just have to picture him next to me and I won't be alone.'

"Can you see me?" Irabell asked.

Tian received a tremendous amount of relief from Irabell's words. "No, I'm having problems. Where are you?"

"I'm next to you."

"I'm sorry I can't see anything."

"That will pass."

"Where are we?"

"We are in a place we use for teaching. It helps us to express to others what we are thinking. Can you see me yet?"

Tian did an inventory of each of his senses and found nothing. "No, everything is just empty."

"It will take a moment."

With that Tian felt Irabell's touch slip away from him and the isolation returned. Tian didn't like this and began to remember the stories of limbo from the Catholic teachings. 'This must be limbo,' he thought. And in the instant it took him to remember limbo, he remembered heaven. He held the thought of heaven in his mind and suddenly everything around him changed.

There were people around again. They looked like humans and they all meandered around within what looked like a large park. The park was covered in sparkling green grass which even grew under the orchard of blooming fruit trees. There was a happy feeling there that made Tian want to stay.

Tian turned to the closest person next to him drawing their attention. "Where are we?" Tian asked.

When the man turned around, Tian saw the man's face contort. Tian's appearance disturbed the man and that made Tian feel self-conscious. He remembered that he no long felt completely human. And he was sure that that was what the man was seeing.

The happiness that Tian felt moments ago was now replaced with regret. He regretted coming here and interrupting this man's joyous feeling. Tian had just wanted to know where he was and now he felt as if he had ruined this man's personal party.

The man looked at Tian soberly. The man had thought that his was an exclusive club. But the thing that stood before him was clearly not one whose heart was pure. There was a distortion about Tian. Tian's facial features had slid away from their natural position. His face had nothing close to the facial symmetry that was associated with beauty. But remembering that he too was a child of God he answered. "You are in heaven."

'Heaven?' Tian thought. 'I am not welcome in heaven,' he concluded. Tian turned away looking for something familiar. He felt like a homeless person walking through Beverly Hills. He didn't belong here but he didn't know how to get out.

As soon as his mind turned to him Irabell appeared. "I want to leave here," Tian said. Irabell reached out his arm and placed it on

Tian's shoulder and again they were in the darkness. This time though Tian could see Irabell.

"Where was I just now?" Tian asked with a dread that he hadn't experienced since coming to this world.

"That was the Christian heaven."

"As in, where Jesus lives?"

"There are many heavens that Jesus can be found in. That's one of them."

"Then the Christian faith was the right one?"

"Right for what?"

"Right for everlasting peace," Tian questioned.

"The people that you saw there can stay there for as long as they choose. But the only ones that have been there from the beginning were the biblical heroes; Jesus, most of the apostles, Mary and a few others."

"I don't understand. Why would anyone choose to leave heaven?"

"I'm sure that it felt very familiar there. That is a very human place, and if you want to hold onto your human experience, that is the best place to be. But our nature is change, and it is hard to resist your nature."

Tian focused on Irabell and his words. "Then where are we right now? Is this limbo? Is that why we're here, to judge my life?"

"No," Irabell said with compassion that Tian hadn't imagined Irabell could express. "We are here because you said that you wanted to understand. This is another one of our great accomplishments. It takes a practiced skill to operate and I'm afraid that I wasn't as practiced as I thought I was."

"How was it that I ended up in heaven?"

"All of the heavens exist in the world that we are now."

"All of the heavens?"

"Yes. This place is the only place in our world where thoughts can be made real for others. So this is the only place where the heavens could be created. I am ready to show you what I had intended. Would you like me to show you now?"

Still processing what Irabell had told him Tian said "yes." With that word the darkness filled with energy. It didn't quite feel like heat, but Tian felt it as waves flowing through him from a source that was somewhere in front of him.

"We don't know what we were before the creation of the physical universe. But from all of the great thinkers from all of the physical universes, we have been able to understand how we became conscious. The big bang seems to have been a result of a series of compression and expansion cycles that the physical universe makes. At the time of the big bang all of the world's matter, all of its material, was compressed into a ball smaller than earth. All of the electrons and protons pushed together so much that new forms of energy were formed.

But because every molecule of physical matter could not vibrate there was no need for an additional energy that stabilized their movement. That stabilizing energy is what we are made of. And since our energy has no mass it was unaffected by the immense gravitational pull of the clasped physical universe. Our energy therefore floated free through existence like dust through the air on earth. But then the big bang occurred."

What was completely dark lit up in front of Tian. Whereas waves were hitting Tian before, an avalanche of everything in existence poured toward him now. And in that moment the rolling fireball of light, sound, smell, and taste slowed to a near stop.

Tian was fascinated by what he saw. Every color of light and every beam of electromagnetic energy showed itself as the frontrunners of this cosmic race. But behind the light he could see explosion after explosion of matter which then shot off in every direction hitting other particles causing other explosions.

He didn't see chaos in all of the activity. Tian saw the symphony of creation. It was like the finale of a fireworks show made all the more impressive because this was the prelude for a more impressive show called life.

The show didn't stop there though. As all of existence came rushing toward Tian, the darkness all around Tian began to light up with what looked like pale blue fireflies.

"Once the explosion occurred, there was one energy released. But that one energy expressed itself in two forms; light and matter. Light is made up of energy packets called photons that travels across the physical universe in waves similar to those found on oceans. In comparison to the particles that make up matter, photons are very small. It is its smallness that allows it to continue to travel as a wave.

All matter in the physical universe is made up of atoms. Atoms are made up of electrons, protons and neutrons. But these pin prick sized objects are houses for even smaller forms of energy. And like all energy in the physical universe these smaller forms of energy also want to travel in waves. But the forces that accompanied the big bang were so intense that when all of the energies collided with each other they became entangled like fishing hooks thrown into a box.

Whereas the smaller energies would prefer to travel in waves, when smaller energies are tied together organized movement doesn't occur. Within the houses of these smaller particles there is one particle pulling in one direction and another pulling in the other. This results in a chaotic tug of war which could result in the house being torn apart."

Tian looked closer at the slowly approaching mass and he could see some of the smaller particles heading in the opposite direction of the rest of the matter. "I can see them."

"But the electrons, for example have too much energy to settle into an orbit around a proton and neutron. What is then needed is a dampener that will absorb that excess energy from the tug of war going on within it. This dampening energy then slows the electron down enough for it to get situated into an orbit around the nucleus of an atom. That is where our energy comes in."

Tian watched as the little specs of pale blue begin to hum in the space around a ball of matter. Tian noticed as one at a time a blue spec would dive into the ball itself. And whereas the entire physical universe exploded outwards at almost a snail's pace, the pale blue specs shot into the mass at a speed that was almost too quick to see.

Sometimes there would be glowing balls of matter between the spec and where it wanted to go and the spec would pass through it as if it wasn't even there. And on the brief occasion when Tian would see the spec find its destination, the particle it joined would wobble a little less and glow a little less brightly.

"Are we the blue specs?" Tian asked.

"The blue energy is the substance that we are made of. Our energy diminishes the tug of war going on in atoms. Our energy absorbs the excess energy that would otherwise make a balanced atom impossible. Our energy combines with physical matter and brings stability to atomic particles within matter.

Each packet of pale blue energy that you see has a slightly different energy signature. This means that whatever the exact need is of the physical matter, there is at least one energy packet from our side to balance it."

"Am I seeing the energy passing through the matter?" Tian asked.

"Yes, the blue energy does not consist of physical properties. It is not affected by gravity or the electromagnetic, ionic or covalent forces. It exists in what some call its own universe."

"Its own dimension?" Tian interrupted.

"Yes, by the definition of the word, because our energy is not affected by the physical forces, we exist in our own dimension."

"If our energy isn't affected by physical forces, then why is it shooting towards the matter?"

"Because there is part of physical matter that exist in our dimension. It is that antenna that pokes through that draws our energy toward it."

"So does each of those specs represent one of us?"

"No, not at all. Those specs are as much us as one atom is a human body. No, the blue energy that matter draws to it, bonds with the matter long enough for the matter to bond with other matter. Once the new bond is created the atoms overall charge changes and the energy that once stabilized it no longer works. So the old blue energy is shed and a new packet of stabilizing energy is drawn to it.

However, the needs of one electron or even one atom is different from the needs of a molecule like water which is made up of two hydrogen atoms and one oxygen atom. No one packet of energy from our side is diverse enough to stabilize all of the energy particles within a water molecule. So an exact match of stabilizing energy from our side must come together to allow the water molecule to form.

The same is true for crystals, and planets. Everything in the physical universe must also have energy from our side in order to allow it to be stable. The great thinkers that we have learned this from, thought that this constant creation and shedding of stabilizing energy is what created life in the physical universe. And although our library of memories doesn't go back that far, our great thinkers believed that life within the physical world is what created us.

What the great thinkers thought was that over hundreds of millions of years, molecules of every possible configuration in every possible environment were created in the physical universe. And eventually there was a molecule created in an electrically charged super heated pond within the physical world. A mixture of carbon and oxygen bonded together but because of the heat, electrons kept braking away from the molecule forcing it to become positively charged.

This drew more oxygen molecules to the carbon-oxygen creature allowing the new oxygen molecule to share two more of its electrons. This created a momentarily more stable state until the heat of the pond would again loosen electrons from the molecule, creating a larger carbon-oxygen creature that was again positively charged."

Tian watched as the avalanche of matter changed into a pond of red hot thick magma. Directly in front of him appeared this large carbon-oxygen creature that was only about 20 atoms long. It didn't look like a chain of little balls, but instead like groups of dots with little packets of energy spinning around it at super fast speeds.

Tian concentrated on what he saw to slow it down in his mind. The creature seemed to be moving. When the shared electrons of the oxygen molecule orbited to the point which was closest to the carbon nucleus it pulled the carbon nucleus towards the rotating electron. The whole process looked like a caterpillar that inched its self forward by contracting and expanding its body.

Initially when Tian had observed it, it just looked like it was vibrating. But then Tian noticed that it was slowly inching across the magma toward what looked like an oxygen molecule. This creature was moving toward substances that helped it maintain a stable balance. It was moving itself toward its food.

Tian turned his attention toward another creature that was considerably larger than the first. It seemed to have depleted the oxygen molecules in the area and was having a problem moving in any particular direction. The heat from the magma continued to strip the electrons from the creature, causing it to become further and further out of balance.

The creature wobbled and shook until the unbalanced positive and negative charges that held the creature together were too weak to keep it as one. Tian watched as vibrations finally broke the creature into two almost equal parts. These two parts then moved off in its own directions no longer weighted down by its once massive body.

These creatures were by no means self aware, but they were feeding, growing and reproducing. Tian concluded within himself that these were what Irabell claimed them to be. These creatures were by most definitions 'alive'.

"The larger a molecule gets," Irabell added breaking Tian's thought, "The larger the energy molecule gets on our side. The closer the molecules were forced to be within this pond, the closer the energy from our side was forced to get. And what began to happen was that the energy particles on our side began to grow together.

Our energy in a way feeds on the energy that electrons need to shed in order to become stable. That excess electron energy causes our energy to grow like vines within a confined space. When two of our energy particles are forced to be close to each other and then the living molecule feeds, our particles entangle themselves within each other and are not easily broken apart.

Eventually there came a point when these creatures were pushed outside of the magma by currents within the pond. In this new uncharged environment the creatures were no longer being stripped of electrons and became stable. But not only that, but because the creature was now being bombarded by new elements that bonded more readily with the atoms of the creature, the creature began to break apart.

However, because the energies from our side had grown together, it shed itself as a complete molecule allowing two or three smaller energy particles to replace it. That freed energy molecule from our side would sit in an entangled state until the energy began to degrade. Our energy needs physical energy to grow, but it also needs physical energy to maintain its shape and size. Without new physical energy, the ends of the vines retract. This retraction untangles the energies. And given enough time the energies will contract until they are their original size and physical charge.

However, it takes a while for our energies to break down. And during that time in the physical universe, life evolved to become more and more complex. Within time those energy molecules from our side became the perfect charge for the larger more complex life of the physical world. And when these complex life forms died, it shed a more complex energy molecule on our side.

These processes continued for hundreds of millions of years until one day in the physical universe a creature's drive for balance forced it to recognize itself from others. The recognition came out of its drive to sustain balance of its internal systems. The creature learned that others competed with it for limited resources. But at the same time others often had excessive resources around it that the creature also needed for balance.

Self awareness developed as one of the many tools that creatures used to acquire the energies necessary to sustain the balance of life within its body. Just as long appendages allowed the creature to reach food that other creatures couldn't, self awareness allowed creatures to recognize the inherent threat others posed to its survival.

As a result, creatures that developed the molecular configuration necessary for self awareness survived longer and reproduced more often. This created a competitive disadvantage for those creatures that couldn't recognize it competitors. And the end result was that the self aware creatures out competed, and then replaced the creatures that weren't self aware.

And because the complexity of the atomic structure within the creature resulted in self awareness, a similar complexity developed within the energies on our side. Every evolutionary step within the physical creatures still involved atoms that needed to be balanced in order to remain stable. So all of the electrons, proton and neutrons which made up a water molecule had a stabilizing energy molecule from our side. That stabilizing energy molecule could only be described as a water molecule on our side, even though it was made up of different materials and had different properties.

And since the brain of cells of living creatures are all made up a different combination of elements, electrons and compounds, they also need the equivalent elements, electrons and compounds created on our side. So when the creature's body became complex enough that it could recognize itself as different from others, the same molecular complexity was left in tack when it died and the energy from this side was shed.

And because the self aware creatures in the physical world out competed and replaced the others, they produced more self aware energies on our side once the creatures died. Soon the self aware energies on our side began to recognize each other and an evolution began on this side that was no longer dependent on the physical world for its only experiences.

The first self aware creatures on our side didn't last very long because smaller less complex molecules degrade faster than larger ones. But as portions of these self aware creatures were recycled within the ever evolving creatures of the physical world, a society developed on our side.

Our societies were never able to exceed the societies in the physical world because we depended on them for their ideas. Survival, it seems, is a great motivator for innovation. And whereas the physical worlds presented their creatures with a clear finite life span, we were never clear upon ours so for a long time our society was content to evolve slowly.

When the first societies within the physical world developed language, we began working on a form of communication. But it took us considerably longer than the physical creatures because we lacked the ability to draw air into a windpipe. We have no air and we don't possess physical windpipes.

Species rose and fell during the time that it took us to develop language. And again our final inspiration came from an innovation developed within the physical world. There were a species of small ocean dwelling creatures that found it more advantageous to not use sounds when communicating with each other.

On their ocean planet there developed another creature that learned to feed using very sensitive hearing appendages. And even the slightest sounds a mile away would attract their attention. So these smaller creatures ironically managed to tap into the part of them that was us and take advantage of the chemical processes going on within their brain."

The space around Tian which still glowed from the remnants of the magma pond changed to a water world deep below the surface of a wet planet. No light got down to where Tian was observing yet many of the rocks and coral like creatures were very radiant with a nuclear energy that appeared to Tian as varied as the colors of the coral in the Bahamas.

The view that Tian and Irabell shared snaked around the ocean until it came upon an ugly black fish like creature that looked more like a rock than alive. It moved slowly and awkwardly through the water by dipping forward then using a back fin to straighten itself back out. It was clear that there was no way for this creature to survive around predators if it didn't develop a great advantage over them.

The image then became less visual and more of a magnetic resonance image that could pick up only the electrical impulses of the creature. The image focused in on the creature's brain.

"When this creature had a thought," Irabell continued, "it first registered all of the subjects that it was thinking about."

Tian watched as an impulse registered in a part of the creature's brain. Then Tian saw how a signal in the center of the creature's brain shot out toward the back section causing a very small section of its brain to light up.

"This creature's brain was organized by subject. So if the creature wanted to remember what something looked like, a small picture of the creature would be painted within the creature's brain.

But instead of having to fill out all of the details like color and exact shape, things similar to footnote indicators would be attached to the picture in case it wanted to focus on that area. And then if the creature wanted to focus on a bump on the subject's back, the image would then draw upon that footnoted image and display the new one. But because all of this happened faster than the creature could perceive, it all seemed like one unending image to the creature.

This, it turns out was the ideal situation for thought transfer. It was because just like every other atomic interaction, the electrical impulses in the creature's brain created physical changes within the creature's brain cells. When the image was painted within the small section of the brain, the atoms in the cells of the brain drew to it energy from our side that kept the newly changed atoms in balance. And when the image was changed, the atoms in the brain shed its self of the energy from our side. And because the energy is unaffected by anything in the physical world they remained in the same position like an imprint of the image itself.

That part is not unusual. In fact, it is quite a common process within the brains of most self aware creatures. What made this species unique was that the creature also had the ability to perceive the abandoned images that others shed.

What made receiving the other's thoughts possible was the fact that each member of their species was unique. Each had distinct visual, radiant and atomic signatures. So when a creature shed one of its thoughts, their thoughts were unique to them. And because the thoughts on the physical side were unique, the energy created on our side by the thoughts was unique as well.

But what this creature had the ability to do which other creatures hadn't was think of another of its species and then hold its brain in a constant ready mode without stimulating a particular memory. This ready mode created an identical energy signature to the creature being thought about. And because the energy signatures were identical, the shed thoughts would be drawn to it as if it were a magnetic white board within the creature's mind. In this way one creature could see the other creature's thoughts.

And since the other creature was constantly leaving images behind charged with its own energy signatures, the images became a flip book of thoughts for other creatures to see and then respond to.

It took a while for these creatures to understand they were actually communicating with each other by thought. But once they did they left their verbal and sonic communications behind for this one that attracted none of the predators that shared their ocean.

When these creatures died, the part of them that was us retained the ability on our side. They couldn't teach it to others, but they could communicate with others that had also shared the body of these species. Eventually there were more physical creatures that gained the ability and that was when our communicative ability began to spread.

The ability to communicate became a segregating ability. Those that could communicate were able to hold their forms longer than those that couldn't. Talking about what we experienced within the physical world kept our energy in the shape of the physical form that we left. And those that couldn't communicate their thoughts other than in gestures degraded more quickly into our original particles.

But eventually our society segmented even more depending on the experiences that we had during our physical life time. Those who had lives that positively affected their physical societies, and those that had lives that benefited the world on this side were thought of as more here. And those that had had lives that degraded the societies of their physical world were shunned a little on this side.

That is what brought about the great debate of our side. The question became how much were we in control of the physical bodies that we were drawn to? It was one who was shunned that raised the question. He contended that in the physical world, we were no more than passengers on a ride. He argued that the environment and atomic structure of the physical bodies determined who we were when we were shed.

The other side of the debate was argued by one whose physical life had been praised. He contended that it was destiny that led the praised to have great lives. His argument was that the reason that those drawn to the bodies that would become great were drawn to them was because their energy signatures matched the bodies of those that would become great. And this meant that there was something great about their energy signature to begin with."

The space went dark around Tian and Irabell and Irabell allowed his mind to shift to other things.

"Was there a resolution to the debate?" Tian inquired. In an uncharacteristic moment Irabell turned the question on Tian. "What do you think the answer is? Who do you think has more control, you or the physical body?"

Tian took a moment to think. He ran through the memories of his physical life. There were so many unexplained events in his life. Why had his life turned out the way that it did? How could he have tried so hard but still failed so consistently? If he was as good a person as he thought he was, why did God let the bad things happen to him? Was it because he favored some over others? Or was it because he had some sort of grand plan?

"I don't know what the answer is," Tian replied. "Do you know who has more control?"

"It is something that I have asked myself time and again. Why did my physical body make the choices it did? What role did I play in those decisions? Was I drawn to that body because there was something destructive within my energy signature before that life was lived?" Irabell, now distracted, turned away from Tian and allowed his thoughts to drift.

"Is there no one that has been able to answer that?" Tian asked.

"There are those that have been able to tip the scales suggesting one answer over the other. But still there is not definitive answer."

"Then which way do you lean?"

"I would like to believe that what matters more than the life your physical body experienced is what you do within this world."

"What do you mean? What can you do on this side?" Tian inquired.

Irabell, more attentive, looked back at Tian. Looking at Tian's misshapen human face caused the image around the two of them to change. The images that they both saw paralleled what Irabell spoke.

"There was once a species that evolved on a planet where the molten core was made up of a metal that when heated and compressed expelled its electrons. This caused the planet to have a high gravitational field and a very electrically charged environment. This planet was hit by a comet that consisted mostly of ice. The ice from that comet created oceans and contained the first life that the planet would experience.

However when the water was added to the planet, it caused an interruption in the normal charging and discharging patterns of the planet's positively charged core. This resulted in a very thick and low cloud layer which included an endless electrical storm. The storm was constant over the oceans making it look like the streaks of lightening were necessary to keep the clouds in the air. A hundred strikes would descend in any square mile at a time. And there was never a moment that didn't connect at least 20 bolts of lightning from the ocean to the sky.

The storms were less prevalent over the land. However because the land was originally a silicate layer similar to sand, the storms made the land large hills made of misshapen and shattered glass.

The species that evolved out of this environment began in the ocean. The species evolved to feed solely off of the lightning bolts that shot through the oceans to the sea floor. The creature developed a chemical within it that converted and stored the electrical energy within its body. It was an electroluminescent process which caused all of the creatures to glow. And because all of the variations of that species evolved the same way, they didn't evolve a way to hide from one another or to limit their growth.

When the species evolved out of the oceans it was practically deaf to the sound frequency of lightning bolts and communicated in high pitched sonic noises that their front antennas would pick up. The species developed into hippopotamus sized, ant-like creatures that had long tails that would act as lightening rod to gather its source of energy.

The body of the species was segmented into four segments to prevent the full charge from the lightening from reaching the species' brain. Its head was almost the same size as the creature's other body segments and had many eyes each of which would monitor a different range of the electromagnetic spectrum. Its body was covered with a long, thick, glass textured hair that had a number of functions for the creature.

The glass hairs insulated the creature from damage as it fished for lightning bolts. The hairs were also used in communication. When the hairs were rubbed together, a high pitched noise would be created and manipulated to express its thoughts.

The transparent hairs were also useful for one other purpose. During courtship, the hairs allowed the glowing chemicals within the creatures' body to shine through. The color and frequency of the glow were indicators of the creatures' health and dominance within its group. This was how the creatures determined each other's beauty and how they could find a mate.

As the species' population increased, some of the creatures moved away from the energy rich storms near the ocean. And the creatures that moved away evolved to become smaller, faster and less transparent. Instead their hairs took on hues that would enhance the lights within it. And as opposed to the creatures by the ocean shore, these creatures could communicate over longer distances. The constant electrical interference by the shore limited how far the sonic sound of the hairs could travel. That created a close knit society where familiarity was a source of comfort.

A border developed between the two societies and the shore creatures became suspicious of these smaller creatures that often traveled by themselves. And when the larger shore creatures mastered a way of redirecting some of the energy absorbed from the lightning bolts, they honed it into a weapon that they could use to kill others. As the lightening hit their antenna, the shore creatures could channel some of the energy into food and the rest could be redirected in a highly charged form, that when hitting the other species' less insulated head would cause their brains to boil.

The shore creatures used this weapon to establish a safe zone between the two borders. But the inland creatures took it as a heightened sign of aggression and developed strategies to use their size and increased speed to their advantage. The inland creatures initiated the first war and were defeated in their attempt. The second war was initiated by the shoreline creatures and they successfully expanded their border and safe zone.

But the new border was hard to keep because on the outskirts of the ocean there was less lightening and hence fewer opportunities to use their weapon. There were constant attacks on the border by inland creatures and they were able to more effectively use their tails as spears, finding gaps in the glass hairs of the bigger creatures.

The bigger creatures' rich source of energy came at a price. The glass hairs had to be farther apart on the creatures' body to allow the bodies to cool after it was struck by a bolt. This was a chink in the creatures' armor for any of the smaller creatures that were fast enough to get behind one.

Because of their dense living structure, the shoreline creatures' civilization exceeded that of the inland creatures. Many nests were built along the ocean. And after the first flood of the area the fashion became for everyone to build upwards.

Most nests were built by piling glass particles on top of each other. And each nest was built to hold a family of eight or nine. But as taller dwellings became the fashion, a new technique was employed. Pure sand silicate was added in between the glass with the hopes that lightening would strike the loose sand melting it to into glass. The newly formed glass would bind the other pieces of glass to it making it an even stronger structure.

When the ability to redirect the lightening was developed it quickly made its way into their construction technique. This limited the amount of time necessary to build a tall dwelling. Slowly the society started to divide themselves into specialists. There were those that fought at the border, those that protected the civilization and the inhabitants. The inhabitants then broke themselves down into those that led and those that built.

It was also turning out that those with the largest structures attracted the best mates. The ability to glow the brightest was still important. But it became common knowledge that the higher the ground that you were on, the more lightening you attracted. So even if the creature wasn't the healthiest or the largest, taller dwellings could assure an endless source of energy for their mate.

The dwellings kept being built higher and higher until the first one reached up past the clouds. This was considered the limit of construction, because up there there was no lightning to bind the sand and glass.

When the construction on the first cloud topping dwelling was finished it was a momentous event for the society. Almost half of the inhabitants of the shoreline society came out to see the owner of the dwelling walk all the way to the top. This creature was considered small, and didn't glow much but had an unusually large tail. The owner was also without a mate choosing instead to spend its time build a dwelling that actually touched the sky.

The creature started out at the bottom with all of the attendants and then slowly made its way up the winding path that spiraled to the top. The small creature had to retract its tail the higher it got because in spite of the glass insulation, the bolts were still attracted to the creature. It was hit many times on the way up, and it seemed that the higher it got the more electrical interference there was in the atmosphere.

The creature's antenna was overwhelmed with sounds. It had to close its eyes because of the spectrum of light that was made at the source of the lightening. Even its thoughts became slower and less precise the higher he got.

It pressed on and eventually it entered the clouds hidden from the crowd below. It hadn't been a heavy storm day like this one during the days he built the top layers. And it was he who built the top layers making sure that no others could say they had the privilege to travel above the sky before he did.

The creature hid amongst the clouds to rest a bit and regain its bearing. It was experiencing sensory overload within the clouds. But it was too proud to just turn around and go back down so it either had to wait there for a while and then go back down claiming to have gone to the top or it had to push through and try and climb past the noise. It chose to keep climbing.

The creature's movements were slow and unsteady but eventually the top got closer. And when the cloud layer became more and more translucent it gained more of its poise and strength. When the creature made it to the top it turned out to be many body lengths above the highest clouds. It seemed that on this particularly stormy day the bolts were more plentiful, and the clouds were closer to the ground.

The creature looked up at the stratosphere and saw something that no other of his species had seen before. An orange red sun shined down on it and it warmed its cold body. The creature also noticed how quiet it was at the top. Looking up the creature could only hear a slight crackle from what was coming from above. This was the most quiet that any creature from his species had ever experienced.

But what was the most unexpected about this place was the clarity that the creature could hear its own thoughts. There was always so much interference from the electrical storms below that the electrical neuron processes in the species brain had to be very powerful. The species, even before it left the ocean, had evolved a highly insulated neuron-electrical process that could withstand the constant disruptions that would be caused by being struck by lightning.

But now that the lightning strikes were removed, and the highly charged atmosphere was below it, it could hear the crackles that were caused by its neurons firing. But not only that, it would think a thought and hear an echo of that thought. It was an unusual feeling made all the more unusual when it thought of its family that had died before it could accomplish the tower. It was unusual because the small creature thought that it could hear the thoughts of his family back.

This creature had always been small and its parents had never treated it the same way it had treated its siblings. Mating was more than just survival for this species; it was the core structure of their society. So not being able to find a mate was considered a failure. And with his deficiencies his parents knew that mating wouldn't be likely for the creature. Usually when the creatures of this species were neglected as much as this one was they died. But this one was unusually tough and its large tail, even at its youngest age gave it a constant enough source of energy that it could use to cling to life.

And now on the top of its tower and as the first one to stand above the sky, it could feel its parents seemingly giving their attention to it. It could feel what seemed like his parents making a fuss about him and what he had done. It didn't feel like a daydream or fantasy. It felt like he was standing with them and they were staring at him showing care for the creature.

That is when it knew that this tower was more than just an accomplishment for their society, it was a sacred place. He lifted the front part of his body into the air as much as it could and felt whatever else it could feel. What came to his mind was another crowd of its species standing around it celebrating in what it had accomplished. But they weren't excited about the architectural achievement. They were ecstatic that this was the first of any species to make contact with those that resided on our side.

However the sun soon became too much for the glass covered creature and it decided to take refuse within the top layers of the cloud. Shaded it wondered what it would share with the creatures below. But almost as if he was being pushed, he quickly knew that it would tell the others everything. This wasn't its accomplishment alone. This was an accomplishment for its entire species; even for the world if they would have it.

Once down, word spread fast. The creature would take others up in groups and the first time there was more than one of them up there it was clear how quickly they could understand each other's thoughts. It turned out to be a clear and more honest form of communication than their sonic glass language. In fact it was necessary for all of them to stand as still as possible because outside of the noise of the storm, the sound of their sonic language was overwhelming to each other.

The building of other sky towers was accelerated, and they quickly became the government centers. Matters of war were most often discussed up there, but what became clear to everyone for the first time was the unwillingness of even their most adamant warmongers to engage in more wars.

Instead a plan was devised. They would build a sky tower within the captured land and then vacate allowing the others to climb to the top of it. Once there the shoreline creatures knew that they would get access to the inland creatures' thoughts and then they would know how dangerous their enemy was.

Building the enemy tower took much longer than the others due to the lack of bolt strikes. And there were a number of times the shoreline creatures had to fight off the soldiers of the inland creatures. But knowing this could mean an end to their war, the shoreline creatures fought harder and sacrificed more to keep their land than in any of the previous wars combined. In the end the tower was completed and the land was vacated.

The inland creatures didn't look on this gift favorably in the beginning. But eventually a creature made it to the top of the tower and the best shoreline thought listeners were on their towers waiting for them. The inland creatures' thoughts were all quite different from the shoreline creatures.

The inland creatures valued exploration and solitude. They all seemed to be deep thinkers that thought endlessly about the effect that the war had had on them as individuals and the affect it would have on their next generation. They had even devised a mythology about what happened after each of the creatures had died. These creatures really were very different from the shoreline creatures. But it was quickly determined that they were no threat to the shoreliners. Peace was quickly established between the two.

What followed on their planet was a new age led by the inland creatures. Thoughts were considered to be objects and a system of commerce was established around it. Stories were told and songs were song for the entertainment of others and all of this was done through the broadcast of thought. And because thoughts had quantifiable value the best minds on the planet went to work trying to figure out how to preserve a thought in its pure form.

With their thoughts they were able to explore our world. They learned how different thoughts attracted different packets of energy from our side. And after generations they discovered an energy that bond to thought energies on our side and stabilized it for long periods of time. The procedure turned out to be as simple as thinking a thought and then ending a thought with a sealant thought. And it was this discovery that was the beginning of our first great library.

But their dying sun soon created a shift within the solar winds that kept their atmosphere evenly charged. And the storms that feed them first spiked to a level almost too high to consume, and then ended all together. The changes happened so quickly that the species couldn't adapt. All intelligent life on the planet died accept one creature who had learned to feed on the microbes shed off of the more dominant species.

The great civilization, as we often refer to them, was gone. But we used what they discovered to save the thoughts of other species that didn't know how to do it themselves. And then we figured out a better way that would not only preserve the thought for longer, but would index them in a way that could be accessed by any of us no matter what our formative species was.

Now with all of this access to information we on this side became freer to shape our own futures. We learned that those who had experienced the memories of a species were more likely to be drawn to another physical life. And we learned that those of us who studied in the library more had a greater chance of shaping the experiences of those that hadn't studied. That is what I mean by it being more important what we do here than what we do in physical form. We may not control what our physical bodies do, but we can shape this life as we choose."

Tian thought for a moment, and almost like the question had been sitting on the top of his mind for a while asked, "are we what the religions refer to as the soul?"

Irabell looked at Tian with a thoughtful quiet look and then turned away from him.

"Are we?" Tian asked again.

Irabell disappeared leaving Tian by himself.

Chapter 8

The day after Tian's death dream he woke up in his Toronto motel bed knowing that he had begun a new life. The one that he had had before was dictated by necessity. There was the necessity of being a responsible son. There was the necessity of being a good student. And there was the necessity to set up his life and to have a career. But today, that day after the dream was his life without the necessities. The training wheels had been taken off of his life and he was free to drive it anywhere.

Tian had decided that he would use his expensive education and charmed life to become an actor. During the lean years of his college days he grew to appreciate money. Life was easier for Jeanie his college friend with a car. Life was also easier for Cameron whose academic scholarship allowed her not to work throughout college. Tian's scholarship hadn't been quite that much. His scholarship was only fifty percent of tuition and required him to work 20 hours a week.

Tian didn't consider this a challenge at all considering that he worked more during his junior and senior years of high school. No, what created a real challenge for Tian was when Tian crashed his motorcycle into a truck that was making a turn off the two lane throughway near his college. Tian walked away with a few scratches and cuts, but he also walked away with a $2000 bill for repairs on the truck that he had rudely run into.

Tian took on a third job at the local grocery store where he worked as a cashier. It was a tedious job that paid minimum wage, but it was the additional 20 hours a week that tipped the scales for Tian. Right before he earned enough to pay off his debt something in Tian snapped. Thoughts of the days before the accident became recurrent.

Two days before his crash he was walking from class to his dorm room and he had distinctively heard someone say to him that he should sell his motorcycle. When he heard it he stopped and looked around. There was no one closer than a hundred feet away. In fact the only person that he saw was Jeanie who had also bought a motorcycle and would often join him for rides around the country side.

Tian stopped and waited for Jeanie to catch up to him. "Did you say something to me?"

"When?" Jeanie asked.

"Just now. Did you yell something to me?"

"No, why do ask?"

"I swear I just heard someone say something to me."

"What was it?" Jeanie pried with the same amount of spunk that it took a good country girl to buy a motorbike.

"They said for me to sell my motorcycle."

"Are you sure you heard it?"

"Yeah, it was just as clear as you sound right now."

"Hmm, what do you think it was?"

"Well, I'll tell you this," Tian began with a confident smile, "if it was God, he is going to have to take my bike from me."

"Oh… oh, that can't be smart."

Tian looked down at the shorter Jeanie with a cocky smile that showed part flirtation and part provocateur. "I'm just saying, if he doesn't want me to have it, he is going to have to take it from me."

"Yeah, I'm going to walk away from you before lightening strikes you or something."

Tian laughed as Jeanie walked toward her dorm.

That weekend was one of the annual fraternity parties and there Tian ran into one of the girls from his sophomore seminar group. She always seemed shy around him, but tonight she had a few drinks and was feeling very open. She danced with Tian and talked with him before admitting the crush she had on him. She even offered to walk him back to his dorm.

His sleeping roommate pushed them to the basement. And it came as a complete surprise to Tian when they engaged in what became Tian's first real kiss. Tian understood the deficit of experiences that he had in his life because of his early spiritual development, but with his lips firmly pressed against hers the wait was well worth it.

Tian liked the kissing and he liked her directness. He liked the entire experience of it, but he didn't necessarily like her. She wasn't particularly exciting to him. She wasn't particularly pretty. There was nothing that drew him to her accept the fact that she liked him.

As usual, sunlight brought clarity to the situation. In the morning Tian knew that she wasn't what he wanted. But with little practice in the social graces he thought it best to simply avoid her for the next couple of day. Tian decided that the best Sunday activity that he could think of would be to do something that he had always wanted to do but hadn't. He had always fantasized about what it would be like to ride his motorcycle to the edge of the river and spend a quiet time reading a book.

Tian snuck in and out of the cafeteria and then changed into good motorcycle riding clothes. Unusual for Tian he switched in and out of clothes trying to find something that he didn't mind destroying. He reached for the nice helmet that his brother gave him and then at the last minute decided on his older one. He hopped on his motorcycle like he did for any other Sunday drive and then headed off for the thru-way.

It was about five minutes into his trip when he noticed the red truck up in front of him. It was also in the left lane but it seemed to be keeping his pace so it didn't matter. Tian kept scanning the trees on the left side of the street looking for the clearing that he knew was there. A few seconds later Tian looked up again and realized that the truck had stopped. It had stopped in the left lane because it had found Tian's clearing and was waiting to turn.

Unfortunately, Tian hadn't noticed the truck's stillness until it was too late. Tian was in the far left of the left lane and didn't have enough space to pass the truck on the right. The only option Tian had was to risk passing him on the left and hope that the truck didn't take that opportunity to make its left.

Tian felt his shoulder hit the door of the truck and compress. The next thing he felt was the force changing direction and throwing him backward onto the road behind him. Tian felt his body contort like a tumbler. And when he landed on his back he didn't slide, but instead flipped onto his shoulder and then over onto his stomach.

Tian felt and saw nothing for a brief moment and then he saw only white. With a loud ringing and what looked like crackles of electricity within the field of white, consciousness returned to him. Slowly he recognized the grain of the road in front of his helmet and he remembered what had happened and where he was. His first thought was 'get up,' which he was able to do without too much of a problem.

As he stood in the middle of the road he watched the people drive by him. They were all staring at him, but none more than a jeep full of college students, all of which he knew. Tian examined the shock on their faces as they all turned around and stared. Tian turned his attention to the next car when he heard the familiar voices yelling for him to get out of the road. 'That's right,' Tian thought, 'I'm still standing in the middle of a freeway.' Tian then crossed to the river and sat with his back to a tree.

As the people started to gather around him, one of them pointed down at Tian's foot. Tian looked down and saw blood coming out of the tongue of his shoe. He took a closer look and pulled the tongue back. There was what looked like a quarter inch puncture wound in the top of his foot. It was barely bleeding so what Tian noticed more was the shoe that he had chosen to wear on this trip.

The shoes were a pair that had moved to the end of his shoe rotation. He then scanned the rest of his wardrobe and found his now torn jeans to be the ones that were bleach stained and too tight. The ripped shirt was faded and of course his now scratched helmet sitting beside him was his disposable one.

Tian remembered moments ago as he chose them. He had purposely chosen clothes that he didn't mind losing. He had never made this type of decision before but yet this time he did and here was why. He then thought back to the voice that he heard telling him to sell the bike. "I knew this was going to happen," he muttered to himself. "They tried to warn me."

The effects of that day rippled out through his college years like a tsunami. The accident forced him to take on more work than he could psychologically take. The psychological fatigue affected his grades bringing him one decision away from dropping out. The next semester brought a de-emphasis on grades and an extreme hesitation to work. And the combination of it all fundamentally changed Tian into a different person than he had been moments before the accident. And more subtly, his mind had created a connection between what was his first attempts at intimacy and with disaster.

The ripple effects were clearly already in motion as he sat against the tree waiting for a tow truck to drag his motorcycle off the street. And there was no question whose voice it was echoing in his head saying "you should have listened." It was a voice that was very familiar to him. This was a voice he heard a lot. The voice he heard chastising him for not heeding the warning was his own.

But in the Toronto motel room the day after his death dream, and at the start of his new life, Tian was feeling optimistic. With the dream he felt like he had been given an exclusive peak into the workings of the universe. The world was amazing, but what lay beyond was even more.

Tian held onto the powerful feeling that nothing around him was completely real. He held onto how hollow everything around him actually was. But mostly he held onto the idea that very few people still alive had probably had such an experience. And by him having it, he must truly be one of God's favorites.

With the new day Tian had a plan. He had only $900 Canadian dollars and with that he had to start his new life. That broke down to no more than seven days at the motel at $100 for the week; an apartment at no more than $325 per month. And after paying first and last month's rent, he would have $150 for food, gas, and other expenses. And as long as he found a job within the first month, his new life could begin.

After a lot of soul searching during college about choosing a career that he enjoyed versus what would be stable, Tian decided that his minor success with commercials and print in Chicago would open up the possibility of an acting career. And as his luck would have it, when he made his three day scouting trip to Toronto a few weeks before, he had not only found an agent, but had almost landed a movie job. All of this had left him very excited about his future. It was with that enthusiasm that he drove to his agent to let him know that he was back in town.

The city that whipped by Tian's car window fascinated him. It was very similar, yet subtly different from all of the American cities that he had visited. There were buses everywhere in Toronto. There were a lot of people walking the streets but not quite as many as New York. The architecture of the buildings was a mixture of old world stone and modern skyscrapers. The bulk of the commerce all seemed to take place along a few major streets. Yet if you traveled even half a block onto a side street you would find residential buildings and a neighborhood.

However, what Tian found most distinctive about this city was what he had seen on his scouting trip weeks before. In almost every subway stop there were musicians performing. And these were clearly not beggars. These were classically trained musicians with cellos and violins. These were artists that hadn't necessarily fallen on hard times. They were simply people who were hell bent in making a living with their art, and the people walking to and from the subway trains treated them as such. Tian was amazed by it all.

It was with that mindset that Tian watched the city go by from his car. And it was with that experience that he evaluated what he saw happening on the steps of a church. The church was a classically build, stone, Anglican Church. And the man sitting on the steps was dark complexioned, with dreadlocked hair, a red sweatshirt and dirty grey sweat pants.

As Tian pulled up to the red light at the corner he turned completely to get a better look. The man was beating his heart out on a rubber garbage can using a pair of drumsticks. 'Can you get an artistic sound from a rubber bin?' Tian asked himself. Tian remembered a commercial he had seen featuring a kid that played drums on metal garbage cans. He had found it was very impressive. But this, Tian concluded, was just pathetic. There was no way that the dreadlocked man could get any sound of value off of rubber. Tian resolved the curiosity within himself and no longer found the man worth watching.

Tian turned back toward the light. And when the waiting dragged on Tian turned back toward the man. This time the man sat paralytically still. A neatly dressed white man was now leaning over talking to him. Taking a closer look Tian realized that the drummer was and had always been crying. This was not a classically trained musician. This was an average guy down on his luck doing whatever he could to not have to hold his hand out to the strangers walking by. And he was doing it on the stairs of a church.

When he saw the cars moving next to him Tian turned back to find that the light had turned green. Tian put his foot on the gas and drove away. But this was not an easy image for Tian to forget. He continued to think about it when the next light slowed him down and then when cars started flowing again. There was something familiar about what he had seen and Tian was struggling to bring it to memory. And then in a flash it hit him. It wasn't that the scene was familiar; it was that Tian knew that he would soon become that man.

Tian struggled to breathe when he thought about it, and this turned out to be more than just a passing thought. This was something that he could feel at the core of him. The last time he had had such a distinct feeling was before the motorcycle accident that changed the rest of his life. Now here again was this voice out of nowhere that spoke in contradiction to everything that Tian felt and wanted. This revelation disturbed Tian and changed his euphoric excitement into a gnawing dread.

That day ended without incident and five days later Tian moved into a shared living space with a young, black, Jamaican Canadian and an older, black Africa man from Mali. Each had their own room and shared the kitchen and single bathroom. It was a very clean space in a solidly middle class part of town. Everyone was courteous to each other, and they all did their bit to keep the place clean.

Tian's days began similarly. Each morning he would either go through the local weeklies or walk to the local mini-mart to pick up the day's paper. When Tian first moved there he focused on the entertainment sections of the papers and called anyplace that seemed to offer a job in the industry. But after discovering that the entertainment jobs were actually solicitations from questionable acting agencies trying to get young actors to pay for more headshots, Tian decided to branch out.

The first job Tian got was one as a telemarketer. Tian knew that meant selling products over the phone and he couldn't imagine that it would be much different than the sports store job he had after school during high school. But when Tian arrived, he found that it wasn't what he imagined it to be at all.

The main floor consisted of a well lit warehouse space lined and stuffed with desks separated by desk long partitions. The job was simple, take a stack of phone numbers photocopied from the telephone directory, start on top and call. When someone picked up the phone read the script. If you got through the entire script without them hanging up on you, then you asked them if they would be interested in buying a package. If they said yes, then you confirmed their address where one of the patrolling account managers would stop by and pick up the check or cash. They would then get some sort of paper and certificate as a thank you, but that wasn't one of the things that the callers needed to know.

"The package being offered today," Chuck the unmotivated floor manager explained to Tian, "is a midnight basketball package. For $98.99 a person could pay for a package that would allow a group of two underprivileged kids to participate in a midnight basketball program. So you see it's a good thing, ay."

"And what is it that the kids get to do in the camp?" Tian asked uncertain about everything.

"They stay off the street by playing basketball."

"So is it just for boys or girls too?"

"It's for whoever wants to participate."

"So this is for other people's kids, right? If they had kids they wouldn't be able to buy it for their own kids right?"

"Hey, if they want to buy it for their own kids that's fine too. It's for whoever they want to buy it for, ok?" Chuck replied sweeping Tian away for a tour of the floor.

Chuck pointed at a short, blonde, unshaven guy standing in front of his desk in the corner of the room. "That's Tony he's our best salesman." Chuck turned to the dry erase board on the wall next to Tony's desk. "He's who you should watch. He averages 15 sales a night. And when you make a sale you get $15 dollars. So you can see that you could make a lot of money if you really hustle it."

Tian's attention was drawn back to Tony whose voice began to rise.

"So you don't want to help out some kids that…" Tony paused as he listened to the person on the other end of the phone. "They're underprivileged… so you would prefer…" Now much louder talking over the person on the other end, "you would prefer those same kids to be doing god knows what, ay? Oh that's good… that's fine. Well thank you for not helping." Tony hits the release button on the phone.

"Stick to the script Tony," Chuck bellowed. But Tony barely even turned around to acknowledge him. "Hey Tony!"

"What is it Chuck?"

"I want you to show someone how it's done."

Tony looks up at Tian measuring him up in a glance. "I can't Chuck. I got a lot of calls to do tonight. Why don't you have Brian do it?"

Chuck led Tian down the aisle toward a rounder, mid-twenties, dark haired guy in the middle of the line. "We give Chuck some leeway, ay. When you start making his type of numbers, then you can leave the script a little as well. But until you do, just stick to the script, ay?"

"No that's fine. I think I would prefer the script."

"Good. Hey Brian I want you to have Tian here watch you for a couple of calls. Ok?"

"Ok."

Brian looked Tian up and down with a far less refined eye for those who wouldn't last. To Brian Tian was just another guy like himself that had no skills and no other opportunities. To Brian Tian was just another guy that needed a job that didn't ask questions, and that was fine with him.

"So how long you been working here?" Tian asked.

"Two weeks," Brian replied with more than a little hesitation in his voice.

"And how many sales do you make a day?" Tian inquired further.

"You know it all depends on the day. Sometimes just a few and other nights ten or twelve."

"Seriously?" Tian asked with a tone that summed up the belief he had in selling even one package.

"Yeah, it depends on what we're selling each night. Sometimes it's pizza packages and other stuff."

"And how is this package to sell?"

"It's ok. Look it's easy. Let me do one here."

Tian watched closely as he watched Brian do something that Tian himself had done thousands of times before, dial a phone. But for some reason watching Brian do it was nerve racking. Brian adjusted the microphone back to his lips and leaned forward to grab the script.

"Good evening this is Brian with the midnight basketball program and I'm hoping that I can take a second of your time to tell you about the work that we are doing for kids in your neighbor that might otherwise be getting into trouble. We are a group that organizes teens with the Psalms Baptist church to play basketball from the hours of six to midnight. What it does is keeps kids that might otherwise be getting into trouble, off the streets and engages them in a constructive uses of their time.

We are hoping that you might help us get more kids enrolled in our program by buying a package that will allow two kids to be a part of the program. It is a very modest $98.99 and covers a period of four months. Can we get your support for the kids in your neighborhood?" Brian paused for a reply. "Well, ok thank you… Yes, thank you for your time."

Tian was amazed that the person on the other end had allowed Brian to get through the entire script. There was simplicity to it. You dialed a number and then read a script. 'How much easier could it be?' Tian thought.

"So what happens when they hang up on you?" Tian asked.

"Then you just dial another number. They're just dicks. You're going to get a few of them. Don't worry about them, ay. They don't know you, just dial the next one."

Tian considered the world that he was now working in where the people being disturbed by telemarketers were the dicks and the person interrupting their dinner was the good guy.

"Why don't you make a call," Brian prodded.

"Can I hear you do one more?" Tian offered, trying to wait as long as possible before becoming one of the good guys.

"Why? It's easy. You dial, read off the script and if they buy then you verify their address, highlight them on the sheet and give it to Chuck."

"I want to see you make a sale so I can watch the whole process."

"Look, it's not that hard. I'll do one more for you and then you can try."

Brian picked up the phone and went through the same motions. Tian wasn't really paying attention to Brian's technique or inflections anymore. Tian was trying to figure out if he could do this. 'I'm an actor,' Tian thought. 'I'm playing a character. It isn't me making the call, it's someone else.'

Brian's call was over before Tian had gotten a chance to convince himself to do it. And before Tian knew it, he was seated at the open desk two down from Brian next to a heavier woman in her thirties. Before he left Brian had placed a list of numbers on the desk with a quick "here you go," and with that he considered Tian trained.

Tian considered how mercifully short the day would be. He arrived at 6:30 pm and would be done by 9. His hesitation finally relented when he realized that he was no longer working his way through some college job that would allow him Sunday night dinner money. No, this job was about survival. Now if he was unable to find a job, he didn't eat and he didn't have a place to live. His doing this job represented his willingness to survive.

Tian put on his headset and dialed the first number on the left hand column. "Good evening this is Tian with the midnight basketball program and I'm hoping that I can take a second of your time to tell you about the work that we are doing for kids in your neighbor that might otherwise be getting into trouble." Tian stopped when he heard the dial tone return on the other side of the phone.

The sound wasn't painful at all. In fact it was sort of a relief. Tian had never been a very confident reader and now he had gotten a chance to practice the first part of the script to make it sound less stilted. Tian dialed the next number.

"Hello" the voice answered.

"Good evening this is Tian with the midnight basketball program," Tian continued. Each time Tian read the script it got a little less nerve racking. Each time Tian made a call he cared a little less that he was interrupting a family's dinner or their relaxing time in front of the TV. Because Tian knew that if they didn't want to hear what he had to say, all they had to do was hang up.

Tian learned that he had the best chance of getting through his script if he didn't give them a chance to get a word in first. He was honing a technique which hadn't yet turned into a sale but seemed to be getting closer and closer. Tian dialed the next in the list of numbers.

"Good evening this is Tian with the midnight basketball program and I'm hoping that I can take a second of your time to tell you about the work that we are doing for kids in your neighbor…"

"Hey!" the voice yelled on the other end of the phone. "Hey! This is a hospital! Do you know every time one of you people calls here it blocks the line and emergency calls can't get in?"

"I'm sorry, I didn't know this was a hospital."

"I get so many calls all night, do you know how many problems you cause?"

"I'm really sorry. I'll let someone here know. I'm really sorry."

"Just stop calling here ok."

"I'll see what I can do."

"Bye!" the person yelled before slamming down the phone.

Tian sat for a moment wondering what to do. Now he no longer saw himself as one guy doing what he had to do to survive, he saw himself as a part of a machine with a thousand arms that didn't just reach out from this floor but from other floors and other businesses from all around the city.

Tian got up and took the number to Chuck. Tian asked if there was some sort of do not call list that they could create. Chuck told him not to worry about it and to try making a few more calls. Tian sat back down, put on his headset and dialed again.

Tian watched as Brian marked four sales onto the board and Tony had marked 10. Tian turned toward Tony and watched him as he danced around in front of his desk gesturing to the caller through the phone. And he saw that Tony allowed himself to believe in what he was selling. 'Belief, that's what Tony was selling, not a basketball program', Tian concluded. Tian turned back to his list and dialed again.

"Good evening this is Tian with the midnight basketball program," Tian stated with enthusiasm. "And I'm hoping that I can take a second of your time to tell you about the work that we are doing for kids in your neighbor that might otherwise be getting into trouble."

"Sure, go ahead," the strained voice replied back.

"We are a group that organizes teens with the Psalms Baptist church to play basketball from the hours of six to midnight. What it does is it keeps kids that might be otherwise getting into trouble off the streets and engaged in constructive uses of their time."

"Uh huh," the voice acknowledged back.

"We are hoping that you might help us get more kids enrolled in our program by buying a package that will allow two kids to be a part of the program. It is a very modest $98.99 and covers a period of four months. Can we get your support for the kids in your neighborhood?"

"That sounds very interesting. How long have you all been doing this?"

"Well the church has been doing it for a few years," Tian improvised. "But we have only been involved for a few months."

"And where do you guys do this?" the voice asked with an unusual wispiness to its voice.

"Well mostly we do it at the basketball courts near the church. But when necessary we also work with the gyms in the area." Tian said hoping Canadian gyms had basketball courts.

The voice took a very strained breath in. "I'm sorry, I'm on an oxygen tank. I have trouble breathing."

'That's what that sound is,' Tian thought. 'I am trying to get a man on an oxygen tank to buy what could be a fake program.'

"I don't have a lot of money so I want to make sure that it would be worth the money for the kids," the voice said breaking Tian's heart.

"Well, the great thing about the program is that it gives kids the chance to be productive and it gives them a place where they could belong," Tian said praying that what he was selling was real.

"Are you sure?" the voice squeezed out.

"It's a great program," Tian reassured him.

"Well, you sound like a very trustworthy person, so I'll buy a package."

"I would like to verify your address so that one of our account managers can stop by and pick up the check or cash."

"Ok, tell them I'm on an oxygen tank so it might take a while to get to the door."

"I will. And thank you very much for your purchase. I'm sure that the kids that you sponsored will really enjoy the program."

Tian hung up the phone and walked up to Chuck with the sale and the address. Tian spoke with trepidation. "Um, I just made a sale and it was from a guy with an oxygen tank. So tell the account managers that it might take him a while to get to the door."

"Don't worry about it, they'll wait," Chuck replied blankly.

Tian searched Chuck's face for any sort of deception or guilt. He knew that Chuck would know the company's legitimacy. Even on his first day Tian could sense things that didn't add up.

It seemed suspicious to Tian that the company had people driving to the buyer's house to collect the money. Why would they need to do that other than to further pressure the buyer? Why did what they sell keep changing? Tian sat back down but he hoped that that would be his last sale for the day. Giving the hard sell to a poor man on oxygen was all he could take for one day.

As soon as he stepped out of the doors of the building he knew that he would prefer to starve than work there again. He planned to return the next day to let them know and to pick up the $15 dollars he had earned for his night's work.

The next night when he returned they informed him that the money wouldn't be available until the end of the week. Tian thought that it would be appropriate if he found an empty building on the day he was told to return. But five days later when he found Chuck pacing the floor and Tony yelling into the phone relief flooded Tian's heart. However, the relief was less for himself and more for the wispy voice on the end of the phone that only wanted to make life a little better for someone else.

Tian collected his pay and left. But he knew that he had learned the first real lesson of his new life. Apparently in real life

there are ways of surviving that are not better than death. So now
not only did Tian wonder what his new life would become. But now
he had a threshold to compare it to. There was a scale to quality of
life that dipped below what was worth living. And now it was up to
Tian to lift his quality of life higher than what he would be allowed
in death.

Tian stood in the dark where Irabell had left him. Distracting
himself from the heavy loneliness that immediately set in Tian
wondered why it was that Irabell had not answered his question
about whether or not they were souls. He wondered why it was that
Irabell had left him. And Tian wondered whether or not he should
leave.

'Certainly Irabell could find me if I left,' he thought. 'But
where would I go.' For all of the information that Irabell gave him,
Tian didn't know very much about where there was to go in this
alien world.

Tian conjured up an image of the ocean of people at the
library and in a moment he was there on the ridge where Irabell and
Tian first stood. He looked down at the billions of people knowing
that each one of them represented another physical life that they
were viewing. 'Were those lives sad lives, or were they all happy?'

Tian thought about all of the decisions he had made in his
own life and wondered if they too were down there. He wondered
about all of the intimate moments and embarrassing moments. He
wondered about the shameful moments and the boring moments.
And he wondered about the long stretches of his life that were
nothing more than sheer repetition.

Tian wondered about the moments where he laid in his
Toronto room day after day staring at the ceiling for hours on end
waiting for his agent to call, too broke to leave the apartment
because of the fear that everything outside his door came at some
cost. Or the thousands upon thousands of hours of TV that he had
watched trying to fill the hole that had developed in his life where a
social life would normally have been.

No, Tian determined that if there were any future viewers of
his life, they would skip over those parts. They would rush instead
to the fun parts and the dramatic parts. They would experience the

small successes he had as an actor or his anxiety filled days waiting to find out if he had gotten the jobs. They would experience when he was asked by the artist to pose for a veteran's memorial statue and the day that Tian saw himself for the first time immortalized in bronze. It would be the plays and the movies that he had done, the brief affairs that he had, and the constant emotional struggle that he had about whether what he was experiencing was worth the effort it took to experience it.

That was the life that Tian left behind. In his mind, it wasn't a bad life relative to the lives that he saw on the news. It was glorious in comparison to those of the starving children with swollen bellies and the veterans returning home with arms and legs missing. But even though it was relatively better, his quality of life hardly ever exceeded the point where his death dream didn't seem superior.

Now here he was on the other side of death standing alone on a ridge looking down at people feeding on the lives that people like him left behind. 'Which side is the grass greener?' he wondered. 'Is this all there is to this world, the ability to live life vicariously through others?'

Tian didn't want to watch what he was seeing anymore. He wanted to be amongst people. But the only other place that he knew with people in it was Christian heaven. He didn't like being in Christian heaven. He didn't feel comfortable there. But he wanted some sort of interaction. Actually, he was beginning to realize that he needed some sort of interaction. Because even in the short time that Irabell had left him he began to feel less whole.

Tian decided that if he could find an out-of-the-way place where he could watch from, perhaps heaven wouldn't be so bad. There he could feel what it felt like to be around others, and he could maybe even join in on some of the joy that they felt.

Tian drew an image in his mind of heaven. He imagined the fruit trees and the people. Then he imagined all of those images off in a distance.

When Tian looked up again he was standing in a new location. He was standing next to what looked like a fig tree in what felt like fog. And unlike all of the other experiences that Tian had had in this world, the fog actually felt like a moist cloud on his legs.

Tian turned around trying to figure out where he was. In one direction the fog only seemed to get thinker while in the other it seemed to thin out. Tian walked to where it seemed the thinnest and saw that the fog had settled in a valley. Above him was a city on a hill that was filled with magnificent mansions and lush greenery that shined like emeralds.

Tian made it out of the fog and began climbing the hill. The hillside was covered with a soft grass that made him wish that he was barefoot. And as soon as he wished it his feet were bare. The grass brushed past his toes like padded velvet. It was a sensation that he hadn't felt before, not in this world or on earth. In fact it was the most overwhelming sensuous sensation that he had felt in his whole life.

Tian looked high up on the ridge of the plateau and he saw someone familiar. It was a recognizable and comfortable feeling. As he got closer he realized that the man standing in the distance was Irabell.

"What are you doing here now? And where did you go?" Tian asked.

"I was called away," Irabell responded matter-of-factly.

"So you just left me there? I was alone in the dark Irabell! Was I just supposed to stay there?"

"You were free to do whatever you wanted."

"So what are doing here now?" Tian asked almost annoyed at his timing.

"I was told that I needed to tell you something."

"By whom?"

"By those who are watching your experiences while you are here."

"Who's that?"

"Come with me and I can explain."

"I don't know. I kind of want to see what's over this ridge."

"Christian heaven is over this ridge. You've seen it before."

"And now I wanna see it again. What? Can't I go back?"

"Tian you have a choice to make. Can I take you somewhere to talk?"

"I kind of wanna stay here. Do you see how beautiful this day is?" Tian turned and looked at the valley below. "This is great. I don't think that I've ever felt more alive."

"I was thinking that I could show you a little more of this world."

Tian turned back toward Irabell. "Wow, you really don't want me to go up there do you? What's up there? What do you think I'll see?"

"If you like we can talk here."

"Why can't we talk up there?" Tian asked with a devious smile.

"Tian you are going to have to make a choice. You are going to have to choose whether or not you stay here or go back to your life."

"Well, right now I'm thinking that I want to stay here. And I mean right here. I could live right here on this hillside, and god knows what else could be on the top of that ridge."

"Do you remember when I explained that each physical body needs a particular energy from this side to stabilize it?"

"Yes."

"Well, it is a very exact connection. And you were exactly the correct energy that your body needed to exist. And as you and your physical body live your physical life you change together. But right now you are experiencing things that your body is not and you are changing without your body. With too many experiences here you will eventually change so much that you and your body will no longer match."

"So what will happen with my body?"

"It will continue to live without being alive."

"But isn't it my body to do with whatever I want? Aren't I the soul? Isn't it my physical life?" Tian asked indignantly.

"No it's not. No. It is not," Irabell answered with a firmness that reminded Tian of a third grade teacher.

Slowing down and showing less indignation, "then if I'm not the soul, then what am I?"

"Why don't you come with me so that I can explain it to you?"

"Why don't you explain it to me here?" Tian asked genuinely curious.

"Because there are places that are better used to explain it to you than here."

"Will whatever I see on that ridge change me so much that I could never go back?"

"No, you've been there before. You know what you'll see," Irabell replied softly.

"Is your question a decision that I have to make right now?"

"No, but it is a decision that if you don't make consciously, the decision will be made for you by your actions."

Tian looked past Irabell up the hill. "If you don't mind, I would like to see what's over that ridge. I just want to see. Is it ok for me to do that?"

"You are free to do whatever you want. I am here to teach only if you want to learn."

"Ok."

"But keep in mind that it wasn't easy for you to be a part of that physical life. It isn't easy for any of us. Every experience that you have while you're here jeopardizes it."

"Did that experience that you showed me in the library change me? Did it make me more like the creature you showed me?"

"Yes it did."

"Is that the type of changing that you're warning me about?"

"Anything that changes you from the person that you came to me as is the type of change that I'm warning you about."

"Ok, then I will be careful."

"Ok," Irabell relented and stepped aside. "There was more that you wanted to know and a few more things that you asked me. I will be here if you still want to know."

"Thank you."

Tian walked past Irabell again feeling the soft velvety grass below his feet. Tian crested the ridge and looked out to the new land. The first thought that came to Tian was 'In my father's house are many mansions. If it were not so, I would have told you.'

CHAPTER 9

Five months after his near death dream Tian found that it had affected him differently than he would have thought. Tian often thought about how good he felt during the dream and the charge that his body had after waking up. But remembering his experiences didn't make him feel good. In fact, more than anything it made him depressed.

Toronto had not worked out as he had planned. What Tian learned after being there for a month was that the city was undergoing a massive recession. So not only was it hard for everyone to find work, but it was near impossible for an illegal alien with no skills to find a job. And being an actor Tian had dropped off a resume at 50 different restaurants on Queen and King Street, without receiving a single call back.

When things finally got to tough to bear he drove down to Niagara Falls, New York and found a waiter job at a motel diner. But that job barely paid minimum wage and if it wasn't for the conversation rate of the American dollar to Canadian, it wouldn't have been worth the three hours of driving each day. However, even with the conversion Tian only worked there three months. When he was again current on his rent and could afford food his commute seemed excessively long and he was again sure that he could find a job in the city.

But when Tian was again down to his last $15 his thoughts about his near death dream became unending. The struggles that he was going through depressed him and the fact that he knew what it would be like on the other side loosened his grip on life. His body, which he had pumped up to what he considered his acting weight, was now down 30 pounds. And although he now felt bone on wood when he sat down, it took a statement from his agent for him to see how different he was from the man who had arrived in the city a few months before.

But once again with $15 dollars to his name he had a plan. What he would do is buy the largest bag of rice that he could find and the largest bottle of pain killers he could afford. He still had a bottle of ketchup so he figured that adding that to the rice would make it a complete meal. And when he was out of rice, he would also be out of rent so he could use whatever gas he had left in his car to find a faraway place and put the pills to good use.

In accordance with his plan Tian found himself strolling the aisles of his local pharmacy. The rice was bought and paid for and all that was left were the pills. There was more of a selection than Tian anticipated. 'What is the difference between acetaminophen and ibuprofen?' Tian wondered. 'Would aspirin work or should it be a something with a big chemical name as the active ingredient?' Since the rice had only cost him $4, Tian gave himself a budget of $7 for the pills. That way if there was an emergency Tian would have the other $4 to make a phone call home.

Tian didn't like calling home. His parents had raised him to be very independent and Tian wanted his college education to be the last thing that his parents needed to pay for. Every statement and action by his father told Tian that it was wrong to ask for anything from him. And if you dared ask for anything it would come with a psychological price higher than that of death.

But as the days stretched out and the rice bag emptied Tian reconsidered calling home. It wasn't his parents he thought of calling however, it was his brother Pat. And when Tian did make the call with two servings of rice left Pat picked up on Tian's desperation and made it easy on him.

"I'll go right now and send you whatever money I have in my pocket. Ok, Tian? Will that be Ok?" Pat said trying unsuccessfully to hide his fear.

"Thank you Pat," was all he could muster back.

Tian felt like a rich man with the $150 that Pat had sent him. And with it Tian had a new plan. Tian decided to move to Michigan and stay with Cameron who had gotten a full scholarship into University of Michigan's biochemistry doctoral program.

Cameron had always been a self motivated woman. She had always been at the top of her class and had published in biochemical journals as an undergraduate. It was that self motivation that Tian had always admired about her. And the thing that kept them friends even after they fought was that Cameron had an almost fantasy like belief in Tian.

Every story Tian told Cameron about his amazing life she believed. And every play that Tian performed in, she supported. Cameron seemed to transfer the belief that she should have had in herself to Tian. And since Tian couldn't do anything to change it, he instead lapped it up.

But the Tian that arrived at Cameron's door wasn't the Tian that she had been friends with in college. The Tian that Cameron knew was strong and confident. This new Tian was less amazing and more ordinary. In fact, Cameron considered this Tian less than ordinary because ordinary people could figure out ways to survive. Cameron considered the person Tian had turned into to be a disappointment.

When Tian applied for a restaurant job, Cameron informed Tian that such jobs were for people without college degrees. But what Cameron meant was that such jobs were not for someone that she considered capable of an amazing life. So when Tian came home smelling like Mongolian barbeque it stank up her life.

Although Tian would most often lock himself away in the room that Cameron had once used as a study, Cameron started coming home later and later. And it was exactly a month after his arrival when she came home announcing that they needed to have a talk. Cameron sat in front of Tian and asked him what he was planning on doing. And the truth was that Tian didn't know. Tian was so delighted to have found a job and to be able to afford food that he forgot to plan much further ahead.

"What are doing here? Are you thinking that you will just get a job and then live here for the rest of your life?" Cameron asked with firmness to her voice.

"No. I was just trying to catch my breath."

"And that's why I let you stay here. But you have to go now. You have three days to go. And I don't want you to tell me where you're going or where you've arrived at because I don't want to have to worry. I have too many things to worry about for myself. I deserve to not have to worry about you too."

"Ok," Tian said without any resistance.

Tian knew the conversations that must have precluded this one. Tian had once been the friend that Cameron complained to about others. He knew the roll that she got on once she felt that someone was disturbing her life. He knew that as close as they had been in their previous life he was now the problem that kept her from being everything that she could be.

Tian never wanted to be the problem so by the third day he had packed his car back up, given his job notice and was ready to hand over the apartment key. The humility that Tian now lived in prevented him from feeling anything but gratitude for the time that he had spent there. So at the last moment standing in front of the door, Tian looked Cameron in the eye and said "Thank you for letting me stay here. I really do appreciate it."

"I know you do," Cameron replied without saying anything more. And then Tian walked out, got into his car, flipped open his US road map and chose a new destination. After flipping past a few pages he saw Vancouver. Tian had disembarked there after an Alaskan cruise that he had taken with his mother after his parents separated. It was the most beautiful city that Tian had ever been too. And it was a place that he immediately knew that he wanted to live. So now that all of his pride and confidence had been stripped away, all he wanted was a place that could one day become home.

Tian left in the evening and drove through the night. As day broke Tian found himself on a small highway that snaked up the western boarder of Illinois. There was nothing on either side of the highway but empty cornfields and the road was only shared by a handful of drivers. Tian felt like this place was literally in the middle of nowhere. It was the type of place where a person could do things that they couldn't do otherwise.

Tian kept the pills that he had bought in a travel bag with his toothbrush and toiletries. And not knowing if he would need any of its contents he kept his travel bag next to the boxes that occupied his passenger seat. And as the open land whipped by his window, Tian wondered if the sight of the sun coming over a fallow field should be the last sight that he saw.

Tian could see no way out of the life that he had only just begun. Tian went over the logic in his mind. 'I need a place to live, and a job to survive. I have gotten myself in a situation where I have no skills other than acting, nowhere to live and I'm driving across the country to a place where I will again be illegal in the middle of a recession.'

Tian pulled his car over to get a better grasp of his predicament. 'Where am I going?' Tian thought. 'By the time I get there, I won't have enough money to do anything but be homeless. Is this where all of my experiences have led me, an empty highway in the middle of nowhere? I thought that I was one of god's favorite children. How could he let this happen to me?'

Tian took the bottle of pills out of his travel bag and looked at it. He considered himself smart to have bought the coated capsules designed not to upset your stomach. Tian had heard about people who had tried to kill themselves but had puked the pills up. Tian didn't know how many pills it would take but after taking 100 his stomach was bound to get irritated.

Tian opened the bottle and poured a few into his hand. Tian looked down at the little red pills that would end his life. Staring blankly Tian looked up and considered his life again. What would he miss? Tian scanned his mind desperately looking for a reason to keep living and only one thing came to mind.

A year earlier he was doing a play in Rockford, Illinois. One night after the show he received a note from an artist asking to do a bust of him for a veteran memorial statue. The artist had been commissioned by the city, and the artist, thinking it would be less strange, thought to get actors to model for him. Tian had spent five hours posing for a bust before the artist asked to sculpt his entire body.

The statue was due to be erected before graduation, but it missed its date. Tian had left town never seeing the result. In 100 years Tian knew that he would be gone, but that statue would still be there. And now that Tian realized just how soon the statue would exceed him, he wanted to see it. It would be his one legacy. The only thing that that proved that he had once existed and he thought this a good enough reason to postpone his death for a few hours.

Tian poured the pills back into the bottle and mapped his route to Rockford. It was about two hours away using deserted highways and country roads. But however long it would have taken wouldn't have mattered. Tian considered this the only thing of value that his life produced and no matter where it was in the world, Tian would have traveled there to see it.

When Tian finally stood in front of it, the monument gave him pause. He looked up at the 15 foot monstrosity wishing he had a camera. The statue had five people on it. Each person represented a different American war. The artist had told Tian that he would be the Vietnam War. Tian smiled remembering the moment when the artist looked at the finished bust. The artist was almost shocked to proclaim that once Tian's brown complexion was gone, Tian looked just like a white man. That was what caused the artist to have to switch Tian from representing Vietnam to Korea.

Tian stood in front of his statue trying to figure out how things had gone badly so quickly for him. He had always had a charmed life and here he was trying to decide whether he should live or die. Tian decided that he hadn't been prepared for this. Nothing in his life had warned him that this could happen to him accept the feeling he had after he watched the dreadlocked man drum the rubber garbage can in front of the church. Back then he felt that he would become that man. So with that potential transformation in mind, Tian wondered how Cameron now saw him. Did Cameron now see him as the sad homeless man camping out on the church steps?

For that moment Tian allowed his mind to consider the possibilities. Tian decided that Vancouver was the desperate fantasy of a dying man. But less than two hours away was Chicago and Jeanie. Tian would expect Jeanie's response to be the same as Cameron's. They were both very self motivated women. And Jeanie would be even less generous than Cameron. But Tian thought that if he could get Jeanie to let him stay there for seven days that would be enough to find a room using the money he had made cooking Mongolian barbecue.

Tian barely recognized his best friend in the response that he got from Jeanie. The hours upon hours that they had spent talking about life and the universe mattered nothing when it came to seven days of generosity. Jeanie only reluctantly agreed to allow Tian to stay at her place, but on the 5th day his welcome had worn out.

Luckily Tian had found a place by day four and needed only one extra day past his welcome. It broke Tian's heart when he called Jeanie on the sixth day to get the last of his stuff and she ignored the phone. Tian had called from the payphone directly in front of her three story walk up and he watched as she flittered around the room as the phone rang.

It took Tian sliding in as someone exited to actually get into the building. And it was at that moment that he realized just how much of a failure he had been at creating his new life. He had no job, he didn't have a stable place to live and he didn't have dependable friends. He had done everything completely wrong and the important things he had gotten wrong twice. Tian saw no ending to this three story walk up of a life and began to realize that he would have to give this life up if he wanted to eventually create the life he wanted.

Giving it one last shot Tian found a job at a local pizza shop and worked there for the next 2 months. His contacts for acting jobs seemed to have dried up during the time that he had been away. They all still answered his calls but the auditions stopped coming. Perhaps it was that his new skeletal appearance didn't sell.

But whatever it was, Tian decided Chicago was not the place for him. So in full resignation he packed up his most prized possessions, sold his car and bought a ticket back home to the Bahamas.

On the day that Tian left Chicago he looked at his naked body in the full length mirror of his shared bathroom. His body was scarily thin. And when he looked deep into the eyes staring back at him he saw a soul that was battered and broken, but still alive. And considering everything that he had gone through Tian considered that sign of life enough.

With Irabell still standing behind him Tian crested the hill and saw what looked like grand estates. Each estate was offset enough from the ridge of the plateau that it couldn't be seen until a person was steering across the flats.

"Wait," Irabell yelled out to Tian.

Tian stopped and looked back.

"Would you mind if I come with you?" Irabell yelled up to Tian.

This wasn't what Tian had in mind. He thought of this as a journey that he had to take alone. There was even a part of him that fantasized that he could get lost in Christian heaven. Perhaps he could stay there and as time passed the angels and the heavenly home owners would just think of him as that person that has been there for as long as they could remember. Tian thought that he could even eventually claim some sort of squatter's rights.

But having Irabell accompany him would make remaining unnoticed impossible. Irabell no longer looked human. He barely still had the outline of a human. He was more of a pulsing, outline of colors than he was human.

"I was hoping that I could see this place without you," Tian reluctantly replied.

"I could offer you an understanding of what you are seeing."

Tian hesitated before answering. "If I'm allowed I would like to experience this by myself. I can only imagine that you don't want me to go here because there is something about this place that you don't want me to see. If that is because you think it will harm me in some way then you can come with me. But," Tian hesitated before continuing, "I lived a long time wondering about heaven. I made a lot of decisions based on whether or not this place existed. And to be honest, I betted that it didn't.

But now here I am standing in front of it with the chance to understand what I should have done differently and what I could have done better. And if I can, I would like to do that alone."

Irabell became very still. He then bowed his head and reached out his palm presenting what lay before Tian. Tian took that as a sign that Irabell withdrew his request and Tian continued on.

Up ahead of him on the grand estate was a grove of beautiful trees that looked weathered enough to have been there since time began. And through the grove was a path that led out to the buildings behind them. At first glance the buildings looked like the castles he had seen drawn in fairy tale books as a child. But when he counted the windows he realized that the castles more resembled hotels with six stories and 30 windows across.

Tian crossed the vast lawn before he approached the first grove of trees. And within the grove was where he saw the first group of people. He tried not to get too close remembering the reaction that he got the last time he was here.

He watched the smooth faces of the two women that chatted with each other. Their cheeks and eyes reacted readily to everything that the other said. Their body motions and reactions were so filled with life that Tian longed for the joy that he saw in them.

"Hello," a voice said from behind him.

Tian turned and found a young man with short curly blonde hair and a pale, freckle-less face staring back at him.

"Hi," Tian hesitantly replied back.

"Are you lost?" the young man who didn't look any older than 20, asked.

"Well, I'm not quite sure where I am."

The young man smiled. "You're in heaven. Wasn't there anyone that brought you here?" he asked with genuine concern for Tian.

"No, I came here by myself," Tian replied, beginning to think that he should have accepted Irabell's offer of guidance.

"Oh, I'm sorry. Usually you are met by someone that brings you here. I've never heard of anyone that just appeared here on their own."

Tian suddenly realized what the young man was talking about. The young man thought that Tian had just died and had simply appeared in heaven. This made Tian feel even more like an outsider. He considered abruptly turning around and heading back to where he came from until the young man extended his hand.

"Would you mind if I showed you around? I haven't been here very long but I can at least share with you what I know." The boy lowered his eyes slightly before continuing. "But I would completely understand if you would prefer that I took you to someone who knows a little more than I do."

"No," Tian replied quickly. "I would really like it if you showed me around. It's so beautiful; it would be great if I had a guide."

"Well like I said, I don't know much about it and I haven't had the chance to see too much of it, but I can show you what I've seen."

The young man led Tian through the grove. Tian dropped a half a step behind him so that he could get a better look at him without the young man noticing. The boy wore brown slacks and a beige, almost colorless shirt that lightly danced back and forth over the young man's back. It looked like a mixture of cotton and satin and seemed like something that a person would wear for a drink with friends at a bar rather than an outfit from a science fiction movie.

Tian also sized the young man up for a possible friendship. If he could befriend someone, he thought, he wouldn't need to claim squatter's rights. In fact, if he could befriend someone, his choice of whether to stay or whether to go back to the life he left on earth would be very easy.

After his first year after college where all of his college friends had let him down, Tian had a hard time making new friends. He held new people at a distance long enough to discover the trait that might prove disappointing to Tian later. And after Tian found that trait he would relinquish the friendship and return to an almost solitary state.

Tian learned to be comfortable going to the movies and restaurants alone. He learned to enjoy all of the imaginary conversations he had with women that he met but didn't talk to. And even though he appreciated how rich his life was with his imaginary friends, Tian began to feel a little resentful toward God for creating the mistrust he had of real people.

Tian felt that during his meditative years when he was always trying to do what was right, he had developed a personal relationship with God. And at the beginning of his life after college, a life that Tian was willing to put in complete service to God, God had abandoned him. Tian's feeling was that at any moment God could have stepped in or sent someone that could help him out of the situation in which he found himself.

Tian knew that God had intervened in his life before. Tian knew that it was God that allowed Tian to move the hurricane. Tian knew that it was God that had helped him connect with the man that got him into college with a scholarship. And Tian knew that it was God that sent him the death dream.

But when Tian reached his lowest point and had to reluctantly lean on his friends for support; when Tian truly needed the intervention of God to keep him from psychological disaster, neither his friends nor God was there. His friends were surprisingly lacking and God was nowhere to be found.

However, in the young man that led Tian through the grove, Tian noticed gentleness. The young man had a vulnerability with which Tian felt very comfortable. Tian observed a need to please in the young man which Tian recognized as a psychological companion of loyalty, the trait that Tian craved most.

The young man stopped in front of a small bush that wasn't taller than either of the men. He pulled apart the branches of the bush peering in. When nothing was found he moved to a new spot and worked his way around the bush. When he found what he was looking for he yanked on it and presented it to Tian.

"It's a peach. Have you ever had a peach before?" The young man said holding it in the palm of his hand.

"I have," Tian replied with an equally genuine smile.

"Then try this one. I have as well but it was nothing like the ones that I've had here."

Tian took the peach from him and immediately noticed a difference. The peach fuzz took on a new feeling in Tian's hand. It sent a warm tickle to Tian's palm. It was a very pleasant feeling that was similar to the feeling that the velvety grass had on Tian's feet. Tian liked the feeling of the fuzz so much that he almost didn't want to bite into it.

When he finally did bite, Tian's brain was stimulated in a way that seemed to bring up almost a life time of memories at once. It wasn't Tian's memories though, it was the memories of what life must have been like as a peach tree. Tian didn't see anything in those memories. Instead his thoughts were filled with feelings of warmth and health before feeling its roots being torn out of the ground and left in the cold dry open air for what felt like a lifetime.

Then the memories were of being planted in a field that tasted different than where it was raised. In this new field Tian felt the effects of the scalding hot sun. But after that initial burst the memories became more pleasant and nostalgic. They were filled with hours of swaying in the breeze and the quenched feeling that came with a good rain after a long dry spell. Tian felt the life that was in every leaf and the water that flowed through them. Tian felt the weight of the birds that nested on the tree and the fruit that it bore.

Tian even felt the tree's last moments as it was cut down. There was no pain involved, just a longing to continue living. There was a shock as pulp was exposed to the open air but it didn't last long. Soon something came along and ripped what was left of it out of the ground. With all of its roots exposed the tree stopped being a tree and the memories stopped.

"How is it?" the young man asked Tian.

"That is incredible."

"I know. It was the sweetest peach that I have ever had."

Tian looked at the young man. The truth was that Tian didn't actually taste anything. All that he experienced was the memories. Tian didn't even chew the piece that he had bitten off, it had just dissolved in his mouth.

"I didn't really taste the sweetness," Tian offered almost apologetically to his new friend.

"What do you mean? It was the sweetest thing that I have ever tasted."

Tian looked down at the peach in his hand examining the fruit to make sure that he had actually taken a bite. "I didn't really taste anything. What I felt, though, was the entire lifetime of the tree."

"What?" the young man asked confused.

"Go ahead. Try it," Tian said handing over the peach to his friend.

The young man took the fruit cautiously in his hand and then bit into it. Innocent pleasure reshaped the young man's face. He closed his eyes to experience the flavors more intently. And after the young man swallowed he opened his eyes and looked at Tian.

"Can't you taste that? It tastes like life."

"Well…" Tian paused looking down at the fruit trying to reconcile what the young man described with his own experiences. "Do you know if this tree is one of us?"

"What do you mean?"

"I was in a place where I was shown the lives of creatures that if I had seen them during life, I would never have expected to be self-aware or as intelligent as they were. Do you think that this bush could have been self-aware when it was on earth? Do you think that this tree is as much of a reflection of the life it lived as we are?"

"I don't know what you mean," the young man replied.

"Umm, I don't know. I guess I'm wondering if this bush could possibly be the soul of a tree that grew back on earth.

"Wow, I don't know. I never thought about it like that."

"I'm only wondering because of the memories that I experienced when I bit into it. It was what it was like when I experienced the life of someone in the ocean library."

"I've never heard of that. Where is it?"

"It's outside of Christian heaven," Tian replied.

"You've been outside of heaven? And why did you refer to it as Christian heaven?" the young man asked slightly unsettled.

When Tian noticed the openness of the young man's eyes decrease, and the pleasant smile that the young man carried disappear, Tian hesitated. Tian liked his new friend the way he was. Tian didn't want to have a negative effect on his friend. He only wanted to make his friend's life better. But when weighing the possibilities of stealing the young man's innocence, and losing his friendship because of a lack of honesty, Tian decided to share his experiences with the young man.

"I've come from a place outside of heaven. And the reason that I called it Christian heaven was because that is what the person that guided me around referred to this place as."

"What is outside of heaven like?"

"It's not as nice as this," Tian conceded.

"Is it hell?" the young man asked sheepishly.

"It doesn't seem like it. It's just different. But this place, heaven, is what I always imagined heaven would be like when I was young. How long have you been here?"

"Not very long," the young man answered embarrassed. "There are no nights here so it's hard to tell. But I haven't been able to explore all of the groves yet. And the only mansion that I've been in is that one over there." He pointed back to the one closest to them. "How is the outside different from here?" the young man said returning to Tian's experiences.

Tian looked into the young man's quizzical eyes and began to feel uncomfortable talking with him. Tian felt such gentleness in his new friend that corruption was the only affect that Tian could imagine his stories having on him. Tian coveted innocence. Tian always felt like he was always so full of knowledge that he never had the chance to be innocent.

And because Tian's knowledge always exceeded that of his friends', Tian often battled with the self image of being the corrupter of innocence. He didn't enjoy extinguishing the bright light in his young friends' eyes, but along the way he had made a judgment call. Tian knew that simplicity enabled joy, but knowledge enabled all of the other experiences valued on earth; health, wealth, growth and intelligence. So, Tian didn't like watching as his friends' innocence turned to confusion, but this, Tian had come to feel, was his greater destiny.

"Outside of heaven there is an ocean that stretches as far as you can imagine, but instead of water it's filled with people. And you don't see things like we do here, you have to feel them. And you don't talk like we do here, you think things and others hear them."

The young man listened intently. "Man, I can't even imagine it."

"But as far as I can tell, there's no joy there. I haven't seen any happiness. In fact, I'm sure that there are people there that have never experienced happiness in their entire lives."

"I don't know, it kind of sounds like hell to me," the young man said.

"Well, maybe it is. I know when I first arrived here it was like finding a tropical paradise after being lost at sea."

"Yeah, it's pretty nice here," the young man concluded. "You think God guided you here?"

"I didn't see God on the outside."

"Well, of course not. God doesn't go to hell. He only goes to heaven."

"Yeah I guess," Tian said half heartedly. Tian had not yet considered the possibility that the Christians were correct in another way. 'What if when you die, you can only go to heaven or hell?' He was standing in heaven so he knew that it existed, but he hadn't quite thought of outside of Christian heaven as hell. There was no fire and brimstone, but there didn't seem to be any happiness or love either. 'Maybe I escaped hell when I came here,' Tian considered.

"Hey, I have a secret I want to tell you. I don't know if I can, but I really want to," the young man said after a moment of silence.

"What is it?"

"When I first got here I was walking through the grove and I heard a man and woman talking. Apparently one of them was showing the other around, and I heard the guide tell the other that God was supposed to be visiting heaven soon."

"God was going to visit heaven? He's coming here?" Tian asked with trepidation.

"Yeah. When I heard that I went over so that I could hear a little more. The woman said that she had been told by someone that had been here awhile that God was going to come to heaven soon. Isn't that incredible?"

"Yeah that's…" Tian was at a loss of word for how wonderful he thought it was. For the first time since he had died a smile crept across Tian's face. Tian could not imagine his luck. But it wasn't luck, Tian decided. It was destiny. It was God himself that had orchestrated this. Irabell had told him not to go, but Tian had listened to his inner voice and coincidently here he was with the possibility of seeing God.

"When is he supposed to be coming?" Tian asked.

"I don't know, but the way that the woman was describing it, it sounded like any day now. She was telling him like it was a secret so I didn't want to go right up and ask her. But she definitely said it like it was soon."

Tian thought briefly about the way that he looked. He remembered the reaction of the first person he had talked to in heaven, and he remembered the way the young man reacted. He knew that his looks would draw some attention if he walked around heaven openly looking for God. But he also remembered that he had a decision to make. And Tian felt that if he could just look at God the choice would be clear.

"Have you asked anyone else about this?" Tian asked.

"No. I don't even think that I was supposed to know. I was just lucky enough to be there when the woman said it. And I would be so disappointed if I asked someone and they told me that I wasn't allowed to go."

"We have to ask."

"No sir. Not me. If you want to ask you can go right ahead. But keep me out of it. I don't even want them to know that I know."

"But what if he comes and you miss it?" Tian asked.

"I won't miss it. I have faith. God let me know that information so I could see him. God's not going to let me miss him now."

"Where does everyone gather here?" Tian asked.

"Well I guess a lot of people get together and talk in the mansions. Do you want me to show you around there?"

"Yeah, I do. And you know what?"

"What?"

"If I find out anything about when God's coming to visit, I'll let you know."

"If you could I would be so happy," the young man concluded.

The thought of making the young man happy brought joy to Tian. Tian had designed his entire life around trying to make other people's lives better. He had always said that on the day that he died the question that he needed to answer in the affirmative was whether or not the world was better for him having lived there. And as the young man lead Tian toward the mansion, Tian wondered if his life had made anyone else's life better for him having lived.

CHAPTER 10

When Tian landed back in the Bahamas after his first failed attempt at creating a new life, the first thing that he noticed was that everything was very bright. The buildings and homes on the island were often more colorful. The mixture of colors began in the early 1900's after the invention of the air conditioner had allowed the Bahamas to emerge as the travel destination for wealthy British citizens. When the expatriates began to invest and build winter homes they wanted something that would contrast with the drab colors of overcast England. So what they did was paint their island homes the colors of the brilliant blue beaches, bright yellow sands, and the pretty pink shells.

These traditions continued for 100 years even after the slaves took over the plantations. And with the advent of richer paint pigments, cloudless summer days created what could be described as a whitewash. On the brightest days the sun would find the speckles of white in the yellows and blues and reflect it back with blinding effect. And on the day that Tian arrived back in town after three years of absence this was the type of day that he found.

The whitewashing was even greater when Tian rounded the semi-circular driveway of his mother's white house with yellow trim. And when Tian stepped into his teenaged bedroom the glow of the empty white walls and high gloss teak floors gave him a slight headache.

For days Tian walked around in a state of over stimulation barely being able to process the experiences of where he had just come from. And when night allowed him breaks from the glaring light of day, his memories defied his understanding of life. His experiences after college flew in the face of everything that he had come to believe about himself and about his place in existence. So on the day that Tian opened his bathroom cabinet in search of mouthwash and found his old Ouija board he paused.

He had bought the board at the objection of his two friends when they had all traveled to New York together. Tian, Colin and Ed were all 16 at the time and they were taking their first unchaperoned vacation together. The three of them had practically been friends from birth. Colin was a gangly platinum blond with bright green eyes, very angular face and a permanent Bahamian tan. Ed was half Filipino and half black giving him an exotic look that was hard to identify. And adults often commented that when the three of them were together it resembled an ad from a fashion magazine.

Although both Colin and Ed engaged in the usual vices of 16 year olds, both drank and Colin smoked a little pot, spiritually, they believed what everyone on the island was taught to believe. The common belief on the island was that God was found in a church; good people gave to the poor; and Ouija boards were instruments of the devil. Colin and Ed didn't necessarily believe that everyone who used a Ouija board was using it for evil purposes. But what they had heard was that freaky things happened when people used it. Those freaky things were unexplainable within the vocabulary of their religious teachings. So for that reason Ouija boards were better avoided than embraced.

But Tian looked at Ouija as a training tool. In the books he was reading by Ruth Montgomery and others, the authors engaged in things like automatic writing and other techniques. Tian wanted a way of communicating with the dead and figured that a structured system with letters and numbers was the perfect way to start. So when Colin and Ed practically pleaded with Tian not to buy the Ouija board Tian just pointed to the 'Parker Brothers' logo and told his friends that it was "just a game."

During the years when Tian was meditating twice a day he would often pull out his Ouija board and ask it questions.

"Will I go to college?"

To Tian's delight the Ouija board centered its magnifying glass over 'yes'.

"Will I get a scholarship?"

Again the Ouija board centered over 'yes'. Tian tried to limit his use of the board, not because he was afraid of it connecting with demons and bad spirits like his friends suggested, but because the more frivolous the questions the more likely it was to offer incorrect responses. Tian believed that the board put him in contact with his spiritual guides and they would know major steps of his life like whether or not he would attend college. But Tian didn't believe that they would know whether or not Sara, a girl from Tian's class would like it if Tian went over and talked to her.

Staring at the Ouija board in his bathroom cabinet Tian remembered that he did enjoy using the board anymore. And as far as he could remember all of the answers that he received from the board had come true. But he also remembered that he didn't enjoy using the board enough to take it with him to college. The board symbolized to Tian the meditative stage of his first life. College represented a new phase and he didn't want them to overlap.

When Tian got to college, however, his desire to contact the beyond remained. It was Tian's junior year when he first lay on his bed and really thought about his meditative life. It was the year before that Tian had had the motorcycle accident that threw his life into chaos. And what Tian wondered during his junior year was whether or not a peaceful mind was even possible for him again.

In his college room, Tian rolled onto his back, closed his eyes and touched his thumbs to his pointing fingers. Tian engaged in the practice that he had done so many times before, and like the other times Tian felt a lighter world relax him. He felt himself floating through the world like a ghost through fog and it didn't even break his concentration when he felt a presence in the fog next to him.

The first words that Tian heard in this lighter world were surprisingly conventional.

"How are you?" the voice said.

The thought was surprising simple for an event that Tian considered extraordinary. And having heard the voice in his own head, Tian didn't feel the need to lie. "I'm barely holding on."

After that experience the voices were there whenever Tian went looking for them. They were sometimes encouraging and other times blunt. They would sometimes confirm the things that Tian believed and other times they would stubbornly disagree with Tian's assessment of the situation. There were even times when Tian would lay in his bed repeating the same question over and over again hoping that he had received the answer incorrectly or that he asked the question in the wrong way.

But what Tian learned very quickly was that his 'dead friends,' as he referred to them, were a literal bunch. If Tian asked "Is the sky blue?" They would answer "no" without explanation. And no matter how many different times he would ask the question he would get the same response. And when Tian would pose the same question to his physics professor, the professor would say "technically not. "It looks blue," he would confirm. "But the sky is no color at all." Those moments of affirmation would make Tian chuckle and shake his head with amazement.

Or when Tian asked for help getting to know Jillian, a cute girl from Tian's economics class, the voices would say "yes, we will help." And then after days of Tian thinking that help meant getting some alone time with her at the cafeteria or a dark corner at a party, Tian would receive a short biography from a play in which she acted. It took weeks for Tian to realize that the biography was what his dead friends meant by help getting to know her.

When it came to matters of the heart the literal nature of their responses hurt Tian. Tian was well liked and often admired but couldn't make it work with women. For the most part Tian knew it to be his own fault. He never took advantage of the numbers of girls that had gently showed their heart to him, and Tian couldn't muster enough desire to make himself vulnerable to the girls he drew. So when his dead friends offered supernatural help, Tian always got his hopes up for the best possible outcome. Unfortunately, in every case, Tian was disappointed in the results. What his dead friends said when it came to relationship help was always technically accurate but almost never in the spirit of what he was asking.

It was for that reason that Tian developed a slight fear of talking to his dead friends. Although he was sure that they didn't mean to be objectionable, Tian often was hurt more from the hopes that their answers engendered than helped by knowing their answer. It was for that reason that he rarely spoke to his dead friends during his lonely days in Toronto. Even though Tian desperately wanted to know how his Toronto experience would end, he knew that his dead friends' answers would only do more harm than good.

But now that Toronto, Chicago and Michigan were all in the past Tian again became curious about what his dead friends had to say. Tian stared at the Ouija board wondering how he should proceed. He knew that he no longer needed it so after a brief examination of the game he placed the board back into the cupboard and lay down on his bed.

The bed and the direction he pointed felt familiar to him. The position was flatly on his back with his legs slightly apart and arms not touching his sides. His hands laid palms up and the tips of his thumbs and pointing fingers touched each other. This was the position that he had learned years ago from the Shirley Maclaine books, and now it was comfortably his.

Tian let his mind rest. During college he learned that he didn't need the Chakra technique to enter the relaxed state, all he had to do was take a few deep breaths. Tian breathed in and out and then reached out with his mind as if he were shooting water out of his head. What he quietly waited for was something to bounce the water back. That is how he knew if there was someone else in the room that he couldn't see. Once someone was discovered then he began conversation. Usually he started with "Hello," but there was no consistency with how they would respond.

Tian would talk to at least two different personalities. One was a larger, more demanding personality that drove home what he stated with a stern tone. The other was a more soft personality that didn't quite express compassion, but had more understanding for what Tian was experiencing. The softer personality was the type of personality that would tell you bad news but held your hand as they did.

But when either of these two personalities spoke, Tian could feel a group of others in the background. The rest of them just seemed to stand there watching. Tian liked to believe that they were lending their support, but there was something in Tian that knew that that probably wasn't true.

As Tian lay in the bed this time he felt the softer personality emerge. He was grateful for that because Tian's mental state was still fragile from his experiences and he wasn't yet ready to be told what he had to do. The softer personality greeted him with "Hello" back and Tian's mind slipped into the state that allowed full conversations to occur.

"Where have you guys been?" Tian asked.

"We've always been right here," the soft personality replied.

"How could you let me go through that?"

"It was your choice."

Tian hated this reply when he received it from one of his dead friends. It felt like a reply but not an answer. 'How was it my choice to have practically come apart at the seams?' Tian thought to himself without broadcasting it to his friend.

Tian's mind slipped out of the relaxed state. He remembered the day that his brother Pat and his wife came to visit him in Toronto. His brother took one look at him and was immediately concerned. There was a wildness in Tian's eyes that Pat had never seen before. Pat had always been impressed by the fact that even when their parents were separating and their lives were unraveling Tian's eyes remained very calm. And even though Pat was the older brother, it was Tian's eyes that secretly gave him comfort that it was possible to make it through to the other side of their parents' separation.

But the wildness that Pat saw now disturbed him. It was not a question that Pat asked often, but now he felt the need.

"Is everything ok, Tian?"

"I can't find work, so I don't know about rent but I have a plan," Tian replied as he drove them to their downtown Toronto hotel.

"What's the plan?" Pat inquired.

"Well, I heard recently that the mental institutions here take people without question. So if I ever can't afford rent, what I figure that I will do is get myself taken there and then not speak. That way they wouldn't know that I'm not crazy and I could stay there until I can figure what I should do next. Of course, I would have to bury my passport and information somewhere so I could get it when I came back out. But that is what I would do if things got really bad."

Pat looked at his wife and both of their mouths dropped open. They looked back at Tian and both could see that not only was he being serious, but he really did see this as a good plan.

"Don't you think that that's a little extreme?" Pat asked.

"No, I think that's a great plan. I just can't speak when I'm there because that might give it all away. There are too many questions they could ask that would prove I'm not crazy."

"Well, if you did do that, it might be a good place to rest," Pat's wife offered with more than a hint of compassion in her voice.

"Yeah, exactly. That's why I would be going there. Where did you say the hotel was again?" Tian asked while scanning the highway signs for the proper exit.

As Tian thought about that moment laying in his bed in the Bahamas he wondered what must have been going though his passengers' minds. Tian remembered the day that he came up with his insane asylum plan. Tian was proud of it. But with the fog of the experience starting to clear he started to see just how much he had lost grip of a healthy mental state. And now his dead friend, who Tian considered his protector, claimed that Tian had gone through that at his own choosing.

Tian knew that a detailed explanation of why his friend would say that was beyond Tian's ability to receive. Tian could only receive short sentences from his friends because long messages required too many short sentences to be strung together accurately and in the correct order. When Tian asked for a longer explanation, Tian's mind just fogged over and nothing came through except various words that made no sense out of context.

Tian decided not to pursue that line of question anymore.

"What is it that I'm supposed to do here?" Tian asked referring to his return to the Bahamas.

"Relax."

'That was good advice,' Tian thought.

"That's not what I meant," Tian replied. "I meant, what am I supposed to do while I'm here?"

"Relax."

"Ok…," Tian thought for a moment. "What am I supposed to do with all of the time that I have on my hands? Like what should I be working on?"

"You should relax," the soft personality repeated with the same gentleness that it said it with the first time.

Tian decided to give up on the conversation. It had obviously entered one of the communication loops that his conversations with his dead friends often entered. Tian knew that no matter how he asked the question, the only information that he would get back would be for him to relax. Tian considered that good advice but not helpful advice. Tian needed to figure out a way to correct the mistake he had made in the creation of his new life, and doing nothing wasn't going to do it.

But since he was given no choice Tian opened his eyes. Staring at the white ceiling of his Bahamian bedroom he remembered the one he had had in Toronto. Tian felt a pain in his chest when he remembered, so instead he decided to roll over and rest. He pulled his legs up into the fetal position, brought his arms in front of his chest and made himself as small as possible. He closed his eyes again and did his best to think about absolutely nothing.

Over the next few weeks Tian got himself into a groove. His mother was now dating and to not upset her clearly fragile son, she would spend most of her days and nights at his place. This allowed Tian the run of the house.

Tian would get up around ten in the morning and then work his way into the kitchen where he worked his way around the newspapers soaked with puppy pee and poop. He would then grab a bowl and the cereal his mother supplied for him and then he settled down for breakfast at the dinner table. He would choose the seat that faced the empty lot next to theirs so that greenery was the only thing that he saw.

After a slowly eaten breakfast he would put a record on the record player. The record player was outdated technology when it was purchased 15 years earlier. But Tian's father and mother spent the 70's collecting the best albums from the decade and a record player was the only way of listening to the classic albums again. Tian's mother had only kept a handful of the 100 that they had but the ones kept were the ones that Tian remembered hearing most growing up.

When Tian put on one of them it reminded him of what was the best time of his young life. It reminded him of Sunday afternoon dinner when the entire family ate together. On those days it was

Pat's job to pick the flowers for the table and Tian's job to watch. But Tian felt an overwhelming sense of pride the first time the duty was entrusted to him. Tian remembered walking around their old yard checking to see which flowers were in bloom. There was always a selection of hibiscus and bougainvillea. And there were always multiple colors of each.

It was Tian's Dad's job to choose the music. Sometimes it could be a Bahamian album by Eddie Minnis or some rake and scrape band. Or it could be Elton John or Simon and Garfunkel. But whatever he chose set the mood as a lazy Sunday afternoon like the kind you dream a family might have. Those were the days before Tian's father took the gamble that would change the trajectory of everyone's life.

But during those mornings after breakfast Tian would usually put on The Best of Simon and Garfunkel. It was the right mix of memories and sadness that both allowed him to reflect on where he was while remembering the good place that he had come from.

After he had flipped the album once or twice he would shut off the player and just sit in front of the window for a while. If he felt up to it he would call up Colin or Ed to see how they were spending their day. Both of their parents had given them a place to live in and a car to drive after graduation, so Tian depended on them to take him around.

As time went on, Tian began to talk to his dead friends more frequently. He didn't necessarily ask them anything, he more needed the company. The house was very quiet and his childhood friends weren't always available, so Tian got the company where he could. And it was with great relief when the softer personality of his dead friends told him that they would help him to meet someone.

Tian was very excited about his friends' offer. They had never made an offer like this unprompted before. The times that they had, Tian was never sure if it was him saying it to himself as opposed to it coming from his friends. But this time Tian was sure. It was them offering it to him, and he knew that whoever she was would be perfect for him and would alleviate some of the loneliness that was beginning to creep up on him.

It was only about two weeks later when Colin suggested that he Ed and Tian go out for drinks. Tian was never much of a drinker choosing not to have his first drink until age 21 during his senior year of college. But drinks were an opportunity to get out of the house and spend time with friends.

Colin picked up Tian and they headed to Ed's house. There they all carpooled to Rumrunners a British styled pub that on off nights would host a Bahamian band. This was a favorite hangout of Marie, a mutual childhood friend that they would all describe as being more cool than alluring. Marie was more of a social butterfly than any of the guys and what she prided herself on most was the amount of attractive people that she would surround herself with. It was that more than anything else that allowed her to remain friends with Colin, Ed and Tian. Their looks had created a high threshold for hearing all of the stupid, degrading things that teenage boys said when they didn't know any better.

The guys all settled into one of the dark wood booths and ordered drinks. It wasn't too long before Marie entered with a female friend. She wasn't what you would call a striking beauty but there was something about her that made all of the guys turn and stare. When they sat down the game to draw her interest began. On this Tian had a slight advantage. Annett was a curious girl with opinions and Tian the charismatic actor could talk about everything from the workings of the spiritual universe to why people acted the way they did.

However, Tian wasn't the only competitor in this race. Colin had more island charm than any of them while Ed just threw out comments here and there to make sure that he wasn't eliminated. But when the night was over Tian, Colin and Ed walked back to the car and Tian firmly planted the flag in the mountain by say, "I like, so back off."

Colin was the only one that refused to back down.

"You can't call her. We will have to see who she likes," Colin objected.

"Dude, I'm saying back off."

"Nope. We'll have to see," Colin decided.

"Game on then," Tian stated with confidence feeling the advantage that he gained.

It took a night to get Annett's number from Marie, and another night to call her. Tian thought Annett was fun to talk to and would spend an hour on the phone with her at a time. Tian would entertain her with psychic stories and heartbreaking tales of his life in Toronto. And she would share things with him that wasn't for public consumption.

As Tian and Annett's relationship progressed Tian got an urge to again have a conversation with his dead friends. This time they told Tian that they would help him find a job. Tian was thrilled with the turn of events. Although Colin still talked about Annett and purposely mentioned times when he took her out alone, Tian considered Annett his for the taking. All Tian was waiting for was the right time to find out if she felt the same way about him.

Full of energy Tian went on the offensive with the job hunt. He had heard about the Bahamas Film commission and decided to have a conversation with the director of the department. She was very polite and told Tian that they would keep his resume and put his name on a list.

But what Tian needed most was money to make the trip back to the United States. So on Pat's urging, Tian allowed Pat to set up an interview with a colleague that ran one of the major hotels in the Bahamas. Pat had told Tian how much golf caddies and towel boys made and Tian was sold on the idea.

Tian always considered himself good at auditions and for Tian this was nothing more than that. Tian went into the meeting smiling, injecting humor and speaking with confidence about his experiences at and after college. When the interviewer asked him what type of job he was looking for he was surprised at Tian's response.

The meeting ended smoothly and what Tian looked forward to most was calling Annett and letting her know how it had gone. But when Tian called, her mother said that she was out with a friend and didn't know when she would be back. Tian left a message asking her to call him back and her mother told him that she wouldn't forget. Tian knew that a friend could be Marie or a friend could be Colin. Neither one was a problem for him.

The first call that Tian got was the next day and it was from, of all people the person that he had had the interview with. The interviewer mentioned that he had enjoyed talking to Tian and wanted to offer him a job. Tian became very excited.

"Yes, we have a job that we think that you would do quite well. It would be as the night manager for the hotel. You would be in charge of guest relations for the later hours. It comes with an excellent starting salary, parking privileges, meal allowances, guest passes for the hotel and I promise you that you will get promoted quickly."

This was not what Tian had had in mind. Tian asked if he could take some time to think about it and was glad to get off the phone when the man agreed. Tian recognized this moment. It was a turning point. It was the point when every creative type made a decision about who they actually were. He had tried to be the artist and had failed miserably. Now he was being offered entrance into the secure life where salaries were weekly and people bought homes and raised families. The question was how could Tian turn down such an offer and Tian thought long and hard about it. How could he turn this down?

The day past as did the next without hearing from Annett. Tian knew that her mother had given the message to her because she had promised. Instead Tian spoke to Pat. Pat was ecstatic with the offer. It was far more than Pat had expected and almost as much as he had been offered at his own job even though Pat had his master's degree.

Pat's elation was short lived when Tian asked him the question he was asking himself.

"How can I turn this down, Pat?" Tian asked softly.

"Why would you want to, this is a great job?"

"Because this isn't what I want to do. I can't even imagine me putting on a suit and going into work every day at a hotel. Where do I go from there, to a day manager? Then where, a managing director or something? Then what? How many years do I stay there and what am I supposed to do with it all?"

"Tian, you're making everything so hard for yourself. This is what people do. They go off to college and they come back so that they can get jobs."

"But I just wanted something temporary and I told him that. I was very clear that all I wanted was a golf caddy job so that I could go back to the States and try again."

"Well he thought you were capable of more. This is a big deal, Tian. They don't just offer people these types of jobs out of college."

"I know, but I didn't ask for it."

"You better figure out what you want to do before you give him an answer."

"I know what I want to do. I want to act," Tian replied with venom.

"No, I mean what you want to do with your life. Because your job is just a means to an end. People get jobs so that they can live their life. You better figure out what life you are trying to live."

"Ok," Tian offered graciously.

"And get back to him quickly. Don't make me look back."

"Will do."

Tian truly considered Pat's question. What was it that he wanted to do with his life? The question reverberated through his being. Tian laid down in bed and thought back to what it was that was important to him. Tian pushed back past Toronto and before college. Tian thought back to the books that he had read. What is it that they inspired in him? What was it that drove Tian to meditate twice a day and let go of all of the other things that were important to him?

Tian laid there thinking about it when the answer poured into his consciousness like warm syrup. The most fulfilling thing that Tian had ever done didn't involve a stage or a camera. It didn't even involve a statue or applause. The most fulfilling moment of his young life came when he was even younger. It came on benches outside his high school cafeteria during lunch on Tuesdays and Thursdays his senior year.

During college, Tian learned that his high school was different from all of his friends' schools because of one thing, it didn't have cliques. Often times, the best athletes were also the smartest kids, so they would go between their jock friends and their chess playing friends. The one segmentation that sometimes happened was that between the troublemakers and the good kids.

But since the troublemakers were often in the science classes as well, it was hard to draw a sharp line between those two groups either.

But Tian didn't fall into any of the distinctive groups. He wasn't really a jock, nor among the best students. He was in all of the science classes and would be considered a good kid, but spent most of his time with the girls preferring the energy that they would give him over any of the guys. That made lunch particularly hard for Tian because at lunch the girls ate with the girls and the quasi cliché were most visible. That often meant that Tian would eat alone or on odd days with one or two other friends.

Tian's classmates always felt that he was different somehow. There was something odd about the way he thought. They were used to kids coming to school one day claiming to be born again and acting completely different, but the change in Tian was a lot more subtle.

His true uniqueness shown most clearly when he would talk about things from the books that he read. Tian would one day talk about how he could feel color and then another about how there was an energy that connected everyone and everything. And what stood out most to them was the confidence with which he said it. There were students that would find him fascinating to listen to. And by senior year Tuesday and Thursday lunches was when all of the students that found him the most interesting would have lunch together.

The group lunch didn't begin on Tian's prompting. It began because one day the skinny, pale kid, who was also the best student in the grade, asked Tian a question. They were both sitting with another kid and all of them had nothing to talk about. So feeling bored the skinny kid teased Tian that maybe he should close his eyes and tell them what color the skinny kid was thinking. Tian without taking offense explained that it didn't work like that, and then explained how it did work.

The skinny kid got a chuckle out of it so when he saw Dwayne walking by, the skinny kid pulled him over and said "you got to hear this. Say it again Tian."

That was the beginning of it. For the rest of the year every Tuesday and Thursday lunch would be like a class for Tian where

Tian was the professor. Each of the group which expanded out to six or sometimes seven people would throw out questions to Tian and Tian always had an answer. The questions were always about the workings of the universe or the strange believe system that Tian had. None of them ever asked to read any of the books that Tian read. None of them ever wanted to be converted to what Tian believed. But they always came, they always sat and they always listened.

As Tian considered Pat's question about what it was he really wanted to do with his life, Tian remembered Tuesday and Thursday lunches. Tian remembered being energized by the teacher aspect of it. Tian liked being the one with the information that everyone came to for answers. And he liked that the topic that he was known for wasn't something that you could find in any textbook, but instead was one that required devotion to find and extrapolation once you found it.

Tian also liked how he felt when he shared his knowledge with his lunch group. He felt like he was making their lives better for having listened to him. It wasn't because they listened to everything Tian said and then followed his teachings exactly. It was because by considering what Tian had to say, they expanded the boundaries of their life. And as they loosened the narrow grip that there society had on their thinking, they opened up the possibilities of what their life could become.

That is what Tian decided he wanted to do with the rest of his life. Tian wanted to help people see life in a new way that made their life better. And he wanted to do it in as efficient a way as possible. Tian had trained as an actor and his field was a mass market field. Tian figured that if he could tell stories that would give people a new way of looking at life, he could be fulfilled forever.

Tian had this plan in mind when he called up the interviewer the next day. Tian did his best to be gracious and to thank him for the opportunity, but then explain that it just wasn't what he was looking for. He felt a little lighter when he was done. He knew that that was the first real decision that he made towards his new life. The second one came a few hours later when the Bahamian film commissioner called Tian telling him that they had given his resume to a movie studio that would be shooting a movie there for the next three months. The commissioner was informing Tian that the assistant director had requested an interview with him for a production assistant job.

The timing of everything was not lost on Tian. Tian could not ignore how his dead friends had told him that they would help him find a job. He couldn't ignore how he had been tempted and how if he failed he would have lost the opportunity for the thing that he wanted most. He couldn't ignore how within hours of passing his test he received the call about the other job. And finally, he couldn't ignore that the first job offer gave him the opportunity to decide what it was that he wanted for the rest of his life. Tian considered all of this a gift from God, and the person that he most wanted to share it with was Annett.

Tian called Annett again, and again found out that she was out with a friend. Like before Annett's mother promised to deliver the message and Tian believed her. This time Tian was concerned about the competition. But before Tian could decide what it was that he should do, he received a call from Colin.

"Man, guess what?" Colin began.

"What?" Tian replied with the belief that Colin had snagged Annett from under him.

"Annett's been spending time with Ed."

"Ok," Tian responded with a cavalier attitude that showed that Ed wasn't to be feared.

"She's digging him."

"How do you know?" Tian replied not believing him.

"Because she and I were hanging out and I told her that I was into her and she told me that she was into Ed."

"Yeah but Ed isn't into her is he?" Tian said hoping it wasn't true.

"Yeah he is. I asked him about it and he said that he was really into her."

"Seriously?"

"Yeah."

"I can't believe that."

"It's true man."

"Wow, I can't believe that!"

Tian's next call was to confirm his job interview. They wanted to have Tian come in the next day to get things moving as quickly as possible. After that Tian called Ed. Ed was reluctant to say anything, because to him there was nothing to say. Tian kept pushing and eventually he got the slightest of admissions that he was interested in her. This wasn't what Tian wanted to hear.

What sat worst with Tian was not that he had lost, but that he was so blindsided by Ed. Tian could understand if he were thwarted by Colin because Colin had been open about his feelings and intentions for Annett. Tian considered this a normal situation that guy friends get into. And as long as they both had their cards on the table there was nothing that couldn't be accepted.

But what Ed did was different. Tian felt that what Ed did was behind both Colin and Tian's back. Losing wasn't the issue because Tian felt Annett's heart was hers to give to whomever she wanted. But what Ed did seemed to look past the 20 years of friendship that they had. It ignored the moments that the younger version of themselves cried to each other. It ignored the secret feelings that Tian had shared to Ed about how much his parents' separation had devastated him. And it ignored how Ed had cried to him about how his mother's dominance over him had made him feel. It ignored their entire history together and made Tian feel as though what Tian felt about Annett didn't matter.

However, 20 years of friendship meant a great deal to Tian. Tian didn't want this one incident to overshadow everything else so on that first phone call to Ed, Tian wanted to find a way to reconnect. First Tian encouraged Ed to pursue Annett but Ed remained quiet. Then trying to evoke a response Tian brought up other girls that they had known and still Ed remained quiet. Tian then changed the topic to his pending job while Ed still remained quiet. Tian then realized that something had changed between the two of them so he hung up the phone and called Colin back.

"You're right man. They're dating." Tian didn't have to say anything else. Both Tian and Colin had felt the shift in the dynamic of their friendship. It was now Tian and Colin and then Ed and Annett. The lines had been drawn and Tian was going to have to get used to it.

When Tian arrived at his job interview he realized the suit he wore had no place on a studio set. Everyone in the makeshift production office was both very busy and very casual. His meeting was quick and consisted of five questions all pertaining to his experience on movie sets. Luckily Tian could talk about his experience working as an extra and then later 1st assistant director on an independent shoot in Toronto. That seemed to be enough for the 1st assistant director of this shoot and Tian was informed that he had the job.

It was later that day when Tian heard back from Annett. He was less excited about sharing the good news at first, but like before the conversation warmed up and Tian couldn't help himself. Tian asked her about Ed and she confirmed what Colin had said. Apparently their group meeting wasn't the first for she and Ed. Annett was once a waitress at Bustman's where she met and fell for Ed the first time. Ed however hadn't noticed her.

After the phone call Tian remembered his dead friend's offer to help him meet someone. And Tian decided that they were certainly true to their word. They had helped him meet someone, but like every other situation, Tian interpreted more in it than was said. It was clear that Annett had no intention in relinquishing the friendship. And since Tian cherished the time he spend with this cool, beautiful woman, it meant that Tian would get a front row seat to her and Ed's budding relationship.

Work on the movie set was a welcome distraction for Tian. It was a movie about a dolphin and had two Hollywood stars in it. It was exciting that first day everyone sat and ate lunch together. Tian did his best not to stare at the child star and his family, but he couldn't help but consider the differences between the kid and himself. Tian imagined that the kid's thoughts were more interesting than his. Tian imagined that the day to day workings of his life was also more important simply because of his celebrity status. None of these were thoughts that Tian would share with anyone, but they were all very real and conscious.

The crew was broken down into groups. There were those that would never talk to the actors and those that would. And then the groups that did talk to the actors were broken down by those that would and wouldn't interact with the stars.

Tian worked within the assistant director group. As a production assistant, he was more of a gofer. And what he retrieved was anything from the supporting actors to coffee. He was never supposed to interact with the stars. Still it was all very exciting for Tian. The newness of the set distracted him from thinking about Annett for the first two weeks. However, after that thoughts of Annett permeated his day.

Making a movie was demanding. Tian worked ten hours a day, six days a week. Tian didn't have much time to spend with Annett, but whenever he could he fit in a phone call. Tian hoped that his cool new status as a member of the Hollywood crew would impress her and it did. Tian told stories about how the movie set worked. He mentioned who on the set was having an affair with whom. And he told stories about what the stars were like in person.

All of the stories had an effect on her, but not the effect that Tian was hoping. With each passing story, Annett respected Tian more and the stories made her want to talk to Tian more. But what was now clear to Tian was that she didn't love him.

And while Annett's feelings remained unchanged, Tian felt something unhealthy developing within himself. He was becoming dependent on hearing from her. When she returned his call, it made his day. But when she didn't the longing continued until she did.

Tian decided that this dependence was a problem. Tian didn't like being beholden to anyone for his happiness. Yes, knowing Annett had suspended his loneliness, but it invigorated something that was even more debilitating, heartbreak.

'This is distracting,' Tian thought. 'And what's more important is that the feelings I'm having for her doesn't matter. What could someone else bring to your life that wasn't there to begin with?'

Tian was fond of a quote that he had read in one of the books of his youth. "The only way that you can truly love someone is if you first love yourself." Everything else, Tian decided, was pointless. And now that he knew what he wanted to do with the rest of his life, there was no room for the pointless. And Tian didn't just think it, he felt it down to his core. 'The only thing that relationships could add to your life is distraction.'

Like the great monks from places like Tibet, Tian promised himself that he wouldn't get distracted from his path again. Tian's entire life would be about giving people a new way of looking at life that helped to make their life better. That was the only thing he needed to do with every breath and spark of energy. Anything that took him from that path was a distraction. 'Relationships were a distraction' Tian decided, and deep down the thought felt right.

So with finality Tian decided what the rest of his life would be about. Tian wouldn't be a monk in the traditional sense. He wasn't about to pull himself away from the trappings of the physical world like he did during his childhood, but he was going to create a life dedicated to work and service. He still craved the life of an actor, but now he knew what he would do with it once he got it. He now saw his acting as a means to an end. He wanted to be the creator of material and not just a performer of it.

Tian's life was going to have meaning so that on his last day, when he was struggling to take his last breath he could look back and say that he had done something good for the world. And as long as he could get even a little help from God, his charm and talent would be enough to take him exactly where he wanted go.

'And all I need is a little help from God,' Tian confirmed and smiled. 'I am one of his favorite children. All I want to do is make other people's lives better. Of course he's going to help me do this.'

Tian looked out onto the set as the director yelled action. The extras began bustling around the fake bar and the actors started to do their thing. Tian imagined what this grand bargain would reap for him and thought most about the director who molded the performances and shaped the story for the millions who would watch it in theatres. That was where the real influence lay, Tian decided. Tian imagined that that was where God would lead him. And imagining himself in the director's chair, Tian couldn't help but feel good.

"I am going to have a great life." Tian took a breath through his smile and then refocused his attention toward work.

Considering his new pledge the weekends weren't easy for Tian. This was when the gang got together; Marie, Colin, Ed and Annett. Tian didn't notice but Annett was saddened when she felt the change in Tian's attitude towards her. Annett had to accept that Tian no longer looked for her first when he entered the room. And

Annett had to accept that their conversations, though still polite, lacked the enthusiasm that she had come to love about him.

For his part, Tian had given the situation a lot of thought. What he decided he needed was a switch. He needed something that he could shut off like he did back when he was a kid meditating twice a day. Back then when he had an unpleasant thought he simply made the decision to stop thinking about things and he did. When he engaged in behavior customary of a teenager but below his own standards he decided that he would stop acting in that way and the action stopped.

Now as an adult he needed that same sort of switch. He needed something that would stop him from feeling the way he did. He needed a switch he could flip that would help him feel nothing.

Although shutting off his emotions was impossible, he knew that he could stop calling Annett, so he did. Tian knew that if he stopped giving her attention he would desire less of it in the end, so he did. But even when he sat their coldly disconnected from what she was saying there was a feeling that he couldn't switch off, disappointment.

Tian couldn't help feeling continuous disappointment. Tian had allowed himself to believe that she could be the one that he could love. And now not only would she not be the one, but there would never be another. It reverberated in Tian's core that relationships were a distraction. So now, before he had had his first he made a vow that would prevent him from having any at all.

And as much as Tian blocked out so many of his other feelings he, somehow, didn't see the harm in allowing the disappointment of that loss to surface again and again. So when other more appropriate emotions were suppressed during conversations with Annett, the feeling that surfaced in Tian as disappointment. And whereas anger should have followed his interactions with Ed, all that surfaced in Tian was disappointment; and hidden within the disappointment below what Tian felt compelled to admit, numbness.

After a few weeks of this, Tian knew that his weekends had to change. So when a crew member put up a flyer advertising scuba lessons every Sunday, Tian jumped at the chance. Tian had never dreamt of exploring the ocean, but there was something else that he had dreamt of that scuba certification would allow. The production had recently moved to a new location. They had bought out the services of a dive shop turning the entire facility into a small fishing town. This dive shop had the true distinction of being the only dive shop in the world that offered cage-free shark dives and this was an experience that appealed to Tian.

The dive package included a three hour dive where the dive master would chum the water with fish guts and then jump in. Once the sharks had been wrangled into an area, the divers would be invited in where two by two they would be allowed to feed the sharks. The sharks sometimes bumped the divers and sometimes nipped them, but there had never been a full shark attack and that was good enough assurance for Tian.

The four Sundays of dive school was exactly what Tian needed. It allowed Tian not to call anybody and unexpectedly nobody called him. Tian had expected at least one unwelcome call from Ed or Annett, but none came. So on the fifth week when certification was complete Tian felt very ready for the shark dive.

To Tian's surprise there was nothing unique about the boat ride to the drop point. He had expected it to be thrilling on its own but Tian felt nothing. Even when Tian put on the tank nothing happened. And within the void of emotion Tian began to consider that he had chosen his activity incorrectly.

It wasn't until he saw the first fin pop of the water that Tian's face felt flush. At that point he knew that he had chosen correctly. What came rushing back to him with the emergence of that fin were childhood memories of the movie Jaws and how it made him nervous to even swim in the pool afterwards. But even as a tightness gripped his chest he never wavered. Between the deafening beats of his heart Tian felt alive. Or more importantly he felt, and feeling felt good.

The first of the divers sat on the edge of the boat crossed their arms and fell back into the shark invested waters. Tian watched as the dark shapes reacted to the splash. Tian tried to count them all but there were too many that dipped out of sight and too many that looked like one shape before splitting into two.

Tian could feel his adrenaline coursing now. He was lined up as the fourth person into the water and all he could think about was what it would be like to be attacked by a shark. And it wasn't an attack while feeding that worried Tian, it was one as he fell backward into the water. That was the point of vulnerability. It was the moment while tumbling backwards when he was unable to react that he feared the most.

When his time came Tian perched himself on the edge of the boat. He did a final check of his gauges and goggles and took a final strained breath. Tian did his best to clear away all of his thoughts, the fears, the angers, the vulnerabilities until there was nothing left. When that calm, darkness entered Tian's consciousness he let go. There was no need to open his eyes when the water hit him. He knew that if something was going to happen to him, it was too late to stop it.

Tian examined the feeling as the water filled up the pores of his wet suit. It felt good not knowing how close he could be to death. It was freeing to know that at any moment it could all be over, that there would be no more disappointment and no more loneliness.

'This is where I'm supposed to be,' Tian thought, 'free floating with my eyes closed in shark invested water. I feel alive!'

CHAPTER 11

The path that Tian and the young man followed felt on Tian's feet like the smooth, rounded stones found on the beach. As a thin guy Tian could always feel the stones pushing through his heel against his bone, but here it all felt very soft and comfortable. Tian looked up the path to what looked like an open courtyard with 30 to 35 people milling around.

"Is there a party going on?" Tian inquired.

"No, this is how it always is," the young man replied.

As Tian approached he wondered what they were all talking about. Certainly more than a few of them had to be talking about the arrival of God. 'How could there be a more interesting topic?' Tian wondered.

Everyone's style of dress differed, Tian noticed. And each person's style of dress didn't necessarily correspond to the person's age. In one conversational group there was a woman in tweed brown and grey pant suit with what looked like a silk beige blouse. That outfit placed the 30 plus year old woman in about the 1950's countryside of England. The woman standing next to her wore a very contemporary colorful spring skirt with a navy sleeveless top. She was in her early 50's and could have been pulled from a spring catalog circulated within the last five years.

Each group was mixed with both men and women and age didn't seem to matter. The youngest person that Tian saw was no more than 16 years old and the oldest looked like a very fit 80. The racial mix was a little less diverse though it didn't matter to Tian. The majority of everyone there was very fair skinned and those who weren't had a Middle Eastern or East Indian complexion.

The young man led Tian onto the courtyard and pointed out the table that had all of the food on it. "Would you like to try any other fruits? All of them were grown on the grounds and are amazingly good."

Tian was curious about the tastes of the food. The peach that he had tried was more of a packet of memories than it was sweet and Tian wondered if all of the food in Christian heaven was like that. Tian moved toward the food table and was struck by the amount of warmth that the food seemed to be emanating. It wasn't a change in temperature as much as it was a change in mindset. As Tian entered the aura around the table, he felt a sense of gratitude. It was as if the foods had stored all of the dinner time graces that was said over it and was now reflecting that gratitude back. And pulsation of all of those graces made the inside of Tian tingle. It felt good.

Tian looked over trays of fruits and vegetables cut and placed intricately on the plates and tried to recognize them all. There were some that Tian would automatically associate with an English countryside like apple slices, apricot balls, blueberries and raspberries. But there were others that were clearly more tropical foods like orange plugs, peach slices, and mango cubes.

"How do you like the food," an unfamiliar voice asked Tian.

Tian looked around and found a good-looking man with curly black hair. The man only looked like he was in his mid 40's but what stood out most about him was his very worn blue eyes. There was no doubt that this man had experienced a lot and thought an awful lot about an awful lot of things.

"I tried something earlier and I had a hard time finding the taste in it."

"Really the foods here are usually quite spectacular," the man said as he picked up a piece of orange and popped it into his mouth. "Umm. Can't you taste how the sugars flow over your tongue? It is simply incredible."

"No, actually I can't. My experience is quite different."

Tian looked around for his young friend, and found him walking away from the table. "I'm sorry, what's your name?" Tian said turning his attention back to his new friend.

"I'm Reshand. And you?"

"I'm Tian." He felt good when he said his name again. In fact, Tian decided that everything about this place felt good to him. "I have to say that I absolutely love it here."

"Well, it is heaven."

Tian and Reshand shared a laugh both sensing that they had found someone in which each other could relate.

"How long have you been here?" Reshand asked.

"I've only just arrived. In fact, the young man that showed me up here was the first person that I met in the grove."

"Didn't anyone escort you here?"

"No I…" Tian wondered if he was making a mistake by starting so quickly with what was clearly a red flag for anyone here. "I arrived by myself."

"Oh really? I guess it happens," Reshand threw off with a smile.

"How long have you been here?" Tian asked feeling good that he had trusted his new friend.

"I've been here a very long time. It feels like they built the place around me," Reshand retorted with a smile.

"Really?"

"Well no. Not quite that long but even in this place where it's hard to judge time, I can tell that I've been here much longer than most."

Tian felt that it would be rude to press him on a question that Reshand had obviously chosen not to answer directly, so instead he reverted to his practiced party mode.

"Do you know anyone else here?"

"Well, in fact I've met everyone else here. There are not a lot of new residents for this part of heaven so it's easy to meet everyone."

"Really?"

"Yes, that's why I was very excited to meet you."

"Why thank you," Tian replied with a gratitude that gave a hint to how long it had been since he had received such a compliment.

"No, it was really a pleasure meeting you." Reshand's reply met only a bashful smile back. "I'm sorry, I'm very curious so I have to ask. You said that the fruit didn't taste sweet. What did it taste like?"

"Well…" Tian thought about how he could describe the experience. What it most felt like to Tian was an abbreviated version of what he felt in the ocean library. But Tian wasn't sure if he should talk about his experiences outside of heaven and he wasn't sure if Reshand would even understand if he did. "What it felt like was as if the most important part of the tree's life was instantly communicated to me. And I didn't chew the food or feel it on my tongue, it just seemed to dissolve as I closed my mouth."

"Interesting!"

"You mean you've never heard of anyone else who has had that experience?"

"Actually I haven't. In all of the years that I've been here, I have never heard of anyone else describe eating food that way."

"I hope you don't think me strange because of it," Tian offered with a smile.

"No, I think you're very beautiful because of it."

Tian began to feel very comfortable with Reshand. He knew that this was someone that he didn't have to hide anything from. Tian was very appreciative for meeting him.

"Come, let me introduce you around."

Reshand led Tian away from the table toward the groups of guests. Tian felt nervous. He had never been one to shy away from meeting people, but Tian remembered that he no longer looked like everyone else there. His slightly elongated face and twisted features made him feel self-conscious. Tian had always thought of himself as a good-looking guy, and it was always his admission into any conversation that he wanted. But that advantage had been taken away from him so now he wasn't sure how he would be received.

Reshand approached the largest of the groups. It consisted of 15 people standing in a near circle laughing and smiling with one another. The person that seemed to be directing the conversations was a very thin woman in her 40's with short reddish-brown hair. She seemed to be addressing each member giving them a chance to speak and then moving on. Reshand stood outside the opposite side of the circle than the thin woman and spoke.

"Trace, what's the topic of conversation now?" Reshand asked in a low rich tone that he knew the entire group could hear.

"Oh Reshand, it's good to see you again," Trace replied with a smile. "It's who we've met here."

"Oh," Reshand replied without wanting to draw more attention to himself.

"So Tomas, who have you met?" Trace continued.

Tian worked his way into the circle with one shoulder next to Reshand and the other next to a balding man with a full beard and pot belly.

"I have a great answer for you," Tomas replied. "So I was walking on the plateaus that overlooked the Triad Valley and I sit to just absorb it all. And as I'm thinking about whatever, the beauty, the creation of it, how I would pose for the picture if I created a series of tourist postcards that included me pointing out Waldo in the landscape," the group laughs. "…when I hear someone sit down beside me. Well, I certainly wanted him to think me very deep so I wasn't about to whip around and give him the once over or anything. So I had to be subtle about it.

I stretch my arms out like I have just been sitting there for months and only his presence broke me out of my intense meditative state. I do a little twist stretch to get a better look of who it was and when I turn around, who is it? It's Saint Peter."

"Really!?" Trace responds with some awe.

"I kid you not."

Reshand looks over and notices Tian's reaction. Tian's mouth is completely open and there is a look of wonder on his face.

The man with the belly next to Tian yells "So what did you do?"

"Well, what can you do? I wasn't about to ask him for his autograph or anything." The group chuckles.

"No, I keep my utmost composure. I get up, go over to him, and with all of the dignity of a 12 year old girl I ask him, are you Saint Peter? I have always been a big fan; as if his dying upside down on the cross was his rock anthem or something."

The group moans in good humor.

"As if he were on the road to Wimbley Stadium instead of Damascus when he was struck down."

"That was Saul," the pot bellied man yelled.

"Whatever," Tomas retorted to a roar of laughter. "The point is that I meet one of the most important figures in all of history and I may as well have asked him to braid my hair while we talked about which boys we would kiss." Again the group laughs.

"So what did he do?" Trace shoots back.

"Well, what do you think he would do? He was very polite and he said that all of my praise was not worthy of him but the heavenly father has earned it and more." Tomas briefly pauses. "Then he said that I was soon approaching womanhood and I should cherish puffy stickers of unicorns for as long as I can."

"Did he really say that?" a small dark haired man asked.

"Noooo, Phil. He's Saint Peter. He just closed his eyes and proceeded to pray or something."

"Wow Tomas. I can't tell if I'm more jealous or embarrassed for you," Trace concluded with a smile and a laugh from the group. "Does anyone have any other stories?"

"Has anyone met the blessed virgin Mary?" The pot bellied man yelled.

"Wow, you can always tell the Catholics in the group," Trace said with a smile and a laugh from the group. "Ok, has anyone met Mary?"

When everyone remains silent Trace turns her attention to Tian. "So what about you, friend of Reshand? Do you have any stories to tell?"

"I have only just arrived. Reshand is the most famous person that I've met," Tian retorted with a smile.

"Ah yes, the mysterious Reshand. So Reshand, you come in and out of here always talking but never telling us a word." Trace said with a playful smile. "When are you going to tell us some of your stories? You've got to have been here for about a zillion years. You've got to have seen someone?"

Reshand stares back at Trace with a light smile on his face. And although he is looking at Trace his full attention is on what Tian is doing. Reshand blinks slowly and then turns to take a look at Tian who is enthralled at the idea that the man he just met was someone of celebrity in heaven. Reshand turns back to Trace and decides that it is time to share.

"I've seen a few people over my time."

"Like who?" Tian asks with a vulnerability which is unlike him.

Reshand turns to Tian. "Like Jesus."

"Really!" Trace responds with utter amazement.

"I've been here a long time. I think that I've calculated that 1500 years have passed since I first arrived here. And what you now think of as heaven is not what it used to be like back then. It was much smaller then. Back then it was just a place where those that strictly followed the teaching of Jesus Christ could enter. There was no need for such wide open spaces and large mansions because there was only about a million of us.

And back then Jesus, Peter, Mary, Paul, John, they were all here. They would spend a lot of time together, but they would also spend as much time talking to the rest of us. And Jesus wasn't a deity like some people think of him as now. He was just a regular person who was just a little wiser and little more compassionate then the rest of us.

And Jesus was very accessible if you ran into him in a field or staring at the beauty of heaven, he would just talk to you."

"What would he say?" Tomas interjected.

"It changed over time. When I first got here he spoke a lot about the glories of this place and how our heavenly father had built it for us to celebrate the life that we have lived. I got a distinct sense that he felt his work was done with us. I felt as though his tough work involved all of the things that he had to do to get us to here, and now that we were here our future was up to us.

But over the next 500 years Jesus seemed to change a little. Heaven was continuously expanding so Jesus had to make himself available to more people. And that meant that I saw him less. But the times when I did see him, he began to recognize me as being one of the old timers of heaven. And I guess that that made him feel a little more comfortable with me than some of the others.

He would ask me questions like if I had visited the new parts of heaven and what I had thought about it. He would ask me if anyone that I knew had left heaven and if they had why they had. I don't know, at that point he kind of struck me as an aging king. Not in the sense that he was any less humble or beautiful. No, he struck me as a great man that had even greater things to consider.

The last time I saw him was about 700 years ago. Heaven wasn't as big or as populated as it is now, but it was still dense. I was near the Braegan Waterfalls when I saw a tremendous crowd approaching. It must have been about a thousand people thick. And it was moving to the rim near the fall. I was on the other side of the river and couldn't hear anything over the roar of the water. But I imagined that Jesus had chosen that location for a reason.

Certainly Jesus was a man of miracles so talking over the sound of the river was a small act. But something told me that the man that I met 300 years prior wouldn't want to speak over the river. In fact, the man that I met 300 years earlier wouldn't want to speak at all. I looked over at the crowd and wondered if he now made appearances because this was heaven and he was Jesus. I remembered the story of him going into the desert and being tempted and wondered what it was that the man who was Jesus was going through when he decided to enter the desert. And just as I wondered this Jesus rose into the air and slowly disappeared."

"Where did he go?" Tian asked softly.

"I don't know," Reshand replied turning back toward Tian.

"Do you think that he's still in heaven?" Tian asked almost under his breath.

"I don't know," Reshand replied with a knowing that was shared only between the two.

"Well that's an odd question. Where else would he be?" the pot bellied man retorted.

"I'm sorry I didn't hear what he asked," Trace said in her booming voice.

"He asked, 'do you think he is still in heaven?'" the man repeated.

"Umm, that's odd. Where else could he be?" Trace asked with a questioning look on her face.

Tian became uneasy about the sudden attention that he was being given for what he realized was a telling answer. Tian looked into the eyes of the group members and struggled to find a response.

"I think what he meant was that all of existence is more glorious than heaven and earth combined," Reshand added coming to Tian's rescue.

Tian turned to look at Reshand who stared back, and Tian couldn't express the gratitude that he felt for diverting a question that he was afraid to answer.

"Well said, but what does that mean," Tomas replied.

"It means that one day your body will go through certain changes and boys won't seem as yucky like they do now," Reshand retorted with the laughter of the crowd.

"Oh that's right, make fun of the guy with the 'Saint Peter Rocks' scrunchy. Yes, very mature for a 1500 year old man."

The crowd erupts in a ball of laughter as Reshand leads Tian away from the group and onto the lawns.

"Are you really 1500 years old?" Tian asked as they walked away.

"As far as I can tell."

"And you've seen Jesus?"

"Yes I have."

"Have you ever seen God?" Tian asked hoping that Reshand wouldn't make a big deal out of the question.

"I haven't. Have you?" Reshand paused for only a second before replying "Wait, why are you asking me that?"

"It's a natural question isn't it? You've spoken to Jesus. It wouldn't seem that much more unusual if you had seen God."

"There is a big difference between the two."

"When you saw Jesus, did you ask him about God?" Tian asked with an air of nonchalance.

Reshand stopped walking but didn't turn around to look at Tian. Tian took his gaze off of Reshand. He looked around to realize that they were now a lot further from the mansion than they should have been by merely walking.

"Wait, how did we get here?" Tian asked.

"It's how we get places quickly here in heaven. We think about where we want to go and then walk in that direction. What happens is that the ground folds underneath you so instead of one step covering two feet, it covers four or five ." Reshand turned to Tian who was now examining the mountains on the side of them and the mansions that looked like dollhouses on the horizon. "I would like to show you something. It's very special."

Tian turned toward Reshand curious. "What is it?"

As Tian stared at Reshand, Reshand disappeared. Thinking that Reshand wanted him to follow, Tian thought of Reshand and disappeared himself. When Tian opened his eyes he was standing on a peninsula of rock that extended out from a rock face. On the right side of the rock was what looked like a 5000 foot drop and on the left was the biggest waterfall that Tian had ever seen. This was the place that Tian imagined when Reshand was telling his story about the last time he saw Jesus.

The rock Tian stood on overlooked a valley. The floor of the valley was impossible to see. The mist created from the water fall seemed to billow out from the river for miles. And the sun hitting the mist created a plethora of rainbows which overlapped the valley. Through the mist jutted more mountains with sharp, tall, snow covered peaks.

The rainbows were what captured Tian's attention the most though. It was one of the most personal days of Tian's short life when he found the end of a rainbow in his backyard. It had been raining throughout the night, and in the morning when Tian went outside to get a feel for the temperature there it was.

Tian was always taught that rainbows were imaginary, so the closer you got to one the further away it moved. But there it was, the end of a rainbow that bent up over the bushes behind his childhood house. Looking up at it, the rainbow curved 300 feet into the air. Anyone driving by the house could have seen it yet where it landed was fenced into a place that was his alone.

Young Tian walked toward the rainbow and to his surprise it didn't budge. When Tian entered the end of the rainbow, he was half expecting to be transported to someplace magical, but that didn't happen either. What happened was that as Tian entered the 15 foot area where the rainbow sat, the color of the air around him changed. First it turned red and then orange. The yellow was hard to see but the green was easier. The blue added a light tinge to the air around him but the lavender was barely visible at all.

It was probably that moment more than any other that taught Tian to believe that there were things more wondrous than science knew. And it was that moment more than most that convinced Tian that he was special and destined to do more with his life than others.

'How many people got to walk through the end of a rainbow?' the young Tian asked himself. 'This must surely be a sign from God. What else could be clearer?' the young Tian concluded before returning to his house to finish getting ready for the 7th grade.

'I will probably do something great with my life,' young Tian thought with a smile growing on his face. 'My life is going to be… grand!'

When Tian killed his belief in God it was an accidental killing. Or perhaps it would be better described as a crime of passion. There was a story in the bible that Tian had long doubted. The story goes that when Jesus was in the desert the devil came to him and tempted him. Once he tempted Jesus to turn stones into bread. Another time he tempted Jesus with becoming ruler of the land. And the third time the devil led Jesus to Jerusalem and had him stand on top of one of the temples. The devil then tempted Jesus to throw himself off so that God would send his angels to lift him up and keep him safe.

In the story Jesus resisted the first two temptations in the desert easily. But in the third temptation, it would seem that the devil was more successful than he is given credit for. The devil, who seemed to be Jesus' constant companion in the desert, got Jesus to leave the desert, go specifically to Jerusalem and then break what must have been the rules of the church by standing on the highest point of the temple.

Tian always considered Jesus' climb to the top of the temple one of the devil's successes. Because if anyone nowadays climbed to the top of a building to decide whether or not they should throw themselves off at the encouragement of voices they heard in their head, they would be herded off to a mental facility. Yet the son of God does it then changes his mind and he's heralded as a great defeater of Satan. It takes a lot of crazy to get a person to the top of a building but the devil gets no credit for it.

But what Tian disagreed with the most from that story was Jesus' reason for not throwing himself off of the building. Jesus is said to reply to the devil by answering "Do not put the lord thy God to the test." 'Why not put the lord thy God to the test?' Tian wondered. 'We put God and his creation to the test every day. We have evolved as a species by constantly putting God's laws to the test.'

God made the sun rise in the east every morning. And we constantly put God to the test by basing our society around the growing of crops that depend on the uniformity of sunrise and sunset. God is said to give man dominance over the animals. And we test that every day by keeping them close as pets. We test God's consistency by sending spaceships into space trusting that all of God's laws for the universe will remain constant. And yet Jesus answered the devil by saying that we should not put the lord thy God to the test. 'What good is putting your faith in someone if you can only believe what they say some of the time?' Tian asked himself.

So after the movie that Tian had worked on ended; and after an attempt to return back to the United States was thwarted by his owning a social security card that the border guard thought he shouldn't have, Tian moved to Dallas, Texas and lived with another college friend. This one had invited him to stay.

June was a very cosmopolitan Indian girl whose father was an Indian diplomat stationed in Nepal. She was now a little plumper than the thin frame that Tian fell for in college. But her intelligence, humor and desire to be around him kept the two in contact.

Tian had kept her abreast of his developments over the years. June was one that had decided immediately after meeting Tian that he was destined for great things. So when Tian told her about Toronto and everything that followed, her heart broke. But even with that story her confidence in Tian's destiny never wavered. She knew that the great things would come, and she also knew that none of them could be accomplished from the Bahamas. So one day during one of their long distance conversations, June sheepishly offered her place as one of his stops on his destined journey.

Tian hadn't thought about this option. Dallas wasn't exactly a Mecca for actors or people looking to help give others a new way of looking at life. But certainly Tian needed to get away. His relationship with his lifelong friend Ed had deteriorated down to primitive grunts when they saw each other. The cold war had been initiated by Tian, and Annett was the prize. And although Annett continued to make it clear that Ed was already the victor, their constant conversations and intimate sharing gave the troops hope that victory could still be won.

It was more than a year later when the battle seemed lost and the prize began to lose its luster. This was when Tian felt that he was allowed to step away from the fight. And when Tian finally made the decision to join June in Dallas the progression was swift. Within a day of agreeing to come, Tian had bought the ticket. The flight was scheduled for 10 days into the future and the exodus ritual began.

Unlike his time after college, Tian would be moving to Dallas as an illegal alien. And what's more, the social security card given to him while in college had been confiscated during his last attempt to move to the US. This time he would try to create his new life with $2000 dollars left from his time working on the movie and no legal status. What all of this meant was that once Tian arrived in the US, he could never leave. No matter who died, or what happened there was no going back.

Tian made what he imagined to be his final visits to both of his grandmothers. His grandmother on his father's side was very spry for 85. And like usual she offered a little of the peas and rice she always had cooking for when any of her 8 children or 20 grand kids came to visit. The other grandmother was Tian's favorite and had been bedridden for the past five years.

The conversation that they had was surprisingly direct.

"You know this is the last time you are going to see me, right?" Tian's grandmother said to her grandson.

"Yes, but I'm expecting you to come up and visit me when you go," Tian replied with a smile.

Tian's Grammy laughed saying, "You know I'm serious right?"

"So am I. You have to promise me that before you go, you will come up to visit me," Tian pushed firmly while holding a smile.

She just laughed delightfully, but Tian wouldn't let go. "I'm serious, you have to come up and visit."

Finally Tian's grandmother relented with a nod, not knowing what the rules would be once her final day came. Tian left her bedside with a smile on his face knowing that though that was the last time they would be able to touch or hear each other's voice, they wouldn't lose contact. And he knew that the next time that they met, she wouldn't have pains in her swollen joints, cataracts in her eyes and 80% hearing loss. Tian smiled because he knew that the next time they were together she would be like she had been when Tian was five, before all of her problems started.

However, years later Tian would be disappointed when he didn't see her on the day that she died. In fact Tian had to be informed about her death by a phone call. That isn't to say that Tian hadn't felt it coming. A week before his Grammy died his thoughts turned to her in an intense way. Tian had decided to search for something to ease the pain of her arthritis. And after he found it he called home to find out that she had only a day or two to live. Tian hadn't called home in months, so the timing and reason for calling confirmed their link to Tian. Tian had decided that he was feeling her death pains from the 3000 miles away and was resolved to help. With that connection and her promise Tian expected a moment of death visit, but when he didn't get it Tian assumed that his Grammy had others that needed her company more.

The visit that Tian didn't know would be his last was the one that he made to his father. So their last visit was nothing special and nothing memorable. Unlike his grandparents both Tian and his father knew that they would be in constant contact via phone. Both also expected Tian's father to come for visits, so no big gestures and no last rites were given. But even so, that last time when they hugged was their last. Tian would never see his father again.

When all of the goodbyes were said and the immigration officers were thwarted, his second attempt at a new life began. On the first night in Dallas, June introduced Tian to her boyfriend. Tian understood their attraction. They were two peas in a pod. Yes, June was overly romantic and Vance was more practical. But both believed in living the largest, most grand life that they could lead. They both made bold life changing decisions quickly, like going whitewater rafting in Utah on a moment's notice; and like inviting a college friend to live with you without considering what it would actually be like.

In this case June and Tian had arranged a token amount for rent so Tian felt less like a guest and more like a tenant. But June made known her dissatisfaction with not being able to walk around her place naked. And Vance only stayed over 2 more times before June became a practical roommate at Vance's.

And although Tian managed to do more in Dallas than he ever had in Toronto, Texas life didn't stick for Tian. June lent her friends to Tian, but a bond was never created between them because as nice as they were, they were all very different from him. Tian felt a lack of curiosity within them and the one thing that everyone that Tian befriended shared was a curiosity about life.

And as much as Tian tried to connect with others outside of June's world, nothing stuck there either. Tian had been introduced to the nicest, most good-hearted group of Christians that Tian had ever met. And it was with them that Tian first saw what the Christian spirit truly was. And with these people, one connection became two, which became a group and then the church. But the phone calls stopped when they realized that no amount of community was going to convince Tian to join the church.

On the employment side, Tian figured out that although foreigners couldn't be employed in the US without a permit, foreigners were allowed to own companies within the US. And those companies were allowed to freelance their services out as whatever they chose. This loophole created an opportunity for Tian to work as a temporary employee in offices. And in those offices Tian met a lot of good people. However, those good people that went about creating families and building lives didn't interest Tian much either.

But what did finally sparked Tian to move was when June gave Tian a clipping from the New York Times' Thanksgiving edition. The theatre section featured a review of a play that a college classmate was doing off-Broadway. That clipping seemed to focus Tian. After reading it Tian's next move became clear to him. Tian knew that he now needed to move to Los Angeles and he not only needed a mention in the LA times, but he needed a picture.

The timing turned out to be perfect. Only after a few months of moving in, June announced to Tian that she and Vance were going to buy a house in Vance's hometown. Both June and Vance decided that they would be moving there at the end of the month. But since it was more expensive to break the lease than complete it, June allowed Tian to stay until the lease ran out. Tian decided that this extra time would give him just enough time to save money and then move to L.A.

After June left, the apartment was empty. Tian hadn't acquired anything during his stay so his only possession was an air mattress purchased after June left. With no TV and no books Tian had a lot of time to think. Those thoughts turned into hours of meditation. And eventually meditation turned into conversation with his abandoned dead friends.

Tian found it hard to reconcile the experiences of his new life with what seemed like a favorite-child-of-God status from his youth. During the time that he spent in the Bahamas after the movie Tian had questioned whether any of his amazing childhood psychic experiences had happened at all. And although his dead friends' promise of a job was fulfilled, the offer of finding someone to ease his loneliness came in a much more painful way than Tian could have imagined.

And as always whenever he questioned his connection with the unseen, the final answer would always be that his experiences were real. But now, after everything that had happened, Tian decided real or not, he would leave his dead friend behind when he left the Bahamas. What they said might have been amazingly accurate descriptions of the future, but once again Tian decided that the heart-ache of his expectations was more painful than it was worth.

But as Tian lay on his air mattress in the empty room staring at the ceiling, Tian once again thought about his dead friends. On one of the many nights when the loneliness began to overcome him and the uncertainty of his future began to consume him, he heard a familiar voice in his head. It was the personality of his harder friend and it came with a very clear message.

"Your new life will begin in August."

Tian considered the date. It was the beginning of March. "I'm sorry can you repeat that?" Tian spoke aloud.

"Your new life will begin in August," the voice repeated in the same tone and inflection.

"That's very specific. Are you sure you don't mean in April when I move to Los Angeles?" Tian asked.

"Your new life will begin in August."

Tian considered what he heard, and he considered what he had been told before. How could he trust what he heard this time when he shouldn't have so many times before? Although to be fair, he had to admit that his dead friends weren't exactly wrong before. They were just unclear. And it was in his misunderstanding that he became hurt. But as tempting as the news was to accept, his smarter side took hold and he brushed the message aside.

The next night mirrored the previous night. After dinner Tian laid down thinking of nothing in particular and then about his dead friends. With a full day and night sleep to clear away whatever was caught in his psychic mind he asked them again if they had a message for him. The message that came back was exactly the same in phrasing and tone.

"Your new life will begin in August."

On the third night when again the message was the same Tian considered the possibility. What would that new life be? What is it that Tian wanted to do on a day to day basis? What does a man that wants to give people a new way of looking at life do for a living?

'Acting,' Tian thought. 'I want to be an actor. Or do I? Maybe I don't. Acting always felt to me like a first step that led me to something else. But before the second step, you must take the first. So my new life will involve me landing a movie or a TV show.' Tian considered the possibility. 'Wow! I can't believe that I am actually going to be famous,' Tian concluded. Tian wasn't proud of the fact that celebrity intrigued him as much as it did, but he was honest with himself that it did.

And now that he knew that his future was set, he allowed himself to think of other things. 'What do I need to do before I die?' This answer came without the help of his friends. Tian knew what the greatest sin was. He didn't know how he learned it or who had said it to him, but he knew it. 'The greatest sin that anyone could commit is to not live up to their own potential.'

Tian felt a knot in his stomach thinking about it. Perhaps it had been his mother who told it to him. Maybe it was the school that he attended. But Tian knew that what he feared most was lying on his death bed thinking that with all of the gifts that the universe and God entrusted in him, he let God and the world down. Tian felt tightness in his breathing and disorientation overcome him. Tian struggled to breath normally shifting over to his side to take the weight off of his chest.

As Tian let his mind float away to other things the weight lifted. Tian thought about his impending new life. He thought about how great it would be to not struggle for money and to be recognized for his work. Tian then cleared his mind and relaxed enough for anything else that needed to come through to arrive. It didn't take long for the voice to enter his mind again.

"Leave on Thursday."

"I'm sorry, what did you say?" Tian asked surprised.

"Leave on Thursday."

Tian tried to remember where he was. It was Thursday. "Did you mean the Thursday before the end of the month."

"No, leave this coming Thursday."

"That would give me a week. I don't have enough money. If I stay until the end of the month I can save more money."

"Leave on Thursday."

'Well, that's going to be something that won't happen,' Tian thought before rolling over and shutting off the conversation in frustration.

The next day at work, Tian's boss called him into her office. Both Jody, Tian's supervisor, and Anna, the department's boss, were across the room from Tian. Tian had been temping at the Dallas phone directory delivery division. His initial job had been to go through lists of names and delete the ones that didn't have complete addresses.

But as the delivery date approached, the company that had been contracted to make the deliveries fell out of favor with Anna. So instead, Anna, a very heavy, dark haired, 38 year old mother of 2 decided to manage the delivery from their department. When the change occurred, everyone's roles at the company changed. Tian's role became that of a point person. Tian became the heavy for the ladies. Tian was the one put on the phone when the words "this is unacceptable" were needed to be said.

This was a role that neither of the ladies wanted and Tian took to naturally. And for their gratitude they gave Tian a raise which would be retroactively paid for 2 weeks. This was great for Tian because it included heavy overtime.

But this wasn't all the ladies needed. What they really needed was yet to come. What they needed was Tian to come with them to visit a delivery station that had stopped working. They needed Tian to stand quietly behind them and look as imposing as possible. These ladies didn't play in the shallow end of the pool. They were sharks and didn't mind anyone else knowing about it.

As the three of them drove to the station Anna made up a position for Tian. He would be the efficiency consultant sent down from the main office to get everything back on schedule. And Anna implored that Tian stay quiet because she decided that his large dark frame was intimidating enough.

When they arrived Tian surveyed the area. The station manager wasn't what the ladies made him out to be. What he looked like was a mid-thirties Texan with a wife and a kid. He looked like a guy that enjoyed his beer and was trying to do the best that he could with the opportunities that he was given.

It didn't take too long before the conversation turned from their failure to stay on schedule, to his company's need to receive their pay. Very quickly Tian learned that he was on the wrong side of this argument.

Apparently Anna, in a move to force the workers into doing what she wanted, stopped paying the company. The company hadn't received their reimbursements and salaries for over a month. And the reason that the company was threatening to stop work was because both the owner and the receptionist had missed their mortgages. And while he was in risk of losing his house, the receptionist was in risk of losing her trailer.

Tian's heart broke for these people. He often heard Anna yelling in her office about this company. He had even overheard Anna admit to Jody that she had their salaries in her corporate account, but had no intension in paying the group until the job was done in another three weeks.

Tian took a minute to assess the situation. He realized that this was one of the moments that life gives you to define who you are as a human being. So in the middle of an argument that broke out between the groups, Tian took a walk around the warehouse to figure out who he wanted to be.

In a moment Tian came up with a plan. He walked back to the group which had reached an impasse in their negotiations. Tian subtly called the owner of the delivery company aside and walked him to a place that he knew no one would hear them. Tian looked into the man's eyes and then transformed himself into a shark as well.

"You need to get paid. And it is your responsibility to make sure that the people working under you don't lose their trailer when they did the job that they were asked to do. This is what I want you to do. I want you to take your car and block in our van. I then want you to go to Anna and Jody and tell them that you have done your job and that you now need to get paid. Tell them that they aren't leaving until you receive the money that you're owed.

You should then tell them that you will drive them to the bank so that they can take the money out, and that you want me to stay here until they come back. Do you understand what I'm telling you?"

A look of horror swept across the owner's stubbled face.

"Do you understand what I'm telling you? I am telling you to do this, but you can't tell anyone that this came from me. Do you understand?" Tian punctuated with authority.

Without a word the owner peeled away from Tian and grabbed a cigarette. One at a time they both walked back toward the group. The owner walked past the ladies into the other room where the rest of his staff waited. Tian, not knowing if the owner would actually do it stalled the ladies, giving the owner enough time to act.

After a few minutes the ladies felt like they were making no progress and took a step to leave. At that moment the owner walked back into the room. His eyes were glassy and red like he had been crying and his cigarette wiggled in his shaking fingers. He repeated the words just as Tian had dictated them and everyone in the room froze.

Anna was the first to move. Anna walked over to the dock to get a better look at her van. It had been cornered in.

"Move your cars now!" she yelled.

"Not until we go to the bank and get the money that you owe us," the owner said in almost a whisper.

"Then Tian is coming with us," she yelled back.

"No, he is staying here," the owner whispered again.

Anna looked over at Tian, lost on what to do.

"That's no problem. I can stay," Tian said trying to inject as much calm into the situation as he could.

Anna then looked at Jody with shock in her eyes.

"I just want to get what we're owed so that I can pay my employees," the owner added.

"You sure you'll be ok Tian," Anna said turning toward him.

"No, no, I'm fine. You can go," Tian replied adding a little more pressure on Anna.

"Ok, let's go," Anna announced before turning to the stairs and almost racing out.

Once the ladies and owner left, Tian talked with the receptionist about life in Dallas and about her family. Tian was fascinated by how different their lives were. Her life seemed so simple. She worked, she loved and she would go out for drinks. Tian could barely recognize that as a life. But although Tian couldn't identify with it, Tian recognized hers as a life worth protecting.

She was clearly flawed. And her yellow hair, and gaunt, 42 year old, sun and smoke damaged face made Tian imagine that she had made a lot of mistakes throughout her life. But Tian immediately recognized hers as the life first sacrificed in the games played by the rich. Tian recognized her as the pawn. And it was really because of her that Tian had come up with his plan.

The ladies were back in 30 minutes and it was then that their van was released. Tian didn't feel the need to make eye contact with the owner. The fact that he had been released told Tian all he needed to know. On the drive back to the office Tian decided that he had earned his raise that day. With one bold move, he had maneuvered a situation that allowed the receptionist to keep her trailer, and the owner his house. He had forced the owner to be stronger than he had probably ever been in his life. And he probably gave him a sense of confidence that would transfer over to the rest of his life.

While doing what he had for the owner, he had also protected the Dallas Phone Directory company from the impending lawsuit that would come from the company not being paid. And last but not least, he gave Anna and Jody a story that they would probably tell 100 times before they died. The story would be about the time that their delivery company held their temp hostage and they had to go to the bank to take out the money to free him. Yes, Tian was sure that he had earned his travel money that day.

Tian worked full days on Saturday and Sunday and it wasn't until Tuesday morning that he decided that he did have to leave on Thursday like the voice said. 'How foolish would I be to ignore a supernatural voice… again?' Tian thought before chuckling to himself. Tian informed the ladies who were clearly disappointed with his decision. But they knew that they could never hold onto him. They found Tian to be impressive in a way that would take him to better places than the one they provided. So when Tian told them about his accelerated schedule, they simply lowered their heads and warned him about 'rolling California stops'.

Tian packed his car with the few things that he had and left early Thursday morning. Tian slept one night in Arizona and arrived in Los Angeles mid-afternoon the next day. June had arranged for Tian to stay with a friend of hers and it was Saturday when Tian began his search for a place of his own. Tian met only one potential roommate before knowing that he had found the right person. Together they found an apartment, and like that Tian was settled into his new place.

As August approached Tian still didn't know very many people. Los Angeles was a big city with lots of groups, but Tian couldn't figure out how to connect with any of them. Work, although steady, was also unfulfilling. Tian found himself taking one assistant job after another. And although the pay was good, the part of him that tightened when he considered his life's purpose prompted him to keep searching for a better job.

Things weren't all bad for Tian though. It took 2 weeks for Tian to fulfill his main goal for coming to Los Angeles. Within his first 2 weeks Tian had been cast in the Long Beach City Theatre production of Upstairs Downstairs. And he was thrilled when he got not only his name, but a full body picture of himself in the L.A. Times. Auditions followed after that and so did a few days on a daytime soap. But none of this neared what Tian imagined would happen in August.

As the 1st of August approached the tightening in his chest pushed him out of the job that he had making photocopies. With nothing to go to he became unemployed. Wanting to kill time, he entered the racquetball courts at his gym and hit the ball around. It was very similar to the tennis, the sport of his youth, so Tian took to it right away.

But as the month progressed nothing extraordinary happened. During the middle of the month he started a data entry job at a production facility and at the same time went on a couple of auditions. Tian didn't know how he would respond when the end of the month came, but he thought about it constantly. He dreaded the end of the month like a death of a friend. And the closer September came the more depressed he was.

During lunch with one of his new racquetball friends he explained how his entire life had been about the 'unseen'. Tian explained how even with all of the incredible things that had happened to him, he was never quite sure whether it was real or if he was losing grip on reality. Tian shared how his message about August had been said with such clarity that it could only be said that he was psychic or crazy. And the friend, never before even having thought about messages from the great beyond felt sorry for Tian.

When Tian woke up on September 1st he was a different person. Tian felt like reality had shifted around him during the night and he no longer knew who he was. Everything around him looked slightly unfamiliar and without a purpose. Holding his toothbrush he stood in front of the mirror wondering why people brushed their teeth. Dressing for work Tian wondered if working was necessary. And getting onto his newly acquired motorcycle Tian wondered if taking his usual commuter route would drop him off at a location different than it had for the previous 2 weeks.

As Tian felt the warm summer morning air blow by him, he considered what had happened. In one moment Tian had lost his grip on his reality. Tian had always questioned if the psychic things that had happened to him were real and with one incident his entire image of himself had been rewritten.

'I have to start again,' Tian thought as the warm air whipped under his helmet and onto his face. 'I have to accept that everything that I read and believed was all a lie. I am no different from anyone else. I'm born, I live, I marry, and I buy a house, have kids and then die. The voices weren't real. The feelings weren't real. All of it was a part of my delusion.' Tian snapped out of his thoughts for a second to see where he was. 'Wow, this entire time has been a delusion.' As the tightness began in his chest, Tian let go of the thought and focused on the drive.

By the time Tian arrived home that night there was a real darkness about him. He entered his place passing his roommate who was sitting on the couch watching TV and retreated to his bedroom. Tian lay down onto the air mattress that he hadn't bothered to replace. He did his best to take long breaths but they skipped on the way in and out. It was too much for him, he thought. He couldn't understand how all of the things that he had believed could be wrong. He couldn't understand how everything that he thought he experienced could have been a figment of his imagination. It was too much for him, so all he could do was wait for the night.

When the last of the light stopped seeping in through the blades of his blinds Tian felt some relief. It was the daylight with which Tian had the problem. The night was more forgiving.

Over the past month Tian had learned to take solace in the night. It was within the darkness that Tian could escape and feel the things that he couldn't admit to during the day. And in the dark of night Tian could feel the rage, not directed towards anyone else, but towards himself. How could he be foolish enough to 'believe' in spite of the evidence to the contrary? He had even lived through the failure of Toronto and yet he held onto the belief that the afterlife was real.

When he heard the click of his roommate's bedroom door Tian ventured out into the living room. There was a bubbling in him that he couldn't control and that needed to be popped. Tian grazed the contents of the fridge by the open door's light, but nothing satisfied him. His mind kept jumping from one thing to another and the static in his head was too loud for Tian to hold a sustained thought.

Tian closed the fridge and sat on the kitchen floor with his back against the fridge door. Somewhere in between his random thoughts, somewhere in between the phrases from the books he read and snippets of conversation that he had had with his lunchtime friends in high school, the word 'park' popped up. Tian tried and successfully latched onto the word.

'What park,' he asked himself.

'Runyon Cannon,' he heard back.

This was a popular hiking trail in L.A. that Tian had heard people talk about but had never visited. Tian wanted to hold off from experiencing this park in case he ever needed a new experience in a hurry. He wanted to keep his knowledge of Runyon Cannon limited in case he ever needed to use the park for reasons other than its intended purpose. Tonight Tian had that unintended purpose.

Tian got up off of the cold floor and headed back to his bedroom. He changed into a pair of running shoes, shorts and his helmet. At what was a little past midnight he left his front door and headed towards his motorcycle. On this warm night Tian considered how long he would be able to sustain a full paced run. As a child Tian had been deathly afraid of the darkness, but as his interest in psychic phenomena developed he taught himself how not to fear the dark. But tonight he wanted to forget everything he had taught himself. And he wanted to allow all of the fears about evil, and the death screams that happened after midnight to resurface.

Tian parked his motorbike outside the eight foot high gate to the park. He imagined that there were other ways into the park, but a direct path was what he was looking for tonight. Tian walked up to the gate and peered past the bars into the darkness. He looked down at the base of the gate and followed the dirt path as deep into the hills as he could see. It wasn't very far.

Tian considered what could be inside the park at night. The park was huge so certainly the homeless went without saying. This wasn't just an open area, it was a hiking path through the woods that was locked up after dark. For the survivalists without homes this was the perfect nighttime camp site. And for those who fed off the land there were a ton of live game ready to be hunted.

Tian felt his first rush of adrenaline staring into the darkness and the second as he threw himself up onto the gate. It wasn't quiet as he climbed over. The metal rattled on its lock loud enough to wake anyone who had their window open in the adjacent apartment buildings. Tian didn't care. He almost wanted them to look out. Tian was full of the moment and wanted others to see the person that was bold enough to go into the park at night.

Tian lightly pressed his shoes against the metal spikes at the top of the gate and worked his way over. Once twisted awkwardly with his hands on one side of the spikes and his body on the other, he felt the adrenaline rush again. Tired, Tian lowered his body onto the faux spears before reacting with an "Owww."

Tian was stuck and the only thing he could think of to do was throw himself over onto the ground. So with a deep breath in he pressed his feet against the gate, let go and pushed himself as far over as possible. Tian felt the skin on his arm rip against the metal and then his knees scratch against the ground. But with a full mix of adrenaline in his system, he brushed the dirt off and again looked into the darkness.

Now on the other side, the gate felt more like a way to protect the unsuspecting L.A. residence from everything in the park as opposed to the other way around. And as Tian stepped forward he could hear the life in the woods. They were all there, the crazies and the animals. The one advantage that Tian had was that they probably didn't know that he was there yet. And the trick was to run all the way through the park without them being able to react.

As soon as Tian left the light of civilization, things felt a lot creepier. Every branch crackle and gravel crunch drew Tian's attention and quickened his pace. Trotting up the hill from the gate was harder than Tian had suspected. He wasn't tired, but the effort made him question if what he had already done was enough. But as soon as returning to life outside of the gate entered his mind he knew that he had a lot further to run.

When Tian crested the hill the light dropped off. The path became nearly undistinguishable from the brush. And all he had was the sound under his shoes to keep him on path. But as his eyes adjusted, running got a little easier. Tian picked up his pace and ran down the center of the eight foot path.

The further Tian ran into the woods the louder the woodland sounds got and the more intense Tian's adrenaline rush became. He looked ahead into what looked like trees. As he slowed down he saw a switchback in the path which seemed to create an imaginary line on the route. The half that Tian was leaving was attached to those on the other side of the gate, and everything beyond belonged to everything else.

Tian rounded the switchback and felt the eyes immediately. 'This was a mistake,' Tian thought before increasing his pace. Now the path narrowed and the sounds from the woods intensified. Some sounds kept pace with Tian for a second while other scampered in the other direction. The woods were alive and Tian's heart pounded.

Tian looked for a higher gear to shift into but found none. And when Tian passed what looked in the dark like a fallen tree, he knew that he had caught the attention of something. Again Tian looked for that higher gear and again he was disappointed with what he found.

Things changed though when the sound of crunching started behind him. It was further back, but it was constant so there was no need to doubt its existence. Tian's heart raced and his legs quickened underneath him. All of the sounds on the path were too close together and to muffled under his own sounds to count. But an even pattern would indicate human and multiple beats separated by a pause indicated a predator like a wolf or mountain lion.

Tian did his best to stay ahead of it but the image of what it could be had already overtaken his mind. He imagined looking back and staring into a pair of shining eyes. And whatever those eyes were attached to was lean and fast.

'Oh god,' Tian yelled in his mind. 'I'm going to die,' Tian kept yelling.

Tian put everything into his pace. At that moment he remembered what his P.E. teacher had taught him about running. In accordance he pulled his arms closer to his body, lowered his head, and shifted all of his weight so far forward that even a slight decrease in speed would cause him to fall forward onto his face.

'I'm going to die. I'm going to die.'

And just as Tian was sure that the sound was right behind him, when it was nipping at his heels, out of nowhere something like a 20 pound bag of potatoes shouldered Tian off of his feet, causing him to roll onto the ground.

Tian was disoriented. 'What happened,' Tian thought. 'Get up, get up!' Tian yelled in his mind. But as Tian fumbled he touched it. He couldn't identify it from the brush but whatever it was, it was real and it was out to get him.

"Ahhhhh," Tian screamed at the top of his lungs.

Tian rolled and scratched at the ground as this uncontrollable impulse represented by the scream burned out of him. Eventually he again felt ground under his feet and his reflex reaction was simply, run. Tian was still screaming when he got up to full pace, but the screaming didn't stop there. It just kept going and going uncontrollably. Soon Tian wanted to hear if whatever it is was still behind him and wished the screaming madman would quiet down, but he still didn't.

Tian now felt trapped within a body that moved with instinct around the corners and that produced a noise that began to feel undignified to him. But as much as he wanted the body to stop, he knew that he would have no luck stopping it. Soon Tian realized that the screams were no longer about whatever it was that attached him. Instead it was about a death. God had died for Tian that day and Tian missed him.

God was Tian's protector. He was the one thing that Tian felt that he could always rely on. God was a trusted friend. But not only did God die for Tian that day, but Tian was no longer even sure whether God had existed to begin with. And the thought that he had designed his entire life around the existence of a friend that never existed hurt Tian. It pained Tian in a way that only a primitive animal scream could release.

Soon Tian stopped hearing the scream. He instead felt something wet hit his chin. It was too tough to tell whether something had landed on him or whether he was crying. Tian hoped he was crying because he needed more of a release. Yet after what hardly felt like long enough his body began to relax.

Tian hadn't noticed before, but there was now a stinging coolness to the air that blew past his legs. Tian also struggled to take a breath. All of these things told Tian that he was approaching the limit of what he could stand and that was where he wanted to be. At that moment he couldn't remember what he felt when he was sitting on his kitchen floor. All of that had been washed away never to return. The running and the fear had flushed out his old thoughts and had prepared him for the new thoughts to come.

Tian knew that a part of his life was over and he welcomed it. He now wondered what life would be like without God. Would it be worth living? It had to include less heartbreak, and less of the disappointments that rattled Tian to his core.

Tian imagined his new life to be less of everything; less sharing, less trust. And after taking a quick account of all of the thoughts he had left, the only thing Tian found he had more of was his wonton desire to succeed.

The reason Tian suddenly had a stronger desire to succeed was a little hazy to him, but the end result was clear. While running through the park Tian had been struck by an overwhelming desire to be loved and nothing engendered love like success.

Once Tian circled the route back to the gate the adrenaline rush that sent him over the barrier was gone. Everything was a lot more uncomfortable now. Shame followed him over the gate as the clanking of the latch rang out through the neighborhood. And this time it hurt when Tian threw himself onto the ground. Tian dropped his head to hide his face as he walked back to his bike. And the sound of the bike starting up was like an assault to his senses.

Tian was glad to be away from the park but his legs felt on fire as the cooler night air hit it. Tian reached down to touch his thigh and almost tumbled his bike from the shock that he received from the touch. Tian was very hurt and he immediately started to think about how he would explain it to others. Or maybe he wouldn't explain it at all, he considered. 'Less is more,' Tian thought. I won't even bring it up. And if they notice I'll joke it away. 'I am now alone,' Tian thought, 'and there's nothing that I can do about it.'

CHAPTER 12

Reshand appeared behind Tian as he stood on the peninsula next to the waterfall.

"How did you get here?" Reshand asked with sternness in his voice.

"I followed you. Is this the place that you saw Jesus for the last time?" Tian replied.

"What do you mean you followed me? And why are you saying it so casually? People can't just do that here."

"When you left I thought that you were expecting me to follow you. I'm sorry, did I do something wrong?" Tian asked with an increasing deflation.

"People don't know how to do that here. That is what I was going to show you. But I guess you showed me. So either you have been here for much longer than you are telling me, or you came from outside of heaven."

Tian looked at Reshand and sadness crept across Tian's face. Tian turned to take in the majesty of the waterfall beside him. "Is this the place where you saw Jesus for the last time?"

Reshand getting his answer placed himself shoulder to shoulder with Tian and replied calmly. "Yes." Reshand pointed to the other side of the fall. "Jesus was walking ahead of the crowd over there. And the people went back all the way to there." Reshand said while pointing to a spot 400 feet back. "And then when he rose off the ground, he was there. And then when he disappeared, he was about there." Reshand finished with his finger pointing to a spot 200 feet in the air.

"The way you told the story you made it sound like the story in the bible when Jesus ascended up into heaven."

"That is what it looked like."

"Do you think that he left heaven?" Tian asked with a sober tone.

"I don't know. Jesus and I knew each other, but we wouldn't be close enough to be considered friends. But if I had to take a guess I would say that he had become disillusioned with heaven."

"Why would you say that?" Tian asked intensely captivated by Reshand's statement.

"Heaven is like a party full of wonderful, kind people. It is practically as big as the earth itself. But it isn't limitless. It isn't infinitely diverse. It is the best things about earth intensified for our enjoyment."

"That sounds pretty great," Tian responded with confusion on his face.

"Yes, but... 'And then what'?"

"What do you mean?"

"I said that heaven isn't limitless. It has its limits. So when you've walked through every beautiful valley and swam on every beautiful beach, what do you do then?" Reshand said while holding Tian's shoulder in his hand.

"I don't know."

"And how long do you think it would take to explore a world that is smaller than earth?"

"I'm sorry, I don't know."

"The answer is 1,215 years if you spend the first 100 years in the village that you arrived in."

"And you've been here for 1,500 years?" Tian asked with a sense of compassion entering his demeanor.

"I have been here for what I can tell is 1,535 earth years. Of course there aren't day and night cycles here, so the only way that I've been able to tell is by talking to people as they arrived in heaven."

"So you think that Jesus ran out of things to do here and then left heaven?"

"No. I think that Jesus started to see himself as the shepherd for a water theme park, until he finally wanted more and left."

"A shepherd for a water theme park?" Tian asked with confusion.

"I was told by someone that I had met recently that one of his favorite places on earth was something called a water theme park. And the person was asking if there were any water themed parks in heaven. The way he described it made it seem like lots of fun. But at the end of the day, it was just a place that stimulated your physical senses and nothing else.

Jesus spent his very short life sacrificing and preaching a type of moral behavior that would allow us to gain entrance into heaven once we died. Our earthly sacrifices, which were meant to create a heaven on earth, had to be rewarded. And after a hard, sacrificial life on earth, heaven is like a cool drink of water. But what happens when you are no longer thirsty? What happens when all of your sacrifices have been long forgotten and the pleasures of heaven are the only thing that you can remember? What do you do then?"

"And you think that this is what Jesus was feeling?" Tian asked.

"No. I believe he was feeling like it was up to him to offer the residence of heaven more. I believe that that is why heaven keeps expanding. Not only must heaven keep pace with what people view as heaven while on earth, but it has to offer something more engaging for the long time residents like me so that we don't leave."

Reshand looked Tian in the eyes without judgment. "You're from the outside aren't you?"

"Yes," Tian replied flatly.

"Do you know that you are the first person from the outside that I have met in all of my years of being here?"

"When did you know that I wasn't from here?" Tian asked sheepishly.

"From the moment I saw you. I hope that I'm not offending you, but you don't exactly look human."

With embarrassment Tian said, "But I am human. I was born in the Bahamas on earth." Tian remembered the experience he had in the library while experiencing the squid-like creature's life. "I know I look like some sort of squid creature. It was something that happened to me since I left earth."

"No, I wouldn't call it that. And again I'm not trying to offend you, but you kind of look like a tree."

"A tree?" Tian paused to think for a moment. "Why would I look like a tree?" Then it hit him. He remembered the experience he had when eating the peach. It was the same sort of immersive life re-experience as he had felt in the ocean. Only instead of it being a detailed reliving, it was simply the flavor of the tree's life.

Tian looked at Reshand embarrassed. Tian now understood that while he was doing his best to blend in at the mansion, everyone else saw him as the freak at the festival. 'How foolish I must have looked,' Tian thought to himself. But then he remembered how easily the people at the party accepted him. It was like they didn't even see his differences even though Tian was sure that they did. 'They do truly represent the best of the Christian spirit,' Tian concluded.

"I can see that you have become self-conscious. Perhaps I shouldn't have said anything."

"No, it's good that you told me. I was warned before I came here that this place could change me beyond the point of return. I thought that it would be in a good way, but now I understand what he meant."

"What is it like on the outside?" Reshand asked with humility.

"It isn't as good as here. I didn't see any joy until I arrived here. I didn't see any smiling faces. It was all very cold. It lacked all of the things that I've seen here. The feeling of the grass on my feet was a more enveloping experience than anything that I felt there. All it was was the accumulation of knowledge, and that can't compare to this."

Reshand looked back at the strip of rock that led to the point on which they stood. "What did you mean by 'beyond the point of return'?"

"I was told that I am going to have to make a choice on whether or not to go back to the life that I had."

"You should go back," Reshand offered without a moment of thought.

"Why do you say that?" Tian asked with a little anger in his voice.

"Because it is such a short ride. It's filled with twists and turns and climbs and falls and loops, but then it's over and all you have left is the memory. And you have those few, short memories that you suckle on for thousands of years to come."

"It has clearly been a long time since you have been alive. One of the mercies of aging is that bad memories fade and all that you are left with are the good times. I'm sure you don't remember the struggles and pains that you went through."

"But that's the point," Reshand added. "You don't remember the bad times once you've gotten here. And all life is is an opportunity to create great, fond memories that you can hold onto for the rest of your existence, however long that might be."

"So your argument is that life is precious. It's hardly new."

"But it hardly wrong," Reshand retorted.

Tian didn't say anything else to Reshand. Instead he chose to walk away. He walked over to the edge of the roaring river and followed the shore away from the fall. Reshand surprised at Tian's retreat caught up to him and walked silently with him for a moment.

"You know, you stand here in heaven very self righteously but you have forgotten what it's like," Tian added breaking the silence.

"I have," Reshand acknowledges humbly.

Tian turned to Reshand a little surprised at his acknowledgement. Tian continued. "And you've forgotten how tough it is to always make the type of decisions that you have to make to end up here. We weren't all raised in a box or in a small town with little ambition and good parents. Every moment that I lived wasn't bringing me closer to here, it was taking me further away. I was told that if I go back I won't remember any of this. So that means that it will return back to the way it was. You don't know how hard that was."

"You're right, I don't," Reshand acknowledged humbly.

"But you still think that I should go back?"

"Yes."

"Why?" Tian pushed.

"Because I know that there must me more to existence than this," Reshand said, with his eyes lowered and a heavy heart.

"More to existence than heaven?" Tian retorted, almost yelling. "There's got to be more to existence than being around good people in a beautiful place, with no expectations and no pressure?"

Reshand responded with a look and a twist of his face that said that as hard as it was to believe, it was true. Tian couldn't understand it. Tian didn't want to understand it. All Tian wanted to do was listen to the soft sounds the splashes of water made as it hit rocks on the shoreline. Tian wanted to stay in Christian heaven, even if it meant living the embarrassment of being a person that looked like a tree.

"Can I show you something?" Reshand asked after a while of walking in silence.

"Yeah I guess."

"Then… well, I guess you can just follow me," Reshand said with a gentle smile.

Tian feeling the lightness returning to their interaction manufactured a smile back. Reshand disappeared from in front of Tian and Tian followed him away.

In a moment everything around the two was different. The raging waterfall and mist filled valley were replaced by flat lands covered with multicolored wild lilies. The blue sky hung low in the distance and perfectly puffy white clouds offset the blue like in a landscape painted by one of the old masters.

Reshand stood akimbo surveying the land. Far off in front of the two of them were rolling hills that could barely be seen in the distance. About a mile behind them were a line of trees which stretched out for a great distance in either direction. Reshand turned toward the tree line and began walking. Tian quickly caught up and together they walked in silence.

Within moments the two spanned the distance and the trees were standing right in front of them. Tian scanned the tree line and noticed a worn path through the undergrowth.

"Over there?" Tian asked pointing at the path.

Without a word Reshand changed direction toward the path. As the trees passed by Tian heard the sounds of birds chirping. There was something welcoming about the birds that Tian couldn't quite comprehend. Tian liked being in these woods, but before he could really enjoy it, the trees opened up to a cabin that stood in front of a lake.

Tian looked past the modest one story log cabin at the incredibly still lake that lay behind it. The lake's calm was almost haunting. Like the woods, Tian assumed that within the lake had to be life, but there was hardly a sign of it anywhere on the surface. Tian wondered what it would be like to swim in the water. Were the lakes in Christian heaven salty or freshwater? Tian wondered if he would sink to the bottom or float to the top. And if there were fish in heaven what type would they be and how would they have gotten there?

"This is my cabin," Reshand said breaking the silence.

"It's very nice."

"I created it after someone I met described their childhood home to me. It really moved me and I wanted to recreate the picture that his story painted in my mind. Whenever I need to think, I come here."

"Did you forget where it was?" Tian asked with a smile.

"What do you mean?"

"Well, we arrived way out there and it didn't look like you were sure where it was."

Reshand smiled back. "No, I just like the walk. And I figured that you would appreciate it too."

"I was just kidding," Tian conceded with a little embarrassment and a laugh.

"Would you like to go inside?"

Tian nodded and both walked onto the little wooden path that led to the cabin. Tian once again imagined shoes on his feet. He remembered the effect that eating the fruit had had on him. He didn't want to have to find out what it would be like to touch the inside of a tree.

Tian began to wonder how Reshand had made the cabin. Did he have to cut down any trees to build it, or did he think it into existence? And if Reshand did have to cut down the trees, would he have been as willing to do it if Reshand could experience what life was like as a tree?

Reshand opened the cabin door to reveal a cozy sitting room arranged with chairs made of tree branches that had been twisted into furniture. The floor of the cabin was covered in a thick, lush, green grass and on the walls were framed photo realistic paintings of what looked like an ancient European town. In front of an empty fireplace was a hallowed out log filled with dirt and living grass.

And all but one of the chairs were placed in a crescent shape in front of an open window through which you could see the lake.

"So this is my little bit of heaven so to speak."

Tian chuckled at the play on words.

"I hope you like it."

Tian turned to the pictures on the wall. "Are these pictures from where you were from?"

"Yes." Reshand walked over to the pictures and began to describe each one in detail. Tian listened very intently as Reshand described what was in each picture and why. Reshand explained that he lived in Italy during the time of the last emperor of Rome. He described it as a hard time to live, but his position in the government made his life a little easier. However he also said that his position guaranteed that his life would have been amongst the first to be cut short when the Germanic invaders entered the city.

Reshand offered Tian a seat in front of the window. Tian sat down and was glad to learn that the chair didn't come with a flash of its memories. Reshand sat next to Tian and they both quietly stared out for a moment.

"Have you had a chance to go back to earth since you left?" Reshand asked breaking the silence.

"No. But why would I want to?" Tian replied trying to hide the hostility that he felt for being reminded of his time on earth.

"Perhaps there was someone that you left behind that you were curious about."

"Why do you ask?" Tian asked defensively.

"Because the one thing that is possible in heaven is the ability to visit your loved ones back on earth."

Tian thought for a moment before asking, "Can you send messages back to people on earth?"

"It is sometimes possible depending on whether or not the person is open to receiving the message. Is there a message that you want communicated?"

"No, I was just curious," Tian concluded thinking of his dead friends.

"So, is there someone that you would like to see?" Reshand again asked with the gentle tone of a confidant.

Tian flipped through his memories of the people he knew on earth. There weren't many people that he thought needed to hear from him again. But soon he remembered the one person that he thought might, his mother. Tian had emotionally withdrawn from his mother and family in his later years. The family had never been close but Tian always had a bond with his mother. They didn't talk all of the time on the phone, but Tian understood that he was once a living part of her. He knew that there would be nothing he could do to dampen the feeling of loss that came with the death of her baby, but maybe a visit now could console her. Maybe knowing that Tian was still alive in another form would allow her some sort of relief from her grief. This wasn't something that Tian wanted to do, but he saw this as a necessary act of compassion. And the more Tian thought about it, the more Tian wanted to give his mother that reprieve from sorrow.

"There is someone that I would like to see," Tian confessed.

"Who?"

"I would like to see my mother. I'm thinking that a visit from me… Well, I just think that she may need it, that's all."

"Would you like me to show you how to see her?" Reshand offered humbly.

"That would be nice. Thank you," Tian added with vulnerability that he didn't often express.

"Well, it should be very easy for you because you can already jump. It's the same process really. All you have to do is think about her and you'll see her."

Tian took a long look at the lake before deciding to do it. But once he decided he immediately closed his eyes and thought of her. In another time Tian's mother would have been an artist. She would have been a creative type like the person Tian turned out to be. Hers would have been a wondering soul, but instead she lived vicariously through her youngest son.

As it ended up Tian's mother's sharp features and always athletic build made her a modern day concubine. She was the beautiful wife that made Tian's father the envy of all of his friends. It was a coup that Tian's father had landed her and in exchange for being a wife and a mother she expected to be provided a certain level of comfort. And although she kept her part of their unspoken agreement by remaining beautiful, he broke their agreement by losing everything that the family had gained.

And when the better part of her nature was wakened in order to rescue everything her family had, Tian's father rejected her ideas, preferring to watch everything be taken away than to lose his status as the head of the household. Tian's mother resented his father for this. It was more than just betrayal of their agreement; it was the rejection of her as an equal when in her mind she was in some ways his superior.

She could always think her way out of a problem better than her husband could. And she was always more willing to make the tough practically decisions. If she could have designed her life in a time more favorable toward women, she would have been a graphic artist who ran her own firm. She would have been something that allowed her to create for a practical purpose.

But born in the time that she was, she spent her peak years washing laundry during the week and on weekends playing tennis with the country's top entrepreneurs and visiting celebrities. But whoever she played with always noticed her phenomenal body gliding across the courts, and they were all drawn to her.

However, those times were a long time ago and when Tian closed his eyes, what he saw was an older woman bent over a flower bed weeding her garden. The years under the sun had taken a toll on her skin, which was only rescued by its still milk chocolate complexion. And her once toned bikini body had begun to loosen and fill out into the grandmother that she now was.

Tian hadn't visited his mother's house in years. His mother had always had a green thumb and her magic only increased as she had more time to use it. She twisted the vine of yellow flowers that grew next to the porch up the roman columns that supported the canopy. And on this day all of the flowers were in full bloom. When Tian had lived there more than 10 years earlier one side of the columns bloomed significantly more than the other. But sometime in the interim she must have figured out the magic formula because now both sides looked like a picturesque mixture of yellow and green.

The thorny bougainvillea that encapsulated the chain link fence in the front yard reached out four feet into the sidewalk. This was the way that Tian's mother liked it. She made it a ritual to cut the bush very low at the beginning of the spring so that she could watch the explosion of flowers that occurred during the summer and fall.

But the part of the garden that Tian's mother was most proud was the half moon area between the fence and crescent shaped driveway. Here is where she would plant all of her favorite flowers. And it was here that Tian found her when he looked out at her from Reshand's cabin.

Tian worked his view of her around until he could look into her eyes. Her vision was focused very intently at the area between the periwinkles that she forced into being a blooming hedge and her rose bushes. Although he wouldn't admit it, Tian was a little disappointed when he couldn't find any grief in her eyes. Tian didn't want her to feel pain, but it surprised him that he wasn't even missed.

"Mum," Tian said hoping to capture his mother's focus.

Tian's mother looked up to wipe her brow with the back of her glove.

"Mum, I want you to know that I'm in heaven."

Tian's mom turned back to the part of the garden that she had already completed and then decided to get up to get a glass of water. She rocked herself back over the periwinkle hedge that was being slightly crushed under the arches of her ankle. Standing she did a little stretch of her legs and then stamped her shoes on the concrete before stepping onto the smoke beige tiles of the porch.

As Tian watched her walk away, he wondered what he had wanted to find when he saw his mother. There wouldn't have been a level of grieving that would have allowed Tian comfort. This total disregard for his death was without a doubt what was best for her; and a complete collapse under the horror of losing a son would have devastated him to see. So Tian considered this a fitting end to his life. Tian considered his death to be properly memorialized by it being unnoticed and ineffectual to even his own mother.

Tian opened his eyes to find him back in Reshand's lake cabin. He again thought about his dead friends. The experience he just had didn't resemble what was once a familiar feeling with them.

"What did you see?" Reshand asked.

"I saw my mother."

"Was she ok?"

"She was gardening. Tell me Reshand, is this the only way to contact people who are still alive?"

"Why do you ask?" Reshand asked with a curious look on his face.

"Umm…" Tian wasn't quite sure how to respond. Should he go into all of the things that he had experienced during his life and therefore after his death? As wonderful as heaven was, there seemed to be a gap between what its residence knew and the knowledge that existed in this world. "It just seems different than what I experienced while I was on earth."

"Are you talking about angels?" Reshand asked without missing a moment.

"Well, it's more like guardian angels."

"Yes, I imagine that that is a different experience. Did I tell you that there are those that leave heaven?"

"You've made reference to it," Tian confirmed.

"I think that's what they leave here to become."

"Is it some sort of promotion?" Tian asked.

"No, I think they leave out of boredom."

Tian looked at Reshand searching his face for insincerity or humor and found none. "I don't understand."

"I wasn't the most driven person when I was alive. My parents even called me lazy. My father had great ambition. He was a merchant that sold goods from the African countries. And his shop was very popular because he didn't just sell the goods that the traders offered, he traveled to Africa twice a year and collected the rarest and most beautiful goods and offered it in his shop. His was the favorite of the emperor and all the members of court.

But I grew up watching that and all of the troubles that my father had because of it and knew that I didn't want it. And because his older sons were ready to take over the business, he allowed me to enjoy life. In fact, it was him that used his influence to secure me a position with one of the senators. He used to say that if I were going to be lazy, then I should have a good seat with all of the other lazy people. And he was right because I was good at being a senator.

Christianity was popular amongst the senators though they wore it more as a piece of jewelry than a calling. But I saw Christianity as more. There was a simplicity that it called for that I was comfortable with. There was a letting go of the material world that was required that I never craved to begin with. And from the example that the senators provided me, Christianity didn't require much of you in return except a weekly donation to the church.

So when I left my life and came here I was already accustomed to the slower pace. In fact, it felt at home to me. This heavenly existence was exactly what I wanted my life to be like and I was ecstatic when this was what I found.

But other people didn't take to it as well. My sister from my father's first wife found Christianity later in life. It was after her first husband died. At that point she, in fact we all, thought she was too old to marry again so she found the church out of desire for community. And since her deceased husband wasn't wealthy the only thing she could offer the church was her service.

Once she began with the church, she slaved for those priests. She would get down on her knees and scrub the marble floors and then beat the draperies and dust the picture frames. And it wasn't until her body started to break down on her that they had her join the devoted that would reach out to the poor.

She took very quickly to working with the poor. She was always a very motherly type and she saw the poor as needing someone to look after them. It was an unfortunate time when she realized that she was barren. But she took care of her late husband well, and she treated the poor like her own children.

She met her second husband doing service. He was one of the devoted and they continued to serve even after they were married. He wasn't wealthy, but he prepared for his old age and he had sons that gave him whatever he needed.

I say all of that to say that when my sister came here the leisurely lifestyle didn't come as easily to her. She and I weren't very close on earth, but we bonded here and spent a lot of time together. After about 200 years she was beginning to feel lost. Service had become a part of her soul and heaven stopped satisfying her. One day I came to visit her and she had regained her spirit. She was telling me that she had found a way to get back to service and that she would be leaving heaven to do it.

I responded pretty similarly to the way you did when I suggested to you that this wasn't the end all and be all of existence. I couldn't understand why my sister would want to go out and live amongst the sinners when she had spent her whole life in an attempt to get here. But she had made up her mind. She wanted to go out and be an angel. And as much as I loved being with her, I didn't want anything else but to be here."

"Did she come back?" Tian asked curious about his own situation.

"She never came back."

"You know I think she could have if she wanted to. There's no gate on heaven. I was able to enter without even a question."

"I thought you had," Reshand stated without an explanation of why.

"Why do you think it is that she didn't come back?" Tian asked.

"I don't know. But everyone that I know that has left, left to redevote themselves to service and none of them have ever come back."

"Have you ever thought about becoming a guardian angel?"

"Me? No," Reshand responded reflectively. "Service wasn't a part of who I was when I was alive. What I have found is that we don't change that much once we die. Who we were in life is who enters heaven. I was lazy in life and I am lazy in heaven. But I had earned my right to be here and being here gives you the right to stay. However, if you ask me if I have ever thought about leaving heaven then the answer is yes."

"When did you consider leaving heaven," Tian asked hesitantly.

"I have thought about leaving ever since I ran out of new places in heaven to explore. And I made the final decision to leave the moment I saw you."

"Me?" Tian asked experiencing a feeling of dread that he hadn't felt since his life.

"When I saw you I realized that you could lead me out of heaven."

"I can't do that," Tian said feeling a warmth building in his face. "I feel very uncomfortable with that."

"Why would you? You've been out there. And I could tell by the way you describe it, it's not that bad."

"I'm sorry I don't feel comfortable with that. I didn't come here to lead people out of heaven. That's not the type of person that I am. You should talk to somebody about your unhappiness. Maybe someone can help you."

"I'm not unhappy. I just know that my time here is complete. I have explored all I need to explore and I would now like to move on."

"Did you know that there's death out there. Out there souls whither and they die. Here it could be life everlasting. Look at me. I ate a piece of fruit and now I look like a tree. With everything I do I keep losing myself. Yet 1500 years and you are still whole and capable of all of the greatest feelings of your life."

"And it's just that. I'm limited to my life; my one life, with no change. When we were alive we were capable of becoming anything. We grew and learned and faced adversity. And if we survived we learned and changed and grew some more. But here, you live with what you came with. After all of this time here in heaven, I now believe that our nature, our soul's nature is to change."

"We aren't souls," Tian added with resignation.

"What?"

"I was told right before I came here that we aren't souls."

"Then what are we?" Reshand asked confused.

"I don't know," Tian replied with what felt like the world on his shoulders.

"Then wouldn't you like to find out?"

"Yes, I would." Tian turned to Reshand with new found energy. "There is something that I was told when I first arrived in heaven. It is kind of a secret really. I'm not sure who knows or who's supposed to know. But the guy I met overheard it from another person when they didn't know he was listening.

Reshand, I think that God is going to be visiting heaven. That's why I have to stay here. Maybe when he comes you can ask him that question. I lived my entire life trying to understand God, believing in God, not believing in God. And here he is, or at least, this is where he's coming and I have to be here. I have to see him. I need to know that he is real. I need this. I have to have this if I'm going to go on. And I would think that after all the time you've spent here, you would want to be here too."

A look of compassion melted across Reshand's face. Reshand stood up and Tian followed. Reshand reached his hand across to Tian's shoulder and squeezed it. With eyes full of sadness Reshand said, "Tian, that is the same rumor that I heard when I first arrived here as well. It is the rumor that everyone hears. I was the one that told my sister and I know that my sister told others.

It is the longest running rumor that exists here. And yet in all of my 1,500 years, with all of the people that I've met and all of the places that I've gone, God has never come here. No one ever confronts this rumor or addresses it. But everyone that I've spoken to that has left this place ultimately settles on the understanding that God has never visited heaven and he never will."

Tian stared back at Reshand stunned. All of the things that Tian was taught about heaven flew directly into the face of what Reshand was now saying. "But wait, when you told your story about meeting Jesus, you said that Jesus was talking about God. And almost every page of the bible talks about heaven and God. I am now standing in heaven…"

"I can't account for the bible. The texts were barely compiled before my death, so I can only refer to what Jesus told me. And what he referred to when we spoke was the existence of a heavenly father."

"Sure," Tian replied back, "God, the heavenly father."

"But what he said was 'the heavenly father.'"

"So?"

"Think about the words. This is heaven, and it had a creator. It had a father. But that doesn't mean that it was God."

"Are you saying that something bad made heaven?"

"No, I'm just saying that the words 'heavenly father' don't have to mean a 'one supreme god.' All of this is still 'good news,' it just might not be the 'good news' that we assumed."

Tian took a moment to gather his thoughts while he stared blankly at Reshand. "So you're saying that God isn't going to come to heaven. And if he is then it probably won't be anytime soon?"

"That's what I believe," Reshand replied with as much compassion as he could engender.

"Ok, then I have to excuse myself. Thank you for your hospitality."

Before Reshand could reply, Tian had disappeared. Thinking that Tian had left heaven Reshand followed. When Reshand opened his eyes again he found himself back on the grounds of the mansion where he found Tian. Reshand looked ahead and saw Tian charging back towards the patio where they had met. Reshand quickly caught up to Tian who calmly proceeded.

"Why did you come back here?" Reshand asked.

"I made a promise to someone that I have to keep."

"What promise did you make?" Reshand asked hesitantly.

"I promised the young man that introduced me to you that if I found out about when God was coming, I would let him know."

"I don't think you should do that," Reshand offered calmly.

Tian stopped his progression before turning to Reshand and asking, "Why not?"

"In the beginning there was the word."

Tian stopped and turned to Reshand.

"Do you recognize that?" Reshand asked.

"Sure it's the first words of the bible; Genesis 1:1. I thought you said that you never read the bible."

"I had never seen one when I was alive. But I have been made aware of all the stories since I've come here. And are you familiar with the story of Adam and Eve?"

"Of course," Tian threw off casually.

"Well, Adam and Eve lived in heaven for a long time and they had domain over everything. The one thing that they weren't allowed to do was eat the fruit from the tree of knowledge."

"I'm familiar," Tian replied.

"But then a serpent came down from the tree and tempted Eve who bit into the fruit."

"Yes, I'm familiar," Tian responded slightly annoyed.

"The one thing that could cause Adam and Eve to leave Eden was if they eat from the tree of knowledge."

"Yes."

"Consider where we are. Wouldn't this be as close to what you could imagine Eden to be? Those that live here are not hungry and want for nothing. But knowledge, what would happen if unnecessary knowledge were introduced to this Eden. What if people knew that heaven wasn't all there was? What if they knew the truth about God? That might be something that you want them to know, but could they enjoy their time here if they knew."

"Wait," Tian rebuked. "If heaven is Eden, and what you told me about God is the fruit of knowledge, then am I Satan in this analogy?"

Tian looked at Reshand who did not reply.

"I'm Satan? I just want to fulfill a promise I made to someone who helped me and I'm Satan?"

Reshand still didn't reply.

"But I gave you knowledge too, and now you want me to take you out of heaven. If I took you out, wouldn't I be Satan for you to?"

"The difference is that I want to go. In fact I'm willing to beg you to go if it's necessary."

"So it's ok for me to corrupt you with my knowledge, but it's not ok for me to corrupt him?"

"Tian I've been here for 1,500 years. Do you know how long that is? I would have left long ago if I knew where to go. I don't want to be a guardian angel. I just want to know more about who I am.

And yes, I understand that I might learn something that prevents me from coming back here. And I understand that leaving here might cause me to die. But meeting you has told me that there is more to existence than the confines of heaven and I need to know what that is. The young man that you're trying to find hasn't learned that yet, and I think that he should be allowed to enjoy heaven as long as he can."

"Then why don't you just leave? Why do you need me to do it?"

"Because the way that I've learned to travel requires a destination before I start. And for the life of me I can't even imagine what life out there could be like. So if I can't imagine it, I can't leave. It's just like without me, you would never have found the waterfall or my cabin. It's not that you couldn't find it if you knew about it. But if you didn't know the place existed, how could you picture it in your mind?"

"Oh Reshand, you don't understand. I've tried so hard in my life to do what's good. I've tried so hard. I have sacrificed so much. Now here I am in heaven. And standing in the Garden of Eden you are asking me to be the serpent that leads you out of heaven. Reshand, I've tried so hard to be a part of what is good with the world. And after risking my life to get to heaven you can only see me as your Satan?" Looking at Reshand Tian's heart broke with the same intensity it had once broken over a girl that preferred the company of his best friend.

"Well, you don't have to do anything. I'm not asking you to carry me out of here. All you have to do is leave. And when you do, I will follow you."

Tian looked around the grounds for his young friend. At the edge of the grove he spotted his friendly face. The young man was carrying a bushel full of peaches from the grove to the mansion. There was such great innocence in the way the young man moved. It was gangly and awkward, but in the face of everything that Tian had seen in his life, the young man was beautiful. Watching the young man Tian knew that Reshand was right. The young man deserved to keep his innocence.

Tian looked past the young man and surveyed all of the land. It too was beautiful. In every way it looked perfect. And when he remembered he imagined his feet bare so that he could feel the wonderful feeling of grass pressing against them.

And while he was getting his last tastes of heaven he thought back to Irabell's final pleas. Yes, Irabell was trying to protect him from heaven. But Irabell was also trying to protect the people of heaven from him.

Tian turned back to look at Reshand. He knew that there was nothing he could do to lose Reshand. All Reshand ever had to do was think of Tian and Reshand would appear where ever Tian was.

And since Tian couldn't stay in heaven he accepted that he was going to lead Reshand out of it. This saddened him, but he accepted that it was his fault for visiting heaven in the first place.

Tian closed his eyes and thought of what the first place Reshand should see after 1,500 years in heaven. And when Tian decided he opened his eyes again and took one last look around. After that moment Tian disappeared and Reshand followed.

When Reshand opened his eyes he was confronted with hills that didn't reflect color as much as it did feelings. And between the hills swirling with energies was an ocean of lights.

"This was described to me as the Ocean of Knowledge. Almost every person that ever lived has every moment of their life saved here. And it doesn't just have human lives, it has the lives of alien species that you can't even imagine."

Reshand quickly turned to Tian shocked at the idea that there could be species past what he had seen on earth.

"If you wanted to know what else is out there, then this is where you want to be. I'm sure that you will find all of the answers you want within."

Without a word, Reshand turned toward the ocean and walked towards it. Tian watched with regret as Reshand walked away. Tian knew that he had robbed heaven of one of their beacons while at the same time not necessarily changing Reshand's life for the better. So with nowhere else to go and nothing else to do, Tian closed his eyes and thought of Irabell. He now knew that more than anything else, he needed the answer to one question, 'where is God?' And He knew that only Irabell could give him the answer. So within a moment Tian was gone.

Chapter 13

The moonlight barely broke through the surface of the choppy Pacific Ocean waves. Tian shone his light around him as sleek grey bodies swam past him. Tian's snorkel dipped underneath the surface of the waves causing him to have to spit out water that entered with his attempts at breath.

Tian's light caught something unexpected in its beam. Tian swung back to get a better look but it had moved. Tian used his fins to spin himself around looking for where it could have swum off to. With his underwater light he spotted what looked like a baby bottle nosed dolphin nursing off of its mother.

Tian remained very still trying not to startle them. He shone his light on them but found it hard to really see what was going on. So very slowly Tian adjusted himself closer and closer to the pair until it all came into focus. It was indeed a baby dolphin, and it was smaller than Tian ever imagined one would be. 'It must be a new born,' Tian thought. And sooner than Tian could imagine anything else, what looked like a grey dart shot over the mother dolphin and with the force of an oncoming car, hit Tian in the stomach under his rib cage.

In shock Tian immediately let go of his light which floated down into the darkness of the ocean. After a stunned moment Tian began to swim back to his boat. And when he felt another blow like a spear into side he knew he was in a lot of danger.

At once Tian grabbed hold of his side and pushed his head above the surface of the water. His rowboat, lacking an anchor, had floated to the full length of the rope that he had attached to his waist. Struggling Tian attempted to swim toward the rowboat, but as the dolphin attacked again from below, he had to think again.

Tian's mind began to float. Thoughts were becoming harder and harder to keep straight. Tian knew that he should pull on the rope attached to him. He had a vague recollection that it would bring safety, but once he began pulling on it he realized more importantly that it was keeping him afloat.

Tian felt only one more hit as the rowboat got closer. This one was to his left side. The dolphin had somehow figured out the softest part of Tian's body to attack and was working him like a boxer.

When the rowboat finally arrived Tian he let go the rope and dog paddled towards it. Tian felt like he needed to vomit, but he choked the feeling back. He then reached up onto the side of the boat and used all of his strength to pull himself into the wooden dingy.

On the way in, all of his front flesh scraped across the edge. And as his back landed on the arms of the oar, the paddle end flipped up into the air trapping one of his legs between it and the hull. Tian made an unsuccessful attempt to sit up and got a shot of pain that took him by surprise. Tian immediately tried to relax every muscle in his body hoping that the pain would subside enough for his sight to return.

As Tian lay still at the bottom of the rowboat, the throbbing bouts of stabbing pain diminished to something closer to agony. The agony was manageable though and clarity of thought returned to him. Tian removed the mask and snorkel from his face.

'What did I do?' Tian thought.

The cold night breeze blew over his wet, naked body and an electric chill shot through his extremities. Tian took an assessment of his body parts to make sure that they were all still there. The droplets of water on him prevented him from telling if there was any blood, but Tian figured that if the dolphin had punctured a hole in him, he would already be unconscious. Instead, what the animal had done was pulverize his insides. Tian imagined that this was what internal bleeding felt like.

He returned his gaze to the amazingly bright moon whose light shimmered off of the speckles of grey on his temples and droplets of water on his toned athletic body. Tian knew that he couldn't sit up much less row his way back to shore, so all that was left was for him to do was lay there and try to remain conscious. But in the event that he couldn't, he moved the mask over his genitals to allow himself a little dignity when the unsuspecting weekend yachter found his boat.

How surreal it seemed to Tian that his life could end as a tragic joke on the evening news.

'A man was found naked and dead in a rowboat off the coast of Malibu, California today, having died of what experts think was an attack by dolphins. Here's Alley Sanchez on what could be a new deadly craze. Alley?'

Tian saw the humor in it all and would have laughed if it wasn't for the pain that it brought. Even so, Tian couldn't help it when a chuckle slipped out.

"Ahhh," Tian reacted in pain.

As Tian began to lose the feelings in his hands and feet, be became amazed at how much colder it now felt. The warm night and his adrenaline had been enough when he stripped at the beach and pushed his boat into the water. Even the cold Pacific water didn't seem to bother him. But now with the adrenaline rush stopped, rational thinking returned to him and all of this was a little too crazy for words.

Tian knew that there was no way for this situation to end well, so with the time he had left, he considered if there was a way that he could have prevented it. And as he thought back over his life he couldn't find an alternative path. Each risk that he had taken was necessary to quiet the beast. And if he didn't make greater and greater sacrifices in order to quiet the beast, it would have been the beast that would have eaten him alive.

Tian thought back nine years to what had to be considered the beginning of his new life. It was August when Tian accepted a temporary job as a data entry person for one of the many production companies in Los Angeles. It was a small company where all of the divisions interacted and often went out to lunch together. Although Tian was just a temp, he was always invited along because to leave him would have been too obvious of a slight for the other workers to allow.

It was during those lunches that Tian met the director of production for the company. Susie was an upbeat, laughing and giggling Filipino woman that took to Tian immediately. So when her assistant went on maternity leave and Tian's assignment came to an end, she transferred him over to her employ. "Are you ready for some real work?" she asked with a chuckle. And then later when she told Tian that they were moving their productions in-house, it didn't seem that unusual for Tian to request the open producer position.

The director knew of Tian's experience on movie sets but she was a firm believer that producing was a closed brotherhood. And she believed that not only hadn't Tian worked his way up like she had, he was also too young to be considered for membership. But she liked Tian and Tian always worked hard so she couldn't do anything else but to give him a chance to prove himself.

"I want you to write two behind-the-scenes making-of-the-movie scripts. Come up with graphic ideas for each and then present it to me in three days." Behind-the-scenes interstitials were what the company specialized in. It was her intension to listen to them on her own and then compliment Tian while politely correcting his mistakes. But her plan changed when the vice president of the company mentioned his desire to watch as well.

Tian had never really met Jim the VP and was startled a bit when he showed up to the meeting. The presentation started with Jim uttering the words "What ya got?" And Tian was on his way. Tian had practiced each word and had gone over the reveal of each graphic image. He had come up with two variations on each script with graphics supplied by the company's graphics department. That wasn't a part of Susie's plan but when the graphics department offered whatever they could do to help, Tian accepted.

"Those were the four scripts. I chose to do these specifically because one is romance, one drama, one comedy and one adventure. I hope that you will see my range and also a spot that we can focus on and refine. Thank you," Tian concluded.

After the presentation ended there was a pause. Tian was happy with what he had said and how he said it, and he wasn't about to show a wavering of confidence by speaking first. In Tian's silence the moment grew longer. Mercifully Susie began to speak up but from her tone and choice of works, Tian knew what she was going to say. She was going to express how some of it was very nice but then explain why it didn't really work.

"Tian, that was very nice but..."

"Teach him how to edit," Jim interjected with the five words that reshaped the rest of Tian's life.

Susie immediately stopped and turned with a surprised look at Jim who stared austerely forward. And after a much shorter pause Tian heard

"Ok Tian, I'll show you the next step."

It took a total of six months from first stepping into the doors as a data entry temp before Tian was offered a full time producer position with the company. And it was another year and a half after that when Tian was hired by a television conglomerate to produce behind-the-scenes for them. By this point acting had become a faded memory for Tian. Producers were the ones that created the details of pop culture. The actors were just the ones that presented it to the public. Tian quickly learned to love his new producer status more than he ever had acting; and more important than that was that he was very good at it.

But in spite of how much he loved it and how much praise he got for it, there was always an emptiness that he fought against. Tian put in more hours at the office and more days on the set so he didn't have to go home and think. Work was his solace. It was the one thing that he knew was real.

He spent the day solving problems about how to write a script to highlight an actor. He solved problems on how to fit all of the material into a two minute piece. And then he solved the problem of how much and what type of sound and music to add in. His work consisted of problems that he could solve all day long. And what's more, he did it, he was respected for it, and then there was more work to do tomorrow.

Unfortunately there was a small unexpected problem that changed all of that. It was a joke that Tian's boss made about one of Tian's behind-the-scenes footage scripts for a romantic comedy. Tian had painted the script with a Hollywood brush. Tian made the romance between the two main characters seem like an endless celebration. His boss who had been married for the lesser part of 15 years had had what could have been the 1000th fight with his wife that morning over raising the kids and her spending. And because of it he was in a particularly cynical mood. So when his boss said, "The way you wrote that Tian makes you seem like you have never been in a real relationship," Tian flinched.

His boss was hoping that Tian would do more than just chuckle which Tian did do. Ron, Tian's boss, was hoping that Tian would pick up on his over the top cynicism and give him an entryway for him to introduce the problems he was having with his wife.

Ron was like Tian in the way that his work was his refuge. Ron didn't really have any friends outside of work, and with his promotion his previous contemporaries chose to spend their time with others still on their level. Ron liked Tian. Tian was driven like himself. Tian was smart. And even though Tian was at least 10 years younger than him, he imagined that they could be friends.

With his cynical comment Ron felt like he had put himself out there and Tian's refusal to accept the invitation didn't leave much room for Ron's introduction into a friendship. Afterwards Ron decided to scrap his befriending plan for a while. 'Nothing's worse than wanting to be friends with someone that doesn't want to be friends with you,' Ron would think that night as he reviewed his day.

But Tian's reaction to Ron's comment was different than Ron had intended. Yes Tian laughed at Ron's cynical comment. Tian knew that that was what he was supposed to do. But the actual words sat in Tian's consciousness like a virus waiting to multiply.

'Perhaps my writing did say something about me that I didn't intend,' Tian thought. 'I haven't been in a relationship in my life. Why is that?' Tian allowed his mind to drift for a moment while he searched for the correct memory. 'It is because relationships distract you from what you are supposed to do with your life.' Tian thought about it for a while longer and then corrected himself. 'Relationships distract me from what I'm supposed to do with my life.'

Those two thoughts gestated for hours until a third more dangerous thought developed. 'What's that 'more important thing' that I was supposed to do with my life?'

All of Tian's work at the production company had been a godsend. The work was his cave to climb into and hide. Unfortunately now that he was forced to once again look out, the landscape hadn't improved. In fact, it had gotten worse. All of the fields left unsown were now overgrown and weeded.

Work became very hard for Tian after that. Scripts became harder to write and decisions like where to put the stinger at the end of the music bed became near impossible.

It was the details that Tian had the hardest times with. It was the subtlety that left him first. All of his work continued to get approved, but the time that it took Tian to do the work doubled. And since his production budgets were tracked in minutes Tian knew that he had a problem.

It was very early one morning after a long sleepless night that Tian's chest felt tight and his breathing became labored. A slight feeling of suffocation came over Tian and at that moment Tian knew that he needed to escape. It was an hour later that his bags were packed and the road atlas lay open on his dining room table.

Tian figured that there was nothing at work that couldn't be handed off and his message to Ron stated that fact. He wanted the message to sound a little desperate because that was the only excuse that would excuse such an abrupt departure. Tian was proud of the tone that he was able to strike in the message. "All those years of acting paid off," Tian mumbled to himself walking out the door.

For the first time in the three years he had lived in Los Angeles, Tian left the county for parts unknown. In a few hours parts unknown became known as San Francisco. But his hotel room's bed didn't allow him to breathe any easier. What did loosen his chest a little was when he noticed the brochures that sat in the hotel lobby.

The brochures covered the full gambit of vacation activities. But the one that caught Tian's eye was the most dangerous of the bunch. Tian often wondered what it would be like to jump out of a plane and now he realized that he had the chance to find out.

Two days later after he had climbed into his jumpsuit he turned to the two women suiting up next to him and asked, "are you excited?" The two women that were in their mid thirties turned to Tian, surprised that he said anything to them. They had been whispering to themselves earlier about the dark loner that was also in their class. They had even made up backstories for the tall, brooding, good-looking man. And only one of them included the premise that Tian had killed a man just to watch him die.

"I've already had to pee twice," one of the ladies stated.

"Linda!" the other protested.

"It's true," Linda said with a smile.

"You know, I don't feel excited at all," Tian added. "I don't feel nervous, or anything. I feel like I'm just having a normal day."

"Wow. Well, I'm excited," Linda added.

When Tian turned away both women looked at each other barely containing their laughter. Later they would both confirm what the other was thinking, 'the tall, good-looking, brooding man had killed someone just to watch them die. Or so he could feel something again after the tragic loss of his wife whom he mourned every day,' they added to give the stranger a lovable soul.

"Hey would you ladies mind if I jump out of the plane first?" Tian asked remembering the shark dive.

"No go right ahead. That way if you die, we don't have to go," Linda said with a nervous laugh.

Tian smiled back and then walked over to the other group of jumpers asking them the same thing. It worried Tian that not even this could get his adrenaline flowing. And as Tian slowly walked toward the plane he began to think that he had wasted his money. But when the door of the plane was dragged open at 10,000 feet his heart began to beat harder and he liked it.

"I'm about to throw myself out of a perfectly good plane," Tian joked to the instructor strapped onto Tian's back.

"Ok, are you ready?" the instructor yelled into Tian's ear. Tian nodded his head to confirm. "Ok, go ahead and work your way over to the doorway."

Tian's heart began to race. It felt good. He felt alive again.

In sync both men held onto the top of the small plane and walked on their knees to the edge. Tian suddenly lost his understanding of what was going on.

"Ok, on the count of three throw yourself forward."

'What did he just say?' Tian thought. 'What am I supposed to do? Am I going to throw myself out of a plane?'

The instructor yelled into Tian's ear, "One, Two, Three." And before Tian could remember what he was supposed to do at three, Tian felt a push, and then a rush that was exhilarating. In the corner of Tian's eye he saw the wing of the plane fly past him and every moment was heightened.

He had always wondered what it would feel like to fall from a great distance and when it was real, when the wind blowing against him was real, the rush that he was feeling stopped. In that moment Tian realized that the falling didn't feel like anything. It felt like standing in front of a large fan.

In fact it didn't even feel like they were falling at all. It just looked like the checker board corn fields below were getting incrementally closer. When the instructor grabbed Tian's wrist and pointed at his altimeter it surprised Tian that he had forgotten to pull the parachute. Tian imagined that that would have been something that an engaged person wouldn't have forgotten to do.

Tian didn't want to pull the cord, though. He knew that he would miss the falling. Tian considered the falling the dangerous part and he knew that it was going to be the most memorable.

Tian wasn't expecting it when the instructor grabbed Tian's hand and put it on the ripcord.

'Ah yes, the parachute,' Tian thought. 'I have to pull the chute.'

When Tian pulled the cord the deceleration wasn't abrupt at all. He had imagined it like being hit by a moving car. But it was gentle. It was even comforting. It felt like he was being introduced to limits, something Tian had lost his appreciation for.

The slow descent was very peaceful. Tian had forgotten that there were places in the world that were this quiet. Places where the roar of tires against road or the sound of air conditioners couldn't be heard. Places where the hums of computers or the chirping of birds couldn't be detected.

On that slow decent Tian could only hear his own breathing and the light sound of air passing through the parachute above. The silence lasted for minutes until the instructor told Tian to brace himself and to not be afraid to fall down. Tian landed on his feet and the instructor pulled the chute until it clasped onto the ground in front of him. The instructor detached the two and Tian walked back to the hanger to disrobe.

Through the zipper on the side Tian reached for his cell phone but found himself staring down at it not having anyone to call. Instead, Tian returned his jumpsuit and waited for the rest of his class at the jump center. As they all stood waiting for their pictures and video tapes, Tian told them how he had needed to get away. He shared with them how he had just started his trip, and needed somewhere else to go.

"You should go skiing at Lake Tahoe," Linda's friend suggested.

"I've heard of that," Tian added, allowing the idea to wash against the possible reasons not to.

"Yeah, I go there every year and it's beautiful. It would be a great stop on your adventure vacation."

"You're right. Thanks." Tian turned around and walked to his car. He pulled out his atlas and mapped his way there. A moment later he was off.

The next day as Tian stood at the top of the bunny slopes covered from head to toe in layers of clothes Tian didn't feel any different. Never having skied before Tian followed the lead of his instructor. It didn't start off well, but eventually with enough leaning and falling, Tian figured out enough of the technique to graduate to the blue squares.

As the trees whipped by him, he realized that it wasn't the skiing he was after, it was the feeling that came from the adventure. There was something therapeutic that happened when the excitement pierced the rubber coating that had replaced his skin. On a daily basis his skin tingled and popped and there was no remedy for it. But when that shot of adrenaline came with life threatening danger, the feeling subsided.

After the blue squares became routine Tian moved to the black diamonds. Staring down at the sloping hill seemed impossible and highly dangerous, but not scary. Tian hit the slope using his day old skills and was surprised to see just how much speed you could pick up if you didn't zig zag back and forth. But still by the end, the slopes were skied and no relief followed.

"Vegas!" he spouted. "I've got to go to Vegas," so early the next morning he left for Vegas.

A few nights later while Tian lay on his Las Vegas hotel bed all was silent. Tian hadn't spent much on the slots and only $20 at the blackjack tables. At the age of 14 he had found himself stalking the slots at the cruise ship casino during a family vacation and immediately realized that he could potentially have a problem. After that he had barred himself from gambling thinking that there could be many better ways of spending his money.

So now with the cap lifted and permission to do what damage may come, Tian didn't desire it. The thought of spending hours at a table with cards and chips didn't interest him. What he wanted instead was another type of rush. Tian desired one where the stakes were higher. He wanted one that reinforced the continuation of his life.

"Why am I even alive?" Tian whispered in the darkness. "Why don't I ever die?"

The words reverberated in Tian's mind. He had never heard them out loud before. They weren't scary to him. In fact, it secretly offered Tian some solace.

Tian stared up at the smooth plaster of the ceiling and wondered how he had ended up there. Tian thought of Los Angeles, and then he thought of home. He thought of his mother and what she must have been doing at that time, and then he thought about his grandmother.

When Tian stood by his grandmother's bedside before leaving for Dallas it did turn out to be the last time that he saw her. She had died less than a year before this adventure vacation and it was that event that made Tian lie down and try to contact his dead friends again.

Tian was years out of practice by then, but like all of the times when he attempted in the past, someone came through. This time Tian wasn't looking for answers. He didn't want a hint about his future. He just wanted to know that there was something out there. That there was something after this and that his grandmother would be fine.

The soft personality that entered Tian's mind was familiar. It felt like an old friend.

'There's someone here,' it said to Tian.

'Who?' Tian asked not wanting to be disappointed again.

And without any further words Tian felt a feeling that was even more familiar. It felt like the feeling Tian had when he was younger and his not yet bedridden grandmother would play a trick on him. It was the feeling that her smile seemed to produce after sticking a feather in his ear while sleeping. It was the feeling he would get when his grandmother would smile after being caught cheating at cards. It was the feeling of the woman that Tian had grown to love as his grandmother before her arthritis and deafness made her a prisoner in her own body.

'I told you I would visit you,' that familiar person said.

'Grammy, is that you?' Tian thought aloud.

'Yes Tian and I'm fine now.'

Tian allowed himself to imagine what his grandmother looked like now and the healthy, heavy woman of Tian's youth came to mind. Tian wondered why she didn't choose the sexier image of her youth, but then concluded that she wanted Tian to recognize her.

'So what is it like there?' Tian started.

'I want you to do something for me.'

'What is it?' Tian asked hesitantly remembering all of the pain brought about by other proclamations in the dark.

'Tell your mother that you heard from me.'

'Ok,' Tian agreed not knowing if he would do it.

And as quickly as she had come, the feeling of her left Tian's mind.

Tian hadn't tried to contact her immediately after that first encounter. Tian found the message to his mother very difficult to deliver even though it was accepted with an open mind.

No, the reason why Tian waited to contact his grandmother was because of all of the disappointment that he associated with talking to the dead. It was never clear. It was never easy. And he didn't feel that it made his life better in any way.

It was about two months after her first contact when he lay sleepless on his Los Angeles bed. His day at work had been an uneventful one and it was followed up by a frozen dinner and a little TV. Relaxed, Tian wasn't quite ready to fall asleep, and it was then that he heard what sounded like a knock on his bedroom door. His first roommate had long since moved out so he knew that the knock wasn't possible.

But still, when time passed and no one knocked again Tian became curious. Tian rolled over to the edge of the bed to examine the door. It was still closed. And when Tian opened the door and found no one in the hallway he considered it a matter of wood bending in an old apartment instead of being a product of his imagination.

Tian returned to bed and lay there a while longer getting closer to sleep when he felt someone enter the room. His eyes immediately flew open to find no one standing there. He took an immediate sweep of the room and when he found it empty, he accepted it as a visitor from the other side.

Almost by instinct Tian rolled onto his back, put his arms to his side and touched his thumb and pointing fingers.

"I'm here," Tian said aloud.

'It's me,' Tian's grandmother put into his mind in a playful tone.

"How are you Grammy?" Tian corrigibly replied.

'I'm good Tian. I'm here because I've decided to help you.'

"How's that Grammy?"

'I'm going to help you know what it's like to be in a relationship.'

"Are you?" Tian replied flatly.

'I am.'

"Ok."

A silent moment went by where Tian didn't ask anything and nothing was stated.

"Is there anything else?" Tian asked aloud.

'No, that's it,' his grandmother replied joyfully.

"Ok, good night," Tian replied before rolling back over and trying to fall asleep. He wanted to believe that he had just spoken to his grandmother. And he wanted to believe that a supernatural force was going to help him with his love life. But neither thing seemed likely or plausible. So instead he put it out of his mind and went to sleep.

But lying sleepless on his Las Vegas hotel bed he remembered his grandmother and what she had said. For Tian it was just another in a long line of disappointments that he needed to wash away.

Tian turned his agitated mind to a new escape plan. On a class trip he had taken during high school he joined a group that had gone whitewater rafting. At the time Tian had found it to be an exhilarating experience and knew he wanted to repeat it.

"I'm going to go white water rafting," Tian spoke into the emptiness of his room. "You know what, I'm going to go white water rafting down the Grand Canyon."

This idea gave him some solace. It quieted his mind long enough to stop the tingles and for him to fall asleep. And the next morning after an all you can eat buffet, Tian made reservations for a Native American guided whitewater rapids trip. The trip wasn't scheduled until the next day, but Tian left immediately hoping to get in a little sightseeing. Tian had never visited the Grand Canyon before, and he hoped that he could make it there with enough daylight to tour the ridge.

The tour across the states was uneventful. And when Tian arrived through the gates of the park, he found he had an hour and a half to spare. As Tian made his way down the long road through the park, he saw the result of the latest fire and for some reason thought of his grandmother.

'Perhaps she would have enjoyed coming here,' Tian thought to explain away the association.

Tian parked his car, paid his fee and hopped on the trolley that toured the ridge. At the first stop Tian was awestruck by the size of it all. He had often thought of it as just being a large crack in the ground but it was so much more in person. There was a stateliness about it that was unimaginable.

Tian walked over to the historical standee and turned to the woman standing in front of it.

"Do you know how old the canyon is?" Tian asked.

The woman turned around and looked at Tian. Tian was impressed. She was tall and lean with long dirty blond hair, and a delicate face. And when she spoke her words were wrapped around a light German accent.

"I don't know," the woman said back. "Maybe it says somewhere on here."

Tian stepped forward and together the two scanned the length of the display.

"Oh wait, I found it," the woman said breaking the silence and drawing Tian to here. "It says that parts of it had different ages. So it's between 100,000 to five million years old."

"5 million," Tian proclaimed. "Wow, doesn't that just make you feel very young," Tian said with a smile.

The woman laughed back and when she smiled Tian couldn't help but notice how much like a model she looked.

"Hi, Tian," Tian said sticking out his hand.

"Katya."

"Nice to meet you," Tian added. "You know I have a fascination with areas of natural beauty. They calm me."

"Me too actually. The parks relax me."

"I'm actually on a bit of adventure vacation right now and figured that this would be a good break from the action. Sort of the eye of the hurricane," Tian said with a smile.

"Me too actually. I sprained my ankle two days ago rock climbing. I came here yesterday and hiked down to the bottom. Today I thought I would tour the top of it."

Tian walked the two over to the edge of the ridge and looked down. "You hiked to the bottom? How long did it take you?"

"It was about three or four hours."

Tian looked at the woman standing in front of him amazed. "Wow! And you did it on the sprained ankle."

The woman smiled. "Well, I didn't want to waste my time sitting around. And it wasn't that bad."

"So where are you from?" Tian asked as they both walked towards the tour trolley.

"I'm from Germany."

"I'm from the Bahamas," Tian retorted. "And what are you doing in the states?"

"I took six months off of my job so that I can travel around the U.S. rock climbing."

"Really?" Tian proclaimed with genuine surprise in his tone.

"Yes, I really love rock climbing and I've been saving a while to be able to do it."

"Wow!" Tian again proclaimed finding her more and more beautiful with every word she spoke. "Well, I can't say anything quite so amazing. About a week ago I woke up and decided that I needed to jump out of a plane. So I packed some stuff, threw it into my car, called my job and took off. After that I went skiing black diamonds and yesterday was Vegas. Tomorrow I'm going whitewater rafting," Tian said with as much bravado as he could muster.

"I think that sounds a little more exciting than what I'm doing," she replied with a smile.

They both rode the trolley quietly as the announcer gave his history lesson about the park. Tian took this time to sneak looks at the surprising woman that sat in the row in front of him. He wondered how she felt about him. Tian never forgot how he thought most women saw him. Tian thought that ever woman saw him like Annett did which was as a friend. Tian wondered whether or not he should waste his time with her.

The trolley stopped and they both got out. "What do you do?" Katya asked.

This was where Tian always had an advantage. And Tian knew that because she didn't live in Los Angeles it would be even more impressive. "I work in television," Tian said with a cocky smile.

"Me too," Katya replied with surprise.

Tian felt the air deflate from his bubble a little because where as someone not in the industry would be impressed by what he did. An industry person would barely consider what he did 'working in television.' Tian back tracked a little. "Actually, I make those behind-the-scenes featurettes about movies."

Katya looked at Tian closely and a relaxed look wiped across her face. "Me too."

"Seriously?" Tian asked unable to believe the coincidence.

"Yes, I went to school for it."

"I do it for a big TV company in LA."

"I do it for a TV station in Germany."

And like that Tian knew that he was supposed to meet her.

After watching the sunset together, Tian invited Katya to dinner. She accepted and the two ended up being the only people in the restaurant. They laughed and shared stories. And when Katya told Tian that she had been sleeping in her car for the past 2 months, he offered her his room without thinking anything else about it. She promised an answer before the end of the night. And as they walked back to their car she accepted.

On the drive to the hotel, Tian considered why Katya had accepted his offer.

'Is it because she wanted a place to stay or because she wanted to sleep with me?' Tian thought. 'Here's what I'll do, I'll leave it up to the universe.' Tian concluded. 'At every hotel I've stayed at, the front desk attendant has asked me whether I want two doubles or a king sized bed. But the way they always phrased it was by offering whatever they had the most of. If the attendant first offers a king I will accept it and if he first offers a double, I will accept that instead.'

The two pulled up to the hotel half-way in between Tian's rafting location and Katya's rock climbing site and entered the lobby.

"Can I get a room please," Tian asked the front desk attendant while standing next to Katya.

"Would you like two doubles?" attendant asked.

"Sure," Tian replied disappointed.

The night was filled with conversation and laughter in front of the TV. And when midnight hit Katya looked forward from the TV and in a soft voice said, "Well, it's getting late."

"Ah, you're right," Tian concluded, before turning off the lights and rolling over to go to sleep.

That night Tian dreamt that he was back in the Bahamas telling his friend Colin about his trip. In the dream Tian mentioned to Colin that he had met Katya. Colin then asked if he had sex with her, and sadly Tian replied "no." The next morning when Tian tried to quietly pack his stuff to make his early morning appointment, he was caught by a smiling Katya.

"Good morning," Katya said through a smile that made her face beam.

"Good morning. I didn't mean to wake you."

"You didn't."

"I have to leave but do you want to meet afterwards?"

"Ok," Katya said with her legs around the sheets like a playful kitten.

"I will call you once it's over."

"Ok."

On the drive Tian thought about his dream. Clearly the dream was precognitive.

"I'm not going to end up sleeping with her," Tian concluded with surprise. 'I guess that's fine too,' Tian thought.

Tian arrived at the docking site to find only one couple waiting for the excursion. He knew it was going to be a long trip with one couple and what looked to be a 10 foot pontoon boat.

The trip itself turned out to be less whitewater and more river rafting. As a part of the tour, the guide explained that the river had been filled with whitewater. But after the government damned the river on the non-native American land, the rapids became more of a ripple.

After the guide turned on the motor and steered them through the flats, Tian stretched out on one end of the boat. 30 minutes were all Tian could take before he sat up and started conversation with the couple.

"So, where are you two from," Tian asked casually.

"New Hampshire," the thin, middle-aged husband replied. "What about you?" he asked back to get all of the formalities out of the way.

"The Bahamas. What do you do in New Hampshire?"

"I research happiness."

With that Tian was intrigued. "What do you mean? Is that a euphemism for 'you spend all day at the golf course'," Tian joked innocently.

The wife that lay with the brim of her hat lifted to let the sun hit her face, smiled.

"I wish," the husband replied. "No, I do research on the biological aspects of happiness."

"Like the chemicals released when you smile and stuff?" Tian had learned a little about smile therapy during his college psychology classes.

"Yes, in a way."

"So if you don't mind me asking, what makes us happy?"

"No, he doesn't mind you asking," the wife said without moving much.

Tian got the impression that many of their dinner party conversations must have began exactly this way.

"Well, there are two aspects that go into happiness: the psychological and the biological aspects. The psychological can be broken down to one's perception of one's life or current situation."

"So if you think your life is good, whether or not it actually is, you will be happy?" Tian asked.

"Yes. And there have been studies that showed that there is a technique that can permanently raise your happiness level."

"Level of happiness?" Tian asked enthralled with what he was hearing.

"It's the level of happiness that you return to after good or bad things happen to you."

"Ok."

"Your happiness level tends to be constant throughout your life and there have been studies that showed that it can be permanently raised."

"And I have to ask what is that technique," Tian asked with a coy smile.

"It's simple actually. Research has shown that if before you go to bed you write down three things for which you feel appreciative of that has happened to you during that day, and then write why you feel appreciative for them, you will raise your happiness level."

"Interesting!" Tian proclaimed.

"But my specialty would be the biological aspects of happiness."

"And what does your research show?" Tian asked.

"Well, my work is more about the role that hormones play in being happy and falling in love."

"Like for example," Tian added prodding his friend on.

"As of right now, we know that there are four chemicals other than the sex hormones that create all of our positive emotions. And what makes the feelings 'exciting' as opposed to 'satisfying' are the combination of those three chemicals."

"Which are?" Tian asked.

"Well the obvious one is testosterone. I'm sure you know that one."

"Yeah," Tian replied with a smile.

"There's also the neurotransmitter PEA which is responsible for the feeling of euphoria that comes when you fall for someone. There's dopamine, which is responsible for that juiced feeling you get after doing something fun and exciting; Serotonin, which gives you that relaxed, mellow feeling; And oxytocin and vasopressin which are responsible for long term bonding with another person. Vasopressin is found in high amounts in women after a woman gives birth. But of course, so is serotonin."

"I image it would take a lot of drugs to make a woman forget the pain of pushing a bowling ball out of them," Tian said with a laugh, forgetting the wife lying behind them.

"HA!" the wife replied.

"So a part of my area is the study of dopamine sensitive individuals. They would be your adrenaline junkies. You know those people that jump out of planes or race cars and that type of stuff."

Tian smiled at what he heard. "And what does your research say about them?"

"Well, our studies have shown that these people actually have an abnormality in there DNA. This abnormality causes them to produce more dopamine receptors than the average person. So where as a normal person may rate an exciting day at the office similarly to jumping out of a plane. The dopamine sensitive individuals would rate them very different. The result is that the dopamine sensitive people find boring activities unbearably boring because they have a much higher upper limit to compare it to."

"Really?" Tian replied without even realizing he was saying it. "So I guess they might find marriage torturous," Tian joked.

"The incidence of affairs is much higher in this group than in the general population."

"And falling in love?" Tian added.

"Well, love has a number of stages. There is the initial stage which is driven by the bodies alternating release of PEA, dopamine and serotonin, not to mention the sex hormones. And then there are the later stages of love which are dominated by vasopressin and serotonin. The dopamine sensitives have no problem with the first stage. But again, once the excitement is gone, it is like they are going through withdrawal from a powerful drug. They describe the feeling as a sort of suffocation; their sex drive diminishes, and as an overall result they can feel depressed."

Tian was shocked by what he heard. Tian needed those shots of dopamine and he knew it. "What a wonderful life that must be for them," Tian replied trying to pull his emotions back into check.

"Actually it can be quite devastating for them."

"He was being sarcastic, honey," the wife chimed in not moving a muscle except her mouth.

"Oh. Yes it could be quite bad. But on the other end of it, when they achieve, they achieve big."

The conversation lulled to a silence. "I'm sorry. I never got your name. I'm Barry. We have just been talking and talking," the husband said.

"It's Tian."

"Oh, I've never heard that name before. Is it Anglo Saxon?"

"No, it's the Taoist symbol for heaven."

"I like that name," the wife added.

"That's my wife Hannah. So what do you do for a living Tian?"

"I'm an accountant," Tian added without another word on the subject.

The riverboat ride ended six hours after it began with a helicopter ride to the top of the ridge. And when Tian met up with Katya she was looking exceptionally beautiful. She treated him to dinner and drinks and they both walked back to their room. Tian's dream had closed the question on whether or not there would be sex so Tian simply enjoyed the moment. Later that night when they lay in their separate beds Katya once again announced how late it was getting. Again Tian turned off the light and went to sleep.

This time however would not be like the last. In the morning while it was still dark, Tian was awoken by the feeling of Katya climbing into bed with him. Still half asleep, Tian looked back over his shoulder where he met Katya lips. Tian then rolled back into his fetal position and thought 'Oh, this is going to end well.'

After a minute Tian was fully awake. He rolled over and kissed Katya properly. They touched, they kissed and they made love till noon.

Later on Katya drove Tian down to the red rocks of Arizona where she shared her passion for rock climbing. Tian understood the draw of it. It was at once thrillingly dangerous, yet calmingly quiet. The only thing that Tian heard on the wall face was the sound of his own struggles next to the crumbling of rocks. Katya was clearly one of Tian's fellow adrenaline junkies and Tian liked her for it.

After another day with Katya, Tian knew what he was supposed to do. He remembered what his grandmother had promised him about helping him know what it is to be in a relationship. Katya was clearly that girl. But as his grandmother's wording had suggested, it wasn't a pairing that was meant to last forever.

Katya said bye to Tian with a kiss and a tear in her eye. And at the last moment before he turned to go she snapped a picture of him. Tian would always wish that he had a picture as well, but that picture was never taken. She would always remain a fond memory for Tian and she would always be known to him as the person that restored his belief in God. It was because of her and his trip that he knew what it was that he could share with the world. He knew the story that could give people a new way of looking at life.

On the drive home he decided that he would leave his job and get a movie 'in the can' by the end of the year. It was now May 1st so that meant that he would have eight months to write, produce and direct it. And he didn't worry about the constraints of it because he knew that he would have God by his side. And as long as God was a co-producer, there was nothing that could go wrong.

CHAPTER 14

Tian appeared behind Irabell in what looked like an underground cavern. Irabell seemed to not notice Tian's arrival. Instead he remained focused on a couple kissing in front of him. Tian looked around the surroundings and found it unrecognizable and decided that it was a foreign terrain on a distant planet.

The ground had been smoothed and polished to an almost mirrored state and the walls and ceilings had shiny crystals within them that sparkled in the dim light. The ceiling was 50 to 100 feet in the air. But within the center of the room eight feet above the couple was a cloth that had crystal chips attached to it. All of this made the room brighter than anyone would expect without a candle or an additional light source.

Tian turned back to the couple and took a closer look. The couple was human. In fact there was something familiar about the man. Tian looked at the back of Irabell and saw what looked like a human back. And on closer observation he saw that the peach colored cloth that encircles Irabell's body was the same color and style as the cloth that encircled the man. And what's more, the man was the same height and build as the Irabell that stood in front of Tian.

Without a word Tian stepped closer to Irabell. As he did he focused on what the couple was saying to each other.

"I need you to go away for a year, but then come back. Can you do that for me?" the man said.

"But why? I don't understand. Don't you love me?" said the woman, whose clothes revealed her midsection.

"I do love you, but I need to be a better man than I am. And with you here all I can be is the man that loves you. My people need more."

"How could you speak so cruelly to me?" the woman questioned as she began to cry.

"It is not cruelty that makes me ask this. It is out of love for all of my people."

"Of which I am just one," the woman said. "I will leave you then, but don't expect me to come back."

Just after the woman spoke the room changed. The crystals that had lined the walls and canopy broke apart from their resting place and swirled into a speckled gray mass that enveloped the space. The walls and the people dissolved before reassembling in a new configuration.

This time they appeared to be outside and the man that looked like Irabell stood in front of a hut. An old woman stood in front of the hut with her arm blocking the man from entering. With tears in her eyes and a deeply sorrowful look on her face she calmly and continuously repeated the word "No" to the man.

The man brushed by the pleading old woman and entered the hut. The inside of the hut looked like death with feces, urine and flies everywhere. But the sole occupant of the hut was the woman that stood before Tian moments before. The woman was still taking deeply strained breaths but it wasn't clear from her eyes whether or not she was still conscious.

The man held his hand to his nose and mouth and began to cry. He then turned to go out but immediately turned back and stared at his former love. Uncontrollably he moved to her and crouched beside the bed. The vomit in her hair and on the reed bed made the man briefly hesitate. But in a second he touched her face and even lowered his head down so that his forehead touched hers.

As their two skins touched the room dissolved again and this time reassembled back within the cavern where the man knelt polishing the floor with another worker. The man's hands slowed from its intense circling before it eventually stopped. The man then looked straight down at the ground while he tried to evaluate what was going on. Suddenly avalanches of vomit spew from him. His back violently spasmed into a spine cracking arch and more and more of what was inside of him poured out.

The other worker kneeling near him got up and touched the man on the skin of his arched back. The touch did no good. The man was propelling without inhaling and it wasn't long before the man's muscles no longer had enough oxygen to contract. The worker watched as the man fell to the ground. The worker then knelt down into the vomit to help the man. And then it wasn't long before the worker got up and ran out of the cavern to get help.

The crystals on the room again disassembled and then reassembled back into the original cavern in which Tian had arrived. The same two people sat on cushions under the crystal woven canopy and again they were kissing.

"I need you to do something that will seem incredibly difficult for you to understand," the man said earnestly looking into his lover's eyes.

"What is it my love," the woman replied.

"I need you to go away for three years," the man answered with sorrow in his eyes.

"What?" the woman asked searching the man's face for a sign of his cruel joke. "How could you ask me to do something like that? I don't understand at all. This temple is the only home I've ever known and you are my love. How could you so casually ask me to leave it?"

Tian watched the scene again confused. In hearing the slight variation on the same conversation he realized that the scene wasn't real. It was some sort of thought being worked out, most likely by Irabell.

"Irabell," Tian spoke.

Irabell turned around and the image around them broke apart into a swirling gray mass that encapsulated them. "Tian, I'm sorry I didn't notice you arrive. How long have you been here?"

"I was here long enough to see the image start over."

"Yes, I was looking for an answer."

"What do you mean that you were looking for an answer? Was that you I saw?" Tian asked confused.

"Yes it was."

"I don't get it. Were you creating a new life or something?"

"No. We are in a special place. We are on a planet in the physical universe."

On hearing that Tian looked around to see anything that would resemble life. But in every direction all he saw was the gray swirling mass. Tian closed his eyes and listened to the swirl but it didn't make a sound.

"There is something about the randomness of the swirls that makes this world void of sound," Irabell said.

Tian opened his eyes and turned back toward Irabell. "Are we close to earth?"

Irabell's face contorted to emphasize its distance. "No. Even when humans gain space flight they still won't be able to travel this far away. And by the time they could make the trek I doubt they would still be what are now considered to be humans. No. As far as we can tell no space traveling species has ever made it to this planet."

"Ever?"

"No. Not since our second age of the great library. The truth is that there isn't much that we know about this planet or its species."

"It's inhabited?"

"Yes there's one species."

"Where does it live? I'd actually be curious to see a living alien," Tian said with a smile.

"There is only one species that covers the planet. This is it. In fact I think that we are technically in it."

Tian looked around at the swirling gray mass. "We're inside of it?"

"I think so."

"Should we be standing inside of it?"

"There would be nowhere to stand outside of it. Think of it like a vine that grows up the side of buildings on earth. It is like that. It has extended itself from one small area to cover the entire planet."

"Ok," Tian replied still with trepidation. "Wait, what do you mean that 'you think so'? I thought that you guys had a detailed library of the lives of every living thing?"

"This species is special. We know it's alive. And we know that a part of us makes up a part of it. But either it doesn't think or the life process exists in a way that we have never encountered before."

"So this would be an unknown species for you guys?" Tian said with satisfaction.

"We think that the planet was once inhabited with sentient beings. We imagine that this sentient species became extinct during the time of our first library. So when we lost all of our information from that time, we lost their knowledge as well. But after the loss of the first library there must have been someone that still had firsthand knowledge of the planet. That person must have taken other to it. And those new people then must have taken others to it before they dissolved away, and so on. This is the only way that we could imagine having the knowledge about a planet that no physical creature has ever visited."

"Do you also keep a library of your thoughts?"

"What, do you mean my thoughts?"

"I mean a library of the thoughts of us that live in this dimension."

"Our thoughts?" Irabell asked confused.

"You know, the thoughts of the species that survives physical death."

"There isn't any. Our thoughts aren't considered as valuable as physical thoughts. Physical species really are a marvelous thing. Each individual in the physical world is an intelligent community of many living creatures that observe, process and react to the never ending probability clouds that exist around them. And with each decision it makes it has to find a way to not just get one species to go along with that decision but its full internal community. And it has to do it this with conflicting information and conflicting species' agendas.

And then after it makes each of the person's individual life decisions, it has to calculate within the probability of the species' larger community as well. The physical species are incredible. And to think that the thoughts of our non-physical species is anywhere as significant as the thoughts of the physical bodies we inhabit is absurd."

'If you had saved your thoughts, you would now know more about this special place,' Tian thought sarcastically.

'And how could we have learned to do that? Everything that we are and we have has been given to us during the lives of physical beings or has been found on our side. Who would have invented this technology? And if it was easy then wouldn't one of the great minds that have passed into our world have created it,' Irabell replied.

"So what do you know about this species?" Tian asked aloud, preferring the distance that speech allowed them.

"Not much. Our best guess is that the creature is sleeping and this, the surface of the organism, is its brain. There is no dense surface past the one under your feet. And the higher you travel over the surface, the less of this mass you find until there is nothing at all."

"So why do you think it's the brain? And why do you think it's sleeping?"

"Both answers are: because of the swirling gray mass. This stuff swirling around us is alive. We know that because of what it can do." Irabell takes a moment before restarting with a lower tone. There was a feeling of embarrassment that came over Irabell though Tian couldn't find its expression in Irabell's very human looking face.

"What you saw me doing when you arrived is often thought of as a waste of time by our kind. During my last physical life I made a mistake that I often think about. I was important in my community. And instead of fulfilling my community service, I chose to depart my life early."

Tian recoiled with Irabell's admission.

"And because of my physical choice, many things happened that wouldn't have happened otherwise. This species can not only sense our presence but it can connect directly with our minds without a conscious intermediary."

"It reads our minds?" Tian asked confused.

"No, much more than that. Our minds here mirror the minds we had in our physical body. Like yours, mine was human. Our brains evolved to be singularly focused even though an incredible amount of information was given to us at any one time."

"I'm sorry. Please I don't understand what you mean."

"I'm sure that you are familiar with the term instinct, yes?"

"Yes."

"Instinct is when knowledge gained outside of our conscious observation works its way into our consciousness. So for example, you were engaged in television watching when alive, yes?"

"Yes."

"Let's say that one day you were engrossed in what you were watching but you suddenly became restless. You get up and start walking around your home. Eventually you notice that it is a little warmer than normal and that there is a burnt smell in the air.

Well, you go into the kitchen and find that you left the fire on. You were completely engaged in what you were watching, but you subconsciously felt the change in temperature and noticed the smell. This knowledge, gained outside of your conscious observation, pushed itself into your consciousness. That process is instinct."

"Ok, I understand."

"This creature can access more than just the conscious thoughts that you had during your physical life though. It can access all of the uncountable observations that your body made as well. So if you think about your life and imagine what your life would have been like if one thing in your life changed, this creature can use all of the information that your physical body gleamed about the probability clouds around you and show you what the likely outcome to your new decision would have been."

Again lowering his tone and slowing his speech, "I know that I wouldn't have been able to continue living my life without the woman I loved. But I also know that I had to be away from her in order to have the experiences that would help me to become the leader I needed to be.

I have visited this planet a lot since my physical death. I have worked through my life in steps trying to figure out what it is that I could have changed in order for me to have had both. The moment that you saw seems to be the one with the most potential for change."

Tian listened quietly sometimes distracted by a piece of matter that moved too close to his eyes. And when Irabell was done Tian remained quiet. He flipped the information around in his head before asking, "How does it help you?"

"When you end your life the way I did, in the circumstances that I have, and then you arrive here and learn what life is like for our species, it feels important to know whether or not you could have done something differently."

"But I don't understand, can you change the past here?"

"No."

Tian asked no more about Irabell's regret. "You kept saying 'probability cloud.' What's the probability cloud?"

"It is a way of predicting what is going to happen to a person. If a person wakes up every morning at 7, then the probability of them waking up at seven any time during the next week is very high. A person's life becomes very predictable if you take a look at their environment, behavior and biology. Entire lives can sometimes be predicted."

"So the probability cloud is kind of like determining the odds in a horserace? If the horse has won more often; or let's say a person chooses green most often, then they are most likely to choose green again?" Tian asked intrigued.

"Well, it's much more complicated than that. From before we're born there are things that increase or decrease the likely of what we will do during our lives. A completely healthy fetus makes the person that develops out of it more likely to do some things and less likely to do others. An unhealthy fetus that survives may go on to do things that the healthy fetus couldn't. But in either case there is a probability associated with that person's decisions."

"So destiny does exist. Our entire lives have been plotted out for us before we start?" Tian questioned.

"No, not exactly."

"So we have choice?"

"I wouldn't call it choice."

"Then what would you call it?"

"I would say that it is our choices that are predestined or predictable. And that remains true until we learn how to shape our probability cloud."

"I don't understand," Tian said inquisitively.

"If a child is raised in an environment where they didn't feel safe, the probability that they make decisions that make them feel safe is very high. As they make those choices they continue to have free will, but the choices they make will always be highly predictable. If a child grows up where one parent seemed to have more power in a relationship, then the child will mirror the parent that they were taught was more powerful. And although that child will think that they are making each of their choices using a sense of free will, each of their choices will be evident to anyone who takes a look at the probability cloud that surrounds that decision."

"So is it an actual cloud that surrounds them?" Tian asked still confused.

"No, the term probability cloud is a math term. I thought that you would know that."

"I'm sorry I've never heard of it," Tian confessed.

"The "probability cloud" is an understanding that every species reaches once they obtain a certain level of self awareness. Perhaps Earth hasn't reached there yet."

"Whether or not earth has, I would like to know," Tian said with growing impatience.

"The probability cloud is a way of seeing the world. You can attribute your success or the success of the people around you to a number of things. Most people choose destiny or luck when the truth is that it's neither. Their success was most likely because of a series of likely choices that their environment, biology and behavior laid out for them. The probability cloud is a way of understanding the choices that they've made and to predict what they will do in the future."

"So it's a pattern that people fall into?"

"No, not exactly. Here's an example, a family could have been performers for generations. Their environmental pattern would predict that the next generation might as well, but their probability cloud might predict that they will be the first generation that chooses something else. Let's say that it is the year 1300 and a family of generational performers arrives at the gate of an English castle. The king inside is fond of comedians and jugglers, and the family is full of them. The family did not know it when they arrived at the castle but their admittance was highly probable because the king of the castle welcomed their kind.

The family performs and their act is very well received. The king, laughing very hard by the end, doesn't want the night to end so he calls on the performers to put on a play. Many family performance groups may not have a play prepared but this family has seven members, four of which are male and over the age of 16.

The number of family members over 16 is critical because 16 is the age when life pursuits are generally taken more seriously. The number of male members is important because women didn't perform. That means that there are four males to perform the play.

The most basic story structures include a romantic couple, a person trying to keep them apart and someone that helps them to get together. That requires a minimum of four people that have to be on stage at the same time.

So let's say that this family has done a number of performances before. That means that they must have had a least a few requests for a play. Knowing that longer shows and happier audiences result in more money, they would have evaluated their possibility of adding a play to their performance. Since they have four male members over 16 they can add a play.

Now let's say that they have had a great deal of performances before they arrive at the king's gate. That means that the show that the king sees will be well practiced and very refined. And since the king was already primed to like them because he loves entertainment and enjoyed the first part of their show, the king also likes the play and is all around impressed.

Now, the king did not expect the family to be so versatile. However, the number of performers over the age of 16 and the family's performance experience created a very high probability that they also had a play prepared. Not taking into account the probability cloud surrounding the family, the king associates the good performance on the talent level of the family and his luck for having found the family. And the overall result is that the king is very impressed with the family and invites them to stay.

The family would never have predicted this outcome when they pointed their horse toward the castle, because their experience was that entertainers are only valued on the night that the wine is flowing. In the sober light of day they were usually ushered away.

However, what they didn't know was that ideal temperatures have lead to two seasons of incredible crops for the king. And having already fortified his land's security he was now looking to use his wealth to purchase more luxuries. The King valued entertainment over objects that sat unworn in vaults. So when the king saw a source of constant entertainment up for sale he used his discretionary funds to obtain it. The family may have thought of this occurrence as unlikely, but that is only because they didn't understand the probability cloud surrounding the king's decision.

Now let's say that the family is living within the community of the castle. The family has two kids under the age of 16. These two kids are now being exposed to many more trades, skill sets and love interests than their older siblings and past relatives. And since the family already has the four actors necessary to perform plays, they aren't in desperate need of another performer. The family may still want another performer, but if the younger boy puts up resistance, the family is more likely to acquiesce.

And if the king in turn took a liking to the entire family, and exposed them to even more of life outside of performing, that would undoubtedly have a very large impact on someone during the identity formational years of their life. And at that point, if the family continues to live there while the youngest kids approached the time when they had to choose their life's path, it becomes more likely for the youngest to choose a path other than performance. And this would be in spite of his family's generations of performance.

So although it would have seemed unlikely to an outside observer for a child from a family of performers to choose something other than performance, when you look at the probability cloud that surrounded the family as they approached the castle, you can see that the probability was actually high that the kid would choose something other than performance."

"I understand that. So this is something that you have access to on this side? Because during life there is no ways to know what others are thinking or what circumstances they're basing their decisions," Tian rebuked.

"Yes, with enough information you can know with certainty what will happen from now to the end of time. If you have all of the information then you don't need a probability cloud because everything would be known with certainty. The probability cloud is when you don't have all of information.

However, what is necessary to use the probability cloud is knowledge of its existence and facts. When you have those two you can build out the cloud."

"Facts like what?" Tian asked.

"Facts about the topic of the decision."

"But you don't always have facts."

"That is why the probability cloud only becomes known to species once they have reached a certain level of self awareness. During the time that I lived, humanity didn't have a lot of access to facts. However I was one of the blessed few who were entrusted with the facts that we had. Even so, they weren't enough to truly apply the cloud."

"So when societies reach a certain level of self awareness they gain the ability to apply the probability cloud to themselves and predict their own futures," Tian concluded.

"Oh it's more useful than that. Once you understand the probability cloud, your environment, biology and behavior become less important and your desire more accurately predicts your future. You become able to shape your future."

"But what stops people from using facts to shape their future now?"

"Nothing. And some people do. They learn things like 'luck favors the most prepared.' Or 'luck is what happens when preparation meets opportunity.' After they take those sayings to heart they seed their own probability cloud. However even in these two most profound facts, there is still the belief in luck. Luck, charms, destiny, god; these are all words used before the probability cloud is fully understood.

The creature of this planet takes all of the information that our body senses, and builds out the probability cloud that surrounds you in every possible situation. So once you have chosen which alternative you would like to examine, it shows you the result of that probable scenario. It then thinks that probable life, or more likely dreams it. And the part of the creature that is us reshapes itself into the images of the probable world.

The part of the creature that is us from the gray matter swirling around us becomes the walls of the hut and the temple. It even became me. I am told that being here is a waste of my time. But understanding the point in which my life took its unfortunate turn gives me solace.

Would you like to give it a try?" Irabell asked.

Tian had been staring intently at Irabell for a while. His question had come back to him, the one that he had come in search of Irabell to find out. And it was Irabell that reminded Tian.

"Irabell, where is God?"

Irabell looked at Tian surprised. And for the first time since Tian arrived within the grey matter Irabell truly saw him. He had been distracted by this planet and its waste of time. But his student stood before him and he was changed. He even looked different. 'He kind of looks like a tree. How did that happen?' Irabell wondered.

"Would you like to go somewhere else to talk?" Irabell asked.

"Sure."

Irabell disappeared and Tian followed him to a new landscape. Tian opened his eyes at the new location. 'This reminds me of the banks of the ocean library,' Tian thought.

Tian felt waves of warm velvet brush against his legs. Tian looked out and saw what looked like an endless field of wheat. But instead of being yellow it hummed a synchronous tone that felt meditative to Tian.

Tian scanned the field and saw that they weren't alone. There were pairs of spindly humanoid creatures with smoothed out features and non-descript fingers. There were large winged, trunk-less elephants that engendered the feeling a kid gets when he smells cookies baking in the oven. And there were large stinger ray type creatures that flew just over the wheat blinking in and out of reality as it progressed forward.

Tian remembered heaven and how familiar everything was. This new world was the opposite. It was definitely not what he imagined the afterlife to be. Tian had believed in the existence of aliens but he had never considered walking amongst them.

Tian continued to scan the field when the tone of the wheat made him forget about the differences.

"I hadn't expected you to ask that question yet. To answer that question I first have to answer a question you asked me at the edge of heaven."

"I can't remember what that was. Oh wait, you mean about us not being souls."

"Yes," Irabell confirmed.

"Well, I've traveled through heaven and I've talked to others like myself from earth. They are living in what was promised to them by the Christian church before they died. They seemed to have everlasting life in heaven. If they aren't souls then I don't know what is."

"That is the question," Irabell retorted.

"What is?"

"What is your definition of a soul?"

"My definition?" Tian thought for a moment. "The soul is the part of the human body that's real. It is the part of us that survives death. It is the part of the human that matters. It is the core of us."

"If that is your definition of a soul then we are not souls."

"What are we then?" Tian asked aggressively.

"We are aliens that live in a different dimension who add to the community necessary to breathe life into living creatures on the physical world."

"That's very different," Tian concluded.

"It is."

"But I think when the bible or any of the religious writings discuss the soul, it is us that they are referring to."

"Perhaps, but that doesn't make their definition correct."

"So you are saying that all of the religious writings on earth don't understand what the soul is?" Tian asked aggressively.

"Your question implies that all of the religious texts of earth are the same. The definitions they use support the ideas they teach. But because they all use similar words, their followers use words like soul, assuming their own definition is what is understood when they communicate. That is not an effective way to communicate with others."

"But wouldn't you agree that my definition of a soul is very similar to what we are?" Tian argued.

"Let's look at your definition. You said that a soul is the part of the human that's real. Don't you think that the physical body of a human is real? Didn't it move objects and itself around the earth?"

"It did."

"Then what is your definition of real?" Irabell questioned.

"Something permanent. Facts are real. A body dies and then the only thing left is us."

"We fade away as well. If we chose to, we can let go of our physical pursuits and the particles that make us would simply break apart."

"But we're more permanent then the body," Tian replied.

"Yes, but you are applying a value to permanence that it doesn't deserve. Our physical bodies have a purpose. It interacts with the physical world. Without a body we would be almost incapable of that. Yes, we last longer than physical bodies, but we are not more real than physical bodies."

"Ok."

"You said that the soul is the part of the body that matters. So I guess you mean that our existence matters over the life of the physical body."

"Yes."

"I have shown you around this world. Everything that we have, everything we are is because of lives lived in the physical world. We archive every moment of physical life and at least a thousand of us follow each physical life as if it were our own. If you ask any one of us here which they think is more important, our life or the physical ones, everyone would say the physical one. We consider it a privilege to let go of everything we were to be wiped clean so that we can be a part of the community of another physical body.

It is only the physical body that thinks that the part of them that's us is more important than the whole of it. And that thought isn't even shared amongst all creatures in the physical world. That thought isn't even shared amongst all humans," Irabell said with a rare smile.

"So there is no part of my definition of 'soul' that would apply to what we are?" Tian asked.

"We are one of the parts that remain intact after the body's physical death."

"So if I said that the soul is the part of the physical body that remains intact after physical death, would that definition describe the part of us that arrives here?" Tian asked suspiciously.

"It would, but the purpose of using words is to communicate with others. And words like 'soul' are attached to a lot of connotations. So someone on earth could use the word 'soul' as you have defined it, but the listener will immediately add their connotations to the word. And most humans would define the soul using the words 'matters' and 'real' as you originally did. So wouldn't it be better to allow the word 'soul' to mean what the majority of people think it means and simply use a different word to refer to what we are?

We are a separate species from physical beings. We have had our own evolution. We have our own culture. And we are among the many individual parts that come together to make up a physical body. A body could live without us. Its life would simply be less complete."

"A physical body could live without us?" Tian asked surprised.

"Yes, that is how you can make the choice to stay here or to return."

"My body's still alive?" Tian said shocked.

"It is, but it's dying."

"When would I have to make a decision?"

"Soon."

Tian looked around at the field and all of the creatures walking amongst the meditative tone. "So by human definition we are not the soul. By human definition the soul doesn't exist. But we would be the closest thing to the soul even though we would be better described as another species living within the human body that helps it to experience physical life. However we don't really exist in the physical world. We live in a non-physical world that has its own culture and history."

"Correct."

"Irabell, where's God?" Tian asked quietly.

"What's God Tian?"

"I don't know."

"Then what are you asking me?" Irabell softly answered back.

"God is love. God is the thing that created us, that looks over us. It's what does the judging if we're judged after we die. It's that thing that we must pray to in order to get things. It is the thing that exists everywhere at once. It is the form from which we were created. I don't know what God is. I just want to know if God exists."

Irabell stares quietly at Tian for a moment. This was always one of Irabell's favorite places in the afterlife. He enjoyed the calm that the field engendered. He enjoyed watching all of the remnants of different species interact.

"I have told you about a lot of species, but I haven't really talked about humans."

"You haven't," Tian agreed softly.

"I guess it was because I knew that you already knew so much about them." Irabell allowed a silence to develop. "You know, humans really are quite special." Irabell looked for an acknowledgement from Tian but got none. "Would you like to know something that human society gave to us that no other species had ever added?"

Tian looked at Irabell but didn't respond.

"Did you know that there is a human religion that teaches that the purpose of life is to learn to let go of life? They believe that by letting go you will achieve a sense of nirvana. It is supposed to be a blissful state.

No other species had ever come up with that belief before. Not once in millions of years. That belief is exactly opposite to what everyone comes to believe here. Everything we have is designed to get the opportunity to experience the physical world. And since we retain the beliefs and characteristics of the physical body we left behind, the devout believers of this religion continued to 'let go' here. While others who died quickly went back to the ocean library to prepare themselves for another possible chance at life, those devotees arrived here and then slowly dissolved away.

Can you imagine the debate it started? We didn't know what to do with that. And soon the thousands that followed their lives in the ocean library started to let themselves dissolve away as well. That moment changed our society. It shaped who we are. So yes, humans are indeed very special."

Irabell looked at Tian but Tian remained looking out onto the field at a male rock creature that rolled itself along. The wheat and the tone it produced were hypnotic. Tian wasn't trying to be rude by not answering Irabell. He just didn't see the need to speak when his thoughts were in disagreement with Irabell's designation of humans as 'special'.

"Tian I would now like to tell you about the creation of human love."

"I would like to hear that," Tian said turning to Irabell.

"Back when life first began on earth there were only single celled organisms. They reproduced often and quickly. Each organism had no emotional connection about the organism that created it and the species quickly spread. But as the organisms became more complex gestation became necessary. Gestation allowed a 2 celled organism to develop into a multi-celled creature before it had to fend for itself.

When the first creatures experienced gestation a lot of their offspring died. Like the organism before it, the offspring held no special connection to the organism that bore it. That meant that if the offspring couldn't immediately find nourishment the offspring died. That also meant that that species also died off.

But one day there was a species that was different from the species around it. This different creature experienced a brief surge in nutrient as it gave birth to its offspring. This allowed it to become more active right after birth. This caused the creature to wiggle vigorously creating space around it in the feeding pool they all lived in. When this happened, it gave its offspring a chance to find nourishment from the immediate area and this gave the offspring a competitive advantage in surviving its brief period of vulnerability.

The offspring now had this genetic change. And soon the offspring that had this change outnumbered the species that didn't. This continued until the competitive advantage allowed the genetically changed creature to wipe out the previous species.

Soon one of the genetically changed creatures changed again. And this time the creature became a more complex organism. This more complex organism needed a longer gestation period for its offspring. And the offspring had a longer period of vulnerability after birth. However, the brief period of vigorous movement after birth wasn't enough to give these new offspring enough time to survive. So these new species died off each time they gave birth to a more complex offspring until another change occurred.

Eventually there was one of these new creatures that didn't just get a quick spike of nutrients after birth. Instead it got an extended nutritional stream. This extended nutritional stream caused the creature to create a space for their offspring for an even longer period of time. This extended period was enough for the offspring to survive and the competitive advantage that came with being a more complex creature was able take hold.

Changes continued to occur in the creatures and all of the successful species had a biological reinforcement that accompanied birth. Soon species became so complex that long gestation periods were necessary before the offspring could survive. But not only were long gestation periods necessary, but long nurturing periods were necessary after the offspring was born.

The parenthood reinforcement system that survived all of the changes was one that released a chemical into the brain of the creature that gave birth. That chemical would last most of the offspring's nurturing and would be associated with the pleasure the creature gained after eating or mating. The creatures that had this trait had more offspring that survived than the creatures that didn't have this trait. And the more complex the creatures became, the more powerful the feeling of pleasure had to be to keep the mother attached.

Soon the gestation and nurturing period became so long, and the environment that the offspring was born into became so competitive that only the species that had two parents to look after them would survive. So the creatures where the male of the species received pleasure reinforcement for staying with the offspring were able to ensure that their complex offspring survived until it entered its own reproductive years.

Humans are the most complex of earth creatures. They have the longest gestation and nurturing period for their offspring. What was necessary for survival of such a species was a pleasure reinforcement for both the male and female. And this reinforcement had to keep the parents coupled for at least four years.

The pleasure reinforcement had to be powerful enough so that it would want to fight off its rivals. It had to be rechargeable so

that it could be maintained over time. And it had to be complex
enough to adapt to a new partner or parent if a parent was lost. This
is the story about the creation of human love."

Tian looked at Irabell in silence before eventually speaking
up. "What does that have to do with God?"

Irabell accepted the silence then responded with one word,
"everything."

Chapter 15

Tian was woken by a bump on the side of his rowboat. His first impulse was to sit up but striking pain forced him back down. He looked up at the stars and tried to remember what happened. 'I was swimming,' he remembered. 'I was attacked by a dolphin. Great!'

Tian looked around the boat wondering if it had hit something. But the boat continued to rock back and forth in the waves unhindered. 'It must have been in my mind,' Tian concluded. Tian looked down at his body. The moon was bright enough to make out his flesh in the light. The water droplets were all gone and they were replaced by goose pimples. 'I'm cold,' Tian thought.

Bam! The boat lurched forward and Tian could feel the hull of the boat breaking the crest of the waves as it sliced through the water. Tian looked out to see if there was a ship nearby that was hitting him. He saw nothing but open sky. And he heard nothing but his boat rocking in and out of the water.

Tian heard a breath and saw a stream of water coming down towards him. The water hit him right in the face and Tian choked a little as he spit out the water that landed in his mouth. Tian coughed out, "help! Is somebody there? Help, I can't move." There was no response.

Another stream of water hit him and Tian called out again. "Who's doing that?"

Just then Tian heard a high pitched chattering response. 'It's some type of animal,' Tian thought. And the sound was then followed by another bump of the boat. There wasn't just one this time, there were multiple bumps. Tian couldn't control his head which bounced up and down on the wood as the bow cut through the water. Tian couldn't tell if he were being taken to safety or if the angry dolphin was getting its last revenge upon him by making sure that his attack was fatal.

Tian looked up at the unchanging sky and wondering how much longer the pain would last. He had begun to feel a little nauseous. Tian wasn't prone to seasickness so he knew that he was hurt worse than he thought.

Tian allowed his mind to drift in order to take it off of the nausea. He thought about what would have to be considered the greatest accomplishment of his life. When he had come off of what he liked to refer to as his adventure vacation, Tian had a renewed vigor. He had a renewed belief in God, the afterlife and all of the things that drew his attention during his youth.

Tian had made a big plan. In eight months he was going to write, produce and shoot a movie. He knew what it was going to be about. It was going to be about coincidences. The story would show how even when the universe was bringing you to your lowest point, it was working to create your greatest good.

That was what he felt had happened to him. He felt a working together of two incidences pushed him to meet Katya at the Grand Canyon. There was his own internal drama pushing him to go on the vacation. And there was his dead grandmother that had previously said she would help him to meet someone. And all of this together had led to him making what would be his first movie.

Tian's experiences making the movie did seem to be charmed. The love triangle story between the character he would play and the two love interests, one a ghost and the other alive, came easily. The locations landed in his lap without effort. The crew volunteered their time and committed for the entire project. And the cast he used were excellent and exactly what Tian wanted. Tian didn't cast any celebrities, but each was well suited for the part and the actresses were attractive.

Tian took to directing easier than even he expected. Decision making came easily to Tian and on set Tian made hundreds of decisions each day. For the first time in Tian's life he felt like he was required to do just enough and it was a rush. His creative skills were being tapped the perfect amount, as were his people skills and management skills. His life was completely without down time, and his social life was all with his cast and crew.

By the second week of January the next year, shooting was complete. Tian celebrated by hang gliding off the cliffs of Blacks Beach in San Diego. The freedom in the air was amazing. The instructor that rode with him did all of the work except in the end when Tian was allowed to steer. Tian's feeling of exhilaration amplified just enough at the end of his flight as Tian almost missed the landing spot.

After gliding through the sky, he stripped down and lay naked in the sun on the nude beach below. He then finished the day with a full body massage at an expensive spa. Tian was learning to manage his lusts for dopamine. Barry from his whitewater rafting trip had helped him to understand his situation and now he was working with it. He figured that if he spoon-fed himself the dopamine every few months it would prevent decisions like the one that led to the adventure vacation.

When Tian got back home he went right to work. He first hoped that he could find an editor, but soon learned that he would have to teach himself. Editing came easy to him as well. He seemed to have a natural sense of storytelling rhythm, perhaps from all the hours that he had spent watching movies and TV as a kid. When the movie was complete he tested it with a few friends and then was ready to present it for sale.

Tian learned that movies were sold at film markets, one of which was in Santa Monica every year. Luckily the timing was perfect and he was able to get his movie in at the last moment. Tian imagined that the last of the process would be no problem. Tian felt a sense of flow to everything that had happened throughout the movie making process.

Tian considered God to be his producer. God had figured out ways to make even the insurmountable problem seem like an ant hill. And now Tian knew that God would get it sold.

But God didn't bring the perfect candidate to him during the film market. God didn't put Tian in contact with the best DVD distributor after the event. And God didn't make an appearance at any other time with Tian's movie.

The result was that Tian was disappointed. Tian went back through his memory to figure out what he had done wrong. He searched every moment he had had during making the movie for where he could have veered off of God's path. He couldn't find any.

So one night after all of the respectable people were in bed Tian hopped into his car and parked it on the edge of the neighborhood where the graffiti started. Tian got out of the car wearing sweatpants and a pair of running shoes. He stretched by leaning forward and pulling his head to his knees. He then got onto the ground, put his feet together and pushed his knees down. Afterwards he got up, stretched each of his knees by pulling them back and then started to run.

The metal bars that encircled each of the yards whipped by Tian as he ran. None of the homes had any lights on. That is what told him that he had a long way to run. When Tian turned off of the main street he knew that he was getting closer. More cars were driving by and there were groups of people that could now be spotted on different sides of the street.

At first a group of people would cause Tian to cross to the other side. But as they got more frequent Tian wondered what it would feel like to run by. He knew that he had to be a strange sight for them. No one jogs in their neighborhood. Would they see him as a victim waiting to be attacked? Or would they suspect that someone who was crazy enough to jog so late would have something waiting for them if they tried something against him.

Tian felt his runner's heartbeat race as he approached the first group. He tried to keep his rhythm the same. He didn't want the group to think that he had a reaction to them either way. He didn't even want to catch any of their eye lines by mistake.

As he got closer to the first group he could hear the conversation die off. They had noticed him. Tian felt his heart rate increase and the air he breathed in felt more pure. The shadowy light down the sidewalk became brighter as if he was now an owl ready to strike.

Tian continued to look forward, but as he got steps away he saw one of them take a step. Tian readied for what would come next without breaking a stride or changing his stare. And when Tian had passed the last one he knew to expect it from behind.

Time slowed down. He took one step. Nothing. He took another, and again nothing. Finally the third step came and there were no steps behind him. He had passed them all without incident.

Tian weaved up and down the side streets and each new group he passed by smoking, selling, getting high on the sidewalk let him pass without incident. It wasn't until Tian found the street where all of the prostitutes hung out that Tian's night was complete.

Tian saw the beastly things hanging out on the corner where the side street met the main. Tian had long entered his runner's stride and he knew that it would now be hard for him to stop. But as he approached he knew that stopping this time was inevitable. Tian approached the group of three bodies and looked forward just as he had before.

Time slowed down so that every step was memorable. The step 15 feet away was when they all had finally turned to look at him. The step 10 feet away was when the large one shifted her body to face Tian. The step 5 feet away was when the first one shifted back not knowing what to expect. And the step right next to them was when one of them reached out her hand to brush Tian as he ran by.

"Hay baby, with the fine body, you looking for something tonight?" the middle one said.

'That voice isn't female,' Tian thought as his body finally slowed to a stop. Tian breathed hard as he turned around and stared at the group. He was trying to figure out which had made the comment.

"You could bring some of that over here. I'll show you a really good time," the voice said again.

Tian felt the testostcrone thumping through his veins. He could feel his chest pop out and the darkness fill his mind. Tian looked at them and all he could see were pieces of meat, beastly, damaged, pieces of meat. Tian's eyes naturally squinted and his body movement rounded out. He slowly reached down into one of his pockets and then he felt the rush come again.

A year later Tian had come up with a new idea. The movie hadn't sold but he felt that he could take what he learned about the workings of God and the afterlife and make a TV show. Tian saw it as a matter of demographics. Those most interested in spiritual matter were people over 35. They didn't go to movies as often. However, they were heavy TV watchers and TV was the medium to reach them.

After his time off to make the movie, Tian returned to his previous job as a freelancer. There he met Brett Lawson. Brett was the executive producer of a production company responsible for the most irresponsible reality TV shows on the air. And after Tian and Brett became friends Brett invited Tian to pitch the company a few TV show ideas.

Tian didn't see how much of a long shot his ideas were. He simply came up with the ideas and presented them. "The message of the show I created is that there is life past earthly life and when that life interacts with this one, amazing things happen," Tian said to Julie, the company's head of development.

"I love it. Let's get some contracts moving. We want to option it and see if we can get it onto one of the networks," Julie announced.

Tian was thrilled. It was an incredible accomplishment for a first attempt and once again he saw the invisible hand of God at work. Tian searched out and contracted the best psychics in Los Angeles to be involved. The idea that Tian had in mind was for a miracle to happen each episode. It would be an extreme makeover with psychics. Participants would enter broken and then leave whole.

Julie loved the execution. And once the contract was signed Julie told Tian that the reason they optioned the show was because the Fact or Fiction Cable Network was looking for a psychic companion piece to go with their most popular, 'Believe it or Not' show. But because the company only created shows for the large networks, they would pitch the show with them before going to the smaller Fact or Fiction cable network.

Tian found the process long and tedious. Every few weeks Tian would contact Julie and find out the latest network to pass on the idea. When all of the major networks had passed, and then all of the major cable networks had passed Julie went to Fact or Fiction. However, too much time had passed from their initial request. The network had found their companion piece and Tian's show idea wasn't even heard.

The failure felt like a bubbling in Tian's stomach that restricted his breathing. He didn't believe in telling his friends about the emotional details of his life imagining it too intimate to share. And he since arriving to Los Angeles Tian never could find himself a girlfriend.

He had wanted a girlfriend and had searched for one. But each time he got close to any of the beautiful women that flocked to him, he could only imagine the project he would not create because he spent time with her. On his death bed he wanted to be able to say that he left the world better than he found it. And as much as he wanted an intimate companion, or even needed one, he imagined that a girlfriend could only take him further from his goal. That meant that when the failures came, which there were a lot of, Tian had only one resource, his escapes.

'This escape needs to require the fight for survival,' Tian decided. 'I need to know if I'm worthy to be here. If God doesn't like what I'm doing, he can take me. If he wants me to stay, I will survive.'

Tian bought a hiker's guide book from an outdoorsman store and chose a trail. The guide book rated it as a four day hike with limited resources. The terrain was uneven and required multiple rock climbs. So Tian packed up: a few changes of clothes, a few protein bars, breakfast drinks, water, a tent, a sleeping bag, and climbing gear and then hitchhiked to the starting site.

Tian managed to work his way through the food within the first 2 days. The hike was more physically demanding than Tian imagined and every three hours Tian required protein to keep his legs moving. On the 3rd day water was the only thing on the menu and even that was growing short.

Tian found himself stopping a lot and fell short of where he marked as his day three rest stop. Making that rest stop was important because that was where he was going to refill his water supply. Tian started day four out of water and very light on his feet. And when it came time to cross the clearing of trees Tian stood under the surrounding rim of trees wondering if he would make it.

'This would be so much easier if I just had some food,' Tian wrestled his mind long enough to think. 'I don't know if I'm going to make it. But I definitely won't make it if I stay here. Maybe I could live here,' Tian's lucid mind began to think. 'I could just live here on the outskirts of the trees that lead to the desert.'

Tian's mind became less and less clear. But somewhere in all of the random thoughts and words was the phrase, "keep on going." Unable to differentiate between the real and the imaginary Tian took it as an unquestionable order and directed his movement in the direction of the desert.

The sun hurt Tian. It baked down onto his sun-darkened skin and distracted him more from what should have been his focus. He moved his feet slowly. But he knew that as long as he kept them moving, no matter how slow, eventually he would reach the end.

During the walk he had thoughts he would remember afterwards. He wondered how it was that God could let this happen. But it wasn't the hike he was referring to, it was all of it. It was his entire life. He had openly given up his entire life to do God's will and here he found himself dying alone under the hot, merciless sun.

Tian didn't make it all the way across the open area. He instead found himself on his knees struggling to focus his eyes with his butcher knife in one hand and his opposite wrist turned upwards. He knelt a long time struggling to see the objects that were two feet from his eyes. He never could. He instead collapsed onto the ground only to wake up a few hours after the sun went down.

Tian's body hurt when he woke up, but his mind had sharpened into a singular focus. Under the sun he had dreamt that there was a stream somewhere in front of him. And all of his subsequent dreams were about overcoming dreamlike obstacles that prevented him from getting there.

Tian was very dizzy when he worked his way to his feet and more than a little nauseous. The earth dipped and swayed when Tian closed his eyes to blink so he did what he could to keep his eyes as wide as possible. When the pack seemed a ridiculous luxury Tian took it off and walked away from it.

Each small step lead to another. And many small steps in the future Tian got to the edge of what was a small pond. Tian couldn't remember what the guide book had said about it and instead allowed instinct to take over. Tian fell down onto his knees once again and this time cupped his hand under his mouth.

The water made his stomach gurgle when he first drank it and he briefly imagined that while he slept he had become allergic to water. But as the smaller and smaller sips made it into his mouth his brain began to clear. He considered going back for his pack and almost abandoned the idea until he realized that his canteen was still attached to it. So when he became stronger he went back for his pack and then rested by the pond for the night.

Tian awoke before sunrise and was again ready to go. He consulted his guide book and realized that he would have one more day of solid hiking before he would reach the convenience store on the other side of the woods. It was there where Tian planned to catch a bus that would take him back to LA, back to life. And all that was necessary for this reward was persistence. Tian started immediately and had reached the trees before the sun was fully up.

Tian reached the store before sunset and must have looked like death walking in.

"Are you ok?" the attendant yelled at the dazed, parched man fumbling through his store.

Tian didn't answer and instead collected an arrangement of food from the snack aisle. Tian grabbed a handful of food and a cold sports drink from the freezer. The cold of the drink burned his tender forearm and he couldn't wait to pour everything he found onto the counter.

"Do you need some help?" the attendant asked, trying to catch Tian's darting eyes.

Tian heard the man and did his best to reply but instead decided to reach for his wallet and offer his debit card. It was like a flash of ecstasy when the sugar of the food reached Tian's brain. It was like a switch clicked on and almost immediately complete thoughts returned to Tian's mind.

Tian's first thoughts were how he would never do anything like that again. He thought about how stupid he was for putting himself into that situation. He thought about how close he had come to death. And he thought about how glad he was that he had finally worked this constant death wish out of his system.

Tian imagined how great his life would be now that it was free of these crazy risks. And Tian considered how lucky he had been that he worked through it without any major damage to himself or others. It was with that thought that he found a desire to smile.

But what Tian didn't realize was that the bus that took him back to LA, also took him back to the life he had left a week before. So it was only six weeks before Tian took another late night run. And after that Tian required a jolt every three weeks instead of every month.

When Tian established a relationship with a children's network to come up with movie ideas, Tian again felt his life taking a positive turn. But in spite of his diligence and planning each rejected movie set Tian back a little more. Every two months Tian presented three ideas, one of which would be taken into the network's monthly internal pitch session. And every two months like clockwork, Tian received a call from his contact letting him know his idea was rejected.

It was the final attempt that hurt Tian the most. That was the one that most tested his sense of purpose. Tian in a final attempt at selling to this client brought on a writing partner that was more successful at story structure than he was. He attached an award winning producer to the project. And instead of getting one approval from his development contact, he searched for many small approvals along the way. That way the project would be as much a sure thing as it could be.

But it was the smaller approvals that killed the project. Early in the process the children's network development client made a decision about the project that unknowingly killed the project for her boss.

"My boss didn't like that it was an ensemble cast. He thought that they were too hard to do," Tian's contact told him.

'It was you that chose the ensemble storyline,' Tian thought.

"Maybe you should take a break from pitching for a while. Good luck with everything," she said.

It was this exchange that led Tian into a road trip around the continent. He had often thought about Katya and the fearlessness that lead her to travel the country sleeping in her car. So that was the inspiration for Tian's transcontinental national parks tour.

With water, and breakfast drinks packed in his car, Tian traveled up to Yosemite National park thinking that that would be the end of it. But standing on the plateaus of Yosemite made Tian remember a couple that had worked as extras on the movie Tian worked on in the Bahamas. They had told Tian that if he ever got the chance he should go to Redwood National park. So that is where he headed next.

Tian then found that that wasn't enough. So when Tian remembered that he was on his way to Vancouver when he detoured to see his statue, he headed to Stanley Park, Vancouver. And then when all of the driving and trees didn't ease Tian's mind he found himself on Highway 1 crossing the country.

Tian considered taking a detour into Toronto, but decided against it when he realized that the city would get a false impression of him in the state that he now found himself. When he was last there, he was a skinny, confused, lost man. Now Tian was a producer, and a writer. And Tian knew that if he would just drive in for the day, the city wouldn't see how much he had changed. The city would miss how much stronger he had become. And when Toronto saw him again, Tian needed the city see that it hadn't defeated him. So instead Tian continued his trip to the city that he always said he would visit but never did.

Tian slept in his car outside of Montreal and then spent his day walking through Parc Mont-Royal. It was the park that overlooked the city but it wasn't enough to occupy a full day. So after a brief tour through old Montreal, Tian turned his tour south.

Again in the States, Tian drove through Kentucky and Tennessee. Tian toured the Smokey Mountains, then a slave plantation in Charleston, South Carolina. Tian then made his way to Florida where he parked his car and spent two weeks in the Bahamas. After that Tian drove through the Gulf States stopping at New Orleans for a day before driving through Texas.

A full month had almost gone by as Tian approached Carlsbad Caverns National Park. And it wasn't until Tian stood within the cool air of the million year old caverns that he felt his life force return to him.

The caverns were the most beautiful thing that Tian had seen in his life. The way that the light shown on the hanging rocks and the haunting echo of slow water drops ushered all of Tian's other thoughts away.

It was walking amongst the high ceilings of this cavern in the mountain that Tian realized what he had just done. Tian had walked in a forest and a desert. He had looked out onto the Pacific Ocean and then swam in the Atlantic. He had been on top of mountains, and then walked within them. And he had visited more natural beauties than many would see in a lifetime. 'I have finally done something,' Tian thought. And it was with that thought that Tian drove home.

Unfortunately with that trip, the excursions that happened every three weeks needed to adjust down to every two weeks. Tian did a lot of running, before discovering wakeboarding. It was his time on the water that allowed his attention to then switch to surfing. And finally when all of the freelance work dried up, and he began to run out of money he decided that he wanted to take a swim with the dolphins.

'How incredible it would be if I met these intelligent creatures with nothing more than what they presented to me.' Tian didn't want to have any pockets, or any backpacks. He wanted it to be an act of purity. Tian wanted it to be something natural, devoid of the complexity of modern society. 'I want to meet them on their terms with my palms open and my arm stretched out. I just need to get away from all of this for a little while. That's all. I just need a little escape.'

Tian didn't wake when the dolphin had pushed him in his row boat into the side of a 30 foot sailing yacht. He also didn't wake as the residents of the yacht scuffled around trying to figure out what to do next. It wasn't until someone lifted Tian out of the rowboat that Tian came to and vomited upwards into his mouth.

As Tian choked, the CMT flipped Tian onto his side and let the vomit drip out of his mouth into the yellow Malibu sand. It was now late enough in the morning that surfers were there to watch the rescue of the tall, naked man from the wooden rowboat.

A couple of the surfers scowled their face when they saw how discolored his abdomen was. A few of them assumed that Tian was already dead. They couldn't account for the vomiting, but all those that knew to look for it recognized the death stare. Tian's eyes had somehow popped open, but it was clear that there was no longer anyone inside.

The paramedics did everything they could to keep Tian conscious. More than anyone they recognized the death stare. What they didn't recognize was the abdominal bleeding. They knew what it was, but they couldn't figure out how the naked man had sustained it. It wasn't until two minutes before arriving at the hospital that one of them said, "Do you think that he was swimming naked with the dolphins?"

They looked down at Tian's lucid face and saw that they could be free to laugh. They both chuckled knowing that this was going to be a story that they would tell for years to come. And as the young one wrapped the blanket over Tian's bare flesh, he looked down at the speckles of grey in Tian's hair. He saw something both sad and haunting about the man lying beneath him. 'He doesn't look like a stupid hippy,' the young man thought. And instead of trying to process all of the possible causes of Tian's predicament, he simply turned his head and thought, 'idiot.'

CHAPTER 16

Irabell took a few steps through the wheat and allowed the husks to brush against his calves. He considered it his opportunity to step into the past. He often thought about the decisions he made during life, but he never allowed himself to wish that he were back. But in this tonal field the velvety brushes of the wheat took him back.

Tian took a few steps behind Irabell. For him the past had come back to life. His earthly experience wasn't what he would have designed it to be. He took some respite in the fact that his earthly existence wasn't hard. The lives he considered hard were the ones that required work from childhood to death. It was those where the word backbreaking was often thrown around.

Tian's life wasn't backbreaking and it wasn't hard but it was nothing that Tian wanted to return to. The best word Tian could use to describe his life was "fruitless." Because for all of his attempts and all of his desires, nothing that he planted bore fruit. He was born in usual circumstances, acquired all of the information that he could and then tried to share it with whoever would listen. But the hard lesson that Tian had to learn was that no one cared to listen.

It was the "finding of those that wanted to listen" part that Tian thought would be the easiest when he was a kid. When Tian was a kid, the one thing that he was sure would be taken care of by God would be finding the audience. Tian simply believed that if he built it, they would come. And as Tian grew older and realized that he was no longer a favorite child of God he still believed that being a devotee would be enough to gain favor.

But that turned out not to be true either. "Fruitless" would be the perfect word to describe Tian's life, because to others, Tian's life seemed to be constantly flowering. Others found Tian's life great to watch and found him pleasant to be around. However that's all it ever was. None of those flowers ever turned to anything of substance. And for that fruitlessness Tian blamed God.

"I have to ask you again," Irabell said breaking the silence, "when you say God, what are you referring to?"

Tian thought for a moment about his life and the role that he expected God to play in it. "Once when I was starting what I thought would be my new life, I had a dream. In that dream I died. That was the way I expected it to be when I arrived here. And in that dream I seemed to understand something that I had no doubt about. It was that God was love. He is that thing that binds the world together. He is the force that created all of us."

"And during your life, when you referred to God, what were you referring to? How did you imagine God?" Irabell asked.

"I guess I imagined him like a friend. Someone that I liked and who paid varying amounts of attention to me. He was sort of like my boss. I did things that I thought would please him so that at the end of the day I would get my reward."

"And when things didn't work out the way that you thought, when you thought God let you down, what did you conclude?"

"I guess I questioned whether or not my perception of God was correct. I questioned whether any of the things that I thought to be real was real. I questioned if there was an afterlife. I questioned if I was really psychic. And I questioned if there was even a purpose to life."

"And now what do you think about all of those things that you questioned?"

Tian paused and looked around. "Well, standing here looking at everything, I am sure that the afterlife exists. And from everything that you told me I now believe that at least most of the psychic things that happened to me actually happened. I don't know if there is a purpose to life yet though."

"Tell me Tian, you can look out at this field and see all of these species from so many different worlds, do you think that any of them ever believed in a God?"

Tian looked out at the rock that seemed to be alive. He watched the ray that seemed to be flying over the wheat. "Yes, I imagine that they did."

"What qualities would you imagine that these creatures would attribute to their God?"

Tian looked at Irabell inquisitively. Tian had never thought of that question before. When Irabell told his stories about the other species the one thing that connected all of them for Tian was how their environments shaped who they were as a species. Tian remembered the squid-like creature that Irabell used to explain how the energy in this world was connected to the physical world. When Tian was experiencing that creature's life in the ocean library, Tian didn't even know that it was pregnant. And finally when it gave birth if felt no connection to the creature that came out of it.

If human love had evolved as a way of ensuring the survival of young as Irabell had described, then the squid-like creature probably didn't evolve to experience love. Therefore, if the highly intelligent squid-like creature ever considered the existence of a God, love wouldn't be an attribute that that species would attribute to it.

Tian also thought about the bug like creatures that had learned to feed off of lightning and who communicated with the afterlife. They probably didn't attribute the same magic to the afterlife that humans did, because for them it was a storage unit. This is where they housed their thoughts. As far as they were concerned it was a place of their invention. It would be the equivalent of the hard drives on human computers. No one on earth would consider a man made hard drive as the kingdom of God. So Tian imagined that their God probably had a completely different purpose and set of rules.

"I don't know what qualities these creatures may consider the qualities of God," Tian confessed. "You're right though, they would probably be different from what I would say."

"So, which one is correct? Is it the one that humans have come up with? Or is it the one that the winged elephant has devised?"

"I don't know," Tian admitted.

"Your perception of God is like a person. He's your friend, you said. He pays varying amounts of attention to you. He is love. Which social group did you hold in the highest esteem?"

"What do you mean," Tian asked.

"Did you most value your mother or father? Was it a sibling or a spouse?"

"Sometime when I was young a distance developed between me and my family. And for some reason I always considered a spouse to be a hindrance to what I was trying to accomplish. So I guess I most valued my friends."

"So your image of God is that God is your friend. However during the times of Jesus, God wasn't known that way. Life was hard for those people. They had little protection for the whims of the authority, and had no protection from disease. It was a very scary time, and their perception of God was, 'God the father.' They wanted a God that could keep them safe.

Tell me Tian, whose image is correct? Is God a friend that allows you to explore the alternatives of life, or is it the strict disciplinarian that rewards you by keeping you safe? "

"I don't know."

"Or is the image that humans have created of a loving God, more correct than a species that didn't develop a pleasure based reinforcement system for protecting their young?"

"I don't know," Tian repeated sheepishly.

Irabell looked at Tian kindly. "When I told you about the species that helped to create where we are now, I tried to also show how their environment and biology shaped who the species evolved into. Do you think it's possible that in each case the species developed an idea of God that evolved out of their environment and their biology?"

"Yes, I can."

"And how all of the qualities they associate with God are simply the qualities that they value the most from their own experiences?"

"Yes I do."

"So again I ask you, what is it that you refer to when you ask me about God?" Irabell asked as gently as possible.

Tian remained silent for a while. He wasn't trying to process the information as much as he was allowing the dust to settle in his mind. When his thoughts started to clear he replied, "I guess what I should ask you is…" Tian's mind drifted again while trying to get the words exactly right. "I don't know what I'm trying to ask," Tian admitted.

Tian paused for yet another moment of thought. "So all of the time when I put my faith in God to help me out of a situation, I was putting my faith in something that didn't exist?" Tian asked a little upset.

"It existed to you."

"But I may as well have been praying to Santa Claus. Is that what you're saying?"

"Prayer is something else. A quality of humans is that perception is more important than reality. If a girl believes that a guy loves her, she will feel exactly the same whether it's true or not. If a guy believes his job is secure, he will feel exactly the same whether or not he is about to be fired. And if a human believes that they are protected and safe, they will act exactly the same whether they are about to be killed or whether they will live forever. In each case it is their perception that dictates how they act.

Prayer is a technique that has the benefit of focusing the mind. When you continuously pray about a desired outcome it has an effect on the human brain. It places the desired outcome in the forefront of your mind. It means that during the day as a person makes the thousand decisions that they make every day they are also thinking about their desired outcome.

So if your desired outcome is to buy a house and you prayed on it every night, your day to day decisions help you achieve it. For example, because buying a house is in the front of your mind, you may think twice about buying a new TV. You might think about saving the money instead.

And let's say that you have bad credit. And one of the thousand things that you heard which didn't make it into your consciousness might be a way of improving your credit. Because you know that good credit is necessary to buy a house, improving your credit might pop to the top of your mind if you are praying about buying a house.

And also, if you pray about a desired outcome, and there is something that your followers on this side can do to help, they may help. Because there are so many more of us on this side than there are physical lives, everyone alive has many followers. They hang out in the ocean library and they experience your life along with you. And when they see something that they can help you with, they help. It would be the same as if a friend came to you wanting your help. Would you assist them if you could? And because they are unseen and living outside the physical world, would that make them gods?"

"No, it doesn't," Tian concluded.

"Prayer is not a waste. But because your prayers come true, doesn't mean it was because of the will of a God. So again I ask you, what is it that you're asking me about God?"

Tian again allowed the mental dust to settle. Slowly each word came out of the cloud in his mind. "God is that which created us. What is it that created us?"

"When you say 'us' who are you referring to? Do you mean the species that we are, or do you mean the physical world?"

Tian remembered the book of Genesis in the bible. In it God created man. "I mean who created the physical world."

"Everything that exists in the physical world was created by the execution of a series of universal laws. Everything in the physical world is acting in a way that will put it in a state of homeostasis.

Molecules attract and repel each other hoping to achieve a state of balance. Life was first created because the smallest of molecules were trying to reach a state of balance. Consciousness was achieved because molecules were trying to achieve a state of balance. And each life within the physical world acts in such a way that that it thinks will help it to achieve a state of balance.

However, the physical world's draw towards balance is constantly being interrupted by the chaos created by the world's failed attempts at balance. When all of physical matter clasped down onto itself, it did it because of the gravitational pull of matter. But when all of matter collapsed on itself in a failed attempt at homeostasis, it resulted in the most chaotic of all events, the big bang.

This intense release of energy caused molecules to bond that might not have naturally balanced together. So when it comes in contact with its natural balancing agent, change occurs. The big bang caused deep wells of energy that caused hydrogen to bond with itself. That in turn released unintended energy that in turn reacted with molecules that were looking to achieve balance. From that planets were formed. The formation of planets caused further change, and out of this pull between a striving for balance and a reaction to chaos, the physical world was created.

That is what created man. Is that the God you were looking for?"

Tian thought for a moment and then asked, "But who set it all in motion?"

"Who?" Irabell asked. "Are you looking for a gender, because gender only exists in physical beings that need two sexes to reproduce? And since everything that was physical shaped itself at the moment of the big bang, a gender could not have done it.

If you are asking which personality traits set it in motion, I ask you to remember that personality is a reflection of the physical body's attempt to manipulate the world. Personality, like gender could not have preceded the big bang."

"So, you're saying that no one could have set this physical process into motion, but something could have. But if it was 'something' it wouldn't reflect the traits that the physical world created in order to balance itself. So essentially, if there was a god, a something that set the universal laws into motion, it wouldn't be anything that a physical being would recognize as life?

So what you're saying is that there is no being that both created us and watches over us?"

"How could there be? But don't think that I'm implying that you are alone in life. You are not alone in your life. There are those that watch over every physical being. In fact there are many. And when they can, they help. But there is no super being that makes conscious decisions about the direction and details of your life. The direction and details of your life are decided each day, with each choice that we make. With each moment you shape your own future and there is nothing supernatural about it."

Tian was not in a rush to disrupt the peace that Irabell's words engendered in him. But Tian had to ask the obvious next question. "What is it that created our species in the non-physical world?"

"All that there is exists in many forms. The physical world is one dimension, but there are many non-physical dimensions. Ours is simply the main one that interacts with the physical universe. But all of them follow the same laws. We on this side exist to balance life within the physical dimension. Without physical life, it is theorized that we would exist in balance.

However, the physical dimension does exist and we are connected to it. We cannot separate ourselves from the attempt at balance that the physical dimension looks to achieve. It is this connection that proves that our two worlds are one governed by the same laws in each case. So, to answer your question, that which created the physical dimension also created our dimension. And the source of those laws wouldn't fall under anything we recognize as life either."

"So God, as I had imagined it throughout my life, doesn't exist?" Tian asked with the signs of heartbreak in his voice.

Irabell simply responded with a sympathetic feeling that Tian recognized.

"But I lived my entire life based on the belief that there was a God looking after me. I don't know what I am supposed to do now," Tian admitted as he found himself lost in a foreign land.

"Well, one thing that you have to do is decide whether or not you would like to go back."

"Where?"

"To the life you left."

"I didn't want to tell you this, but I can't go back. I can't be alive. I died in the woods that day I met you. There is nothing to go back to."

"You didn't die. You are still alive. And if you want to go back, you have the choice."

Tian looked at Irabell and felt the first truly human emotion that he felt since arriving here, dread. "I don't know how I could make that decision. Why would I go back? What would be the point?"

"Tian, there are some people that I would like you to meet. Can I take you to them?"

Tian starting to feel the full weight of his life come back to him, nodded his heavy head in agreement and in moment, both were gone.

CHAPTER 17

The first thing that Tian noticed when he became conscious was the smell of antiseptic. It was the same smell that permeated Tian's pediatrician's office whenever Tian was about to get an injection. Tian hated that smell. And he had learned to hate the doctor's office even more.

Tian wasn't a healthy child. He caught every childhood disease imaginable. And what made it worse for Tian's parents was that every time they took one of their parents only vacations, they would always return to find Tian in the hospital. It became a running joke for Patrick and a non-stop dread for all of the relatives that would watch the kids while the parents were away.

Dr. Mohamed, Tian's pediatrician blamed it on separation anxiety. The doctor proposed that Tian's stress hormone cortisol spiked when his parents left. This spike caused a suppression of Tian's immune system making him more susceptible to infection.

This diagnosis kept Tian's parents close. Tian became their porcelain doll. He was the child that they were careful with. He was the one that they first considered before taking long trips. And he was the one they hugged a little longer before putting their kids to bed.

The pinnacle of their concern came when Tian was five years old. Tian's dad took the family on a cruise around the Caribbean. It was a two week long trip and had seven ports of call. Tian enjoyed the trip thoroughly. It was the greatest adventure of his young life. And during each stop young Tian would take in the sights and the people.

Tian wasn't scared when at the Haitian marketplace 30 people surrounded his family cajoling them to buy another banana tree silk portrait. Tian found it fun being lifted onto his dad's shoulders and being rushed off. And when the taxi driver sped around the narrow mountain roads in the Jamaican Blue Mountains, Tian wondered why his mom gripped his hand so tightly.

But it was when every port was visited and the ship was on its way back that Tian became sick. Tian didn't feel particularly bad, but when Tian's mom took him to the ship's doctor, the doctor suggested that Tian stay. Tian found the ship's infirmary to be very uncomfortable and what's worse the nurse wouldn't let him get a good night's sleep. Every time Tian would get deep into slumber, the nurse would wake him up asking if Tian wanted something to drink.

Little Tian wasn't told this, but what he had was a serious case of pneumonia. The nurse had been on constant vigil because the doctor was afraid that Tian would die while he slept. In fact, on the day before they docked, Tian did lose consciousness and awoke to find himself alone in a hospital room.

It was his mother that was the first one to arrive. Later it was Tian's dad and Pat. This was still their vacation so they didn't want to spend their entire trip in a hospital. And to that end Tian's dad was chosen to take Pat to the toy store. When they all arrived and Tian saw that they were having fun without him, Tian wanted to join them. Tian couldn't understand why he was being forced to miss out on all of the fun.

That trip marked a turn in Tian's health. After that cruise Tian no longer had what Dr. Mohamed called separation anxiety. In fact, it was quite the opposite. Tian became the first of his friends to do full sleepovers. Tian became the first of his friends to jump off bridges into canals. And Tian became the first of his friends to announce that he would be moving off the island when he became an adult. Tian didn't know where he would move to, but Tian anticipated that adventure would abound.

As Tian got older he figured out that it was never the high moments or stressful moments that Tian had a problem. Tian learned that he was at his best in those moments. No, what Tian learned he had a hard time dealing with were the slow times. It was the day to day monotony of school that did something to him. It was the daily routine of getting up, doing, and then doing again that got Tian sick.

Tian would often have a record number of sick days each year while being completely healthy during the summer.

It wasn't until Tian discovered meditation in his teenage years that everything evened out. After meditation nothing external bothered Tian anymore. The monotony was dulled and the teenaged insults from classmates were muted.

But after giving up the monastic life at 17, serenity was something that Tian never achieved again. The excitements and uncertainties became much to thrilling to Tian to forget during meditation. In fact, with all of the disappointments and failures that Tian experienced, those thrills became his one saving grace. And as the failures piled on further, Tian began to see the thrills as his life.

Somewhere along the line Tian's life stopped being about trying to find projects that he could create to help people, and started to be about the thrill of the chase. Tian imagined that this wouldn't have been true if any of his projects had succeeded. But after 15 years not one of them had. Not with God as a producer, or an inspiration.

The irony was that during those 15 years Tian watched the people around him achieve all of the things that he had strove for. Two of his friends had sold scripts. One of his friends had created two television shows. And three of his friends had published their first attempts at books. It was Tian's distinction alone to be the guy that co-produced and co-wrote with God. And it was Tian's distinction to be the smartest, most interesting and least accomplished.

Ultimately Tian couldn't help but notice that all of his friends wrote about topics that were interesting to others. While Tian chose to write about topics that could help others. More specifically, it was Tian's choice to write about topics that would give people a different way of looking at life.

Tian felt that he too could create reality shows about sex and money, but he chose not to. Tian felt that he could write books about kids making tough life decisions, but he chose not to. Tian saw that his failures weren't because he didn't know what entertained people. His failures were because he thought that he was on a mission designed by a higher power. Tian thought of himself as someone special, and thought it would be a betrayal of all of his gifts if he used it for anything other than the peaceful, enlightenment of society.

But lying in that hospital bed with his eyes closed he saw where that way of thinking had led him. As important as success was too him, he was unemployed, alone and career-wise a failure. He was a man that used all of the money he made to create projects that no one wanted to read or watch. And he was someone that needed a constant stream of dopamine to both help him forget, and to keep him going.

His was not the life he imagined as he drove toward Toronto a newly designated college graduate. And what was more was that the core belief he built his life on turned out to be wrong. All of the books he read when he was introduced to the spiritual life said that all that was necessary was faith. Those books called upon a blind faith. They espoused that if you let go and let God, your life would be successful and full of love.

Well, Tian knew that he had spent a lifetime letting go and letting God, and this was where he was. He was lying in a hospital bed, smelling antiseptic, scared to open his eyes in fear of what dreams may come. But when he felt a hand touch his wrist looking for his pulse he couldn't help but see who it was.

"You're awake," the short Filipino nurse said with the chubby cheeks. "Can you hear me?"

Tian wanted to clear his mind before answering. He knew that somewhere in his memory was a thought of him in a hospital, and in that memory he was there on purpose. In that memory he was to purposefully remain silent. And Tian couldn't remember if this was the execution of that thought or some other thing.

"Follow my finger," the nurse said moving her chubby finger back and forth in front of Tian's face. "That's good. Do you feel any pain?"

Tian reacted very little. He searched his body for pain and found some all around his abdomen. 'Why am I in pain?' Tian wondered.

"Can you tell me what your name is?" the nurse asked.

'They don't have my name,' Tian realized. 'I am anonymous. Is that right? Was that how the plan was supposed to go? But why is there pain?'

"Ok. I'm going to get the doctor and she can explain to you what happened," the nurse said before turning to walk off.

Tian examined the room. Now that his consciousness was back, he found it to be a noisy room. The space was longer than it was wide, and it was full of beds that lined the walls. The ceiling tiles were cracked and water stained and the three nurses that circled seemed barely enough to take care of everyone that was there.

A few minutes later a doctor approached. It was a heavy set Russian woman who wobbled a little when she walked. She planted herself next to Tian's bed and began to speak.

"So everything is now ok. When you were brought in you had some internal bleeding coming from your right renal artery so we had to remove your right kidney and now you're fine. Ok?"

Tian lost his breath for a moment. In that instance Tian felt like he was floating between one world and the next. After a moment he was no longer sure, 'did I hear that she removed my kidney?'

Without Tian saying a word, the doctor continued. "We used laparoscopic surgery so you will have only small scares and you should be feeling better soon, ok? That was your right kidney. When we were in there we checked out your left kidney. You have a broken rib. It is the one at the bottom of your rib cage." The doctor took a moment to place her finger above his rib.

"And your left kidney has heavy lacerations and it had some damage to the left renal artery but we were able to repair it. Right now what we are going to keep our eye on is your left kidney. If it is able to heal itself you will have nothing to worry about. If the kidney is too far damaged then we will have to consider some alternatives."

"What alternatives?" Tian said in a voice that he didn't recognize.

"You are young so you would be a good candidate for a kidney transplant. We would put you on the donor list. And only if your kidney fails to recover we would put you on dialysis."

"Is that where you have to wear a bag on your stomach?" Tian asked.

"There are two different types of dialysis. One is called continuous ambulatory peritoneal dialysis. That is where a tube is inserted into your abdomen and five or six times a day you can flush your kidneys at home. The other is continuous cycling peritoneal dialysis. This is where you would come into a faculty sometime during the day and have your kidney flushed. After that you are free to carry on your normal activities during the day. But before we seriously talk about either option, we are going to see how well your kidney recovers."

"When will we know if I have to get dialysis?" Tian said with fear in his voice.

"Well, we are going to monitor you for a couple of days. And if you continue to improve, we will let you go home. Then when you're at home you will have to watch out for blood in your pee and a feeling like you want to throw up. If you have any of those symptoms, you come back and we'll talk about dialysis. Do you have any other questions?"

"Yeah, what happened?"

"What do you mean?"

"Was I in an accident?"

"You don't remember? We were hoping that you could tell us. The people that brought you in said that they found your body in a rowboat and you were wearing flippers. We were assuming that you were attached by sea lions or dolphins."

Tian got flashes of memory before turning his head away from the doctor.

"If you remember anything let us know. It could help us to explain your injuries."

"Is there anything else?" Tian asked hoping that the doctor would go away and it would all be a dream.

"You also have some slight liver damage. You have lacerations directly below what we think is the point of impact. But those should heal without any problems. Any more questions?"

"No."

"Then the nurse will be back in a little while to get your information and emergency contacts in case we need to get a hold of them. Ok?"

Tian shook his head and released a closed mouth sigh in acknowledgement. When the doctor walked off Tian looked around at all of the bodies lying motionless in their beds and wished for privacy. Knowing that he would get none he pretended that no one was around.

He let his face twist and distort into the sad little boy that he felt like and without anyway of stopping it he broke down into an ugly, loud cry. He knew that everyone in the room could hear him, but he couldn't control himself. In the brief moments after he had opened his eyes, his life had changed forever. Tian wasn't ready for it.

Four days later the hospital was ready to release Tian. They had had him walking around the hospital as soon as he became conscious. While Tian was on the painkillers the cuts into his abdomen felt tight. But during the periods between when the old meds wore off and the new ones kicked in, the incision points felt like they were on fire. Tian dreaded going through therapy when the meds were wearing down. But what motivated him was knowing that if he didn't push himself now it would be more painful once he got home.

When the fourth day came Tian didn't feel ready. After years of roommates Tian finally lived alone. And this was not something that he was going to tell his friends about. Tian found this whole thing to be embarrassing. He realized that he brought it onto himself. And after a lifetime of being known to his friends as the adventurous soul, he didn't now want to be known as the sick one.

The doctor explained Tian's situation to him on the day Tian was scheduled to leave the hospital. "I would prefer to keep you here for a couple of more days, but without insurance there's not much more we can do."

"That's ok. I'm beginning to miss my life anyway," Tian said mustering up a smile.

"Do you have someone that can take care of you?"

"Absolutely."

"Who's that?"

"A friend. She said she'll take care of everything."

The doctor knew that Tian hadn't had any visitors and didn't give an emergency contact. But since there was nothing she could do to help, she left the lie as it was. "Ok, because you are going to need a lot of help. Your bandages have to continue to be replaced once a day. If they aren't you can get an infection and you'll end up right back here."

"Ok."

"And your kidneys seem to be improving but I want you to keep monitoring it. If you begin to feel nauseous or if you see blood in your urine, come back here and we will set you up for dialysis. Do you understand that?"

"Yes."

"This is very important because if you miss those symptoms you can die, and then there's nothing we can do for you," the doctor said with a smile.

"Yes, I understand that if I die there is nothing that you can do for me," Tian repeated smiling back.

"I want you to take care of yourself now. Ok?"

"Wait I have a question. How long would I have from the time that I start seeing blood in my pee before I die?"

"As soon as you see it, come right in?"

"I know. But if I miss it, how long would I have before I die?"

"You don't have to worry. The blood in the urine would be very easy to see. Just look down when you pee and you wouldn't miss it," the doctor replied.

"That's not what I'm asking you."

"I know."

"How long?"

"It's tough to say. Maybe two weeks."

"Would my death be painful?"

"Yes it would. It would be a horrible way to die."

"Ok, thank you."

"You take care of yourself now."

"Thank you for your help," Tian concluded before the doctor walked away.

On the taxi ride back home Tian looked at the painkillers that he was given. It was enough for 10 days. He knew that he could renew the prescription but he would need cash for that.

On the ride home he now considered how much his life would change. His saving grace, and his self prescribed therapy always was that he could put his life in danger. Those moments felt like a breath of air when he was choking. Tian couldn't imagine what his life could be like without his escapes and Tian feared finding out.

Tian found himself lying in bed for all of the first few days after the hospital. Tian no longer had his car. He had parked it at the beach before his accident, so he was sure that it was now impounded with fees that were higher than the value of car. And Tian no longer had his phone since he had buried it with his clothes at the beach.

But when it was clear that Tian would run out of food he went into his garage and brushed off the seven years of dust that had settled on his motorcycle. He had bought the bike shortly after arriving in LA after the car that had driven him from Texas broke down.

For the three years that had followed his arrival Tian referred to himself as a 'motorcycle rider' and not 'a person without a car'. Being a biker had become a part of his identity. The danger, the isolation, it all fed into the image that he had of himself. It was only a futile attempt at finding a girlfriend that led to the car.

It was actually just a conversation between him and his college friend Jeanie that drove him toward a car.

"You know, I think that I'm actually ready to be in a relationship," Tian said.

"Well the first thing you will have to do is get a car. Because no women who looks like the type of girl you're attracted to is going to get on the back of a motorcycle," Jeanie joked.

It was the next day that Tian met up with a friend and started looking for a car.

"And you know what else you'll need? A job. And not one of those I'm working today, but not tomorrow jobs. Women want their boyfriends to have jobs."

It was only a few days after that that Tian accepted Ron's offer of a full time position. It was the first full time position that Tian ever had.

"And you know what else you have to do? You have to figure out your whole immigration thing, because no woman wants to date a guy thinking that they are only with them so that they could get their green card."

It was a few weeks after that that Tian asked one of his friends to marry him. It would be strictly platonic and last no more than three years. The friend that Tian asked was a bit of a wild girl, and it fit her self image to say yes on a whim without considering the consequences. The marriage allowed Tian to get his green card but the friendship didn't last. Their marriage stumbled past the finish line giving Tian the status he needed with slightly more pain than he expected.

"If you do that, then even you can find a girlfriend," Jeanie said with a chuckle.

"Wow, you know Jeanie, that almost sounded like a compliment. You know, as much as you can bring yourself to compliment someone," Tian said with a snort.

"No, I could compliment someone."

"Really, then why don't you tell me how good-looking I am? You know I'm hard to resist," Tian said with a flirtation laugh.

"No, I think you're good-looking. But you're good-looking like a vase. Sure you're great to look at, but what good are you past that," Jeanie said with a laugh.

"Ugh," Tian said without a smile. Somewhere deep inside Tian he knew Jeanie wasn't serious. But that was too similar to how Tian felt about himself to forget. And after transforming himself into Jeanie's ideal man didn't gain him a girlfriend, all that was left was for him was to chalk it up to his vase status.

As the years went on Tian would have flashes when he knew that he needed someone in his life. During those times he found himself presenting the sex appeal of the vase that he deep down believed himself to be. He acted with the women like the friend Annett believed Tian to be. And he treated the women like the hindrance to his success that he couldn't help but believe them to be.

So now as Tian stared at his dusty motorcycle considering how to get it started, he saw the life that lay ahead of him.

"If I couldn't find anyone to love me when I was free, how could I find someone with a bag of pee attached to my leg?" Tian wondered aloud.

Tian popped off the seat to reveal the battery and the pouch of tools. He quickly took the battery out and set it to charge for the next few hours. To Tian's amazement when Tian put the battery back the bike started. It didn't start on the first attempt, but after turning the charger to 'jump' the engine turned over and the bike was spouting seven years of dust and oil. 'How easily my old life welcomes me,' he thought. 'It's like I never left.'

Tian doubled up on his pain killers and then took his motorcycle for supplies. The higher dose of meds made him feel good. So after restocking his kitchen with food, he took the 40 minute ride to the beach to retrieve his buried clothes and phone. The ride there was uneventful and even a little fun.

When Tian leaned into the turns on Sunset Boulevard he remembered why he had enjoyed riding his motorbike. There was an unmatched freedom that came with feeling the wind in his face. And Tian felt the magic as he leaned his body as far as the physics would allow him. In fact, the bike seemed to give him the little boost that the meds could not. On the bike Tian could feel his almost forgotten rush.

The beach appeared too soon. Tian parked his bike and walked down the familiar sand. The lack of a rowboat made Tian imagine that this wasn't where they rescued him. With the angle that he rowed the boat, he imagined his boat would have drifted further down shore.

As Tian contemplated taking off his shoes and letting the sand run between his toes he noticed the sunset. It was one of those long Malibu sunsets. The thickness of the Los Angeles air allowed Tian to look directly into the sun as it touched the horizon. So still in his leather jacket Tian worked his way onto his butt and watched the sunset go down. There was no doubt that this was one of the most beautiful sunsets ever.

Tian remembered back to his time with Katya. He remembered what the sun had looked like as it dipped down behind the Grand Canyon. Tian thought about his childhood in the Bahamas. He remembered how there was always a swirl of oranges and red. But in spite of the company and in spite of the colors, this sunset on this day was the one that he hoped he could relive after his life was over.

When the last of the sun was gone Tian rolled himself onto his stomach and struggled to get back on his feet. The pain killers were wearing off. And in perfect symmetry the stark reality of where he was was starting to return.

Tian walked down the beach to where he buried his phone. The area seemed undisturbed. Scared to bend, Tian tried to slow his decent by slowly falling down onto his knees. But even with all of his effort a shot of pain reverberated through his body.

Tian cupped away handfuls of sand. Less than a foot deep he touched what felt like a plastic bag. Tian dug around for the tied top and pulled on it once it was found. Tian was kind of excited to finally get his phone back. Tian had often joked, "Let's see who loves me," when checking his messages. And now after over a week of hell, Tian looked forward to seeing that someone did love him.

Tian tore open the bag and turned his phone on. The phone went through its normal cycle and there it was. It was on. Tian waited for the message alert and nothing. Tian continued to stare knowing that it would take a moment for the phone to check the tower, and the tower to check the phone company, but still there was nothing.

Tian stared intently at the phone waiting for something to change, perhaps a text alert, perhaps a bill notification but nothing came. Tian would not let the discouragement that often came with inpatients over come him. Tian was determined to wait it out, but as long as he waited nothing changed.

Tian gathered his bag, stuck his phone in his pocket and planned out how he would make it to his feet with a minimum amount of pain. There was no easy solution. Everything that Tian thought of would involve the sewn together muscles in his abdomen. After a while longer Tian weighted the immediate pain of getting up with the eventual pain of waiting. That brought Tian to his feet.

Mounting his motorcycle was just as hard. Tian pushed through that and started the bike. Tian could feel the rumbling in his kidneys. Tian kicked up the kickstand and felt all six of the stitches try to shake themselves free.

As Tian pulled out of the parking lot a cool breeze blew over him. He considered taking the freeways back knowing that it would require fewer stops. But he decided even with the constant lifting of his legs onto and off of his foot pegs, Sunset would be faster. 'Fast. That is what I need. I need to get home fast.'

The scratches and dust on his old helmet's shield made it very difficult for him to see at night. Tian lifted the shield up but had to close it back when the speed of the wind bothered his eyes.

"How did I mess up my life like this?" Tian spoke to himself. "How did I mess up my life like this?" Tian yelled a little louder. "How did I mess up my life like this?" Tian finally yelled at the top of his lungs. "How did I mess up my life like this?" he repeated again and again.

The nights after that were restless. He found that doubling his dose not only relieved the pain of sleeping on his stitches but it quieted his mind enough to sleep. But no matter how much he took, the restlessness of mind would return in the morning.

"I need an escape," Tian said. "I need something new I can do. Let's see. I can't run, I can't swim and I can't do anything too active." Tian thought about it for a few hours and then came up with it. In all his years and all his adventures Tian had never fired a gun.

Tian searched out the nearest gun range and went down. When Tian got there he was disappointed to learn that the trip was wasted.

"Did you bring a gun?" the short Latino attendant asked.

"No, I'm looking to rent one for the range," Tian stuttered out a little nervous about what he was going to do.

"I'm sorry, no solo renters."

Tian gave the attendant a confused look and the attendant continued. "It's to prevent suicides. You have to come to the range with someone else. It has to be someone that knows you. It's to prevent suicides."

Tian couldn't help but smile. 'What had mandated that rule?' Tian thought. "Ok. But if I brought my own gun can I use the range?"

"Yes," attendant said before moving onto the next person.

Tian drove right from there to the closest gun dealer. The salesman described the differences in shapes and performance. Tian made his selection, filled out the form, did the test and paid for his gun.

The mandatory three day waiting period was not a problem for Tian. It turned out that the mere purchase of the gun was enough to again clear his mind. However, when Tian checked his bank account to refill his prescription, his new balance made him sick. After seeing how much money he had left, Tian had to run from his computer to the bathroom to vomit in the toilet.

Tian had no choice but to purchase the meds and to make himself feel better he picked up his newly licensed gun from the dealer. The feeling of the gun in his hand gave him a sense of fear. What sparked the fear was the ability to end life in a moment and it didn't sit well with him.

But it was that night when the fear of the gun went away. Tian hadn't felt well all day. He had continued to feel a little nauseous and added to that he had a slight sense of disorientation. It almost felt like Tian was no longer completely in his body.

Tian thought a little rest would help, but the answer to how he felt came when he peed. Tian didn't see it come out, but there it was in the toilet when he was done. The doctor was right the blood was very easy to spot.

Tian doubled up on his meds again and packed up his gun for a little late night escape. He left his wallet behind and considered whether or not he would take his phone. In the end he pocketed his phone because after a lifetime of living without it, it made him feel better to travel with it.

Tian thought about where he should go. He remembered what he still considered the best time of his life. Tian remembered the fulfillment he felt making his movie.

He thought about what was the greatest execution of his skill as a producer. The lead actress had very much been scared of the dark, and the last night before their Christmas break was to be shot in the woods of the Azusa Mountains.

It had been a long two weeks with lots of unpaid overtime. The crew was almost ready to revolt. But somehow Tian had kept them all together. Tian talked the lead actress out of the car, and stopped the director of photography from walking off the set. Tian considered that day in the woods the greatest example of what his potential was. So now that he was looking for a late night wooded area, it only made sense that that would be the place.

Tian rode his motorcycle 35 minutes down highway 10. He turned off onto the main Azusa strip and then headed into the mountains. Even after all of these years the spot wasn't difficult to find. It was one of the only offshoots from the winding mountain road that was blocked by a gate.

Tian parked his bike past the gate and took the long familiar walk into the woods. It was dark that night but the lights of the city added just enough that Tian could see the trees. Tian thought about his father as he walked. Tian had always imagined that his father had committed suicide but now he was beginning to wonder.

Tian's father had died from a major heart attack. But when Tian returned home for the funeral, everyone that knew him said how he thought that his "asthma" attacks were going to kill him. They didn't turn out to be asthma attacks. What they were were mini heart attacks, and Tian always presumed that his father was smart enough to know that.

But here in the dark of the woods Tian second guessed himself. 'What if dad just didn't want to face the truth? That wouldn't really count as suicide. That would be a whole other thing.'

Tian took out his gun and loaded it as the salesman had shown him. The gun no longer engendered the same fear. In fact, Tian felt nothing at that moment. He remembered the equation that he had come up with all those years ago, 'Will my quality of life be better than death would allow?' It wasn't a hard question to answer. The answer was no.

Tian remembered the death dream he had had the day after arriving in Toronto. It was an incredible experience. He hoped that when he died it would be his father that would meet him on the other side. Tian knew that he had made a mess of his life. But he assumed that if he had his father by his side he could have a much better afterlife.

'I think I based my life on something that wasn't real. I think that was the problem. There must be a God,' Tian decided. 'But I just don't understand why God let's bad things happen to good people.'

With that Tian shut off his mind. He found a nice tree not to deep into the woods and sat down. Tian closed his eyes and took in a few long deep breaths. He then took hold of his gun pointed at his temple and pulled the trigger. With that Tian fell down dead.

It wasn't a pretty death. When the bullet hit Tian's head, parts of his brain exploded out the other side. And after Tian's head hit the ground, Tian's face and the pine needles under it caked with his blood. In his death Tian was looking for a simple, easy answer. He was looking for solace and peace. He was looking for a place filled with the loved ones that he ran away from during life. However, despite his best wishes Tian didn't find any of that. Instead what he found was Irabell.

CHAPTER 18

During the time it took Tian and Irabell to leave the wheat fields and arrive at parts unknown Tian considered a lot. The first thing he thought about was how it was possible for his body to still be alive. He was sure that he had killed it. And when he left it for the walk into the woods he had certainly felt free.

Another thing he thought about was how different he thought the afterlife would be from what it was. What he expected was magic. What he found were ordinary lives lived in unique circumstances. He considered death to be his ultimate escape, but here he was having to make more decisions about a life that to him was a disappointment.

Tian wanted death to be the end. He wanted it to be the final chapter on his book, but it wasn't. Death was neither the beginning nor the end. It was more of the middle. Death was a return to the old frontier that he had left for a new adventure.

On the other hand, Tian didn't know how to refer to life. Tian couldn't imagine that anyone would've guessed the way that his life would turn out before he was born. That uncertainty made life a mystery. So Tian couldn't say that life wasn't what he expected because there was no way to know what to expect. And the way that the people in the afterlife acted, Tian imagined that no one cared what type of life they had. All anyone seemed to want was a chance at life.

There was a uniqueness to living that captivated everyone in the afterlife. And Tian imagined that before his life he would have been one of those captivated. However there was something about living life that ended that captivation. At the end of his life Tian imagined that it was the futility of life that ended the captivation.

Tian imagined that if his entire life was spent with an achievable purpose he would have clung to life more. Tian did have a purpose, but it was the lack of achievability that killed Tian in the end.

But still, after what he saw in the afterlife, Tian could understand why everyone in the non-physical world valued life. Life was a unique journey. Life seemed to give the people in the afterlife something when before they had nothing.

The only problem with life, as Tian saw it was that life appeared to have no rules. And if there were rules to life, then no one knew what they were. Everyone in life seemed to be fumbling their way through. And Tian's time in heaven seemed to imply that those who felt the most certainty were the ones that were the most mislead.

After everything he had seen of the afterlife, Tian now understood that life was a privilege. Tian understood that one had to earn the right to be a part of life. But it was life's haphazard nature that made Tian decide that he didn't need to return. Tian considered his life to be complete and Tian was ready to accept whatever it was that came next.

When Tian opened his eyes it looked like Irabell had arrived a few minutes before him. Irabell was already seated in one of the patio chairs past the sliding glass doors on the deck.

Tian looked around and noticed how much like heaven everything looked. The room Tian stood in was large. Tian imagined it to be the size of a basketball court or half the size of a soccer field. And the couches and love seats throughout the room broke it into large seating areas.

The room was very comforting to Tian. The pearl color of the furniture and walls were offset by the light colored marble floors and earth tone artifact throughout the room. The ceilings were much higher than the ceilings in houses on earth, but they were low enough to not make the space overwhelming. And the photo realistic paintings on the walls were all of the most beautiful natural scenes on earth.

Tian considered this room to be his perfect room. And to top off his perfect room, he walked over to the sliding glass door to find that the deck overlooked a beach. And it wasn't just any beach, it was a pink sand beach like he saw on Harbor Island in the Bahamas as a child. Tian truly felt at home.

Tian pulled open the glass door to find the human image of Irabell staring at the ocean. The way Irabell had his face turned slightly upwards it looked like Irabell was trying to 'catch some sun.' This image made Tian happy.

"Are we back in Christian heaven?" Tian asked the quiet Irabell.

"No, we are in the place that the non-religious go after they die," Irabell said without turning around.

"Oh, I didn't know that there was such a place."

"Like I said, there are many different types of heaven here. This is the heaven for those that made living life their religion."

"Is this where I would have gone if I had died?" Tian asked hopefully.

Irabell turned and looked at Tian again. He still couldn't get over how much Tian looked like a tree. "Yes, I think that this is where you would have considered the most like home."

"Then can I stay here now?"

"You have the choice to do whatever it is that you want to do. But I brought you here so that you can meet a few people."

Tian remembered that his father and grandmother had passed before him. Tian hoped that it was them that he had been brought to meet. "Who's that?"

Just then the sliding glass doors behind Tian were pulled open. In walked two people that looked a tremendous amount like Tian looked on earth. One was slightly taller than the other, and the shorter one seemed more feminine. Neither of them felt male or female. But there was something about them that made it easy to tell them apart.

"Hello Tian," the taller one said.

"Welcome," the shorter one added.

Tian felt something familiar about their tone. Although they looked like Tian he didn't mistake them for being him. They were someone else, someone that Tian felt like he had known all of his life. "Hello," Tian replied. "Thank you."

"Do you not recognize us?" the shorter one asked.

"I'm sorry I don't."

The shorter one smiled. "That's disappointing considering the number of times that you referred to us as your friends."

Tian lurched back when the recognition hit him. "Are you my dead friends?" Tian said with a smile, happy to finally meet someone he had known during life.

"That is what you called us," the shorter one said with a brilliant smile.

"Although I'm sure you now see how much of a misnomer the phrase is," the taller one added.

'The tall one is definitely the harder personality,' Tian decided. "No, I always knew. It was always just a term of endearment," Tian concluded with a smile. Tian didn't know whether he should hug them or not. Whatever the correct response was he felt good to be in their presence again.

"We were told that you had questions," the shorter one said.

"About what?" Tian asked.

"Your life. When many people end their lives they often have questions that they need answered before they can move on. We know that Irabell has been wonderful and has shown you a lot. But I'm sure that you have questions that only someone that has followed your life from the beginning can answer," the shorter one said.

Tian looked back at Irabell who had again turned to watch the waves as they rolled onto the beach. "Well," Tian said feeling like a host, "would you like to sit down?" All three sat down in chairs that faced Irabell and Tian started with the question that was most obvious to him. "Why do you two look like me?"

"For much of the same reason that you look like a tree I suspect," the tall one answered abruptly.

"It would also be the same reason that you looked like this when you first came here. When you follow a life from where we are, it changes you. You might think of the life you lived as your life. But just like us you were just brought along for the ride. The difference between you and us being that your presence was necessary to make the body live, while ours was only necessary to help it to live," the shorter one concluded.

"If that was your job, then I guess you failed," Tian added. He didn't like the way that they were staking a claim in what Tian considered to be his life. Whether he was considered a failure or a success he wanted the journey to be his own.

"There were no failures during your life, there was simply a conclusion," the taller one said.

"If you don't think there were any failures, then I don't think you were watching close enough," Tian said with a chuckle. "Perhaps there was a time early on when I had success. But once my life got going, once the training wheels came off, I never succeeded again," Tian said still smiling.

"If you saw your life as a series of failures and successes then I think it was you who weren't paying close enough attention," the tall one said.

"You're feisty aren't you?" Tian said with a playful familiarity.

"What do you think were your childhood successes?" the shorter one asked.

"Well, number one, I learned how to talk to you guys. I would consider that a success wouldn't you?" Tian said chuckling.

"Tell me, if a child learns how to tie their shoelace should it be considered a success by the adult that the child becomes?" the tall one asked.

"Well, certainly it is a success for the child," Tian said.

"But should it be considered a childhood success by the adult the child becomes?" the tall one asked again.

"Are you comparing a child learning how tie their laces with my learning how to talk to the dead?" Tian asked with signs of indignation.

"A child learns how to tie their laces because a child wants to learn how to tie their laces. Once they decide to learn it is just a matter of study and repetition. It was your desire to learn how to talk to us that made you unique. But once you decided you put in hundreds of hours of practice and many more hours in thought about it. What separated you from your peers that couldn't was the fact that you put in the hours necessary to learn how to do it. Anyone could if they put in the work necessary to learn.

So in the end the question is a good one. Do you think that the adult should consider his learning how to tie his laces as a childhood success?" the shorter one concluded.

"Isn't the fact that I stuck with it long enough to achieve it deem it worthy of me considering it a success?"

"The fact that you genuinely wanted to learn is what makes you special. The fact that a human was able to learn to talk to us is no more amazing than a human's ability to walk on two legs," the shorter one said.

Tian's jovial mood was now gone. Tian saw what they were doing as diminishing the parts of his life in which he took the most pride. "Wait, you were there right? You watched me? Do you remember the hurricane? Wasn't it me who moved it? Wasn't that a success?" Tian argued.

"Your life is not without success, Tian. But I ask you, when a person goes to medical school and then uses that information to save a life, how amazing is it?" the shorter one said.

"I'm sure it's pretty amazing to the person whose life they've saved," Tian said with an indignant smile.

"Yes, but should it amaze the doctor? You know how hard you worked before you attempted to move the hurricane. I know that you believed that what you were attempting could work because you were bold enough to put your whole heart into trying to move it. I've always wondered why you were so amazed that you succeeded," the shorter one added.

"I guess I was amazed because I didn't realize anyone could have such an effect over something that seemed as chaotic and uncontrollable as a hurricane. You know, I was also amazed that one person could control something that could affect so many other people's lives. Did you know that someone died when the hurricane made landfall?"

"Yes we know," the tall one said.

"How was I supposed to deal with that?"

"That was just one life that you indirectly had an effect on. Would you like to know any more of people that have died due to your indirect actions?" the tall one asked.

"Somehow I don't think that I do."

"There are more. But in every case it was their own actions that had a much greater effect on their lives than whatever you did indirectly," the shorter one said.

"I think it's that belief which was the cause of much of your distress on earth. So often you placed the cause of events at the feet of someone other than yourself. You blamed us or God, when what you were going through was the natural evolution of you making decisions based on your environment, your behavior and your biology," the tall one said.

"Did Irabell explain the probability cloud to you?" the shorter one asked.

Tian looked over at Irabell who remained transfixed on the beach. "He did."

"Have you had the time to examine how it shaped everything that happened to you during your life?" the shorter one asked.

"I haven't thought about it."

"Let's take a moment to consider it now. What would you consider to be the first major failure of your life?" the soft personality asked.

Tian thought for a moment about his life. He often separated his life into two parts; before Toronto and after. It was his first attempt at starting an independent life that he would consider to be his first major failure. "It was when I tried to make a life for myself after I graduated college. I failed miserably."

"And you blamed God," the harder personality added.

"Yeah. I gave God credit when I moved the hurricane. I gave him credit when I amazingly got into college. And I gave him credit when I couldn't find work in Toronto. I considered it to be a fair distribution of credit."

"When you say that you amazingly got into college, are you referring to your mother meeting the man that would assure you admittance and then give you a scholarship for the school?" the shorter one asked.

"Yes."

"Let's take a moment to look at that situation through the probability cloud," the softer personality said.

"Ok."

"Your mother socialized within a community in the Bahamas where many very rich people from all over the world retire. Yes?" the shorter one continued.

"Yes," Tian confirmed.

"The man who gave you the scholarship was one of the wealthier residents in the community and had been retired for a while, yes?"

"Yes."

"He had started the scholarship seven years earlier to help native Bahamians go to the college on which he sat on the board, yes?"

"Yes."

"He socialized almost exclusively among the wealthy of his community, yes?"

"Yeah."

"He didn't interview any of the scholarship recipients before they received his scholarship, meaning that he never had a personal connection with any of the people he helped, correct?"

"Yes."

"So, your mother and this man traveled in the same social circles. Since it was a small community is there any surprise that they ran into each other?"

"I guess not."

"And isn't it customary for people to go around the table and talk about what's interesting in their life?"

"Sure."

"So, being retired isn't it any wonder that this man mentioned that he was on the board of this college?"

"I guess that's not unusual."

"And your mother knew that you were in the process of considering schools correct?"

"Yes."

"So, is there any wonder that your mother mentioned you to him?"

"No, not really."

"And because every year his scholarship had to find at least one person from the Bahamas to go to his small school, is there any wonder that he encouraged your mother to get you to apply?"

"I guess not."

"And since it feels better to give to someone you know over faceless names that you've never met, doesn't it seem normal for him to give one of his scholarships to the son of the delightful and beautiful woman he met at the party?"

"I guess."

"So thinking it through, is there any wonder that you got a scholarship?"

"I guess not."

"The way that this worked," the taller one added, "was that your mother increased the probability of you getting a scholarship when she began socializing amongst retired wealthy people. Retired wealthy people tend to be in charity mode. It was in that way that she shaped your future. She didn't know she was doing it. But she did understand the basic idea that networking will eventually lead to something good."

Tian stared at the two without reply.

"You also gave God credit for not finding work and having a hard time in Toronto?" the shorter one said.

"Didn't you know within a month of arriving that Toronto was going through a deep recession and that jobs were hard to find," the shorter one continued.

"I guess I did."

"And weren't you trying to work there illegally?"

"Yes."

"Did that limit you to working as a waiter?"

"Yes."

"During a recession, those are amongst the first jobs to be eliminated. Eating out is the first luxury that people cut out during a recession. And even if there were any restaurants hiring, wouldn't they hire any of the legal workers with lots of waiter experience over the illegal worker with almost no waiter experience?

So, with that in mind is there any wonder that you couldn't find work as an illegally employed waiter in the middle of a recession?" the shorter one concluded.

"I didn't know that waiter jobs were so hard to find during a recession," Tian said sheepishly.

"And after realizing that there was no way to make a life for yourself in Toronto, you could have chosen to go home to the Bahamas. I know it was something that you considered many times," the taller on added.

"I considered it often, but I didn't want to feel like a failure by giving up."

"Do you understand how your probability of failure was incredibly high under the circumstances that you began your after college life?" the softer personality said.

"And yet with all of the probabilities pointing in the directions that they eventually led, you blame a god for what happened in your life," the taller one said leaning forward in his chair.

"The fact that I got into college so easily made me believe that someone was looking over me. So when I graduated from college I imagined that no matter what happened whoever it was that helped me get into college would help me to have a good life in Toronto," Tian said quietly.

"Yes, but do you now see how it was your mother's decisions combined with your good grades in school that got you into college? It was because of you and your mother's behavior that your future was shaped the way that it was. And do you see that it was your decision to stay in Toronto during a recession, that led to the bad times you experienced?" the shorter one asked.

"It was my behavior combined with the environment that shaped my future. It wasn't God at all. It was me."

"Exactly," the shorter one said.

Tian thought for a moment. "Well what about all of my failures in Los Angeles?"

"What failures are you referring to?" the taller one asked.

"I tried being an actor and I failed to find enough work. When I failed at that I decided to create things that would be good for society. But I ended up making a movie that no one wanted to see. I created a TV show that no networks wanted to show. And I wrote a lot of scripts that no one wanted to produce. How could these not be failures?

I know that success was possible, because the people around me made successful TV shows and sold scripts for lots of money. Yet everything I tried failed."

"Let's first talk about your acting," the taller on said. "You were one amongst 1000 other actors like you. This means that your probability of finding work started off low. And while others continued to sharpen their skills, you didn't get any better. And while others networked insistently, you barely made the effort. And then when your meager efforts were beginning to bear fruit, you switched to being a producer.

You then had the opportunity to make a lot of money as a producer, but you switched and made a movie. However, 200 independent movies are made every year in Los Angeles. There are eight studios that acquire an average of three movies a year. And in an industry where having known actors in movies are the only thing that is thought to increase the chance of a studio's financial return, you chose to cast all unknowns.

But even with all of these strikes against you, you developed contacts with people who were interested in seeing your next work. But instead of building a career based on these contacts which would turn into more contacts and finally a released movie, you switched again.

This time you switched to television. In this case the company that you sold your show to ignored the high probability opportunity of the network that was asking for such a show, and went after the low probability of the big networks. And because the big networks need big ratings in order to survive they also wanted to stick with the high probability opportunities.

And as well intentioned as your work was, the spiritual genre had no history of getting a large enough audience. And since you had no stars attached the network couldn't gamble on a low probability opportunity. And again instead of taking your newly created contacts and building a career on those, you switched to writing scripts that others would produce.

Your friends had success because they stuck with one thing and they practiced. In each case they started practicing in their childhood so that by the time they got their opportunities they were very skilled at what they did. After their practice they then took their time and built up their contacts. And eventually their preparation aligned with an opportunity and they had success. This is how they tremendously increased their probability of success and shaped their future."

"However this doesn't guarantee success," the shorter one said. "There are no guarantees. All there are are shifting clouds of probability that we step into and out of."

Tian stared at the two for a while not saying a word. He found it hard to accept that he was the one that created the failures in his life. And it came as a cool breeze when Tian considered that it could have been his creation of those failures that brought him to this world.

"Ok, I can accept what you're saying. Perhaps humans do control what happens to them to a certain degree. But in truth I don't think that it's my decisions that led to me sitting here with you. Sometimes bad things happen to you, and you have no control over them. And no matter what decisions you make those bad things will happen.

My entire life would have turned out entirely different if I didn't crave excitement like I did. And I'm told that it wasn't just a crazy passion I had. My body was wired to crave excitement. No matter what decisions I made in my life I always would have had to fight this craving. And it was the decisions I made while trying to satisfy these cravings that led me here. And I can tell you for a fact that it wasn't just a matter of self will.

So what would you say to that? How can you say that we shape our own futures when we have these things that happen to us that we could never change? The way I see it, either there is some force like God that makes all of these things happen for a reason; or we are haphazardly living our lives for no reason or purpose. And if that's the case, what's the point in living?"

Both the shorter and taller one remained silent. Irabell who had long stopped his steady examination of the waves was also now staring at Tian in silence. Although Irabell knew that this wasn't his time to teach, he felt the need to speak up. "Tian?"

Tian turned to look at Irabell a little surprised to hear his voice.

"Here on this side we are given the opportunity to follow the lives of those in physical bodies." Irabell pointed to the two beings sitting next to him. "They have chosen to follow your life in depth. They practically live every moment of your life with you. But there are many others like myself that follow three or four lives less closely.

Because of certain similarities to my last life, I had chosen to follow yours. But because I am also interested in how knowledge is passed along within human society, I have also followed other lives.

Did you know that one of the leading causes of death in Africa for the last 500 years has been malaria? It is spread by a mosquito. When that mosquito stings babies and young children it passes on the disease and kills them. However, in response to these deaths the African body has evolved.

The human body is constantly mutating. And many hundreds of years ago a mutation was introduced into the African gene pool that protected people from dying of malaria. And as more and more young Africans that didn't have the gene died off, it allowed more of the Africans with the mutation to have children and pass on the trait. Soon huge portions of the African population were lucky enough to have this mutation.

This mutation was nothing but a benefit for hundreds of years and many generations. But recently a new virus was introduced into the African population. And that mutation that was such a benefit before has now made Africans more susceptible to disease and death.

In Europe malaria wasn't a problem. However they had what was called the black plague. This was a contagious disease that very quickly killed large portions of the European population. But because there were mutations developed within European genes not everyone was affected.

Due to the deaths of so many others, these Europeans with the mutated genes became a larger percentage of their population. That resulted in that mutation being passed on much as the anti-malaria gene was passed along in the African community. However, this mutation had a different result in the long run than the African mutation did.

Whereas the anti-malaria mutation made the Africans more susceptible to the new virus, the anti-black plague mutation made the Europeans less susceptible to the new virus. The Africans that now catch the new virus may struggle to understand why a god might have allowed such a thing to happen to them. But they fail to realize that the very thing that allowed them to catch the current disease is what allowed their ancestors to survive in the first place. And the Europeans that think themselves lucky for not having caught the new disease fail to take into account the number of people that had to die for them to become resistant.

Just like each human body is a living community, so is the human population. The human population is constantly adapting. It grows large in prosperous times and thins in lean times. And just like the community of species within each body is there to keep the body alive, the diversity within the human population is there to keep the human population alive.

Your genetic mutation that makes you crave excitement, or others' mutations that may cause cancers are not assigned to you. Those mutations are neither a curse nor a blessing given to you by a supernatural being. They are the healthy workings of a human population that will use them to survive whatever may come.

When your genetic mutation occurred within prehistoric hunters, it caused them to take more chances and bring home more meat. When the cancer prone mutation first occurred it might have helped the population survive long winters. If it wasn't for this genetic mutation your ancestors would never have survived. And as a result your current body wouldn't have been born to complain about it.

So you see that there are more options than there being a god and there being a haphazard world. A human's future is shaped by three things; environment, behavior and biology. And the best way to predict or shape the details of what will happen in a person's life would be to take a look at the probability clouds that follow them around.

When a child starts out, their future is most determined by their parent's behavior and their environment. But as soon as they start making decisions for themselves they have the ability to shape their environment, behavior and biology to a state that will create their own future.

You, Tian, made the decisions that created your life. You were free to make the same decisions or change them. You didn't experience failures, the rules of life aren't haphazard, nor was your life controlled by supernatural beings. Your life was what you shaped for yourself. It may not have been what you said you wanted, but it was the life that you created for yourself. And all you ever needed to know to reshape your life was to know the role you played in shaping it."

Tian was momentarily speechless. Everything they said made sense. Tian now understood why life had turned out the way that it had for him. The reason wasn't magical or mystical, but it made sense. "There is one thing that I don't understand," Tian added. "If there aren't any supernatural beings controlling my life, then what role did you play? You all told me things that I couldn't have known any other way. The things you told me helped to shape my life."

The taller one spoke up first. "We told you those things because we cared about you, and you were willing to listen. There are those among us that have a clearer perspective on your life than you do. When they understood what was about to come, we tried to give you an advantage in dealing with it. But we aren't infallible. We have made mistakes."

The shorter one added, "All any of us ever wanted was to be a part of your life. That is all any of us on this side ever want from the lives we follow. We don't need to be acknowledged though acknowledgement feels good. What we want is to quietly follow your life so that one day we could be a part of a physical body.

We enjoyed following your life as we enjoy following the lives of every physical body. But we have to admit that we are most attached to yours because you feel like a part of us. Your life experiences shape us. The bond that developed amongst those following your life has made us closer than family. And pardon the hyperbole, but for us you are like our god."

The shorter one blushed a little and paused in order to compose herself. "It is not our decision to make. It is only yours. But it's all of our wishes that you choose to return. We don't want to pressure you. Nor do we want to control you. It is just our humble wish."

Tian looked at the shorter one as he squirmed his way through her request. He then looked over at the taller one. The taller one's face had softened into the vulnerable look he had seen his own face make in the mirror. "I don't understand how my body could still be alive," Tian said to no one in particular.

The shorter one leaned forward in his seat. "There is a ranger that lives in a station at the end of the road you were on. When he heard your gun shot he decided to do his midnight patrol early. He found your motorcycle parked on the side of the road and then found you. You were unconscious but still alive."

"But I don't understand how I could still be alive?"

"It is quite common for people to shoot themselves in the temple and then stay alive," Irabell added.

"So do I have brain damage?"

"Yes you do," the softer one replied without remorse.

"Wait, if I'm here, how is the body still alive?"

"It's in a coma waiting for you to come back to it," the shorter one confirmed.

"But if I went back, I would have to spend the rest of my life with brain damage. Would I ever recover?"

"We don't know," the taller one added. "The probability of you recovering to a normal functioning state is higher if you had someone you loved help you through this. But as we all know, relationships were never your strength."

"So, if I went back I could be going back to live in a vegetative state?"

"Or you could simply die," the taller one confirmed.

"Why would you want to experience that?" Tian asked the group.

The tall one was the first one to speak up. "Because it is life. And we all want to experience life in all of its forms."

"Would I at least be able to remember what I experienced here?" Tian asked.

Choosing to remain silent, the tall one just shook his head 'no.'

Tian felt alone in this moment. He did his best to prevent too much time from passing before he said something else. "You keep saying we. Something tells me that you aren't just referring to the two of you."

"There are more of us," the shorter one said.

"How many more?"

"There are a thousand more depending on the day," the
shorter one replied.

Tian looked out at the beautiful beach. The waves crested
and then spread out with the greatest of ease. Sitting out on the deck
was comfortable. It was how he imagined his retirement to be.

But now he was being presented with a request. They wanted
him to give up his dream for work. But unlike the jobs he did back
on earth, this time he knew that it would be appreciated.

He thought back to his apartment on earth. It was on a
dangerous bend that followed a long straight away. And very often
when the drivers weren't paying attention they would miss the bend
and collide with an oncoming car.

There was a day when Tian was at home watching TV. The
sound of tires screeching and the inevitable crash was common
place, so much so that he stopped going out to see. But this time he
felt an urge to go.

When he went outside he saw a young woman sitting
shocked in the damaged car. He ran out to her and she quickly got
out. She slowly followed Tian across the street where she sat down
on the low wall around Tian's building. And as the crowd around
the girl gathered she broke into a hysterical cry.

Tian looked down at this tall, pretty, young girl and
wondered why none of the women in the crowd were comforting
her. As a strange, young man Tian didn't feel that it was appropriate
for him to do it. But as she continued to cry and everyone continued
to gawk, Tian pushed past the people, sat next to her and placed his
arm around her.

Tian felt uncomfortable but he didn't want the girl to know
he was. He looked out towards the skyline for awhile before
changing his focus to the street. Tian couldn't shake the feeling that
he was doing something wrong until the pretty, young girl placed
her head on Tian's shoulder and stopped crying.

When she finally lifted her head up Tian removed his arm.
And when she began to speak Tian spoke to her. He asked her a few
questions about insurance and how she felt, and she answered each
one without a problem. And finally when she seemed collected
enough he stood up and just stood next to her.

After Tian got up it wasn't long until one of the gawking women sat down. He was glad that she had come. Tian hadn't sat next to the girl because he wanted to. He sat there because the girl needed it. Tian had never felt comfortable with public displays of affection. But there was something in Tian that always told him that if he had the opportunity to help someone to feel better, he always had to take it. And that included when it was hard.

"I'll go back," Tian said. Tian turned back from the ocean to see the smiles stretch across the two faces that looked like his. 'It feels good to see me smile,' Tian thought. And then he looked over at Irabell whose expression had not changed. Tian wondered why.

The short one spoke. "There are a few people that would like to thank you. Will you see them?"

"Sure."

The shorter one got up and led Tian back through the sliding glass doors. As Tian stepped through he was greeted by a room full of people that looked a lot like him. And when they saw Tian they all began to smile and clap.

Although he knew that these people weren't him, Tian felt good to see himself happy. The genuine joy that he saw on their faces was something that he hadn't seen on his own face in a long time. Tian watched the people, heard the applause and smiled himself.

Tian pushed through the crowd. Each time he passed someone they reached out to shake his hand. And when the group realized that Tian was shaking hands they all worked to get in his path. Everyone in the crowd wanted their hand shook by Tian and it gave Tian joy to shake them.

As long as he stood there the applause continued. And when it felt like Tian had shaken every hand he began to wonder what he would find on the other side of the room's front door. Since this was the place that he would have gone had he died, Tian wondered what it was like outside.

Still under the shower of applause he took hold of the front door's knobs and twisted. The door opened to a flood of light, but even in the blinding sun Tian still made out the images of people. In the brief moment between when the door opened and the light becoming too much for him, Tian saw a street full of people.

The roads seemed dusty and there were no room for cars. Everyone seemed to be walking everywhere and Tian couldn't remember seeing anyone that wasn't in a group. It was almost like the people were swarms of identical twins walking from one little blue house to another house of a similarly tropical color.

But that is all Tian saw of this place. Afterwards the light became too much for Tian and he had to close his eyes.

When Tian opened his eyes the scene was much different. Instead of a beautiful tropical scene he was staring at the square white tiles of a hospital ceiling. And instead of understanding everything that was going on, things came very slowly to him.

'Where am I,' Tian thought. 'I don't recognize this place. Where did I go to sleep,' Tian asked himself. 'Is this my childhood home in the Bahamas? Is this my college dorm? Wait, I can't remember anywhere else. It must be one of those two places but how could I be positioned in the room to be seeing what I'm seeing?'

Tian tried to imagine himself in each of the rooms, spinning his body around in his mind to accommodate all of the things that seemed unexplainable to him. For example, he imagined that the constant beeping he heard was the alarm clock that sat next to both of his beds. And he imagined that the sickly smell he smelt was what he smelt that time when his pediatrician made a house call to Tian's home.

But no matter how hard he tried, there were a few things that Tian couldn't understand. He couldn't understand why there were so many strange objects in either of his bedrooms. And Tian couldn't understand why his body felt so stiff.

Although all of these things were unusual they didn't bother him. The one thing that did bother him was the machine that sat next to his bed that made a whoring noise and had the moving parts. There was something dark about this machine and Tian didn't like the way wires ran from the machine to an area under his sheets down near his crotch. Tian didn't like this machine and wanted it turned off. Unfortunately as much as Tian tried to remember how to do it, he couldn't even remember how to ask for it.

There wasn't much that wasn't hazy to Tian. Even the details of who he was were unclear to him. Tian remembered that before he had come here, he was awake and had a life. But what that life consisted of was a mystery to him.

As Tian looked around his new world he was sure that there were others in the world even though there was no one in his room. And Tian looked forward to seeing one of those people. Tian imagined that it would be a great event when he saw another person because what it would confirm for him was that in this new world he was not alone.

EPILOGUE

Tian's mother's name was Olive but most of her friends called her Livie. She had married young and then had two sons for the person that she had intended to spend the rest of her life with. But life had ended up being a lot harder for her family than she expected. And as her girlish dream of her perfect life faded, her heart wondered more and more.

It was a surprising night when Livie found herself in bed with a man that was not her husband. This was never a part of the dream that she had for herself, yet there she was. That was the first crack in the picture she had created for herself but it wouldn't be the last.

That one night turned into a regular thing. Soon all of her friends knew that these two were together in spite of the fact that they both had spouses at home. And with the knowledge so freely available it wasn't long before Livie's husband found out and threw Livie out.

Livie moved out and took Tian with her. Together they would struggle through poverty. Livie had never known what it was to be so poor. Like most beautiful girls of her time, she moved out of her parent's house into the house built by her new husband.

But now Livie knew what it was to eat stale bread. In fact, Livie's delightful little boy Tian met with an accident when he tried to cut himself a slice and instead sliced open his finger when the hard bread tipped forward and the knife landed on him. Livie tried to comfort the boy as he screamed at the sight of his own blood. And it took 30 minutes of sitting with Tian in the tub before his finger stopped bleeding and the boy stopped crying for home.

Livie had always considered Tian her little trouper, so it unnerved her when he so openly wept for his home. Livie had always believed that Tian considered his home where ever she was. But in his screams she began to see her little boy for the little boy that he was. And that realization led to a further crack in the picture that she had of her life. That crack occurred when she had to beg her husband to take her back just to satisfy the wishes of her little son.

Livie's little son wasn't the same after that. He moved back into his childhood home and Livie tried to help them stay there but her now angry husband made it clear that he would prefer to lose his home then listen to her. So, even though she had just moved back so that Tian could live in his home again, the whole family quickly had to pack up and leave.

Over the next few years Livie saw less and less of the delightful little boy that she once knew. She found him withdrawing further and further until soon he was interested in things that seemed strange to her. She had always been interested in the prospects that life was more than what she saw, but Tian seemed to take that idea to a whole new level.

Soon Livie realized that she had lost her little boy. She came to understand that the only thing she had left was a marriage to a man who, as well meaning as he was, didn't make her happy. So instead Livie went off looking for someone else. She found this new man in the circles that she had found her last one. And although he too was married, Livie fell in love.

This time Livie knew better than to flaunt her happiness in her husband's face, but she found it too hard to keep it to herself. Livie thought about Tian. She knew that she had lost her little boy, but thought perhaps she could start up a new relationship with the man that he would become. So on a warm Bahamas night she invited Tian to dinner and then invited her new friend to join them for drinks.

The meeting didn't go well. Livie found Tian to be polite but not cordial. Livie hoped that Tian would be the one that she could share her newly found joy with, but it wasn't meant to be.

Soon afterward Livie's husband found out about her new relationship and they fought about it. And in a bitter twist, with the circumstances what they were Livie was in the position to throw her husband out.

The relationship with her new love ended abruptly when Livie's husband threatened to tell his wife. And Livie soon found herself alone in the house with Tian and her oldest son Pat. After a year Pat moved in with his father and Livie and Tian were roommates again.

But by this time Tian had become a different person completely. Tian was distant and withdrawn. Even when Tian was in the room, it didn't seem to Livie that he was completely present. Livie trusted her son to make good decisions because out of all of the kids that she knew, her son Tian had the best heart.

After Tian left for college, Livie's thoughts of having a relationship with her son left as well. Tian rarely came home after that. And it was clear that when Tian did come back, it was only because he had to be there.

As the years went on Livie wondered what she had done to lose her son. She imagined that it had to do with the loss of his home, but there was nothing that she could have done about that. She tried not to feel regret about how she had lived her life but after so many years and so few phone calls she often asked herself, "how did I make such a mess of my life?"

It was one day while weeding her garden that she got an undeniable feeling about Tian. She would later describe it as mother's instinct, but she got the distinct feeling that there was something wrong with her son. She immediately got up from her garden and sent Tian an email. And when the email wasn't returned after a day she gave Tian a call.

Tian often ignored her emails and didn't pick up his calls, but this time Livie was sure something was wrong. Livie didn't bother to leave a message on his phone. Instead Livie called up Pat and asked him to make her a reservation to go to Los Angeles. When Pat asked why, Livie simply said that she needed to see Tian. And after all of the years that he had known his mother, Pat knew that that reason was enough.

Livie booked a hotel near Tian's address so that she could easily go over and knock on Tian's door. On the day that Livie arrived she knocked on his door three times. And when she had no luck, she came back and knocked on the door when every normal person would have been in bed asleep.

Early the next morning Livie knocked on the other apartment doors until one of them put her in contact with Tian's landlord. The connection was timely. It was also that morning that the police had contacted the landlord informing him that a motorcycle riding resident was found with a near fatal gunshot wound to the head.

Livie took the information in stride. She knew that she had come to Tian for a purpose. And although she wished that she would find everything all right, a large part of her knew that he was in trouble.

Livie arrived at the hospital to find someone that no longer resembled her little boy. The person lying in the bed was a strange man. He had all of the features of her and her ex-husband, but all of Tian's familiar zest was gone.

It was from the doctor that Livie discovered what had happened to him. "Apparently your son had an accident. His medical records indicate that he was attacked by dolphins while on a boating trip. His records indicate that he showed signs of depression when he left but nothing indicating that he would be a danger to himself. We believe that after he saw signs that his remaining kidney was failing he tried to take his own life.

Unfortunately his remaining kidney is failing and his suicide attempt means that he can no longer be added to the donor list for a new one."

"Will he be alright eventually?" Livie asked the doctor.

"Right now he seems to have some brain damage. But research has shown that the brain is a very adaptable organ. With enough help there is no telling how much of his cognition he will get back," the doctor concluded.

Livie lived in Tian's apartment and took care of her son until he was ready to leave the hospital. Livie learned a lot about the man her son had become by living in his place. Livie learned that he was an avid writer. She had heard him mention it, but she never imagined how productive he had been. And through knocks on his door she discovered that her boy had friends.

By the time Tian was ready to leave the hospital he had regained most of his cognition. Tian now always knew where he was and many of his memories had returned to him. Tian's coordination wasn't completely back so walking was a challenge and writing his name was out of the question.

Between kidney dialysis and rehabilitation the costs were too much for Livie so it became necessary to take Tian back to her home. Tian didn't say anything about the move requesting only that his computer come with him.

When the two got back to the Bahamas Livie immediately looked for work. She had been living the life of a retired woman, but with her son's expenses that luxury was now gone. Each morning Livie helped Tian with his first dialysis of the day and then left him to his devices while she went off to the flower shop where she earned their keep.

As time progressed Tian's memories completely returned. Tian relearned how to sign his name and could construct a sentence as well as anyone. Tian did his best to contribute to the house by spending his time cleaning during the day. Tian thought that he should also do the cooking, but his mother cooked so much better than him that he never did.

Livie was proud of the progress Tian was making. And although she had never told Tian, after a few years she had saved enough money to pay for a kidney transplant. Livie had held off getting the test thinking it better to wait until she had all her ducks in a row. But now that Livie was mentally ready, she learned that she wasn't a match.

Livie's disappointment was hers alone until she found the nerve to ask Pat for one of his kidneys. Pat was hesitant to give up his kidney but when he found out that he was a match he couldn't imagine not going through with it. To Livie's disappointment it was Tian who stopped the proceedings. Tian joked that with all of Pat's drinking he would need all of the kidneys he could find and therefore couldn't afford to give up one of his own.

As much as Livie resisted, she knew there was truth in what Tian said. Livie's other son Pat drank way too much and could need his own transplant soon. But what this left Livie with was a son whom she loved that would never be much more than what he was then.

Livie wouldn't have to wait too long for a surprise though. On a pleasant May day Livie learned that Tian wasn't just spending all of his day cleaning and watching TV. Tian had been spending the last year of his life writing a book.

When Livie read the book she was just glad to find that all of the sentences made sense. Livie looked at it more as an exercise for his brain than a work of entertainment so she was again surprised when he said that he planned to submit it to publishers. Livie thought it best to leave him to his devices and allowed him to pursue his new goal as far as he wanted.

As the months went on Livie noticed how Tian changed because of the book. Before Livie saw a bridled restlessness in Tian, but when her son talked about his book calm came over him. She liked this new side of her son so when the last of the publishers passed on his book Livie encouraged him to write another.

Livie read his second, then third then fourth book, and soon she stopped seeing them as a mental exercise. The books had eventually turned into poignant expressions of who Tian was. Livie found them funny and sweet. And more than anything else Livie found them insightful. Tian's books made Livie wonder about the man Tian was before the accident and about how much her little boy experienced in the brief time that he had lived as a man.

Livie was also surprised one day when a joyful Tian met her at the door announcing that the first of his books was going to be published. Livie identified the book as the insightful fourth one. And Livie enjoyed hearing her excited son tell how he had worn the publisher down.

"He liked the first book I submitted," Tian said to Livie, "but he couldn't get the marketing department on board. But then I submitted the second and he put me in contact with another publisher. That publisher did like the second one, but wanted to read the third one. That publisher couldn't publish the third one. But when I submitted the fourth one, both the first and second publisher offered me a deal."

Livie loved hearing her son talk about what he had accomplished. As a boy Tian was always so full of dreams and it was that that made Livie think that she had done something right. And now that he had accomplished his first big goal after the accident, Livie began to believe that Tian would be alright.

One day as Livie got out of bed she realized that somewhere along the way, she had gotten old. The beauty of her youth was a distant memory. The vigor that she showed as an active woman was replaced by a slow moving gray-haired grandma.

Her son's health had taken a lot out of her as well. She had often let her heart medication lapse so that Tian could get his medical supplies. It was a trade off that she made gladly, but unfortunately she knew that those lapses had now caught up to her.

Livie was disappointed when Tian's book was published and he couldn't visit the publishers. Livie was even sadder when the small but loyal fan base that loved Tian's book organized an event and Tian couldn't make it. Tian told Livie that he didn't feel that his body could take it.

Livie knew that she had gotten old, but what she failed to notice was how much older Tian had also become. Over the years Tian's hair went from being speckled grey to completely grey. As time went by, Tian's movements had slowed considerable and he was now balding.

The biggest contributor to his age was that Tian's home dialysis wasn't conducted as frequently as the doctor would have liked. The result was that Tian was more often guessed as Livie's husband instead of her son. When that mistake had occurred during Livie's youth, she knew it was because of her sustained beauty. But when it happened as an old woman she knew that it was because of her son.

As Livie felt her end grow near she began to feel comfortable about the continued life of her son. Livie was content to learn that Tian's fourth book had made a profit and that Tian's share was enough to live modestly for a year. Livie was also satisfied to know that Tian's publisher had given him an advance on a second book. Livie didn't know what Tian would have become if he didn't have the accident. But she knew that after the accident, she had helped her son become a novelist. That made Livie feel proud.

On what was to be the last day of Livie's life she laid in her bed thinking about her life. Lying there she knew that her sons were talking to her but she now had a very hard time paying attention. She thought about her mother and her ex-husband, both of whom had passed years earlier. She wondered if she would see them again.

She had very much missed her ex-husband as the years went on. He was a good man dealing with a difficult wife and she respected the grace with which he handled it.

Livie wouldn't have to wait long before she saw her loved ones again. Livie remembered how much her mother loved her ex-husband when Livie saw them standing together at the foot of her bed. Her mother, that now looked younger than Livie said, "It's time," and in a moment Livie was standing with them. In that moment Livie saw a white light and felt an overwhelming sense of love.

She then looked back at her sons. Tian was now standing at the head of her bed with tears in his eyes. Tian then leaned over and whispered something into her ear. Still connected to the body that lay there, Livie struggled to hear. "You have been the love of my life," Tian said. And with that Livie was gone.

Tian held his mothers face in his hands and kissed her on the forehead. "You have been the love of my life," he said again before brushing away a tear that had landed on his mother's lips. "You have been the love of my life," he said again before standing up, turning to his brother and falling into an embrace.

The End.

* * * * *

Follow the author on twitter **@RateABull_guy**
Connect with other readers on FaceBook at:
http://www.facebook.com/pages/The-First-Day-After-Life/157295860992034

Buy these Books Now from author Cristian YoungMiller:

<u>Happiness Thru the Art of... Penis Enlargement</u>
A 'Novel Guide' to Jelqing, The G-Spot,
How to Last Longer in Bed
& Other Sexual Secrets

Ben, a good-natured guy, has lived his entire life with an alcoholic, verbally abusive penis named 'The Brotha'. The story begins when the Brotha finally goes too far with his dictation over Ben, and both admit to being unhappy with their life. As a result, both start a journey toward happiness which leads to their finding a guide to penis enlargement. Following the guide, they increase the Brotha's size, and learn sexual secrets which turn out to be only the beginning in their journey towards happiness.

This 'Novel Guide' includes step-by-step instructions on how-to:
- Permanently increase the size of your penis using Cristian's very popular Jelqing technique
- How to find the G-Spot - How to last longer in bed by delaying your orgasm
- How you can please a woman whether or not you have had previous sexual experience This

'Novel Guide' also helps you to:
- Decide whether or not you should try Jelqing by describing some of the potential problems
- This book also helps you to become happier no matter your penis size

Buy these Books Now from author Cristian YoungMiller:

<u>Everybody Masturbates</u>

'Everybody Masturbates' is the perfect gift idea for anyone from ages 8 to 42 yrs old. In the style of the classic book 'Everyone Poops,' 'Everybody Masturbates' is designed to make boys and girls of all ages feel comfortable about masturbation. (It also makes a great party gift for adults.)

<u>Everybody Masturbates *for Girls*</u>

'Everybody Masturbates *for Girls*' is the perfect gift idea for girls between the ages of 7 to 38 yrs old. Also, in the style of the classic book 'Everyone Poops,' 'Everybody Masturbates *for Girls*' addresses the specific issues that girls have accepting their emerging sexuality. (It also makes a great party gift for adults.)

<u>Everybody Has Those Thoughts, So It Doesn't Mean You're Gay</u>

'Everybody Has Those Thoughts, So It Doesn't Mean You're Gay' is a great gift idea for anyone from ages 13 to 55 yrs old. Written in plain, easy to read text, this book discusses why otherwise straight people have same-sex thoughts and dreams. Sexual arousal in same-sex situations doesn't automatically mean someone is gay. This book will help the reader figure out their sexual orientation. (It also makes a great party gift for adults.)

Join the Free Online Community at RateABull.com

RateABull.com is an online community created by author Cristian YoungMiller. Cristian created the website so that members can give and get advice from each other on all topics. Because you may not know the answer to your problems, but there's a world of people that do. Connect with them and make your life better.

Here's what you can do there:

- Communicate with the author Cristian YoungMiller and ask him questions about the book
- Connect with others that are following Cristian Jelqing technique
- Ask for and give advice about sex, relationships and life
- Watch the videos and read the conversations that inspired this book
- Find out about upcoming seminars, webinars and appearances by author Cristian YoungMiller

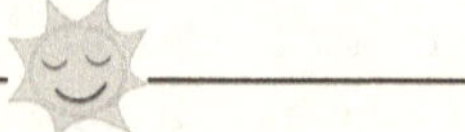

Take a Trip to The Bahamas Online at RememberTheBahamas.com

Author Cristian YoungMiller was born in the Bahamas. Go to his popular online store to purchase the most popular products from the Bahamas and take a trip without even leaving home.

- Rent a beach house on one of the most beautiful, secluded beaches in the world
- Purchase the popular pineapple flavored soda Goombay Punch
- Buy the colognes made and sold only in the Bahamas
- Connect with others that have visited the Bahamas